As Haden got out of his car, he heard the motorcycle rounding a bend, and glanced toward it automatically. Both the driver and the passenger wore helmets and visors. Long blonde hair protruded from under the helmet of the smaller, slimmer figure of the girl on the pillion.

As he fitted the key in the lock, Haden heard the motorcycle's engine suddenly cut off. He looked up, but only the rider was getting off. Haden turned around quickly. The other one, the girl, was approaching him from behind. In her hand was what looked like an iron bar.

Haden backed away until the iron railings behind him pressed into his shoulders. The driver, coming from the other direction, was swinging a heavy chain.

"You know what we want," the driver said, his voice low.

BLOCKBUSTER FICTION FROM PINNACLE BOOKS!

THE FINAL VOYAGE OF THE S.S.N. SKATE   (17-157, $3.95)
by Stephen Cassell
The "leper" of the U.S. Pacific Fleet, SSN 578 nuclear attack sub SKATE, has one final mission to perform—an impossible act of piracy that will pit the underwater deathtrap and its inexperienced crew against the combined might of the Soviet Navy's finest!

QUEENS GATE RECKONING   (17-164, $3.95)
by Lewis Purdue
Only a wounded CIA operative and a defecting Soviet ballerina stand in the way of a vast consortium of treason that speeds toward the hour of mankind's ultimate reckoning! From the best-selling author of THE LINZ TESTAMENT.

FAREWELL TO RUSSIA   (17-165, $4.50)
by Richard Hugo
A KGB agent must race against time to infiltrate the confines of U.S. nuclear technology after a terrifying accident threatens to unleash unmitigated devastation!

THE NICODEMUS CODE   (17-133, $3.95)
by Graham N. Smith and Donna Smith
A two-thousand-year-old parchment has been unearthed, unleashing a terrifying conspiracy unlike any the world has previously known, one that threatens the life of the Pope himself, and the ultimate destruction of Christianity!

Available wherever paperbacks are sold, or order direct from the Publisher. Send cover price plus 50¢ per copy for mailing and handling to Pinnacle Books, Dept.17-305, 475 Park Avenue South, New York, N.Y. 10016. Residents of New York, New Jersey and Pennsylvania must include sales tax. DO NOT SEND CASH.

THE NINTH CIRCLE

N.J. CRISP

PINNACLE BOOKS
WINDSOR PUBLISHING CORP.

PINNACLE BOOKS

are published by

Windsor Publishing Corp.
475 Park Avenue South
New York, NY 10016

First Pinnacle Books printing: January 1990

Printed in the United States of America

Never did Danube in Austria or
far off Don under its frigid sky
make in winter so thick a veil on
its course as was here.

From Canto XXXII, "The Inferno,"
The Divine Comedy of Dante Alighieri

Translated by John D. Sinclair

Chapter One

The plane had been in for some time. He was waiting at Arrivals, watching the trickle of emerging passengers dwindle. Broad-shouldered, slim-waisted, he remained still and relaxed, but his unblinking blue eyes set above high cheekbones, the hard line of his jaw, expressed an impatience that caused passersby to glance at him twice, and skirt him carefully.

He had begun to suppose that she had missed the flight, which would not have surprised him, when he saw her.

She was talking animatedly to a slender young woman with frothy blond hair, who would have caught anyone's eye.

They paused, she looked around, saw him, said something to the blonde, pointed, ran on ahead, threw her arms around him, and hugged him. In the past few months she had changed from a girl into a young woman.

"You're filling out," Stephen Haden said, now wearing another face entirely, one in which the mouth was spread in an affectionate smile, and the blue eyes were not cool but shone warmly.

"Not bad, eh?" Christa peered down at her chest proudly. "I was beginning to think I'd be stuck with two mini-bumps for life.'' She looked up, studying his face. ''You look pretty good.''

''I feel pretty good,'' Haden said.

The eye-catching blonde had followed. She looked even better close up.

''Petra, meet Stephen,'' Christa said, introducing them.

''I've heard nice things about you,'' Petra said, with a slight diffidence that was somehow unexpected. Her accent was American.

''Petra's a parent,'' Christa explained.

''Really,'' Haden said, not quite eliminating the note of surprise. Making every allowance for grooming and makeup, the concept of this willowy creature's being the mother of a teenager strained credulity.

Petra smiled faintly. ''My son is in the junior school,'' she explained. ''It's his first term.''

''He's only eight,'' Christa said, with the superiority of a girl who had recently celebrated her fifteenth birthday.

''He was kind of homesick for a while,'' Petra went on. ''Christa was sweet, looked after him, took him under her wing.''

''A mother hen, deep down, that's me,'' Christa said. ''I told Petra we might give her a lift. Will that be okay?''

''Fine,'' Stephen Haden said.

The sheet of deep snow swept unbroken from the roadside, capping rooftops, to the rising mountains beyond, but the traffic stream moved smoothly and unhindered as they drove toward the city.

''In England,'' Christa babbled with amusement from the back seat of the Mercedes, ''a few inches of snow, and it's a crisis. Frozen points, trains canceled, roads closed. Headlines in all the papers.''

"The English like to believe it'll never happen," Haden said. "The Swiss know it will."

"In general?" Petra inquired from beside him. "Or just in particular?"

"Snow in particular," Haden said. "Will you be staying in Zurich long?"

"No," Petra said. "It's a business trip."

"Oh, Helen sends her best," Christa said.

Haden glanced at her in the rearview mirror. "Have you seen her?"

"She's been to school a few times," Christa answered. "It was fun. She took me out. Peter, too, one weekend."

"Peter told me how kind she'd been," Petra said.

"He was a bit down that day, and Helen said he could come along," Christa continued. "Helen's great. She cheered him up in no time."

They were entering the city, and Haden concentrated on his driving in silence. He had received a note from Helen Lloyd that had read simply: "Glad to hear you're okay. Helen." Its form and brevity had not struck him as much of a signal that a response was expected.

A porter materialized as soon as the Mercedes pulled up outside the City Center Hotel.

"Thanks for keeping Christa company on the flight," Haden said politely.

"Maybe you'd care to lunch with me tomorrow?" Petra said. "Or dinner, if you prefer."

Haden looked at her. The porter was removing her luggage from the back. In the reflection from the streetlights, he saw a degree of strain in her expression that had not been apparent before; he thought her smile was manufactured rather than easy.

"I'd planned to spend some time with Christa," Haden replied.

Petra said, "The truth is, my business is with you, Mr.

Haden. Do try, please. Call me, will you? Ask for Mrs. Baron.''

Her smile wavered fractionally; she got out and closed the door. Haden drove off.

"You don't have to spend time with me, Stephen," Christa said.

"There are some shows I thought you might like to see."

"All I want to do is just flop for a couple of days after a hard term's work. I have been working, Stephen, honestly."

"I believe you," Haden said. "And time will tell, anyway."

"Except I'll cook for you, if you want to risk it."

"You, cook? Since when?" Haden's eyebrows rose.

"Since I started classes at school. I like it. I'll cook tonight, if you want to be my first real guinea pig. But don't expect Cordon Bleu. Not yet, anyway."

"I won't," Haden said.

That evening, they ate in the spacious kitchen. Haden praised the meal extravagantly.

"It wasn't all that good," Christa said. "The steak was overdone."

"Just the way I like it," Haden said. "I'm a philistine."

"There's no pudding," Christa said. "I haven't got to puddings yet. Ice cream?"

"Nothing more for me." Haden lit a cheroot, thought longingly about a cognac, but settled for the remaining wine.

Christa had saved herself a huge bowl of ice cream. He watched her, reflectively, as she ate.

"Petra Baron seems nice," he said. "How did you come to meet her?"

"When she brought Peter, halfway through term," Christa said, scooping busily. "We got talking."

"And she asked you to keep an eye on him?"

"People in my year, we're expected to help out with the kids in the junior school. It's supposed to give us a sense of responsibility." She chuckled at the thought.

"Why Peter in particular? Any special reason?"

"Mm." Christa waited until she had disposed of her last spoonful of ice cream. "They'd been living in Germany."

"Where in Germany?"

"I forget," Christa said. "But all Peter's friends had been German kids. I think he had a German nanny, and he's more at home with German than English. Maybe that's why they sent him to school in England, I don't know. Anyway, since I was brought up to speak German as well as English, I could communicate with him more easily. That's why. He's settled down now, but he was sort of a pain at first." Haden was content to smoke and watch her as she rambled on. "He says he wants to study Russian, but of course he can't do that until he's in the senior school. He knows a bit already, though."

"Where did he pick that up?"

"It might not be Russian for all I know," Christa confessed. "He says it is, but he could be having me on. He's a funny little boy, I mean, he's sweet, but you never know if he's pretending or not."

Haden blew out smoke and tapped his cheroot on the edge of the ashtray.

"Does his mother have any other business in Zurich, apart from seeing me?"

"I don't think so."

"Without making an appointment, she flew out on the off-chance?"

"Well, she knew you'd be meeting me," Christa said. A small flush tinged her high cheekbones.

"What business do you think she might have with me?"

"Your line of business, I expect," Christa said.

13

"You've discussed it," Haden supposed, "and you gave her the hard sell."

"Sort of," Christa admitted. "I suppose I should do the washing up."

"The dishwasher swallows it," Haden said. "Right now I'm more interested in what Petra Baron wants of me."

"She didn't say. She asked about you, and that's all I know. Most of the time she looks like something out of a glossy magazine, but now and then you can see from her face there's something wrong. Didn't you notice?"

"Perhaps she was tired," Haden said.

"Will you see her?"

"I'll think about it."

"The thing is," Christa said, "I sort of promised you would." Haden gazed at her in silence. She blinked but did not look away. "Did I do something wrong, Stephen?"

"Make some coffee while I call her," Haden said.

Christa's face lit up in a smile of eager relief. Lavish payment, Haden thought wryly, for the sake of a telephone call. Besides, why not? He was mildly curious anyway.

From out of her one small suitcase, Petra Baron had some-how contrived to conjure up an evening outfit that was both discreet and dazzling. The hint of strain in her face had gone, either consciously erased or vanished on its own with a change of mood—Haden could not decide which. The face itself repaid close scrutiny across a table.

It could have been pixielike with its tip-tilted nose and small chin tapering from a broad forehead, but it was not. The green eyes were clear and steady, the mobile mouth shapely and sensuous. It was the kind of face to which a man's eyes returned as if it were a magnet. She seemed entirely unconscious of the effect her appearance induced; either that or she was used to attention.

14

They were eating in the hotel dining room. It was early evening and the room was as yet only half full, but it was a place where Stephen Haden was not entirely unknown.

"You seem to attract some interest," Petra Baron observed as she sipped her wine. "People are looking at you."

"Wondering who the lucky fellow is, I expect," Haden said.

Petra smiled. "I think they know who you are." She put her glass down. "Will you be spending Christmas with Christa?"

"She's only with me for a few days. Then she'll go to her mother for the rest of the holiday."

"What will you do for Christmas?"

"Ignore it," Haden said. "Treat it as just another weekend. You?"

"Spend it with my son. Some friends in London have invited us."

"Is that where you're living now?"

Petra said, "We all live where we happen to be, don't we? Christa's a lovely girl. If I had a daughter, I'd like her to be like that. You're very lucky."

"She's my stepdaughter," Haden said.

Petra nodded. He could not decide if she had already known that or not.

"She refers to you as her father, and it's obvious you care for her. The difference seems to be something of a technicality."

"She feels like my own," Haden said.

"Is it true that you smuggled several Poles dressed as priests out of Warsaw on board the Pope's special train?"

"Someone else did, if it happened at all," Haden answered. "I always thought it was just a press story."

"I heard it was you," Petra said.

Haden shrugged, finished his Sole Bonne Femme, and waited. He supposed that this was where they would get to the point, but she only switched to more talk of Christa and of her son. She asked for his opinion of the school and its staff, subjects on which Haden was not notably well informed, so she gave him her own views. She was easy to listen to and the time passed pleasantly, but if she wanted to fill it without revealing anything much about herself, she was succeeding. Perhaps she subscribed to the getting-to-know-you-first-and-talk-business-over-coffee convention, which Haden usually considered tiresome and a waste of time. On this occasion, with this companion, however, he had no objection.

"You haven't mentioned your husband all evening," he said, having declined a liqueur. "Or isn't there one?"

"His name is Alex." She put her coffee cup down. Her expressive mouth suddenly revealed that tension he had noticed upon her arrival. "I don't know where he is," she said. "That's why I want to talk to you."

"Where did you lose him?" Haden inquired.

The green eyes suddenly flashed the color of sea ice, but her voice was steady.

"In Vienna," she said.

"How does your eight-year-old son come to know Russian?"

Her smile was rueful, resigned, but the sea ice had melted.

"Christa gossips about you, too," she said. "You're a kind of latter-day Scarlet Pimpernel who slips in and out of enemy countries, his only aim in life to rescue those in danger and distress."

"Do you believe in Santa Claus, too?" Haden asked.

"Let's continue this conversation in my room, okay?" The nearby tables were occupied now, the place was full. "Or we can go to your place, if you'd prefer."

"Your room is nearer." He looked around for the waiter. "I'll get the bill."

"It's on me," Petra said, "unless you're the kind who can't bear to see a woman picking up the tab."

"No, I like it," Haden said. "It makes a nice change."

The room was not a suite, but a large double, with a separate sitting area, and at the upper end of the price bracket in a hotel that was far from cheap at the lower end. Haden mentally added the cost to that of the meal plus a round-trip ticket from London to Zurich. Whatever Petra Baron wanted, she wanted it badly. In Haden's experience, it all added up to the proposition's being riddled with unpleasant problems. However, in his line of work, that was not too unusual.

Petra sat on the couch. Haden chose the armchair, facing her. Past her, he could see the double bed. She would have more than enough room to stretch out as she slept.

"About my son's smattering of Russian," Petra said. "It's sometimes spoken at home. He's picked up a bit."

Haden supposed that. Petra seemed to be waiting for him to say something.

"Are you sure you don't mind this?" he inquired, referring to the cheroot he had lit.

Petra shook her head. Her small smile had nothing to do with the negative gesture.

"I'm used to it," she said. "Alex chain-smokes cigarettes. Please just sit and listen, if that's your style."

"For the time being, that's okay," Haden said. "I didn't fly anywhere to talk to you."

Her mobile mouth could express a certain sulkiness, he noted.

"Okay," she said. "Back home, in my student days, I majored in Russian. After that, I went to study in Moscow. I met Alex. He was a journalist. We became lovers, and I thought that that was all there was to it. He wasn't my first,

17

by any means. But it grew into something else. The authorities might have agreed to marriage if I'd been willing to live in Russia, but I wasn't. I went home, back to California, but we kept in touch. Through friends we could trust, that is. I guess his people believed it was done with. When he was sent to Helsinki to cover some arms talks, he defected.''

''The Finns are in no position to annoy the Russians,'' Haden said. ''Defectors are usually handed right back.''

''The plan allowed for that. Alex crossed into Sweden first—with help, I guess, he said it wasn't safe to tell me. I was waiting for him in Stockholm, and then he flew to the States. After he was granted U.S. citizenship, we got married.''

''Baron doesn't sound like a Russian name,'' Haden said.

''It was Alexander Baronin. He changed it to Baron to sound more American.''

''Gossip has it your son was brought up in Germany,'' Haden remarked.

''Munich,'' Petra said. ''Alex got a job there in broadcasting, working for Radio Liberation, mostly as a translator and researcher.''

''We're still not in Vienna,'' Haden said.

''Last summer, he had an assignment there. I went with him. For me, it was a holiday. I saw the sights, shopped, went to concerts—that kind of thing. One evening, I went to the opera. We had arranged to meet after the performance at Sacher's, but he didn't show up. I went back to the hotel. All his things were in our room. I lay in bed, waiting, ready to give him hell, still not realizing there was anything wrong. I haven't seen him since. Nor heard from him. Nothing. Just silence.''

She was fiddling with the rings on her left hand, and a certain huskiness had entered her voice.

18

"The Austrian police should come into this somewhere," Haden prompted her. "It's their territory."

"Naturally," Petra said. She sighed. "They couldn't find any trace of him. Not a thing. He'd simply disappeared. He's still in their missing-persons files. They say they'll re-open the case if any further evidence comes to light."

"Your embassy?" Haden suggested. "He was a U.S. citizen."

"Yes, I've spoken to the embassy, too," Petra said. "I was told that all possible inquiries have been made over the last several months, but they haven't been able to find out a thing." A touch of doubt pursed her lips. "Or maybe they don't want to tell me. I can't be sure."

"From Austria, it wouldn't be too hard for Alexander Baronin to cross the border into Hungary," Haden suggested, "should he have decided to go home again."

"He wouldn't do that," she said.

"Or been taken home whether he liked it or not," Haden continued.

Her nod was one of acceptance, with no surprise.

"I know," she said. "That's what I'm most afraid of. Which is why I've come to you. If you can only trace him, he may be someplace where he'll need help to get out."

"They wouldn't keep him in Hungary," Haden said.

"I didn't come to you blind," Petra said. "I looked you up. You're the man who once said he could get a man out of Moscow, if need be."

Haden didn't bother to correct her, but she had culled the line from a tabloid intent on printing something more striking than what he had actually said.

"Not if he's in the Lubyanka, I can't."

"If he is in the Lubyanka, at least I'd know," Petra said. "I must know, for Christ's sake."

"I'll consider it," said Haden. "But my services don't come cheap."

"The Scarlet Pimpernel worked for free," Petra said. "Christa tends to overlook that."

"Sir Percy was a rich aristocrat. I'm in business."

"Well, I need help. Whatever it costs."

"Ten thousand dollars for a start," Haden said. "That's for thinking time and for expenses. You'll get my yes or no in the New Year. If it's yes, I'll quote my full fee then."

Petra said fiercely, "But I want you to get started now."

"You've been waiting since last summer," Haden retorted. "You can wait another two weeks."

She stared at him, not blinking, for a full half minute before she stood up, crossed to the writing desk, sat down, dipped into her handbag, took out a checkbook and a pen, and wrote a check.

"Also, where can I reach you?" Haden said. "And I'll need a recent photograph of your husband."

Petra took a sheet of hotel notepaper from the rack and scribbled on it. She dipped into her handbag again, and then stood, holding out the two slips of paper and a photograph.

Haden got to his feet and took them.

"What else do you want to know?" she asked.

"What haven't you told me?"

"There's nothing else," Petra said.

"Then there's nothing more I need to know, is there?" Haden said. She eyed him with a mixture of doubt and something else. "When husbands disappear," Haden continued, "most often it's for very mundane personal reasons." He glanced at the check and noted that it was properly made out.

"I don't believe it's another woman," Petra said. "If it is, I'll hate him, but at least I'll know where things stand. I can get on with my own life."

"Write him off," Haden said.

"Why don't you like me?" Petra demanded. Her lips

were pursed like a petulant child's. "You were okay over dinner."

"We weren't discussing business over dinner," Haden said. "I'll tell you this. If your husband has run off with someone else, she must really be something."

The indirect compliment was sufficient to induce a smile and the kind of look that raised speculations.

"It may be business to you," she said, "but not to me. I need a man around. I haven't had one for a long time."

Stephen Haden was far from certain whether, had he wished, he would have been welcome to stay a good deal longer. Part of him contemplated the idea with interest.

"Good night," he said. "Until next time."

Anna was late. She sat in her car outside the house, sounding the horn. Haden opened the front door, carried Christa's luggage to the car and put it in the trunk.

"Sorry," Anna apologized, winding down her window. "I got held up. I won't come in, if you don't mind."

"No, fine," Haden said. They chatted briefly, inquiring about the other's welfare with that blend of friendliness and distance usual between two people who were once married and who had parted without too much rancor. Then Haden went back inside to find Christa.

"Your mother has your present," Haden said.

"Thanks," Christa said. "I left yours in your room, but you mustn't open it till Christmas Day. Promise?"

"I promise," Haden said.

He led Christa to the front door. She waved to Anna, but paused before going outside. She looked up at him seriously.

"I have to ask, or I shall burst," she said. "Are you going to help Petra?"

"I don't know," Haden answered.

"She didn't tell me anything, but the way she was talking, I knew she needed you and that it was something very important. I hope you can."

"We'll see," Haden said. In this young girl's eyes, he was really someone.

Haden saw them off. As the car drew away, Christa turned, waved, and called, "Happy Christmas."

"And to you," Haden called back.

He closed the door and went up to his bedroom. The carefully wrapped package was propped up against the bedside telephone. The card attached said: "For Stephen. Lots and lots of love. Christa." A row of X's for kisses followed.

Haden sat on the bed and tore off the paper. Inside was a silk tie. It was all right. She had a good eye. He thought he would wear it when he left, for luck.

He lifted the receiver, and dialed Swissair.

At London Airport Stephen Haden went to a car rental desk and hired a Cavalier. Then he made some phone calls. Although it was early evening, one of them was to the International Information Institute in Mayfair, just on the off-chance someone was still there. An answering device began telling him that the office was closed. He rang off without listening to the rest of the message.

London had no snow. The rain had stopped falling, but the roads gleamed under the streetlights. He turned off Bayswater Road, left his car on a residents' parking strip near Cleveland Square, and walked around the corner, a shopping bag in his hand.

Outside the large house, one of many divided up into flats, he pressed the button for the ground-floor flat. There was a long pause before the soft American voice answered.

"Give me a couple of minutes, okay?"

"It's Stephen," Haden said.

There was an even longer pause before the buzzer sounded. Haden pushed the street door open and walked in. The door of the flat opened as he was about to knock.

"You would turn up now," said Helen Lloyd.

She looked as if she were dressed for a party, although there were no sounds of revelry coming from inside.

"Happy Christmas," he said, handing her the bag, and walked past her. She closed the door and followed him into the living room. It was much as Haden remembered it.

Helen took the bottle of champagne from the bag he had handed her, unwrapped it, and studied the label.

"It's not chilled," Haden said. "I'll have whatever else is going."

"There's nothing," she said, and stood the bottle on a bookshelf. "I just ordered a cab. I thought you were it. I'm going out."

"We could go somewhere instead," Haden suggested.

"My chief wouldn't like that," Helen replied. "It's his party."

Haden nodded. "Still in the same line of work, then?"

"Like you," she said.

"This evening, try mentioning the name Alex Baron, born Alexander Baronin," Haden asked. "See if anyone's interested. You've met his son, Peter. His wife, Petra too, maybe." Helen stared at him without expression. "She's mislaid her husband," Haden explained. Still she said nothing, her direct gaze fixed on him. He was thinking that outwardly, anyway, she had not changed. The same short, dark hair casually styled in the same way, the same inner glow to her skin, the same flawless, discreet sense of fashion. And she still moved him in the same disturbing way. "I'll call you and we'll fix a meeting when you have more time," he said.

"Only you would choose Christmas Eve," Helen said

23

tartly. "I won't have any time. I'm not a woman at loose ends. I get invitations."

"Bear mine in mind," Haden said. "Put me on your list. Since you're still on your own." She gave him a look that told him nothing. "Is Harold Leyton still an Institute client? Still in need of commercial information?"

"Harry hasn't been in touch for a long time."

"Okay if I call his office?"

"He won't be there now."

The buzzer squawked while he was dialing Leyton. He heard Helen tell the driver she was on her way.

The answering device at the other end told him that he had reached a photographic model agency. He hung up. Somehow, models did not strike him as Harold Leyton's scene.

Helen was coming out of her bedroom with her coat on as he walked into the hall. He remembered that bedroom. He went outside and waited while she locked up. A thin drizzle of rain had started; more threatened to come. Helen ducked her head into her coat collar and hurried toward the taxi. Haden opened the door for her.

"Where are you staying?" she asked. "Can I drop you off?"

"No need," Haden said. "I'm just around the corner. Walking distance. It was all I could find." Her eyes registered some disbelief. "Have a good time," Haden said.

He pushed the door shut and watched the taxi drive off. Somehow, her sitting in the back seat alone, without an escort, her face framed by the high collar of her coat, seemed unnatural. The thought induced a momentary, passing twinge of loneliness, a feeling that rarely afflicted Stephen Haden.

He walked through the intensifying rain toward the Cavalier to fetch his suitcase. He wondered if she would return home alone.

* * *

The hotel faced onto Bayswater Road. A neon strip advertised a cocktail bar. The obligatory Christmas tree stood in the foyer, its colored lights winking unevenly. The cocktail bar was jammed, the dining room noisy with revelers letting their hair down.

The noise penetrated to Haden's room, which looked comfortable but was stuffy and stifling hot. He tried to turn the heat down, but the controls wouldn't budge. He took his jacket off, loosened his tie, and sat down on the bed. He looked up a number in his diary and dialed. The answering voice had an eager, expectant tone. "Hullo?"

"Hullo, Harry," Haden said. "How're things with you?"

"Who is this?" The eagerness had vanished.

"Stephen Haden."

"Good God," Harold Leyton said. "I heard you were dead."

"No, you didn't, Harry," Haden said. "What are you doing over Christmas?"

"Not a lot. Why?"

"Invite me over for a drink," Haden said.

There were more cars on the roads than he had expected. Some of the driving was decidedly erratic. Haden kept his distance from the offenders and watched a police car as it switched on its siren and took off after some weaving celebrant.

He turned off Earl's Court Road and found a space the Cavalier would just about fit into. The block of flats was Edwardian and looked as if it had recently been renovated. He took the newly installed elevator to the third floor.

A short, pudgy figure was standing in the open door of

the flat. The mouth beneath a neat mustache split into a broad grin.

"Well, well." Harold Leyton beamed. "Good to see you, Stephen. If it weren't for you, I'd have spent Christmas Day alone, do you know that?"

Haden shook the outstretched hand.

"How's the spy business, Harry?" he inquired.

Harold Leyton clapped him on the back jovially, looking around to make sure no one else was there.

"And I thought this was just a social call," he said. "Come on in."

Chapter Two

Stephen Haden had never before seen Harold Leyton wearing anything but a sober business suit. Today, he was clad in jeans and a silk shirt. Given the man's rotund build, Haden thought the jeans were a mistake. But that was Haden's business.

"I wondered how much had changed," Haden said. "Aside from your being just a businessman."

Harold Leyton swirled his glass of Scotch and concentrated on the eddies that it created.

"That's exactly what I am now," he said.

"No difficult interviews with Special Branch? No unpleasant talk of prosecution?"

"I spun the firm a yarn," Leyton said. He smiled guilelessly. "The gist of which was that I was merely trying to put things right, and all the blame lay with Stephen Haden."

"Thanks a lot," Haden said.

"They didn't believe a word of it, of course," Leyton said. "But it suited their purpose to buy it. On the understanding that I would no longer be required to serve Her Majesty. They didn't have much option. The whole thing had to be covered up or all hell would have broken loose. Offing someone like me was a luxury they had to forgo."

"I wondered about that, too," Haden said, "for my own selfish reasons."

"If nothing ever happened, you couldn't have been involved, could you," Leyton said pleasantly. "Forget it, Stephen, it's been buried by experts." Haden sipped his wine, which was light and dry and went down well. Leyton leaned forward, and topped up his glass. "Why, is there something on?" he inquired with interest.

"You've given up your office," Haden remarked.

"Working from home now, with a partner," Leyton replied.

"Where is he?"

"His parents wanted him to spend Christmas with them," Leyton said. "He'll be back for New Year's Eve." He tilted his glass and swallowed a mouthful of Scotch, his small eyes fixed on Haden over the rim. "I've gone into the franchise game," he said, putting his glass down. "European agent for an American outfit. Not a bad little number. Nothing to it. Hold meetings now and then, sell the concept to men of substance willing to invest, who in turn appoint group sales executives whose job is to flog the franchises to the public. Everyone takes a cut, right down the line, of course."

"It sounds more like pyramid selling to me," Haden said.

"Certainly not," Leyton said, affronted. "It's multilayer marketing. No resemblance. Tell you what, though. The Swiss marketing rights are still available. I could put them your way at a discount. You'd be the Zurich supremo. How about it?"

"Harry," Haden said, "don't try to sell me things I don't want."

"I thought you called yourself an entrepreneur," Leyton grumbled.

"I stick to the business I know," Haden said. He studied the high ceiling, with its original plasterwork. "But with a place like this and a flourishing business, you wouldn't be interested."

"My service charges have been horrendous since they did this place up," Leyton said promptly. "Cash in hand, naturally. What's the deal?"

"Consultation and advice," Haden said. "Five hundred dollars to start."

"Make it a thousand," Leyton said at once. Haden took an envelope from his breast pocket and handed it to the plump, short man. "And the rest?" Leyton said, holding out his hand.

"There's a thousand dollars in there," Haden said. "I know you, Harry."

Leyton smiled, but counted the money anyway. "I'll let you know when you've had your money's worth," he said.

"The other way around, Harry," Haden said. "I'll tell you." Leyton seemed disposed to argue the point, but changed his mind and tucked the envelope away in a drawer. "You used to do business in Moscow," Haden said.

"Not for a long time," Leyton said cautiously.

"Cast your mind back ten years or so," Haden went on. "If you came across a Russian called Alexander Baronin, I'd be interested."

"Moscow's a big city, Stephen," Leyton said. "And anyone who met Russians socially would attract attention. You were liable to get yourself tailed everywhere. The last thing I needed."

Haden said, "This particular Russian could have moved in the same circuit you did—the hotels, restaurants, shops used by Westerners." Leyton screwed up his eyes and frowned, but no sign of enlightenment appeared. "Alexander Baronin," Haden said again. "He was a journalist."

Leyton unscrewed his eyes; his face cleared.

"Oh, him, yes," he said. "A journalist. You should have said so."

"You know him, then?"

Leyton shook his head. "Hardly at all," he replied. "Saw him around, may have spoken to him casually once or twice, but no more."

"But you remember what he looks like," Haden said. It wasn't a question. He handed over the photograph. Leyton studied it with care before replying.

"He'd have been about thirty at the time," Leyton said at last. "But this is the same man, all right. A bit older, but the same friendly, good-looking face."

"I'm told he had an affair with an American girl called Petra, a student."

"Don't know anything about that," Leyton said. "Never saw him with a woman. But then he wasn't off duty. He was doing his job. A popular man with the Western press corps, Baronin."

"Any special reason?"

"Good English, approachable, told the same kind of sly joke," Leyton said. "He'd talk off the record, drop hints, pass on gossip, speculations about possible policy changes that would turn out to be right. He understood what the Western press wanted."

"And gave it to them," Haden said. "More or less openly, the way you tell it. Without any official disapproval?"

Leyton said, "He was the Russian equivalent of 'informed sources' in London or Washington. His leaks were deliberate, everyone knew that, but at least they made better copy than official handouts. That's why the press liked him." He grinned and swallowed some Scotch. "That and the fact that it happened over drinks."

" 'Informed sources' have connections, East or West. What were Baronin's? The Kremlin? The KGB?"

"Either or both," Leyton answered. "Or maybe he was just a reliable Party man with nice manners and a good memory for briefings. I really couldn't say. If it was anyone's business to find out, it wasn't mine."

"Baronin defected to the States and married his American girlfriend," Haden said, eyeing Leyton closely. Leyton's chubby face remained expressionless. "Later he worked in West Germany." Still no reaction. "No comment, Harry?" Haden inquired.

"Oh, come on, Stephen," Leyton said, resigned. "I was a very small fish in a British pond. People defect all the time. Usually they're not important. If they are, whoever gets lucky uses them. The Americans play their game, we play ours. Baronin's name never came my way. I'd forgotten all about him until you mentioned him."

"Even if you have been drummed out of the Brownies, Harry," Haden said, "I expect you're still on drinking terms with a few old pals inside. It's still a club, even if you have broken the rules."

"Well?" Leyton inquired cautiously.

"Look up any likely ones," Haden said. "Talk about Alexander Baronin. Keep the photograph. Jog memories."

Leyton considered that for a while. "I think I'd like to know what this is all about," he stated eventually.

"You'll figure it out, Harry. You're not stupid. When you've talked to your friends, it'll come to you."

"I hate to strike a sordid note," Leyton said, "but were it a question of checking records than memories, some further inducement might be required."

"Well, I calculate I've had ten dollars' worth so far," Haden said. "Dip into the balance."

"You bloody cheapskate," Leyton said indignantly.

"Harry," Haden said, "you've told me nothing I couldn't have got for a few large whiskies from any journalist who served in Moscow at the time, and I know a lot of journalists. I don't think you've been trying."

"If you're going to cast doubts on my integrity," Leyton said coldly, "I suggest we forget the whole thing."

"Okay," Haden said. He held out his hand. "Call it a hundred dollars, and I'll have the rest back."

Leyton's flesh face broke into a sudden smile. "I thought you said ten dollars," he said. "A hundred I could agree to, this time, for a start."

"Just don't try to screw me too much when you bill me for your conversations," Haden said. "I'm working on a tight budget." The telephone began to ring. Leyton did not move, but directed a look at Haden. "All right, I'm going," Haden said.

As he made his way out, he heard Leyton's voice.

"Hullo, love . . . How are the aged parents? . . . What? . . . No, there's no one here . . . No, I'm all on my own . . ."

Leyton stepped back into view and waved a warning gesture. Haden closed the front door with considerate care.

"How was your Christmas Day?" Helen Lloyd inquired.

"Twenty-four hours long," Haden answered. "How was yours?"

"It started quiet and ended late," Helen said, "that's why I was a bit sleepy when you called."

She had yawned as she answered the phone. Her voice a blurred murmur, she had sleepily recited her day's engagements. Lunch was out; she was tied up that evening. Haden pointed out a gap around teatime.

"Four o'clock?"

"No, come around about six for a drink, okay?" she had said. "That'll give me time to shower and change."

And now they were sitting in her living room, sipping the

32

champagne he had brought on his first aborted visit. It was chilled now. Haden did not really like champagne much, no matter what temperature, but Helen seemed to be enjoying it. Her choice of evening clothes reflected an infallible taste for the deceptive simplicity that suited her so well. She looked stunning.

While Haden was almost certain that Harold Leyton had been genuinely surprised to see him, it had been the opposite with Helen Lloyd. Only the timing of his arrival just before Christmas had taken her aback.

"Any nice presents?" Haden asked.

"Some," Helen said. She smiled across her near-empty glass of champagne. "But I like yours, too."

Haden lifted the bottle and topped up her glass.

"I wonder where, or if, Alexander Baronin is celebrating," he said.

"If anyone knew that, his wife wouldn't have approached you," Helen said. Haden smiled at her, took out a cheroot and lit it. "How can you smoke those things while you're drinking a great champagne like this?" she asked. "Don't you have any taste buds left?"

"It's a bad habit. Like the way you avoid answering me." He put away his lighter. "I suppose it's the way you've been trained," he added.

There was a momentary gleam of irritation in her eyes, but she let go of it.

"I've mentioned Baronin," she said carefully. "There's some curiosity about what happened to him. Or why it happened, for that matter, since he only defected to get married."

"From what I hear, he was treated rather exceptionally back in Moscow," Haden said. "Free to mix with Westerners, be one of the boys, make cracks about the regime, pass on rumors, but no KGB minder on his back."

"They have licensed court jesters, too," Helen said. "All that was undoubtedly looked into."

"So it was all for live, then. Nothing for reward."

"It may surprise you," Helen said, "but that happens." She met his eyes, sighed, and shook her head. "Okay, I withdraw that. You, at least, care for one other person. Christa." Her smile was both apologetic and mischievous. "You have this great gift for irritating me."

"You have quite a talent in that direction yourself," Haden retorted.

"I sent you a note," Helen said. "You didn't answer."

"You didn't expect me to."

Helen made no reply to that, other than to lean forward to pick up her glass. Their brief lapse into personal remarks had, paradoxically, slackened the tension between them. They were nearer to being close than at any time since they had last made love.

"Baronin was rewarded, though," said Haden, returning to the subject. "Radio Liberation is a CIA operation, that's no secret."

"All kinds of people would be involved in running a radio station who weren't CIA personnel."

"As with the International Information Institute, Miss Deputy Director, London Office?" Haden inquired.

"I thought we'd called a truce," Helen said.

"Baronin has useful connections back in the Soviet Union. I would think he'd be on the payroll."

"Have it your way," Helen said.

"If a CIA man goes missing in mysterious circumstances, that sounds like CIA business to me. How come I get approached to look for him?"

"For a long time, you weren't," Helen said. She studied her watch. "I have to go. I did warn you."

"I could wait here until you get back," Haden suggested.

"I'll be late."

Haden said, "My hotel room's grossly overheated. I'm not sleeping well. There's still some champagne left."

Helen had switched on a couple of table lamps. In the shaded light, her face was very soft. She was perhaps unaware how tantalizing her small smile was.

"Stephen," she said quietly, "I don't want to start anything again. It would get in the way." Haden nodded and waited for her to continue. "You got to me," she said, not looking at his face. "I didn't think that would happen. If I had to define the kind of man I prefer, nothing about you would meet the specification."

"You could be speaking for both of us," Haden said.

Helen said, "I'm not someone who goes looking to get hurt. So, I'd rather you weren't here when I get back."

Haden stood up. "You're probably right," he said.

Helen sat where she was, looking up at him. "You use people, Stephen."

"So do you," Haden said.

Outside, a thin, chill wind had sprung up, and it felt much colder. He turned up his coat collar. In one respect only, he recalled with a nostalgia akin to regret, he knew a great deal about Helen Lloyd. Otherwise, he knew very little. She had simply vanished from his life, bound for who knew where, like a stranger.

As he walked away, he heard the sound of a taxi somewhere behind him. A change of engine noise signaled that it was slowing down, but not to a stop outside Helen Lloyd's house. Haden kept on going and did not turn his head, although his body tensed and he listened intently, mentally tracking the cab's movements. His ears told him that it had turned off toward Queensway. He walked on, his hands in his pockets, his senses searching for anything untoward, but finding nothing.

In the preceding twenty-four hours, he had begun to suspect that he was under surveillance. It was an instinct, a feeling, indefinable, impervious to reason. Haden treated instincts with respect. Yet he could find nothing to support that one, not the flimsiest trace of evidence, no recurring figure, face, or vehicle. Nothing.

Logically that should mean that he was wrong. The alternative—that he was the object of surveillance conducted with such skill that he would remain ignorant of the exact quarter from which danger might spring—was what kept his nerve endings tingling. He had the sensation that the back of his neck was exposed, and that hunching his shoulders would prove to be useless.

By way of random twists and turns along residential streets and quiet, ill-lit mews, he reached Bayswater Road and the entrance to his hotel. No evening stroll could have been more uneventful than his walk back from Helen Lloyd's, no sight more innocent than the lighted Christmas tree in the foyer. He should have felt foolish for his suspicions, but he did not.

Haden had asked the desk to do something about his hothouse room, and the heat was now at an acceptable level. He slept lightly. The feeling refused to go away.

Scattered snowflakes were drifting down halfheartedly when Haden stepped out of the hotel, but they melted as they fell and merely wet the roads and pavements.

He considered taking a taxi but decided to drive instead. He chose the most brightly lit route, which involved Oxford and Regent streets, both still ablaze with colorful Christmas illuminations. Already the great stores were advertising sales. A few hardy bargain hunters, some with sleeping bags, some perched on canvas stools, had begun their nightlong vigil.

Haden turned off Regent Street and crawled around the traffic-clogged streets of Soho. He finally insinuated the Cavalier into a space fortuitously vacated by a small Renault.

Earlier, after making an illegal maneuver to turn into Regent Street, he had been confident that no private car was following him. Taxis were another matter. All black cabs looked the same. But any taxi that had remained in his rearview mirror during his random tour of Soho would have become conspicuous. Surveillance was either intermittent, or he had evaded it, or it was nonexistent. As he walked to Shaftesbury Avenue and toward the theater, he felt almost relaxed.

"You mean you're in London?" Petra Baron had sounded surprised and a touch fretful when he had telephoned. "Hold on a minute." There had been a long silence. "Listen, I've arranged to go to the theater tonight, but suppose we meet afterward and have something to eat? Would that be okay?"

Haden had said, "I'll be waiting outside."

"Make it the stage door," Petra had said. "I have to go backstage afterward."

Haden tapped on the stage door's glass panel and spoke to the doorkeeper. She nodded and invited him to wait inside. On the other side of the door was a very small vestibule furnished only with a pay telephone and a tattered leather bench. Haden sat on the bench. The aging doorkeeper seemed glad to have someone to talk to. She told him the play was running for just a limited season. One of the leads had other commitments coming up. He only half listened.

From somewhere behind him came the sudden sounds of voices, bursts of conversation, shoes tapping as the owners hurried up or down stairs. Dressing-room doors slammed shut, and then there was silence again. Soon after, Petra Baron came in. She smiled a greeting at Haden and turned to her companion.

"Ralph, this is Stephen Haden," she said. "Ralph Janson."

"Happy to know you, Mr. Haden," Janson said, shaking hands with a well-practiced smile.

"We'll make this quick," Petra said.

They went past Haden and out of sight. Not long afterward, voices and the patter of feet on stone steps broke the silence.

"Someone should have embalmed that audience tonight."

"Somebody already has."

The three actors, two men and a girl, appeared, turned in their dressing-room keys, and went off in search of consoling food and drink. When Petra and Janson came back, the three of them walked to Old Compton Street. They were expected at the Italian restaurant, and fussed over.

Haden was indifferent to Italian food unless it was authentic and good. Here, it proved to be both. Ralph Janson conversed easily, seemingly about nothing in particular, as did Petra Baron.

Neither of them referred to the reason for Haden's presence, perhaps because the restaurant was full and its acoustics required raised voices even across a table. Or perhaps Petra was waiting for Janson to leave. Haden didn't know which. Nor was it clear what they were doing together, anyway.

Ralph Janson explained that the director of the play was something of a friend. "He was acting tonight as well, and he knew we were coming. That's why we had to go around and say hello afterward." By the time Janson had worked his way through the meal, Haden had learned that he had at one time been a lawyer but had for some years served his government in various capacities. He spoke of ambassadors, high-ranking officials, and secretaries of state in a familiar way. He seemed to know the President. How well was not clear.

Ralph Janson was the kind of American who gave the impression that success had arrived without his really trying for it. Ostentation, his dress and style made clear, was foreign to him. His voice was deep, with a resonant timbre, the sort that compelled and received attention. There was something weighty and formidable about Ralph Janson.

Haden supposed from Janson's groomed silver hair that he must be somewhere in his early fifties. The face, though creased with lines of experience and humor, might have been that of a younger man, with its white, even teeth and determined, firm jawline. When Janson studied the wine list, he took out a pair of glasses and held them briefly in front of his eyes to read the rather small print, but otherwise he did not use them.

Haden thought that Janson was a man who could easily appeal to women a lot younger than him. Since Petra Baron did not know if she was a wife or a widow, and since Haden had a skeptical view of human nature that veered to low, Haden watched them carefully to try to figure out the relationship. But although they evidently knew each other well, and exchanged smiles and glances, and although Ralph Janson watched Petra attentively when she took up the conversation, Haden could not detect any of the tiny give-away sexual signals that would support his half-formed hypothesis.

Eventually Janson said, "Well, I guess it's time to have Mario call a cab."

"My car's not far away," Haden said. "I can drive you, if you like."

"That would be kind," Janson said, "if it's not too much trouble."

Haden, guided by Janson, wound his way out of Soho toward Little Venice, and Janson directed him into a quiet road lined with trees whose branches were bare and stark. They stopped outside a substantial, elegant house that fronted on the canal.

"You'll come in for a nightcap, I hope," Janson said.

An ornate chandelier lit the large entrance hall. As Janson closed the front door, a small, pajama-clad boy appeared on the upstairs landing. A middle-aged woman wearing glasses was holding his hand.

"He heard the car," she said, with a touch of resignation.

"I'll settle him down again," Petra said to Haden. "You talk to Ralph."

Janson led the way into a spacious drawing room. A gaslog fire was flickering. Janson turned it up, and the flames licked high.

"I like to see a fire," he said. "What can I offer you?"

Haden succumbed to the idea of a cognac. Abstinence could be carried to excess.

The drawing room was furnished with a mixture of antique and modern pieces that blended well. Haden knew something about antiques and gave them an admiring glance. The cognac was impressive, too.

"Petra worked in my private office for a while when she got back from Moscow," Ralph Janson explained. "She left when young Peter was on the way." They sat in armchairs near the fire. Haden allowed the cognac to caress his palate. At his elbow was a standing ashtray. He lit a cheroot, enhancing his pleasure. Janson sipped his own drink, a single malt whisky, and pointed to their surroundings with a small gesture. "I spend time in London now and then," he said. "When I'm here, I like to have my own place." He crossed his legs comfortably and added, "The way London house prices are going up, it's also an investment."

"With plenty of room for guests," Haden added.

"Exactly so." Janson nodded. "That fine boy of hers deserved a good Christmas. I like to think that having people around her, going places, is helping Petra through a bad time."

"Did you know Alexander Baronin?" Haden inquired.

Janson said, "I was at their wedding. Alex is both clever and intelligent. Two qualities," he said dryly, "found in conjunction less often than most people imagine."

"What do you think happened to him?"

"I wish I knew," Janson answered. "I hope there is some simple explanation and that he's safe and well somewhere. Suffering from amnesia, or whatever. Who knows." He smiled slightly. "Of the many speculations put forward, there's nothing to back any of them. Including yours," he added. "Petra told me about your conversation."

"There's plenty of time to find out," Haden said. "And endless resources, if anyone was really interested—CIA personnel stationed in Vienna, American agents in the East. Inquiries, formal or not, could have been made through your Moscow embassy."

Janson gazed at Haden for some time, appearing to consider his reply.

"You seem to be taking rather a lot for granted, Mr. Haden," he said at last. "However, I will tell you that as much as possible has been done without making waves. If that answers your unspoken suggestion."

"Only up to a point," Haden said.

"Inquiries were accomplishing nothing," Janson continued, "thus, they have been allowed to go cold. An able outsider with a fresh mind might be able to turn up something." He shrugged. "No harm in trying. I imagine you have your own unorthodox methods. Free lances are not infrequently used in undercover capacities, as you surely know.'' Haden wondered if that was a veiled implication that Janson knew of his previous involvement with the intelligence services.

''Did Baronin settle down well in the West?'' Haden asked.

''No question of it that I'm aware of,'' Janson said. ''He married his girl, had a son, a well-paid job. Why shouldn't he?''

''His defection, through Finland and into Sweden, was arranged,'' Haden said. ''Petra says she doesn't know how.''

Again, Janson paused, weighing his words before responding.

''Petra came to me with her problem,'' he said eventually. ''I have contacts, a certain amount of influence. On the practical side, it was agreed that Alex would be useful. And he has been. I was glad to help Petra then. I hope you will feel the same now.''

''For me it's a commercial proposition,'' Haden admitted.

''That is well understood,'' Janson assured him. ''It's in your favor. You're not an ideologue. A man working for money is much safer. Less likely to get carried away and do something silly. To make it attractive, suppose we construct a deal on this basis: all expenses covered, plus guaranteed payment, with a bonus for results. Would that be acceptable?''

''What results are you looking for?''

''In the best of all possible worlds, the return of Alex Baron. Failing that, information, susceptible to proof, as to his whereabouts.''

''And if he's dead?''

''Then he's dead,'' Ralph Janson replied.

Stephen Haden drove thoughtfully toward Bayswater. It was well after 2:00 A.M., and the roads were almost deserted. Petra Baron had not reappeared before he left. Ralph Janson was either acting for her or was the principal in the matter. Possibly both. How or if Helen Lloyd entered the equation was not apparent.

Alexander Baronin's death would be sad news, Janson had said somberly, but if established beyond reasonable doubt, it, too, would be regarded as a result. For any of the various positive results, he had suggested a bonus of fifty thousand dollars. Haden had suggested double, testing the temperature of the water. It seemed to be on the warm side, for Ralph Janson, although he had hesitated, had acquiesced. The agreement, however, was in principle only. Haden had postponed final acceptance.

He turned the proposition over in his mind as he drove along, approaching it from all angles. A substantial guaranteed sum with a possible extra hundred thousand dollars had undeniable attractions. On the other hand, no one discussed that kind of money for anything easy, even though he would be very well paid for his time even if he failed to uncover anything. It looked like a no-lose proposition.

The lines of parked cars were continuous, occupying all the meters and residents' parking spaces. Haden did not feel like searching at this time of night and pulled his car in on a yellow line. He would move it in the morning.

As he got out, he heard the motorcycle rounding a bend, and glanced toward it automatically. Both the driver and the passenger behind him wore helmets and visors. Long blond hair protruded from under the helmet of the smaller, slimmer figure of the girl on the pillion.

43

As Haden fitted the key in the lock, he heard the motorcycle's engine suddenly cut off. He looked up, but only the rider was getting off. Haden turned around quickly. The other one, the girl, was approaching him from behind. In her hand was what looked like an iron bar.

Haden backed away until the iron railings behind him pressed into his shoulders. The driver, coming from the other direction, was swinging a heavy chain.

"You know what we want," the driver said, his voice low.

Haden was far from sure that he did. Both of them were wearing running shoes. When, simultaneously, they began to run, their feet made no sound in the night silence.

Haden's reaction was instinctive. There was only one way to go, and that was down. His fingers found the gate behind his back. He shoved it open with a clang, turned, and leaped down the steps into the basement area. In the shadowed half-darkness, he missed his footing, slipped, and fell, painfully grazing his face against the wall in his descent, and tumbled into a trash can that went over on its side with a metallic clatter, spewing out a collection of bottles. The noise reverberated in the quiet of the night.

The one with the chain was coming down the steps first, the girl following. Noise struck Haden as a very good idea indeed. He picked up an empty whisky bottle and hurled it. The driver ducked, but it hit the girl's helmet and shattered. "She" fell backward, swearing in a deep male voice.

The chain flailed at Haden's head in a vicious whirling arc. It hammered and rattled against the trash-can lid Haden had raised as a shield. Then he rammed the lid upward, violently, toward the driver's head. From the strangled, gurgling noise that followed, it seemed to have caught him somewhere in the throat, and his body lurched sideways.

There was a plentiful supply of bottles available. Haden slammed one on the knuckles of the hand holding the chain.

44

A grunt of pain joined the choking, and the chain fell onto the upturned trash can.

One or two lights had gone on nearby. Voices inside were raised in alarm. For good measure, Haden threw another bottle through the window of a downstairs room, smashing the glass. More alarmed voices joined in.

The "girl" had had enough and was on "her" way.

"For Christ's sake, come on," "she" growled to her companion, who needed no urging. Heads were looking out of upstairs windows, and someone shouted about phoning the police. The driver was scrambling away up the steps.

Haden groped for the chain, found it, and went after him, his shoes crunching on broken glass strewn on the steps.

The iron bar sailing through the air as he reached the top of the steps almost caught him unawares. He ducked, and it ricocheted off a spiked railing and onto someone's front steps.

The motorcycle engine roared before he could reach them. He threw the chain at the receding bike, hoping it would entangle itself in the spinning spokes, but it bounced off the tail pipe.

Haden walked away, ignoring the voices calling after him from open front doors. The two men were gone, and he had not seen their faces.

He heard the approaching scream of a siren when he was within yards of his hotel. The police car passed at high speed, turned off Bayswater Road on squeaking tires, and disappeared from sight toward the scene of the incident.

The night porter handed over his key and wished him good night without noticing that Haden had averted his head. In his room, Haden examined his face. The left side was an angry red.

Haden went into the bathroom and sponged the raw skin gingerly, wincing. He was annoyed. He preferred to shave with a blade. A blade would be out of the question for a few days.

Chapter Three

Stephen Haden was cautiously experimenting with his electric razor, trying to skim off stubble without removing inflamed skin, when the telephone rang. It was Reception.

"A Mr. Hamilton is on his way up to see you, Mr. Haden," the girl said.

Hamilton was a large man with a round, fortyish but still boyish face and a polite manner. When he smiled, his eyes crinkled pleasantly while somehow failing to reflect any inner humour.

"I'm from the Home Office, Immigration Department, Mr. Haden," he said as he stood in the doorway. He offered identification without being asked. "There may be some query concerning your passport. May I see it, please?"

Haden stepped aside. Hamilton walked in, glanced around idly, and gazed at Haden with interested concern.

"What have you done to your face, Mr. Haden?" he asked.

"Window-shopping," Haden said. "Walked into a lamppost." He opened his briefcase and handed over his passport.

"Yes," Hamilton said, testing the document as if weighing it. "A British passport. But you are not a British subject, are you."

"My father was British, my mother was Swiss," Haden answered. "I was born and brought up in Switzerland. Eventually, I took Swiss nationality. When I was working in England as a young man, I found I could apply for a British passport. It was granted. Your own records could have told you that."

"Do you happen to have your Swiss passport with you?"

Haden delved into his briefcase again. With a polite smile, Hamilton took the second passport, sat down at the writing desk, opened both passports, and studied them slowly and carefully in silence. He was paying particular attention to the entry and exit stamps.

"There's some coffee left," Haden said. "Help yourself."

Hamilton nodded, continuing his scrutiny. Haden went back into the bathroom to his experiment with the electric razor. He left the door open and kept an eye on Hamilton.

When Haden wished to cross a frontier on serious business, he rarely used either of these passports. The man could pore over them to his heart's content, but he would find no irregularities, and even if he had powers of search, he would find no forged passports among Haden's possessions. Hamilton did move once, leaning in the direction of Haden's briefcase, but he lifted the coffeepot instead. His coffee poured, he remained at the writing desk, his head bent, his fingers turning pages, glancing from one passport to the other, perhaps checking dates for inconsistencies.

Haden switched off his razor. The side of his face that rather resembled half a red traffic light was not as smooth as he would have wished, but it was the best he could do. He went back into the bedroom and sat down. Still Hamilton did not look at him or say anything. Haden checked the time. He should have moved the Cavalier before now, but he could cheerfully tear up a parking ticket. He would have left the country long before the cumbersome machinery traced him. But it would be tiresome if the car were towed. At last Hamilton sat back and placed one passport neatly on top of the other, although he made no move to return them.

"If you've finished, I have things to do," Haden said pointedly.

"Yes," Hamilton said. "What exactly is the purpose of your visit to the U.K.?"

"To see friends," Haden replied.

"And you propose to stay how long?"

Haden said, "Perhaps until early January. My step-daughter's at boarding school in Hampshire. I may meet her at the airport and take her back. I haven't decided yet."

Hamilton nodded gravely, as though this information were of intense significance. His fingers played with the passports, until he'd aligned the covers to his satisfaction. Only then did he direct his opaquely discomfiting eyes at Haden.

"Might these friends be concerned with your business activities?" he inquired.

"I have no business interests here," Haden said.

"My question requires a yes or no response," Hamilton advised.

"My answer contained the word no," Haden pointed out.

"To me, the phrasing was evasive," Hamilton replied.

"Please yourself," Haden said indifferently.

Changing his tone, Hamilton said agreeably, "By profession, you are a *Fluchthelfer*. You operate an escape organization. You smuggle human cargo from Eastern Bloc countries into the West, usually West Germany."

"Where it's not illegal, as you should know."

"We are not in West Germany," Hamilton observed.

49

"Even there, you have caused embarrassment. Your organization has been the subject of a report by their intelligence service. Your own country is less than happy about it."

Haden said wearily, "What I do is not illegal under Swiss law either."

Hamilton said, "Many of your activities are illegal under any law, including British."

"Everyone's happy when refugees gain freedom, most of all the poor bastards themselves," Haden said, irritated. "If they can manage it on their own, it's cheers all around. Most can't. They need help. And that's what I provide."

"But only for money," Hamilton added.

"It costs money," Haden snapped. "Freedom's fine in theory, but governments don't like to accept responsibility for the means. They want to play Pontius Pilate. Now the British want to wash their hands, too. Is that the message?"

"I'm glad you mention the means you use, Mr. Haden," Hamilton said, unmoved. "Among them, I'm given to understand, is the acquisition of stolen blank passports from West German criminals, the use of false number plates on motor vehicles, the forgery of documents, the unauthorized possession of firearms, and the smuggling of firearms into other countries, which may well include the United Kingdom. For all I know, there are more. Whether you are a White Knight to your clients is irrelevant. Any person known to have been engaged in criminal activities is likely to find his presence regarded as unwelcome if there is the slightest hint of anything amiss. Such a person would be well advised to behave with great care."

"And may well find himself under surveillance," Haden said.

Hamilton eyed him bleakly. "Really? Do you have reason to suppose that is the case?"

"As a personal favor," Haden said, "make it around the clock. Then you'll feel happier and I'll feel safer."

"Have a good holiday," Hamilton said, his eyes crinkling agreeably. "Early January, you said. I'll wish you a pleasant flight home. Good day, Mr. Haden."

The door closed behind him. Haden crossed to the telephone and dialed. A voice he did not recognize answered.

Haden parked as near to the block of flats as he could. Why he had been asked to wait outside was not apparent. He sounded the horn when he saw Harold Leyton emerge. Leyton came down the steps and walked toward the car. He was followed by a tall man of about thirty, with a lean, handsome face. Haden wound down the window.

"Stephen, I'd like you to meet Ian," Leyton said. "Stephen Haden."

"How do you do, Mr. Haden," Ian said, with a nice smile, offering his hand. Haden shook it. "I'll be in the pub, then, Harry," Ian said. "I'll set them up, shall I?"

"Okay," Leyton said. Ian walked away with an easy, athletic stride. Leyton watched him go. "He rather wanted to meet you, Stephen," he said. "He's a bit insecure, poor soul." He sighed. "No reason. I'm not one to go cruising, but there it is. He'll be all right now he's satisfied you're straight."

"What is he? Another actor?"

Leyton managed a pained smile.

"Despite the looks, no," he said. "He's an accountant. A very sharp one, too. Let's talk in your car, if you don't mind. We're meeting some chums, and as you gathered, I'm not supposed to be long." He walked around the car, got into the passenger seat, and noticed the left side of Haden's face. "Stephen!" he said. "What . . . ?"

"Later," Haden said. He wound up his window. The incipient snow had gone, but the damp air was cold.

"You've had drinks with some old pals, then," he remarked.

"What makes you say that?" Leyton inquired warily.

"I've had a visitor. He said he was from Immigration. What was I doing in the country, whatever it was kindly don't do it, and the sight of my back would be a pleasure. He smelled like Special Branch to me."

Leyton considered for a moment, but shook his head. "My pals wouldn't have talked," he said.

"Someone did," Haden remarked. "Suddenly I'm not welcome."

"When you were welcome, you caused a lot of trouble," Leyton said. "Probably just a warning shot. No encore, by request."

"You told me all that had been buried."

"The tombstone bears my name," Leyton said sadly. "I'd be surprised if yours didn't figure, too."

Haden supposed that was not only plausible but likely.

"I also have the feeling I'm under surveillance part of the time."

"Given your caller, that wouldn't astound me," Leyton said.

"During the other part, two bikers tried to mug me."

"Hence your Technicolor face," Leyton said, smiling. "Another American import we could have done without. Time was, no one had heard of muggings. Now it's all the rage."

"They didn't wait to find out if I was going to hand over my wallet," Haden explained. "They were set on using a chain and an iron bar."

"You got off lightly," Leyton said, studying Haden's face. "What happened to them?"

"They went away," Haden said.

"Yes, you can be a vicious bastard, Stephen," Leyton reflected. "Someone wanted to put you in hospital for a few weeks, is that it? Stop you trying to find out what happened to Alexander Baronin." He wagged his head dubiously. "They were probably just muggers, high as kites."

"I told you that what it's about would come to you," Haden said. "So what have you got?"

"Not much," Leyton answered. "The wheels are in motion, though, but I'm afraid they'll need oiling. One little item did emerge."

He broke off and gazed at Haden significantly.

"Which is?" Haden inquired. Harold Leyton was being coy.

"After he defected, Baronin was tried and sentenced to death *in absentia.*"

"No one's mentioned that to me," Haden said slowly. "I wonder why. Unless your pal had nothing worth selling and served up a tasty rumor instead."

"Rumors can be true," Leyton said. "This chap was serving in Moscow at the time. He mentioned it to a friend at the U.S. embassy there as a piece of Allied goodwill. He got the impression they already knew about it."

"If it's true, I find it surprising," Haden responded. "For quite a long time, their policy has been to try to get defectors back again."

"That's right," Leyton agreed. "One way or another. Even highranking KGB officers. More propaganda mileage in news conferences about how they were kidnapped and tortured by Western agents, and so on."

"They've sentenced serving officers to death who've defected," Haden reflected. "But Baronin wasn't a military man. Or was he? If not, why him?"

"Could be they thought he wasn't important enough to bother getting back again, but what he was up to annoyed them," Leyton suggested. "They regard the output of Radio Liberation as an attempt to stir up dissidents and subversives. Which, of course, from their point of view, it is."

53

Haden tapped his fingers on the steering wheel and considered the various implications, if the report was accurate. Among them was the elimination of one possibility.

"That means he wouldn't have gone back to the Soviet Union," he said. "Not if he had any choice in the matter, anyway."

"Not unless he was suicidally inclined and riddled with guilt," Leyton added cheerfully. He smoothed his small mustache with his forefinger. "Suppose I said 'Dante' to you," he asked. "Would that suggest anything?"

Haden looked at him. Leyton's face was bland, but his eyes were intent.

"Dante? As in the Italian poet?"

"As in, but not—if you see what I mean," Leyton said, with a gentle smile.

Haden shook his head. "Then it doesn't mean a thing."

Leyton regarded him carefully before nodding acceptance.

"Should it?" Haden asked.

Leyton said, "I looked up a certain Freddy. His role in counterintelligence was keeping an eye on our friends rather than on the opposition. Put crudely—what the Americans were up to that they weren't telling us about."

Haden gazed at the chubby face with approval. "That's more like it, Harry," he said warmly. "Go on."

"I said 'was.' The Americans rumbled him and made hostile noises. Now he's stuck at a desk in London instead of living it up in Washington. So he's out of date, but nursing a grievance and inclined to talk more than he should. We had a few jars. He drinks too much, too. The word 'Dante' cropped up."

"In connection with Baronin?"

"The reverse, actually," Leyton said. "What he said was, to quote verbatim, 'Fuck Baronin, he's a nobody. Who cares

54

about fucking Baronin? Dante now, that'd be different, Dante would.' "

"What does that mean?"

"I don't know. He was pissed and none too coherent," Leyton said apologetically. "I played along, fished, tried to find out. It turned out he'd picked up the word 'Dante' in Washington. He didn't know what it meant, but he was convinced he was on to something big. Then he got the elbow. Now he has this fixation about Dante." Leyton shook his head uncertainly. "He used to be good. But he was hitting the bottle over there, too. That's why he blew it. I'm not sure what to think. Oh, well." He looked at his watch. "Time I went. Sorry I haven't got more for you, Stephen."

"Perhaps that's all there is," Haden said.

Harold Leyton scratched the back of his neck. "If you do go looking for Baronin, Stephen," he said, "how would it be if I stayed on board? Would you mind?"

Haden said, "There wouldn't be much in it for you. You'd make more loot flogging franchises."

"Yes, but cash in hand from you is tax free," Leyton said. He smiled slyly. "Well, so is flogging franchises, virtually, thanks to Ian. I'm not after your cut, Stephen. Just on an expenses-paid basis. How about that?"

"You look fine, Harry," Haden said. "You sound delirious."

"I know," Leyton said sheepishly. "The truth is, I try and make light of it, but I miss the Brownies. There's something about this Baronin business doesn't quite click." He met Haden's gaze. "Don't ask me what because I couldn't tell you. It's a hunch. A gut feeling there's something more to it. Christ knows what. Maybe I am raving. But if anything interesting did turn up, perhaps I could use it to pay my way. What can you lose?"

Haden handed him a plump envelope. "Oil for the wheels, Harry," he said.

"See you, Stephen," Harold Leyton said. He got out and slammed the door.

Stephen Haden sat for a while before he turned the key in the ignition. He shared Harold Leyton's instinct. Something about Baronin did not quite add up.

"You should have been a nurse," Haden said. Whatever soothing emollient she had applied to his face had been instantly effective. He looked at himself in the wall mirror and fancied that the redness was subsiding, too.

Helen Lloyd said, "I don't suppose you reported it to the police."

"I preferred some sleep to making statements and looking at mug shots I couldn't identify anyway. How much time do we have?"

"It's open," Helen said. "All evening, whatever you need."

That meant, Haden supposed, that matters had been hurriedly advanced after his unexpectedly early arrival.

"Suppose I'd agreed to Petra Baron's proposition in Zurich? She wanted me to start there and then."

Helen smiled faintly.

"Petra doesn't know you," she said. "Even if you had, you'd have needed more information."

"Which is suddenly at the fingertips of the Deputy Director of the International Information Institute. I thought I was *persona non grata* with your outfit."

"You were," Helen replied patiently. "The requirement for a certain type of person arose. There aren't too many around. So, temporarily, you're *persona grata*." Haden grunted dismissively. "Stephen," she said, "if it riles you to talk to me, I can arrange for you to meet with someone else. It wouldn't be good for personalities to get in the way."

Haden grinned at her. "It's a pipe dream," he said, "but I sometimes think it would be nice if you were just a woman, that's all. Open, no secrets to hide. Instead of a lady whose prime loyalty is always elsewhere, come what may."

"If I weren't what I am, you'd have forgotten me long ago."

Haden wondered if it were true. It might well be. "We all want it every way," he said. "You're the same. Okay. Information. Ralph Janson. You know him?"

"To speak to," she said. "Not well. I know about him. He's a behind-the-scenes man, one of those people almost unknown to the public, but carrying a lot of clout. He specializes in sensitive issues."

"You mean like security issues?" Haden supposed.

"High-level advisers are concerned with assessments," Helen went on. "He ranks high. He'd like to go higher. He's ambitious. Very."

"For what? Not money—he has that already."

"His wife has the real money. She's an heiress. A Burnham. Supports an opera company. Her father was the one who set up the Burnham Foundation for Foreign Policy Studies."

"I was at his house in Little Venice. If there was a Mrs. Janson there, he didn't mention it."

"Should he have? Maybe she had already gone back, I don't know. She doesn't visit the London house much. She prefers the social scene in Washington."

"Ralph Janson talked about money as though he personally would be loosening the purse strings."

"Maybe he meant the government purse. But the source of the funds is outside my competence."

"You weren't briefed on that?"

"I guess no one imagined you'd care where your money came from."

"Helen," Haden asked, "does government funds mean the CIA budget? That's all I'm asking."

"No, you're not," Helen said. "You're asking if Ralph Janson is in a position to authorize CIA expenditure."

"Not necessarily," Haden insisted. "I could be inquiring if there's more than one outfit in on the act. I've been caught in the middle before. It's nicer when everyone's pulling in the same direction. His links could be with the National Security Council, for all I know. They don't always see eye-to-eye with the CIA, I'm told."

Helen sighed pointedly. "You adore looking for complications where none exist, don't you?" she asked. "If the White House were interested in Alexander Baronin for some reason, a man like Ralph Janson could be entrusted to overlook developments and report back. But that's only a guess," she added.

"Janson behaved like a man in the driver's seat, not a messenger."

"Maybe it was felt that his considerable standing would be helpful at this stage."

"His standing meant nothing to me," Haden said. "I'd never heard of him."

"Well, you have now," Helen commented tartly. "You should be able to read the cards for yourself. If you take this on, you're acting for Petra Baron, no one else. That's how it has to be. But Ralph Janson's intervention should show you that no one, not even me, is trying to get you involved in some private game on the side." Haden wondered why he had not read the coded message for himself. It seemed logical enough.

Helen glanced at her watch. Then her clear hazel eyes returned to his. "If you insist, we can go on discussing

Ralph Janson," she said, "but I'm getting bored with saying 'I don't know.' "

"It must be tiring," Haden agreed. "When did you suggest Christa's school for Petra Baron's son?"

Helen's face remained composed. "When she asked me. It's a good school, right for Peter."

"Sometime last autumn," Haden said, nodding. "Why the delay before I was approached?"

"Inquiries into Baronin's disappearance were still in hand. Had the matter been cleared up, it wouldn't have been necessary to try a different angle."

"But the groundwork had been laid," Haden said. Helen gazed at him steadily but said nothing. "I don't like Christa being used," Haden said. "I think I take serious offense."

She gave him a sudden mocking smile. "Cant like that doesn't seem natural coming from a bastard like you," she remarked.

Haden shook his head and laughed. Helen's smile took on some warmth and lost its mockery.

"Don't be misled," Haden told her. "A high moral tone from you is funny, that's all. Okay, tell me about Baronin."

"You're mostly aware of the known facts," Helen replied.

"Helen," Haden said, "your intelligence people must have come up with something, for Christ's sake."

"Nothing conclusive, or we wouldn't be talking. It's thought best that you make your own judgments."

Haden said, "I need to know Baronin's real function inside the CIA. If he wasn't on the payroll, none of this makes sense."

"His work at Radio Liberation involved research, some monitoring, translation, very occasional broadcasts—for all of which he was well qualified. He was a useful employee, but it was all pretty run-of-the-mill, low-level stuff."

"Just a small, unimportant cog in the machine?" Haden

translated. Helen nodded. "Then I wonder," Haden said, gazing at her, "why Petra Baron suggested he might be somewhere behind the Iron Curtain and might need to be smuggled out again, courtesy of Stephen Haden."

"That isn't thought to be very likely," Helen said. "Petra fears such may be the case, but she's personally involved."

"My name still came out of the hat, picked by those who aren't," Haden remarked. "But who would know that organizing escapes is my trade?"

"Unlikely doesn't mean impossible," Helen emphasized. "You represent a good bet. But the odds are heavily against. If he went back willingly, he wouldn't cooperate. And there is no known reason why the KGB should take the trouble to kidnap Baronin. They go for big fish, not minnows."

"If I were a Soviet defector who'd been sentenced to death in my absence, I wouldn't go back willingly," Haden assured her.

"Why that should have happened simply isn't understood," Helen said frankly. "He just wasn't important enough."

"Then why is he so important to your people?" Haden inquired softly.

Helen shook her head slowly. There was uncertainty in her eyes, and her expression conveyed honest puzzlement, as if she were confronting some inexplicable riddle. Haden privately reserved his position, but he thought that it certainly looked like the genuine article.

"I don't know, Stephen," she said. "I can't even guess. I only know that it's important."

"How do you know? Who told you?"

"It's not been expressed in words," Helen explained soberly. "There's an atmosphere. Something's going on, or has been, and people are worried, but no one knows what it is."

"Someone must," Haden said. "Have you tried ing?"

"I've given you all the information accessible to me," Helen assured him.

"Perhaps Ralph Janson has more," Haden suggested.

"Maybe," she said dubiously. "But I'd think he's here to show the flag—to express the concern felt back in Washington. Anyway, I doubt your premise that someone must know. You can become convinced that something's wrong without knowing what it is."

Haden nodded a silent amen to that. That particular feeling was a constant companion.

"But somehow the disappearance of the low-level Baronin is thought to matter," he said. Helen nodded. "And you'd like me to try to come up with one of Ralph Janson's 'results,' " Haden said. He leaned forward and took her hand before she could nod again. "I don't mean 'you,' the lady who works for a CIA front organization in some capacity she'll never tell me," he said. "I mean the 'you' who's not looking to get hurt."

Helen smiled at him with a touch of sadness, her fingers pressed against his.

"If you were someone else," she said quietly, "a safe man, trusting, vulnerable, I guess I'd say no." She turned her hand, and her fingertips caressed his palm. That simple touching unlocked suppressed desire. "But you're everything that kind of man isn't," she continued, her soft, velvety voice very low. "So I guess the answer has to be yes." Their fingers played gently, each with the other's. Her eyes were wide and veiled, the same look she'd had when she had first seen the scars on his naked body. "Besides," she murmured, "you only need to do your best to trace Baronin. No one wants you to take any risks." With one fingernail she began to trace an intricate pattern on his palm.

"I definitely do not," she said. Her smiled lingered, but the touch of sadness had gone. "Okay?"

"Whatever you say," Haden told her abstractedly. He leaned forward a little farther. She met him halfway. Her lips touched his and settled, warm, soft, compliant. It was a gentle kiss, a recollection, a meeting after a long absence, a promise. She laid her cheek against his. Her fingers stroked the back of his neck.

"I guess I could fix something to eat here, if you like," she said. "If you're ready."

"I'm ready," Haden said. "Whenever you are."

"I'll do it now."

Haden was sitting back comfortably, watching her as she moved away toward the kitchen, and contemplating the prospect of the next few hours, when the telephone rang.

Helen lifted the receiver, her back to Haden.

"Hello . . . Who is that? . . . Hold on." She turned, covered the mouthpiece, and gazed at Haden with eyes no longer veiled in the slightest. "This number is unlisted for very good reasons," she said in a tight voice. "I don't like it being handed around."

Haden stood up. "I only left it in case of emergency," he said pacifically.

She handed him the receiver without commenting and walked out. Haden spoke into the telephone, jotted down the number he was given, and hung up. Helen had left the door open. He could hear her moving about in the kitchen. He closed the door, returned to the telephone, and dialed the number.

It proved to be a club in St. James's. His call was evidently being awaited. After the polite male voice said, "One moment, sir, please," he heard a brief murmur of conversation and then a more familiar voice, saying, "I'll take it in the private booth, George." Then there was a pause before the lines came to life again.

"Hullo, Stephen," said Harold Leyton. "I'm with the Freddy I mentioned. He claims to have something but insists on speaking to the man with the money, in person. Can you be at your hotel in about twenty minutes?"

"Remember my friend from the Home Office," Haden said.

"I mentioned that to Freddy," Leyton said. "He says it's safe."

"Is he sober?"

"As the proverbial judge. Listen, he'll only meet you without me. But if it's anything ripe, I'm in on it. I hope that's understood."

"Of course, Harry. Goes without saying."

"Be in the lobby," Leyton told him.

Haden wandered casually into the kitchen. Helen was closing the oven door. He gave her an affectionate smile.

"I have to meet someone," he said. "It's probably nothing, but I think I should find out."

"By all means," Helen said sweetly. "Fine with me."

"It shouldn't take long."

"Don't worry about it. I've decided on an early night, anyway. You have fun."

"Helen," Haden said, with as much humility as he could muster, "it was only a message. It could have been important."

"I'm not mad about that," she said. "Just for a minute there, Haden, I nearly forgot. But for that phone call, I could have done something I'd have regretted a lot."

"I don't believe that," Haden said.

"On that subject your opinion doesn't count." She began to chop vegetables with deft, quick strokes. The click of the gleaming knife on the cutting board ceased for a moment as she glanced at him sideways with the small, mocking smile that, Haden reflected, usually appeared on her lips only when there was a safe distance between them. "Go keep your appointment, Stephen," she said. "I hope it's interesting. Good night."

She resumed chopping.

Chapter Four

Harold Leyton and another man walked into the hotel lobby and stood talking near the revolving doors. Neither looked in the direction where Stephen Haden was seated. Haden stood up, crossed to the desk, collected his key, and entered the elevator.

He got out on the third floor, walked along the soft carpeted corridor, and unlocked the door to his room. Once inside he sat down facing the door, which he had left slightly ajar, and lit a cheroot. A few minutes later, he heard the elevator arrive. After a pause it whined down again. The door opened wide. Freddy walked in, closed the door, nodded cordially, took off his smart tweed overcoat, and sat down.

"I've sent Harold home," he said.

"Something to drink?" Haden asked.

"No, thank you, I'm on the wagon," Freddy said. "For the time being," he added, with a gentle smile.

If Freddy was the lush prone to four-letter words that Harold Leyton had portrayed, his appearance belied it. His bland, soft, benign face could have belonged to a bishop who had retained his innocence, and his immaculate clothes were those of a City gent. His fingernails were manicured, his full head of hair graying and stylishly cut, and his accent fruity, with a tendency to render *r*'s as *w*'s.

"I gather surveillance is off tonight," Haden said. "I wonder why I'm honored with any at all."

"More of an occasional check than close surveillance," Freddy said. "There are people whose presence in the country is noted. You're one of them. Routine stuff. Not to worry about it. If it concerns you, I suggest you use one of your funny passports next time."

"It only concerns me if it gets in the way," Haden said.

"The British have no interest in Baronin," Freddy explained. "Even if they knew your purpose," he continued, "which they don't. At least, not from me."

"Meaning Harry?" Haden inquired doubtfully.

"Do you trust him?"

"Yes and no," Haden answered. "It would depend."

"Harold is outside," Freddy said. "He craves to be back inside. For him, it's like a womb. He wants that comfort very badly."

"What do you want?"

"Money," Freddy replied blandly. "A great deal."

"Good luck," Haden said. "Find a benefactor."

"You have access to certain people," Freddy said. "I can't approach them. You can. For suitable recognition of your services, naturally."

"Uh-huh," Haden said. "A front man."

"An ambassador," Freddy corrected genially.

"While you remain in the background." Freddy nodded. "Because it wouldn't be safe for you to be in the foreground." Freddy shrugged. "So you want someone to stick his head over the parapet," Haden said. "While you stay in the bunker. I sympathize. I'm a bunker man myself."

Freddy chuckled tolerantly. "A poor description of Stephen Haden the *Fluchthelfer*," he said. "But on this occasion you would simply be the negotiator. You would play no part in the actual arrangements. That would be my province, in which area I am reasonably skilled," he said modestly. "Your commission would be substantial. Think in terms of, say, fifty K for two or three short meetings."

Haden thought about it. "The subject of these negotiations being what?"

"You will receive a perfectly innocent object," Freddy said, "which your contact will recognize. You need not." His expression was complacent, his eyes dreamy.

"Dante," Haden guessed, although not, he considered, too wildly.

The face remained complacent, but the eyes changed, although only momentarily. For a fraction of a second, they lit up hard and dangerous. Then they were innocent once more.

"When in my cups with old friends," Freddy said, apologetically, "the tongue sometimes wags out of turn."

Haden studied the bland, sleek man. In less time than it took to blink, Freddy had examined the possibility that Haden knew something—and if so, what to do about it—identified the source, and decided that what Haden knew was insufficient to prejudice anything. Haden, who liked to think he was pretty quick himself, was impressed. He remembered Leyton's saying that Freddy used to be good before he took to the bottle.

Freddy was saying nothing, waiting, apparently placid and composed, but Haden had noticed Freddy wet his lips with his tongue and swallow—quick, small movements, but perceptible. He was not finding it an easy ride on the wagon. Perhaps he was still good when he was sober. Haden wondered how long he could hold out.

"Don't just sit there, Freddy," Haden said. "Tell me who or what 'Dante' is."

"I really don't know," Freddy said, with the open honesty Haden had encountered before from members of the intelligence fraternity.

"You ruined a promising evening," Haden said. "Find yourself someone who'll negotiate blind."

"You think I'm lying," Freddy said sadly. "I'm not."

"Then you don't need me," Haden said. "You've nothing to sell."

Freddy said, "You don't quite understand how these things are." He abandoned his relaxed pose and leaned forward with earnest intensity. "It's scraps, disconnected threads, disjointed leads, none of which mean anything on their own or attract any attention in the department. Unless you know what you're looking for. You might call it a hobby of mine," he said dryly. "One advantage of being shunted into a dead end behind a desk is that material crosses desks. Occasionally I have access to information I shouldn't. Codes I understand. Quite recently, for some reason I can't identify, it's begun to form a pattern, although without a final configuration. Rather like an immensely complex crossword puzzle, if you like. With one entry missing. When I have that, I'll know all about Dante."

Haden said, "Even unfinished merchandise can provide samples. Come up with one."

Freddy, thoughtful, nibbled his lower lip, with every appearance of reluctance.

"I hesitate," he said eventually, "not because I've so much to choose from. Far from it. Without the final link, there's no cohesion, so this is speculation, but it's the best I can do. It looks," he said carefully, "as though somewhere there's some kind of . . . there's no other way to put this," he said apologetically, "some kind of shadowy group, in effect a secret society, at work."

Haden's eyebrows rose. "Like the Freemasons?" he inquired.

Freddy's bleak smile acknowledged the sarcasm. "Nothing so innocent," he said. "Although perhaps I've misinterpreted the indications. Within twenty-four hours I'll know. I'm that close." He held up his thumb and forefinger, half an inch apart.

"After you've cracked it," Haden said, "why will you need me?"

Freddy leaned back comfortably again, crossed his legs, and adjusted the knife-edge crease in his trousers.

"It's big," he said. "I've known that from the beginning. Really big. Duty suggests I should pass the information to my superiors. They're the same slimy bastards who demoted me. They'd take the credit. The alternative is to sell it. I think it's worth a small fortune. I prefer that option."

"It all began in Washington," Haden said, watching Freddy's face. "Logic suggests that payment for silence would come from that direction. I've only two American contacts I could take it to. Helen Lloyd and Ralph Janson. Which would you prefer?"

Watching Freddy's face was a waste of time. There was no reaction, not a flicker. He simply smiled knowingly. "That's your logic, not mine," he said. "I haven't mentioned anyone paying for silence. We'll come to your contact when we're ready to move."

"Does Baronin fit into your crossword puzzle?"

Some impatience modified Freddy's clerical visage. "Not to my knowledge," he said. "Never mind Baronin. This'll be more cost-effective for you than Baronin."

"It would be nice if one stone killed two birds," Haden said.

"Well, I can't promise you that," Freddy said, jovially, taking Haden's remark as an acceptance. "But if so, consider it a bonus. Tomorrow I'm duty officer," he said in a more businesslike way. "Saturday's pretty quiet. I'll have access to certain traffic. If I've got it right, that'll be it."

He scribbled on a piece of paper and handed it to Haden. "This is my modest home," he said. "I used to have a decent place in Kensington, but divorce is a costly business. Two are crippling. Unless I call you in the meantime to say otherwise, be there at ten-thirty on Sunday morning. If you don't hear from me, you'll know it's a go." Haden took the slip of paper.

Freddy stood up, eased himself into his overcoat, and buttoned it. "One rather important thing," he added. "Surveillance may be back on. I can't be certain. Were you to be followed to my house . . . well, I needn't elaborate."

"I'll be careful," Haden assured him.

Freddy made his stately way to the door, but paused before opening it.

"I need hardly add, I'm sure," he said, "that Harold Leyton is not a party to this."

"No Harold," Haden agreed.

"If all goes well tomorrow," Freddy continued, "I'll see you Sunday morning. We'll have a drink on Dante."

He smiled with some anticipation, and left, closing the door quietly behind him.

Haden sent for some roast beef sandwiches and a Danish pastry. He might as well imitate Helen Lloyd and have an early, if separate, night. He undressed, and, when the sandwiches arrived, sat eating them in his dressing gown, thinking about Freddy and whether, driven by his private obsession, he was wandering in some fantasy land, or if he should be taken seriously.

Haden left half the Danish uneaten and thought he would have preferred dinner and dessert with Helen Lloyd.

Saturday seemed as good a day as any to catch up on outstanding matters. Haden called his Zurich office, expecting to leave a message on his answering machine, but Anna picked up instead. He had been obliged to replace two of his key personnel, and Anna had agreed to look in now and then to make sure things were running smoothly.

She brought him up-to-date briskly. There appeared to be no outstanding problem that couldn't wait. He asked her to try to establish the whereabouts of one of his agents, Erwin Matz—to find out whether he was in the East, and if so when he would return—and suggested she call him back. Anna told him to hold on and gave him the answer in seconds. Matz had not yet left and was standing by at the usual number in West Berlin. Haden thanked her and hung up.

Anna was a highly efficient woman. He had offered her the job of office manager, but she had not wanted to be tied down on a full-time basis and had declined. Haden understood her reasons but still rather wished she had accepted. The man he had recruited instead was competent enough but lacked her quick mind.

Erwin Matz answered at once in his quiet, unemotional way.

"I may need a policeman in your hometown, Erwin," Haden said. "Someone who's kept his eyes and ears open, who's willing to talk off the record."

Erwin Matz did not ask why. He took his time before answering.

"Only one I could recommend," he said. "But he's careful, and it's a personal contact."

"Understood," Haden assured him. "I'll come back to you if necessary. This may not mature. How are things otherwise?"

Erwin Matz replied concisely and without elaboration. Haden found no need to offer advice or comment.

He had lost the man who had run his all-important West Berlin branch. With some reservations, he had put in Erwin

Matz on a temporary basis. Matz lacked experience, but Haden was beginning to warm to the young man.

Later Harold Leyton called and chatted discursively, without mentioning Freddy. Haden supposed he did not wish to display undue curiosity. Finally, Leyton casually let the name drop indirectly.

"I thought you told me he hadn't been drinking," Haden said.

"He hadn't," Leyton protested. "I was watching him all evening. He was on mineral water. And his breath was sweet as a baby's."

"Vodka doesn't smell," Haden said.

"You mean there was nothing in it?" Leyton sounded both disappointed and not entirely convinced.

"He burbled on about his grievances," Haden said. "Harry, I have a long-distance call coming in. Talk to you another time."

Haden hung up, took a break, and smoked a cheroot while he glanced through the newspapers. Then he tried Helen Lloyd and discovered that the number was no longer in service. He sighed, called the International Institute, and spoke briefly to the answering device. Twenty minutes later, Helen Lloyd called him back.

"I gather you've had your number changed," Haden said.

"It can't be handed around," Helen said.

"It won't happen again," Haden promised.

"Make sure it doesn't, please." She gave him her new number. Haden wrote it down. "What did you want me for, anyway?" she inquired.

"Just that," Haden said. "I think you gave me everything else, or nearly."

Her chuckle was musically agreeable. "Have a nice day," she said ironically.

A few minutes later, the phone rang. It was Ralph Janson, who, without in any way appearing anxious, evidently thought it was time to check in with Haden.

"We haven't been in touch, Mr. Haden," Janson said courteously, without reproof. "I hope you don't mind my contacting you."

"I'm looking into Baronin's disappearance," Haden reported.

"Petra will be happy to hear that," Janson said. "Take such time as you truly need. Anything I can do, you know where to reach me. I remain available."

Haden stayed off the telephone after that and remained in the hotel in case Freddy rang to cancel their appointment. He did not.

Sunday was a grim, raw day, biting cold, with intermittent icy rain. Haden rose early and left the hotel before nine. He walked fast through one of the piercing showers, with his head bowed and eyes to the ground, wishing joy of it to anyone assigned to follow him. At Kensington Gardens he circled the Round Pond. That early on a Sunday morning, there were no children sailing their model boats. The only living person in sight was a daintily attractive, middle-aged woman dressed with some style for the weather, who was exercising an Irish wolfhound. Haden admired the beast, and he and the woman fell into conversation, mostly about dogs. She talked openly and amusingly in a slightly offbeat way as they strolled along, side by side.

The Round Pond topped a small rise, and the view of their surroundings was excellent. For a few minutes Haden thought that they were alone in the park and that his precautions had been superfluous. Then he saw the distant figure with the walking stick.

Too far off to identify, little more than a finger-sized outline, the man gave every appearance of being engaged in

taking vigorous exercise. Yet, somehow, his brisk peram-
bulations never quite took him out of sight.

When the woman decided that the weather was unbearable, Haden walked away with her. The massive hound
padded along obediently behind. For a small lady, she set
a fast pace. The distant figure strode off in the opposite
direction, toward the Albert Memorial.

As they neared the exit, the woman called the wolfhound
and put him on a leash. Haden waited for her and noted
that the man had reversed his direction. But he was a long
way off. If they were serious about it, however, he would
have a radio and a colleague somewhere. Haden thought it
possible that they might also have become interested in
whomever he had apparently arranged to meet.

As they neared Holland Park Underground station,
Haden bade his newfound companion goodbye in mid-
conversation and dodged across the road into the station.
He heard the rumble of an approaching train, sprinted, and
squeezed through the doors before they closed. He got off
at Shepherd's Bush, hurried outside, and took a taxi from
the rank to Sloane Square, where he caught the above-
ground District Line train to Ravenscourt Park.

Ravenscourt Park was never a busy station. In the bitter,
hostile weather of that Sunday morning, it was deserted.
On Sunday, trains ran infrequently. Haden found a corner
where he could see incoming trains without being seen, his
gloved hands deep in his trench coat pockets, and watched
three come and go. No one got off.

Numb with the cold, he was glad to walk away toward
his destination. Either he had shaken them off or they were
engaged in identifying and checking on the unknown
woman. He sent her his mental apologies.

The house was in a conversation area, a series of streets
and narrow lanes, composed of workmen's cottages built in
the 1850s, now Grade III—listed buildings of architectural

and historical interest, preserved and protected, desirable, somewhat fashionable residences, if on the small side.

Haden could hear the uneven rumble of light traffic on the A4, the main road leading into London from the west, but otherwise the area appeared still to be fast asleep. He pressed the doorbell, heard it ring inside, and waited. There was no answering sound of movement. The chilling rain spit down at him again. He rang once more and looked around. He was still alone in the street. He stepped back, glanced upward, and saw that heavy curtains were drawn across the two upstairs windows. Perhaps Freddy was sleeping off the excesses of triumph or failure. He tried a third time and met only silence after the bell stopped ringing. The upstairs curtains did not move. He could not see much through the living-room window. The sill was high, but it struck him that the television set was oddly placed.

Only a minute or so had passed, but Haden began to feel prominent. He walked decisively away, took the first left turn into a narrow lane scarcely a car's width across and then turned left again.

An entranceway led to a builder's yard, with the builder's premises on one side and a wall on the other. He could just see over the top of the wall.

Haden counted the backs of the houses facing him and moved along until he was nearly at the locked wooden gates beyond which was Freddy's yard. He stood on tiptoe and peered over the wall.

The enclosed back gardens were small, perhaps thirty feet long. The adjoining one was of flagstones, laid out patio-style, but Freddy's boasted a tiny lawn, lined by tall, over-grown shrubs and one forlorn, ancient apple tree. The rain had increased and was lashing down on the dripping shrubs. He studied the back of Freddy's house through the down-pour. The curtains were open on the windows facing him, but he could not see inside. There was a small lean-to that

75

may have been used for garden tools. Beside that was the back door. At first sight it looked to be closed; but, his vision impaired by the driving rain, Haden could not be sure that it was.

He came down off his toes and thought. He was probably wrong about the back door. He could walk away and get out of this bloody freezing rain. That would be sensible. But he remained troubled, with that indefinable sense of unease that had served him well in the past. He took another quick look over the wall. Neighboring windows overlooked that back garden, but the neglected shrubs and the garden walls would provide some sort of cover, although far from perfect. Yet, at worst, he would only be exposed for moments.

Haden decided to take a chance. He heaved himself up onto the wall and was over it, gaining the shelter of Freddy's back entrance in seconds. He stood, listening intently, but could hear only the gurgle of rainwater in the gutters. He turned to the door.

Splintered wood had prevented it from being pulled closed completely. The lock had been forced. With one leather-gloved hand, he pushed gently. The door opened with a squeak, and he was inside. Carefully he eased it closed again.

He could hear only the ticking of the hall clock. He went past it and turned up the stairs. At the top, he moved along a short passage and into the front bedroom.

Heavy floor-length curtains spanned the width of the room. Only a few streaks of dim daylight leaked in around the edges. A fetid, sickening smell hung in the air. Haden switched on the light and looked at the bed.

On it lay a man clad in pajamas. His hands and feet were bound to the bed frame. A vomit-stained gag clung to the remains of his face. He had been savagely battered to death. The pillows were dark with blood. There was blood everywhere, spattered on the walls and on the bed linens. All of it, including that on the shattered head, had dried.

The room had been ransacked. Drawers and their contents littered the floor. Haden picked his way through the debris and touched the limbs of the body. They were stiff.

Haden stood looking down at the body, trying not to breathe in too much, quelling nausea. The man's build was Freddy's, what was left of the face was Freddy's, the single intact, staring eye was Freddy's. The crumpled suit lying on the floor was the one Freddy had worn. Haden lifted the jacket and checked it. There were door keys in one pocket but no wallet. Somewhere, not far away, church bells began to ring.

Haden went downstairs and opened the doors. He did not bother to enter the kitchen. The floor was covered with utensils and food someone had emptied out of boxes and packages.

The dining room had been turned upside down, the period sideboard emptied and its contents thrown on the floor. Among them was a large cutlery box, lined with worn velvet—Victorian, Haden guessed. An engraved plate bore the name of a silversmith. The box was empty. So was the glass-fronted display cabinet lying on its side in the living room. The television set had been pulled forward into the middle of the jumble. The hanging wires, Haden thought, should have connected to a video recorder. There was no recorder. Nor, he noted, were there any cassettes.

Haden went back upstairs. In the bathroom, the medicine cabinet had been emptied over the tiled floor, and the cupboard doors underneath the sink stood open. So did the wardrobe in the small guest bedroom, whose dressing-table drawers also had been emptied onto the floor.

The remaining bedroom had evidently been Freddy's study. Files, books, and papers were scattered everywhere. If there had been a typewriter on the desk, it was gone.

The house was warm, the central heating system no doubt having obeyed its timer, but an inner chill gripped Stephen Haden. He stood in the doorway and gazed hopelessly at the obscene litter of Freddy's possessions. Freddy had claimed to be "that close," and now Freddy was dead. If whoever was responsible had been looking for something, Haden did not know what that might be. Some perfectly innocent object, perhaps? But a man like Freddy would have had his own methods of concealment, and Haden did not know what they might be, either.

He looked at his watch uneasily. He felt as though he had been there for hours and was surprised to see that it had only been minutes. But how long did he have? He forced himself to think. Freddy had expected him at ten-thirty. Freddy would have made certain that they would not be disturbed. Surely it would be safe to spend another few minutes there. He grimaced. Safe? It was never safe to linger at the scene of a brutal murder.

Five minutes—he would give himself that, on the off-chance the intruders, for there must have been more than one to overcome Freddy, bind and gag him, and wreak this much havoc, had overlooked something.

Freddy, assuming he had remained off the bottle, was a professional. He would have taken precautions. Even if they had beaten what they wanted out of him before killing him, there was a chance that he had kept something back. But what? And where?

Freddy had been trained in the arts of intelligence, and Haden was not. He looked at his watch again. The minute hand seemed suddenly to have accelerated. Think, for Christ's sake, think. Not the files. Too obvious. Besides, he thought, the intruders would have had plenty of time to go through them all, and he did not.

Obvious. That struck a chord somewhere. He remembered the Edgar Allan Poe story about the best place of concealment being under a man's nose. God Almighty, in this house of turmoil, everything was under his nose.

One word was the only flimsy clue in his possession. Dante. Not what it meant. Nothing but the word itself. Dante. He eyed the empty bookshelves—the books lay everywhere, all over the room.

Haden crouched down and, trying to be methodical but fast, worked his way across the floor, checking all the titles. None of them was a work by Dante.

He stood up. There were, he remembered, more books lying around the living room. Another remote possibility struck him—one that was certainly obvious enough.

He started again, but without much heart. The odds were, he realized, that the intruders had not been searching for anything, anyway. Leaving the house like this was probably only to make it look as though they had been.

This time, he peeled off the dust jackets. It was slow, clumsy work in his gloves, but fingerprint men would be going over all the house's contents in the not too distant future.

He had crawled across the floor and had nearly reached the last few books. He noticed that it had stopped raining and the sky was lightening. He glanced down and noted that he had picked up a book about cricket. He shook the dust jacket loose. The spine of the book informed him that the contents had nothing to do with cricket.

Haden glanced at the text to make certain before he replaced the dust jacket and slipped the volume into the capacious inside pocket of his trench coat. He had stayed longer than he intended. It was time to go.

He was halfway down the stairs when the doorbell rang. The long peal jolted him as though he had been struck in the chest. He froze and waited. It rang again, persistently. Then whoever it was used the doorknocker as well.

Cautiously Haden inched his way into the living room,

keeping well back, until he could see who it was. An erect, tall, elderly woman, her gray hair gathered in a bun, had stepped back from the door and was gazing up at the second-floor windows. When she looked down again, her eyes met Haden's through the window. Common sense told Haden that she could not see him nearly as clearly as he could see her. But the fact that she had seen him at all was enough.

As he closed the back door, he heard the doorbell ring again. He crossed the lawn fast and went over the wall like a pole vaulter. In the street he dodged into the first turning he saw, to get away from the old woman. He forced himself to walk and not run. He took one turning after another at random, came to a church, and found himself looking at the A4, its six lanes much busier now than they had been an hour before. He didn't see any way of crossing it. His alternative, to turn back into possible danger, was unacceptable, so he walked on.

He came to an underpass, dived into it, and hurried under the A4. Unsure of his bearings, he kept going and found himself on an embankment alongside the Thames. Haden swore silently. He could see Hammersmith Bridge in the distance and realized that he had to get there before he could hope to find any means of transport other than his own legs.

He strode toward it quickly. Perversely, shafts of sunlight were breaking through the clouds, as England's fickle weather took another turn. He passed a pub overlooking the river, considered the merits of joining the pre-lunch drinkers he could see inside, but decided to keep going. The old lady struck him as the kind who might take decisive action, and she could have seen just enough. There could be police patrols in the vicinity very soon looking for a man wearing a trench coat.

When he came to the bridge, there were people waiting at the bus stop but no sign of a bus. Nor were there any taxis in sight. Haden headed instead for Hammersmith Broadway and its Underground station. Only when he was sitting in the train, and the doors were closed, did he let out a deep breath and feel reasonably secure.

Haden spent the rest of the day and most of the evening carefully studying Freddy's copy of Dante's *Divine Comedy*.

Haden went to sleep late and awakened early. He sent down for the morning newspapers. The murder, lacking any sexual connotations, had failed to make the tabloids. Among the heavies, only the *Daily Telegraph* had devoted much space to it, and that in the lower part of a column on an inside page.

The victim was described as Frederick Webb, fifty-five, a civil servant. The murder had come to light when Miss Prudence Baker, seventy-four, a committee member of the local residents' association, had called to secure Mr. Webb's signature on a petition opposing a development that would encroach upon the local conservation area. She had not received any reply to her persistent ringing of the doorbell, but she had seen a man inside the house, whom she described as well built, about six feet tall, with dark hair, about forty years old, and wearing a trench coat. Becoming alarmed, she had telephoned the police. The detective in charge of the investigation called the murder a particularly vicious one. Robbery had clearly been the motive. A number of articles of value were missing. He was anxious to interview the person glimpsed by Miss Baker. Anyone who had seen a man answering her description in the area on Sunday morning was asked to contact he police.

Haden folded the *Daily Telegraph*. Should he manage to reach her age, he hoped his eyesight would be as keen as Miss Baker's.

Haden considered the various possibilities. He had not discovered one he liked much when the telephone rang.

"I'm in a phone booth," said Harold Leyton. "I think we should talk."

"Have you got plenty of change, Harry?" Haden inquired. "Or shall I call you back?"

"Don't be so damn silly, Stephen," Leyton said evenly.

Chapter Five

Haden ate breakfast in his room. He received no telephone calls, and the only knock on his door was delivered by the chambermaid at her usual time. He strolled to Praed Street, found a photocopying shop, and had Freddy's Dante reproduced in its entirety and bound. Then he took a taxi to Charing Cross Road. The third bookshop he tried came up with a pristine copy of the same edition, which he purchased. He was back at his hotel in time for a quiet lunch, over which he lingered.

He drove straight to Earl's Court without troubling to check his rearview mirror any more than was necessary for normal driving. It was safe to assume that Harold Leyton knew what he was doing, whatever that might be.

Leyton opened the door of his flat with an affable smile and directed an admiring glance at Haden's dark gray overcoat.

"Very smart," he said. "Quite the businessman."

"Like you, Harry," Haden said.

"This way," Leyton directed, and led him along a corridor. Haden had not previously penetrated beyond the living room. The flat was larger than it at first appeared. Leyton opened the door of a room furnished as an office, where Ian was speaking on the phone. "We'll be in my study," he said. Ian raised a hand in acknowledgment. Leyton closed the door again, turned a corner, and entered his study.

Venetian blinds obscured the view of the back of another block of flats. The room held a rolltop desk, filing cabinets, rows of books, and armchairs angled around a coffee table.

"This is where I hold private business meetings," Leyton explained. "Allow me to hang up that expensive coat for you."

Haden took off his coat and sat down, putting his briefcase beside the chair. Leyton arranged the overcoat on a hanger to his satisfaction.

"This one may not be too private," Haden said. "I took you at your word and came straight here."

"Why shouldn't you?" Leyton inquired. "We know each other. That's no secret. What did you expect, that we'd fart around meeting in cinemas or something?" He snorted. "That would attract the buggers' real interest."

He sat down facing Haden, looked at him reflectively, smoothed his small mustache, and said no more. The silence grew until it was oppressive.

"You called this meeting, Harry," Haden reminded him eventually.

"I don't think you've been entirely open with me, Stephen," Leyton said, with the gentle reproach of an honest man unexpectedly deceived. "I don't suppose you'd care to make amends of your own accord without further ado?"

"About what?" Haden asked.

"No, I thought not," Leyton said sadly. "Smudging the truth is a bad habit of yours, Stephen. You should try to break it. I'll kick off, to perhaps facilitate things for you."

"I'm listening," Haden said. He took out a cheroot and lit it. Leyton watched him until he had completed the process.

"Ready to concentrate?" he asked then. "Good. A former colleague has been in touch. He was not a chum. Far from it. Now he'd like to be friendly."

"It always gives you a warm glow when something like that happens," Haden said. "You feel you've been appreciated at last."

"Exactly," Leyton said. "His approach concerned you."

"I'm always happy to make new friends," Haden said. "You must introduce us sometime."

"You wouldn't like him. He's an evil shit." Leyton clasped his hands behind his head, sat back, and stretched his short legs comfortably. "Yesterday morning, you left your hotel in filthy weather, walked to the Round Pond in Kensington Gardens, where you met a woman with an Irish wolfhound, talked to her for fifteen minutes, and then walked back with her. You were wearing a trench coat. When you dove into the Holland Park Underground station, there was a moment of confusion. Where you went isn't known."

"I'm a tourist in this country, Harry," Haden said. "I tour. See the sights."

"Later, a man wearing a trench coat was seen inside Freddy's house."

"Yes, I read about that," Haden said, with interest.

"It was put to me," Leyton continued, crossing his outstretched legs, "that were I able to establish that there had been contact between you and Freddy, and for what purpose—say, if a meeting had been arranged at his house—it could prove to be to my considerable advantage."

"I smell an auction coming up," Haden said. "What's the existing bid?"

"A recommendation for my reinstatement," Leyton said.

"It's a good offer, Harry," Haden said judicially. "I hope it's in writing."

"I wouldn't trust the bastard if it was sworn on the Bible," Leyton said. "He's quite capable of sticking to the spoils and welshing on the deal. But then, regrettably, Stephen, you're no better. So I'm in a dilemma." Leyton unhooked his fingers and consulted his watch. "I think we might have tea and biscuits soon," he reflected.

"Fine," Haden said. "Perhaps after we've resolved your problem."

"As I see it, there are two courses of action," Leyton said. "There's the path of pure honesty—that Freddy met you on Friday night, in private and without me. That I had the impression he had something to sell. That when I asked you about it, you were evasive and implied he was pissed. That I didn't believe you and strongly suspected you'd arranged to meet him again—for what nefarious purpose, I don't know. In short, I drop you firmly in the shit and claim my reward."

"I don't think you're any keener on that one than I am," Haden said. "Since you believe your prospects of reward are slim."

"Ah, but," Leyton said thoughtfully, "slim is something. If I tell him the truth, it might just get me back in. At worst, I'd chalk up a good mark, demonstrate my devotion to the old firm, take a step in the right direction."

"Let's examine your second alternative," Haden suggested.

Leyton said, "I could assure him that, to the best of my knowledge, you've never even heard of Freddy, much less had dealings with him, and that our meetings have been to discuss the assignment to you of the Swiss marketing rights in my franchise operation."

"I rather like that one," Haden said.

"No doubt. But then again, he could be on the level. Also, he's not the most trusting soul in the world. If I spin him a yarn, he'll want evidence. Proof that you've paid over a substantial option fee for the Swiss rights would do, I expect."

"No comment," Haden said.

"None required, not yet," Leyton assured him. "I may decide to withhold the valuable rights in question. That depends on whether you come clean with me. I need to know how the percentages look from where I sit before I come to a decision."

"I was going to tell you about it, anyway, Harry," Haden said.

"Bollocks," Leyton said kindly. "You intended to freeze me out."

Haden sighed. He supposed that Leyton could be right, although perhaps not for the reason he imagined.

"Freddy was going on about Dante," Haden said. Leyton sat forward intently. "That may thrill you to the core, Harry," he continued, "but not me. Not unless Baronin was involved in some way. Freddy didn't think he was, but said he'd know by Sunday. He claimed he could get the final piece on the Dante thing on Saturday, when he was duty officer."

Leyton's forehead wrinkled in thought. "How? Some expected incoming message?" He eyed Haden sideways. "Or access to the secret computer room?" Haden shook his head and shrugged. "Freddy used to be hot stuff with computers," Leyton said. "I wonder if that's what he'd been up to. Hacking into someone else's system."

"I don't know," Haden said. "That's it. He was going to tell me the rest on Sunday."

"No, that is not it, my dear Stephen," Leyton corrected coldly. "Freddy was selling. So what were you supposed to be buying?"

"Nothing. I was supposed to act as his front man. To negotiate."

"Who with?" Leyton demanded.

"Contacts I had and he couldn't approach himself. He wouldn't say who. Our American friends, I suppose."

"You underestimate your flexibility. You also have contact with the East German State Security Service, and through them the KGB."

"Hardly the friendly variety," Haden said coolly.

"They might get friendly fast," Leyton retorted, "if you were offering something juicy. Or," he went on, a gleam of excitement in his eyes, "there's Baronin. Not because he had any connection with Dante, but because he disappeared in Vienna. Freddy'd guess you might be going there. Perhaps your contact was to be in Vienna. And you'd have the perfect cover." His plump face expanded in a beam of pleasure. "This becomes of increasing interest."

"Well, you'd better share your enthusiasm with a good medium," Haden said. "He didn't tell me who—or what—Dante was. When I got there, he'd already been dead for some time. I think he was killed Saturday night."

"Clever of him to let you in, then," Leyton said.

"When facetious, Harry, you're tiresome," Haden said. "They went in the back way. So did I. The time of death will have been established. Even if you put me there, it'll be obvious I didn't kill him."

"Oh, I don't know," Leyton said agreeably. "You could have gone back in the hope of finding something you'd overlooked the first time around. I could build that up," he said enthusiastically. "My former colleague would like it."

"My first evil speculation," Haden said, "was that your old firm had discovered what Freddy was up to and decided to put an end to it. And possibly to recover something."

Leyton pursed his lips but seemed willing to consider the possibility. "If so, they must have been scared shitless," he said dispassionately. "A panic measure, rough stuff like that. It would render my information even more valuable, though, Stephen. They'd have someone to hang it on. Dubious character, Haden, suspected accessory to murder, won't say who his associates are. I wonder if that old bat could pick you out in an identity parade?''

Haden wished he had held his tongue. "On the other hand," he said, "it could have been your average robbery, with a sadistic killing thrown in."

"I hear that's how it looked," Leyton said. "Or was made to appear."

"I decided to have a good look around," Haden went on.

"Hoping to find what?"

"If Freddy wasn't raving, he'd have planned my eventual approach. I'd have needed something that meant nothing to me and everything to my contact, whoever that was to be. A perfectly innocent object, Freddy called it. That's what."

"Did you find it?"

Haden handed over his briefcase. Leyton opened it and took out the book. He glanced at the cover briefly and then turned to the title page.

"Did you put this dust jacket on?" he asked. Haden shook his head and screwed his cheroot into the ashtray on the coffee table. "Ah," Leyton said. His eyes were gleaming. He examined the title page more closely and began to flip through the text.

"I've been through it," Haden said. "Nothing written in it, no words underlined, marked passages, nothing. If there's a message somewhere, it's concealed, needs infrared on it or something, I don't know."

Leyton wrinkled his nose in doubt. "As you convey your supposed scenario," he said, "you're guessing you were supposed to hand this to someone, who rapidly gets the point and starts bargaining, even though you don't know what he's buying." He gazed at Haden with some suspicion.

"Harry," Haden said, "if I knew, I wouldn't be showing it to you."

Leyton found a stray, untrimmed hair in his mustache and smoothed it sideways, reluctant, it seemed, to concede the point.

"All right," he said at last. "But a copy of Dante isn't enough. And I think that if it's designed to give your unknown contact instant greed and a desire to part with money on a large scale, it has to be reasonably obvious. People don't carry a bloody laboratory around with them."

"Perhaps there's nothing there after all," Haden suggested. "Or perhaps it was supposed to be taken away for examination. There's no Freddy to ask. But if there is some cryptic code in that book, he'd have used one of the dodges of your old espionage trade. You know the techniques. I don't."

"It'd take a bloody long time to examine it properly without facilities," Leyton grumbled. "And I don't have them to hand anymore."

"Ah, but your former colleague does, the one who's holding the baited hook you're eyeing," Haden said.

"I'm considering that," Leyton said. "What do you propose to do with yourself when you leave here, Stephen?"

"What an innocent man would do," Haden replied. "Stay put. Go about my business. Unless you choose to interrupt it. Otherwise I think I'll pick up the Baronin thing. I begin to like the idea of being paid to visit Vienna. It's not London." He checked his watch. "Let me know when you've decided where your percentage lies."

"On reflection, I think I shall yield, since you beg so humbly," Leyton said sanctimoniously. "Because you are my friend, I shall take the risk of shielding you from the consequences of your illegal actions." He glanced at the book in his chubby hands. "Which include theft," he said absently. "Also because, if my bones tell me right, and I

90

can unlock Dante, I shan't need to suck up to any loathsome creep. I shall be invited back in, trumpets sounding. The red carpet will be out. Whereas the same bones tell me that if I let said creep have a sight of it, he'll steal it. So, my dear Stephen, the deal is this. You recompense me for my expenses. Should my honest endeavors turn up anything about Baronin, that's yours. In return, *everything* about Dante is mine. Okay?'' Haden nodded agreement. Leyton tucked the book under his arm and stood up. ''We'll take refreshments now,'' he said, ''and Ian will draw up the contract for the Swiss rights.''

''Harry,'' Haden said, ''your franchise operation stinks. I don't need it. I don't want it.''

''You don't have to pick up the option,'' Leyton assured him. ''Only pay for it. Have your checkbook ready.''

He went out, leaving the door open. Haden got up and browsed over Leyton's rolltop desk without finding anything of interest. He had little doubt that the portly man's option fee would be wildly ambitious. There was some hard bargaining ahead. By the time he returned to his hotel, he might have suffered a loss rather than gained a profit, but he was not dissatisfied with the deal.

Most likely the whole Dante thing was a product of Freddy's vindictive grudge, a fevered figment of his imagination. If, however, it was not, it was a matter people somewhere appeared to be ready to kill for. Which rather supported Freddy's claims as to its value.

Haden considered that aspect could be worth bearing in mind.

Christa telephoned, and they made plans for her to fly into London early to spend a couple of days with Haden before she returned to school. She was to arrive that very day, and he offered a theater outing for that evening.

"Oh, smashing," Christa said. "Can Helen come, too?"

"I'll see," Haden said. "But I expect she's tied up."

He called her. She was not tied up at all. After the show, they went out for dinner. His two female companions chatted and gossiped and laughed like two fond sisters reunited. Haden felt somewhat superfluous.

Over breakfast the next morning, Christa said, "You're wearing my tie again. I'm glad you like it. And thanks again for my watch. It's fantastic." She gazed at her wrist in admiration. "A knockout," she said contentedly.

"It's supposed to be a dress watch for special occasions," Haden said.

"Well, tonight is a special occasion," she said. "So I shall be all dressed up."

It transpired that she was invited to a party that evening at a house off Sloane Street. Haden suspected that the real reason for her early return had just emerged.

"Will your boyfriend be there?" he asked.

"Who? Oh, Paul. He may be," she said vaguely. "I think nearly all my crowd have been invited."

"Okay, I'll take you," Haden said. "And pick you up at eleven."

"Eleven? Stephen," she said loftily, "it's an all-night party."

"Not for you," Haden said. "Eleven-thirty is my final offer.

"You can get really old-fashioned sometimes," Christa said mutinously. "I suppose you'll want to meet the parents, too."

He did. When they arrived at the large house, he sought them out and learned without too much surprise that they wanted the house cleared by midnight.

"All right," Christa said cheerfully. "So I got it wrong."

She joined the flock of teenagers, looking, Haden thought,

quite the prettiest of the girls. He drove off and met Helen Lloyd for a drink.

There was no edge this evening; she was entirely at ease. Haden thought it an agreeable enough way to kill a few hours even if it somewhat resembled an outing into some distant limbo, isolated and with no reference to anything of any consequence.

After a couple of small lagers, Haden switched drinks.

"Mineral water?" Helen queried. "That's new."

"I'm driving," Haden said. "Picking up Christa later."

"Being careful. Good for you."

"I'm always careful to respect the law," Haden said.

She smiled at him, but any ironic comment in her eyes remained unspoken, and she went on about Christa. She avoided talking shop and made no reference to the untimely death of the British civil servant, although, Haden imagined, there was a pretty fair chance that she had known, or at any rate known of, the man whose task it had once been to monitor, on behalf of British Intelligence, those clandestine CIA activities the Agency preferred to keep from their friends and allies.

She did not mention Dante, and neither did Haden. His previous inquiry, even though she had professed ignorance, now struck him as having been on the careless side. He had no intention of repeating what could have been a bad mistake. Dante might mean nothing at all, but a man had come to an extremely unpleasant end, possibly because of his obsessional interest.

Helen Lloyd the woman was one thing. Just listening to the melody of her voice made it hard to forget their brief affair, past though it was. Helen Lloyd's chosen career was another matter entirely. She held a high-ranking position in what was certainly a CIA front organization. Her duties embraced the legitimate commercial side of the International Information Institute, but she carried out other duties as well. In that other role, or so she conveyed, she merely acted as an intermediary. She was, for example, only maintaining contact with Haden concerning Alexander Baronin, without either being informed or having direct involvement in any deeper implications.

Haden found that hard to believe. He thought it was all part of her cover to play the innocent. He believed her when she said that he had gotten to her. The evidence of experience supported that. He also believed that, whatever her private feelings might be, her enduring loyalty would always rest with the organization that had recruited her from college, trained her and promoted her, and in which she seemed set to rise high. She was part of a closed circle. If only in that respect, she resembled Harold Leyton, who mourned his enforced exclusion and valued a return to the fold above all else. In the last resort, that made her equally unreliable and even, if she ever had to choose between him and the interests of those she served, a potential source of danger. For there would not, he thought, be a choice.

Haden would have liked to believe that he was doing her an injustice, that his detached suspicions, even when he desired her, or in the moments when he had possessed her, were unworthy. He hoped they were. He thought it prudent not to test that hope.

The name of Alexander Baronin did not pass Helen Lloyd's lips that evening, either. Haden supposed that she knew about his phone call to Ralph Janson and saw no need to refer to the Russian defector unless she was asked. He did not ask.

"Thanks for this evening," Helen said when they parted. "It was nice to be off duty for once." That made Haden feel remorseful for about half a second and wish that he had spent less time giving her his warm smile with inner reservations and more time enjoying her company. "You'll be leaving tomorrow, I guess," she said.

"After I've dropped Christa off," Haden said, the half-second over. She knew, she didn't have to guess.

Helen took his hand and gave it a squeeze. "Don't get into any trouble," she said lightly.

"Not if I can help it," Haden said sincerely. "I don't like trouble."

"Well, good luck," Helen said. "And watch yourself, anyway, okay?"

She released his hand, gave him a smile, and turned away. Before getting back into the Cavalier, he watched her go into her house. That was about as much of a warning as he had ever received from Helen Lloyd or was ever likely to. Against what, would be asking too much. It was quite possible that she did not know herself. But she knew something. More than he did, anyway. As he drove toward Sloane Street, he wondered what it was.

"Come on, party girl, get up," Haden said.

Christa's breakfast tray was on the floor, but she was still in bed.

"There's no hurry," Christa said sleepily. "We don't have to be back until four."

"For the junior school, it's before lunch," Haden reminded her. "You're required to do your mother-hen act, and don't ask 'Who says?' I say. So wake up and start packing."

As they drove to the school, in the guise of idle talk, he briefed Christa concerning where her mother-hen act should take place.

Most of the parents delivering their seven-to-eleven-year-olds were young, smart, and solicitous, and most of their offspring were either chirruping boisterously or mildly moody. Parked at a corner was a large limousine, its uniformed chauffeur sitting behind the wheel, reading a newspaper and smoking a cigarette.

Haden helped Christa carry her luggage into the main building and agreed to join her later in the junior-school wing. Huge logs burned in the majestic fireplace in the mock-baronial hall that doubled as a games room. Ralph Janson rose from his seat beside the fireplace as Haden approached, shook hands warmly, and introduced him to his wife.

"Honey, this is Stephen Haden," he said. "My wife, Marianne."

Marianne Janson was a slim, still beautiful woman about Janson's age, elegantly coiffured, with the easy confidence of one who took being rich for granted.

"I'm sorry we didn't get to meet before, Mr. Haden," she said. "I had to cancel the theater that night. I was in bed with a chill."

"A pleasure delayed," Haden said, being gallant. She smiled at him approvingly. "I hope you're better now."

"She's fine," Ralph Janson said. "Petra's gone to see the headmaster."

"If you'll excuse me, I must find Christa and say goodbye," Haden said.

Christa had given him directions on how to reach the junior-school wing, and he duly found her there. She was pink-faced and harassed.

"Peter, get off that banister," she was saying. "It's not allowed. I warn you." She saw Haden and made a face. "He's being a brat," she said, resigned.

Haden lifted the little boy off a banister and spoke to him in German. Peter responded, and after a while agreed to show Haden where he slept. As they walked along the corridor, Christa slipped away with relief, her job done.

Haden spent twenty minutes with the boy, conversing in

German. Peter listed the Christmas presents he had received from his mother and Mr. and Mrs. Janson.

"And my daddy sent me this," he said proudly.

"I gave Christa a watch," Haden said.

"She showed me. Mine is better. It talks. It does *everything.*" He demonstrated. Haden admired it and casually mentioned the boy's father again. "He couldn't come for Christmas," Peter explained. "He had to go away for his work. He often goes away. Never as long as this time, though." His face brightened as he added, "But Mummy says he'll be coming to see me soon."

"That'll be nice," Haden said. He switched the conversation to Munich, and the little boy chattered away quite cheerfully about his mother and father, his German nanny, his German school. Haden casually mentioned Dante in such a way that the name could have referred either to some friend of Peter's father or to the subject of a conversation overheard at home, but the little boy did not register any recognition. Haden dropped it, in favor of asking what the boy would like to do when he grew up. He was informed matter-of-factly that Peter would work for a radio station, as his father did.

Eventually Haden said, "We'd better go downstairs, young fellow. Your mother will wonder where you are."

He took the boy down and handed him over to Petra, who was talking to another young mother. He felt sorry for the child, but told himself that while he had learned little, he had done no harm, either.

The Jansons were no longer sitting beside the fire. Haden gave Christa a hug and promised to call her when he could and perhaps come to see her should he return to England in the next few weeks, which he thought was possible. He waited at the bottom of the stairs for Petra.

Petra smiled at him when she appeared, but she looked ready to cry, and she shivered when they walked outside, although the breeze was from the west and the day was relatively mild for the time of year.

"I don't know how much longer we can keep this up," she said.

"Perhaps you should tell him," Haden suggested.

Petra came to a stop, looked back at the school, and then at Haden.

"I can't," she said, subdued. "Not until I have to. Not while there's any hope left." Her eyes searched his, as if seeking reassurance. "Ralph says you're leaving today." Haden nodded. "I do know the chances are not good," she said, "but I want to thank you for trying. If there's anything I can do—some way I could help—you will tell me, won't you?"

"This is where I'll be," Haden said.

She looked at the card he handed her in a puzzled way, as if it were not what she had expected. Haden led her across to the limousine. Marianne Janson was sitting in the back. Ralph Janson was talking to the driver. Haden said goodbye to the ladies, walked across to the Cavalier and got in. Ralph Janson joined him, slid into the passenger seat, and took a package from his pocket.

"In one-hundred-dollar bills," he said. "Any unforeseen expenses over and above, call me, and I'll authorize it at once. Do please check it."

"Not necessary," Haden said. He pointed at the glove compartment.

Janson smiled, put the package inside, and shut the lid.

"Quite so," Janson said. "If you find it's short, you stop working until it's made good. But of course the bonus is in escrow. Give me proof of a result, and it's released. Someone will contact you." He tapped the glove compartment with one finger. "It's in there. He's one of the best operatives available. Very knowledgeable. He won't interfere, he won't ask questions. He knows it's your show. But anything you need, anyone you need to talk to, he'll fix it. Anything else?''

"I'll be in touch," Haden answered.

"Well, then, I guess there's nothing left to say, except good luck, Mr. Haden."

They shook hands, and Janson got out. Haden watched him climb into the limousine, which then drove away. Petra Baron twisted around in her seat and waved to him out of the rear window.

In another window, high up in the junior-school wing, Haden could see the pale outline of the small boy's face. The boy was slowly moving one hand from side to side. Then he turned away and was gone.

Inside the main school building, the lunch bell was ringing.

Bad Gastberg was on the map, but as a village it was so small as to be almost nonexistent. It was set on a lonely side road, deep within densely wooded hills. Snow lay everywhere, a thick white blanket, as far as the eye could see. The trees wore clinging coats of snow.

Despite its apparent remoteness, however, the hotels, guesthouses, and other buildings scattered in the forest surrounding Bad Gastberg generated very large sums of money year in, year out—and year round, too. There was no off season in this business.

Stephen Haden had chosen to stay in the central complex, which included all the comfort and facilities of a luxury hotel and was the spa's center of activity. He turned his Mercedes in through the main gates and followed the long drive. He passed tennis courts no doubt much used in the summertime but now heaped high with drifts of snow. The building that came into sight was set on a rise and commanded a view of the distant Danube Valley. The dull sheen of the river was just visible. Someone in years gone by had built the place of gray stone with turrets and towers to resemble an old *Schloss*. Accretions of modern low-level, interconnecting buildings clung discordantly to its back and sides.

When Haden pulled up outside, staff appeared at once, unbidden. Outside the warm car, the cold, still air caught his throat and chilled his nostrils. He left the porters to deal with his luggage and went inside to check in, making an appointment for an examination, and was shown to his room.

Stephen Haden was not so much a connoisseur of hotels as a reluctant user, jaded by the number of occasions he was obliged to stay in them. This room, however, was enormous and opulent, and the view from its windows was magnificent. Its ornateness suggested not a hotel room but a chamber the owner of some great mansion might provide for his most honored guest.

Haden smelled the fragrant fresh flowers in a bowl, flown in from God knew where, and decided that he might as well enjoy the sybaritic comforts of this establishment, considering that it was at someone else's expense.

Dr. Wolfgang Gottl exuded reassurance. His voice was deep and calm, his gaze direct and friendly. The smile on his handsome face was welcoming, his handshake manly, his skin smooth, his nails manicured, and his discreetly dark suit immaculate. The touches of gray in his hair lent a suitable hint of knowledgeable experience. He looked as if he had recently been polished.

He welcomed Haden to Bad Gastberg, inquired solicitously about the comfort of his journey, and conversed for several minutes as though he had nothing else to do for the rest of the day. But finally, spurred by some mental timer apparently, since his watch was concealed under a spotless white cuff, he rose from his desk, opened the door to an adjoining room, and suggested that Haden might care to undress therein. He was encouraged to use the dressing gown and blankets if he felt the slightest chill.

Haden took off his clothes and lay on the examining table. No artificial aid to warmth or comfort was necessary. The mental timer, this time telepathic, brought Dr. Gottl back a few seconds later. He resumed their cordial conversation as though it had never ceased. Now wearing a brilliantly white coat, he washed his hands and scrubbed his fingernails before turning to the prone Haden and using his stethoscope. He issued instructions softly.

"In . . . Out . . . Good . . . Again . . . Splendid . . ."

He continued with his listening and finger tapping, his close-shaven face looming over Haden's, his eyes straying now and then, but always returning to the same point. After he had taken and warmly praised Haden's blood pressure, he remarked on the objects of his scrutiny.

"These scars, Mr. Haden, rather resemble those one might expect to be caused by gunshot wounds."

"A shooting accident," Haden agreed.

"Very nicely healed . . . Excellent . . . Would you turn on your side, please, Mr. Haden." Dr. Gottl bent down. Haden felt the gentle touch of his fingers. "You were shot twice in the back, perhaps?" Dr. Gottl murmured.

"That's right," Haden said. "The gun went off twice."

"I see . . . Again, excellent. You were in good hands."

The examination continued, perhaps even more thoroughly and painstakingly than previously, and with rather less conversation. Finally, Dr. Gottl gave Haden another of his brightly reassuring smiles and asked him to get dressed.

When Haden returned to the office next door, Dr. Gottl was studying copious notes. He looked up at once and leaned back in his chair. Haden sat down.

"Your general health is good, Mr. Haden," he said.

"Very good. However, the wounds you suffered in your shooting accident must have been very serious. There could have been some abdominal injuries, perhaps to the spleen or kidney. Might that be so?" Dr. Gottl, unruffled, spoke calmly, and smoothly contrived to convey both concern and lack of curiosity. Haden thought that for a doctor who must deal to some considerable extent in hypochondria, he knew his stuff.

"The spleen went," Haden said. "A small part of the left kidney was removed. Everything's fine now."

"Splendid," Dr. Gottl said heartily. "Splendid. However, a note from your own doctor or hospital physician would be most helpful to us in the circumstances. Have you brought one with you?"

Haden shook his head. "I didn't think it was necessary," he said.

Dr. Gottl said earnestly, "I'm sure you have been warned that certain complications may just possibly arise in your case. If you are seeking treatment, more detailed medical information would be most desirable, indeed essential."

"There were some disagreeable symptoms at first," Haden offered, "but not for a long time now."

"Just the same . . ." Dr. Gottl began.

"I'm not here for treatment," Haden said. "Just rest and recuperation."

"Ah, well, we can most certainly offer that," Dr. Gottl said, his enthusiasm decently masking a degree of relief. "The waters here are highly beneficial, with a worldwide reputation, as I'm sure you know. And you will find our mud baths deeply relaxing. Our mud is ten thousand years old." Haden wondered how the doctor knew that. Mud was mud in his experience. "Massage, a little gentle exercise," Dr. Gottl continued. "I shall draw up a personal program for you. On one point, however, I must seek your cooperation. There is no prohibition on alcohol here. We are not

102

a health farm," he explained, with dismissive contempt. "For those who enjoy it, in moderation, of course, that is fine. But in your case, Mr. Haden, no strong spirits, if you please. We wouldn't want to undo all our good work, would we?"

Haden agreed that indeed "we" would not. Dr. Gottl rose to his feet and gave Haden one of his strong, manly handshakes. Haden had had his one hour, precisely.

The large, discreetly lit bar offered a choice to moderate drinkers. Low-voiced waiters flitted efficiently to and from elegant tables and banquettes for those who preferred to imbibe that way. There was a bar with high stools for those who liked to look at the extensive selection of drinks available and to talk to the bartender—who, however, did not initiate conversations, only replied to them.

Haden ordered a cognac. Doctors had that effect on him. A couple of stools away was a man with a firm grip on a large Scotch with ice in it, as if he did not want to let it go. He folded the American newspaper he had been reading and glanced in Haden's direction.

"Hi there," he said. "Just arrived?" Haden nodded. "Taking the waters?" Haden agreed that he was. "Listen, I hate talking across bar stools. Mind if I join you?" The man shifted to the stool beside Haden's. "My name's Gorman," he said. "Walter Gorman."

"Stephen Haden."

"A pleasure to meet you, Mr. Haden," Gorman said respectfully. He twisted around on his stool, his back against the bar, and surveyed the scattered tables. The bartender, having evidently decided that his services, either as waiter or companion, were no longer required, moved away. "These things always give me a crick in the back," Gorman remarked. "What do you say we grab that quiet table over by the window?"

"Suits me," Haden replied.

He followed Walter Gorman, whose cover was special political officer at the United States embassy.

Given the polite title the Central Intelligence Agency usually assigned to its station chiefs, Haden wondered if that meant that Gorman was senior to the CIA station chief in Vienna. On the evidence of first impressions, that seemed unlikely. But then, first impressions could be misleading.

Chapter Six

"A very fine view," Walter Gorman said. "If unlimited snow happens to turn you on. Me, it doesn't—I was born in Florida. My stint here's coming to an end soon. Back to Washington would be nice. It'll be goddamn Finland with my luck," he said gloomily.

The curtains were looped back. Through the double-glazed windows, the scenery, for snow lovers, was spectacular—a panorama of rolling, snow-encrusted forest. In the far distance the glimmer of reflected light in the night sky indicated the location of the city of Vienna.

Haden supposed that Gorman was going through a getting-acquainted routine, and he let him get on with it. Haden was getting acclimated, too. From London, he had flown to Zurich, where he satisfied himself that the business could continue to run smoothly for a while without him and made such further arrangements as were necessary. Then he climbed into his Mercedes station wagon and set out on the long drive that would take him across Austria to Bad Gastberg.

When the muggers had gone for him in London, Haden had been unarmed, and he hadn't liked the feeling. Underneath the carpet beside the driver's seat of the Mercedes was a concealed compartment in which he had placed a small Beretta, as well as his preferred Smith & Wesson .38 revolver. Its accessibility improved his sense of well-being. Whether the presence of Walter Gorman was similarly comforting, he was not certain.

Gorman was of average height, average build, average everything. His voice was level and monotonous, with few inflections. In all but one respect, his face was that of a lugubrious, worried clerk. The structure was bony, the cheeks hollow. If he ever grew a beard, it would be ebony. Although he was cleanshaven, the field of incipient stubble straining to reach the light stood out darkly against his waxy pale skin. But set in his mournful visage were eyes of a glittering, unnatural intensity, and when he smiled, which he did frequently, and usually for no apparent reason, the mouth simply stretched sideways, baring his teeth. The fleeting combination made him look not so much saturnine as satanic.

"Don't comment if you don't want to," Gorman said, "but there are plenty of good hotels in Vienna, where you'd be on the spot."

"Baronin disappeared while he was staying at a hotel in Vienna," Haden said. "I'm superstitious."

"Okay," Gorman said, with one of his meaningless smiles.

"What does your job entail, exactly?"

"Oh, the usual crap. Safety and proper behavior of personnel, like they don't start screwing KGB-planted females. Or handsome males, according to taste. Plus a load of special responsibilities on account of these goddamn arms talks. Security of documentation. Policy briefing and background material are highly sensitive. Security of communications. It sometimes feels like every goddamn thing has to be referred back to Washington, including permission to shit."

Gorman continued with his flat, sardonic account. The

list could well be genuine, Haden imagined, if somewhat edited.

The talks on conventional arms limitation in Europe had meandered well into their second decade in Vienna. Teams of negotiators and ancillary personnel had talked, adjourned, reconvened. Conceivably, one day, some sort of result might be achieved. Meanwhile, the years came and went, and the talks progressed with the mounting pace of a glacier.

Walter Gorman seemed to be willing to explain his role in Vienna more or less indefinitely. Haden stretched out a hand and touched his arm. The flow stopped, and Gorman looked at him inquiringly.

"Am I one of your security problems?" Haden asked.

Gorman bared his teeth in what Haden supposed was a friendly smile. "Please," he said. "You come with credentials I don't argue with. My job is to help. If I can, that is."

"Well, I'm getting hungry," Haden said, "so unless you're staying to dinner, let's get to the point."

"I guess it's not very interesting, but you did ask," Gorman said defensively, and with an unconvincingly docile expression on his lean, ascetic face.

"Did you know Alexander Baronin?"

"Personally, no. I knew of him. I handled the investigation when he disappeared."

"Tell me about that."

"Like trying to track a wisp of smoke," Gorman said. "The instructions were to keep it low-key. No fuss, right? It seems Baronin was in Vienna to meet someone. The presumption is that the meeting went wrong."

"Meet who? And why?"

"That isn't anything I'm in a position to know. The indications are," Gorman said cautiously, "that it could have been a Russian, maybe someone Baronin hoped to persuade to defect. The identity of the Russian isn't known. There is some evidence—circumstantial, I have to say—that the meeting was a KGB trap. That the intention was to kidnap Baronin, but that he was accidentally killed in the ensuing struggle, when he resisted."

"Killed how?"

Gorman shrugged dejectedly. "Chloroformed to death, maybe. It's guesswork—I like to think informed guesswork—but I have to leave it at that. The word from above is that you are to roam loose, without preconceptions. Someone up there doubts our conclusions," he said, full of dull resentment. "It's true that we haven't come up with definite proof, but the best estimate is that Baronin met his man and got himself killed."

"In which case, there should be a corpse," Haden observed.

"Any corpse could have gone into Hungary or Rumania," Gorman countered. "Or, if it's still around somewhere, this is a country of mountains, forests, rivers, pastures. I'd say there was more chance of a body remaining undiscovered than a live man walking around somewhere."

That sounded pretty reasonable, Haden reflected, but he didn't think repeating it to Ralph Janson would qualify him for a bonus.

"This last meeting Baronin had with someone took place where?" Haden inquired.

"It looks as though it could have been somewhere near Sacher's Hotel."

"*Could* have been? Wasn't there CIA surveillance?"

"There was not," Gorman stated.

Haden stared at the saturnine countenance, the deep-set, glinting eyes. It occurred to him that Gorman's unusual facial structure made his expressions uncommonly difficult to fathom.

"All right," Haden said, "we have Alexander Baronin working for the CIA in Munich. He travels to Vienna—to research something, according to his wife, and to meet a possible Russian defector, according to you. And there was no CIA surveillance of a CIA man when he kept an appointment you believed was a KGB setup? Why not? The risk must have been obvious. Did someone screw it up?"

"There was no screwup," Gorman insisted. "Had we been informed in advance of any such meeting, surveillance would have been routine. We were not. What I've told you is hindsight."

"It sounds bloody strange to me," Haden said skeptically.

"I'm not exactly thrilled about what happened," Gorman said. "Nor are you the first to suggest a local blunder, and that the can should be attached to Walter Gorman's tail. I'd like to know the answer, but I can't get one. No one knows. Or no one wants to say. Or someone's covering up a mistake elsewhere."

"Or Alexander Baronin was working on his own account," Haden suggested.

"That, too," Gorman agreed. "Although, since the idea doesn't find favor up top, I have no opinion."

"Give me your opinion on just how frequently Baronin visited Vienna on CIA business," Haden asked.

He received one of Walter Gorman's unnerving smiles, which he imagined was intended to be a compliment.

"Our approach to this is similar," Gorman said. "Some information on that emerged during our investigation into his disappearance. I can't provide a definitive answer, but it must have been several times a year during the last several years. I can't be more precise."

"But you weren't told of those visits, either?"

"If he was researching material for a radio station, there'd be no reason to tell me."

"Well, whether he was researching material for Russian-language broadcasts or laying the groundwork for a future defection—or both, come to that—there are plenty of Russians in Vienna. But you don't know of any contacts he might have had with them?"

"Baronin was never observed with any of those we like to keep an eye on. If there were others, I couldn't tell you."

"You must maintain contact with someone on the other team, someone willing to gossip," Haden said. "But I'm told that line of inquiry was ruled out."

"Absolutely," Gorman agreed. "Why, who knows? Sure, the comrades I'm on nodding terms with might have lied to me, but then again, they might not. And even lies can sometimes tell you something. Me, I'd have tried it. But it was a direct order. No contact with the other side about Baronin, period. So that was it. My job is to take orders."

"Well, mine isn't," Haden said. "Nor am I interested in affairs of state. I don't care what Baronin's role was. I'm here on an errand of human mercy in behalf of his anxious wife."

"Human mercy," Gorman said. "That was good, the way you said it with a straight face." He scratched his prominent chin. Haden could hear his fingernails scraping against the stubble. "Let me consider the implications," he said finally.

"You do that, Walter," Haden said cordially. "Then you call me. And give me your number so that I can contact you if I don't hear."

Haden's program as a patient was not unduly taxing. He soon established that no one much minded whether or not he showed up for the various curative treatments, but for the first day he stuck to the schedule, except for the medical lecture in the afternoon. He spent that hour in his room,

110

where he continued the tedious task of comparing his photocopy of Dante's *Divine Comedy* with the virgin copy of the published work he had acquired in London. It was painstaking, time-consuming, and discouraging work.

He had spent several hours on it after dinner the night before, until he began to go word-blind and was forced to stop lest he miss the tiny discrepancy that might exist between the two texts. "Might" was a very big word, he thought at the end of the hour, as he laid the copies aside and wondered if his diligence would pay off. He was beginning to think that he was not pursuing a well-reasoned, logical probability at all, only a monumentally ill-founded piece of guesswork. He returned to the next treatment period.

During the day he drank the mineral waters derived from four different fountains—"rich in natural carbonic gas," he was informed—and later bathed in the stuff as well. The earnest and extremely pretty attendant assured him that such applications were "very effective as a prophylaxis against cardiac infarction."

Haden received a personal lecture about the ten-thousand-year-old mud as his mud bath was being prepared, in which he learned that the mud had first been analyzed in 1890, had a curative effect on any number of diseases, and had even been used with surprising success to treat infertility in women. He promised to convey the information were he to come across any infertile women, but the look he received told him that his attitude was not at all serious enough.

The massage and electrotherapy were rather more to his taste, as were the sauna, the solarium, and the final swim in the indoor pool. After that, he changed, spent another fruitless hour comparing pages word by word, without any regard for Dante's grandiloquent poetry, put on an overcoat, muffler, fur hat, and gloves, and walked outside to his car.

A slice of moon hung in the clear sky. The temperature had descended even further, and the snow was frozen hard. The still air bit icily against Haden's face, and he was glad to get the car engine started and the heater going.

The Mercedes displayed some inclination to slip and needed careful handling until he reached the village of Bad Gastberg. Once he passed the village, the roads were meticulously snow and ice free, and progress was uncomplicated by nature.

Haden drove steadily, warm and comfortable in his metal cocoon. He felt alert and healthy. Perhaps, for all his skepticism, the spa had been mildly beneficial, as well as hedonistic. Thirty minutes later, he was entering the outskirts of Vienna, and renewing his acquaintance with that very cosmopolitan city.

Embraced in the dense stream of early-evening traffic. Haden crossed, one after another, the three broad roads that, in concentric rings of diminishing size, encircle the city. He drove on into the center, where blue-and-white trams, as well as buses, served the traveler. The trams ran with such remarkable silence they constituted a hazard to the unwary pedestrian.

The city itself, with its sumptuous and fashionable shops, wore an air of opulence. Almost all the buildings were pure Baroque, excessively so to an eye unused to such grandeur. And yet Haden found a curiously parochial feel to the place. Vienna had once been the capital of a powerful empire. Now, that empire long gone and the original purpose of its grandiose buildings lost, the city sat virtually unchanged on the eastern edge of a neutral country, and the power it had once wielded was in the hands of others. In the modern world it governed only itself, a glorious fossil from another age.

Born and brought up in a country long neutral, for all that the Swiss had once provided the most ferocious and feared mercenaries in Europe, Haden imagined that the citizens of present-day Vienna probably preferred things as they were, if they ever even thought about it. Quite likely, it was only to outsiders that such reflections occurred, or to those who viewed the city as a beautifully preserved relic of a once great imperial power.

Pride and efficiency remained. Haden passed the magnificent opera house, lovingly rebuilt and restored to its former glory by the Viennese after it was destroyed in World War II. All the city's many statues and all the fountains that spouted and played in summer had been carefully encased against the bitter winter in solid structures that looked as though they were reused year after year.

Haden parked his Mercedes as near to the café as he could get, but the chill had entered into him by the time he reached it. Inside, a small vestibule, its doors heavily curtained, acted as a kind of air lock. Beyond it the cozy warmth of the café itself denied the subzero temperature outside.

Haden hung up his overcoat and made his way to the table. There were cafés that catered to all the divergent tastes of Vienna. This was one of the small, intimate, and smoky variety, a largely male preserve, with deep voices rumbling in quiet conversation that was broken only by occasional laughter. There was no music to intrude.

Erwin Matz stood up and shook hands in his polite, reserved fashion. "This is his regular table," he explained.

Haden nodded and sat down. The regular table—*Stammtisch,* in the German Matz was speaking—was a feature of café life in Vienna. This one, despite the intimate, nearly cramped ambiance of the place, was set in a corner with more room around it than its neighbors enjoyed. The nearest table was occupied by a group of neatly dressed old gentlemen, mostly smoking pipes, for whom the café clearly served as a club, the place they always met. Unless Haden or Matz raised his voice, there was no risk of being overheard.

Haden ordered coffee and a cognac. When they arrived, the coffee was accompanied by the inevitable glass of ice water. Why this was the custom, summer or winter, Haden had never worked out. Ice water in this weather was not to his liking and he always left it untouched.

"He won't take anything from you," Matz said. "He is a very careful man."

Haden nodded, and pushed an envelope across the table. Matz pocketed it. They talked business for a while. Haden was interested in the escape, which had looked like a difficult proposition, of an East German surgeon and his wife, resident in Leipzig, who declined to be separated from their two small children. Children were always chancy—too inquisitive, too prone to say the wrong thing at the wrong time.

Matz replied laconically. With children involved, an escape by car would have been too risky. He had decided to use Czechoslovakia and had accompanied them from Prague into the West by train. There had been no problems. The surgeon had paid in full, and the money had been remitted to the Zurich office, less Matz's "royalty." He offered no details of how the dangerous journey had been achieved.

Haden approved of that. Erwin Matz encountered problems less frequently than most, which Haden did not think was any accident. Matz was still in his twenties. Born in Vienna, well educated, he had followed his father into the civil service but had rapidly decided that a comfortable, conventional life was not for him. He had resigned, moved to West Germany, drifted around for a while, earning his keep as a driver, and finally arrived in West Berlin. It was there, during one of Haden's periodic visits to that city, that Matz had sought him out. He had heard, he said, of Ste-

114

phen Haden and his *Fluchthelfer* business, and had decided that he would like to work for him.

Haden was accustomed to such approaches, usually from young loners who fantasized about daring exploits or who were just looking for trouble. He firmly showed them the door, without an explanation.

There was something about Erwin Matz, though, that was appealing, something different. Under his mop of unruly black hair, his face was lean and intelligent. His build was slight, his movements casual, his manner introspective, his words few and precise. This one, Haden had thought, was neither a romantic nor a troublemaker, and so he decided to take a few minutes to let him down lightly before showing him the door.

What was Matz after? Fun? Excitement? Danger? And why did he want to run the risks of crossing into the East? Was he a politically committed anti-Communist?

Matz thought for some time before replying to Haden's questions, although his direct gaze never wavered.

"My family lived in the Russian-occupied zone of Vienna," he said at last. "They suffered. My grandfather died. My father's health was affected. I was born into freedom. I expect most people in the East are content enough. Some wish to escape. To help a few may not be much, but it's something. The world is as it is. I don't want to fight anyone. Or court danger. Just to do the job as safely as possible." Haden had been prepared to discourage the young man. He had paused before replying and considered whether he should discourage him after all. Then Erwin Matz had added, straightfaced, "Also, I hear the work pays very well."

Haden decided to employ Matz in the workshop where vehicles were modified. Matz soon graduated to doing dummy runs across the frontier into East Germany, then to acting as backup man, then to conducting escapes on his own. His success rate was high.

Perhaps it was time, Haden reflected, his cheroot adding to the drifting smoke in the café, to confirm him as chief of the West Berlin branch.

"Excuse me," Matz said politely. He got up, crossed to the door, and shook hands with the man who had just come in. After helping him off with his overcoat, he carefully hung it up. If the envelope had changed hands, Haden had not detected its passage, but the man went off to the cloakroom while Matz waited for him, so Haden supposed that it had.

When the man returned, Matz brought him over to the table. "May I introduce my friend Willi Hofer," he said. "Stephen Haden."

They shook hands, and Hofer sat down. A waiter arrived at once with an open-face salami sandwich and a carafe of wine. Haden ordered another cognac.

They talked about the weather and future holiday plans while Hofer, in a neat, unhurried fashion, disposed of his sandwich. Then Matz stood up and shook hands all around.

"If you will excuse me," he said, "I promised to go to see my grandmother this evening."

"My wife tells me that your grandmother is failing," Hofer said.

"She's very old, very frail," Matz said. "We hope she will see another summer."

"I hope so, too," Hofer said. "On behalf of my wife and myself, please convey our best wishes." Matz nodded and left. Hofer folded his napkin neatly and gazed at Haden. "I understand you are making inquiries concerning Alexander Baronin, or Baron, on behalf of his wife," he said.

"Sometimes the police had suspicions or knowledge they can't prove. Anything like that, I'd be grateful."

"In Vienna," Hofer said, "we have something of an inherited tradition of missing-persons cases. My father was a

116

policeman, too. During the four-power occupation of the city, many people were reported missing. Sometimes they turned up in another zone, sometimes not. My father learned much, and we have learned from men like him.''

He reached out and replenished his glass of wine. Whether he had paused for refreshment or had no more to say was unclear. Haden had not yet made up his mind about Willi Hofer. The man was about forty years old and a little overweight; he had carefully arranged his thinning hair to cover its creeping loss, although here and there the skin of his scalp showed through. He was a guarded, wary man and his face reflected his caution. So far, he had smiled only once, and that was when he said goodbye to Erwin Matz. Haden would have preferred a more easygoing, sloppy cop who might become talkative and let things slip after a few glasses of wine. This watchful individual was going to say nothing he might regret later, cash in hand or not.

''You were involved in the police inquiries,'' Haden began.''My own inquiries are quite independent of that and not confined to Vienna. Should I come across anything, naturally I will pass that information on to you.''

Willi Hofer's second smile of the evening was a small one, with his lips pursed, indicating a degree of wry disbelief that, Haden supposed, indicated the man's good judgment.

''Our investigation was extremely thorough, and the results negative,'' Hofer said. ''What happened to Baronin remains unknown.''

''I've talked to Walter Gorman,'' Haden said. ''I expect you know him.''

Hofer's expression neither admitted nor denied the assumption.

''I am aware of Mr. Gorman's belief,'' he said. ''It rests on the statement of a passerby who claimed he saw Baronin being forced into a car in a street behind Sacher's Hotel.

117

The statement was looked into and is considered wholly unreliable."

"Do you mind telling me why?"

"The passerby had been drinking heavily on the night in question. He did not report the incident immediately, but waited until the following day. He could not describe the car. He could not describe the men. When shown photographs of Baronin and several other men, he picked out the wrong person, not Baronin. His statement did not constitute evidence, it was worthless."

"Okay, worthless for the police," Haden argued. Trying to steer this conversation was like stirring cold porridge. "But even a drunk with a bad memory can get something right. Off the record, with all your experience, do you think he *could* have seen Baronin being kidnapped?"

"When the wind is in a certain direction," Hofer said tangentially, "aircraft leaving the Vienna airport are obliged to enter briefly into Hungarian airspace. We are that close to the Hungarian border. It is a drive of some twenty minutes. Anything *could* have happened. What did happen is not known. And it is not my habit to speculate."

"Baronin is supposed to have been due to meet a Russian that night," Haden said.

"His wife merely said 'someone,'" Hofer corrected. "She was not able to say who, or of what sex; nor did she indicate the individual's nationality."

"This information didn't come from his wife," Haden said.

"I glanced at the file before meeting you. I recall no statement of that kind."

"On file or not, I think you've heard it," Haden responded tartly. "You have quite a Soviet colony in this city. Have you made inquiries in that direction?"

Hofer's eyes opened a little wider, indicating the need for extreme patience.

"No," he said flatly. "There is no evidence to justify any such action. And even if there were, I am simply a police officer; that sort of inquiry would be handled on another level entirely. I could do no such thing."

"I'm not a police officer, and I could," Haden said.

Hofer finished his glass of wine and consulted his watch. "I must go," he announced.

"A likely KGB man attached to the Soviet delegation," Haden continued. "Someone willing to chat off the record frankly and honestly, the way you have."

Hofer's third and final smile of the evening indicated real, appreciative amusement. Perhaps he enjoyed sarcasm. He stood up and offered his hand. "My supper will be ready soon," he said. "I promised my wife I would be home early."

"Erwin Matz knows where to reach me," Haden said, returning the handshake.

"So do I, Mr. Haden."

Haden wondered about that as he watched Hofer stroll across the café unhurriedly, don his overcoat, muffler, gloves, and fur hat, and leave. Erwin Matz would not have mentioned where he was staying.

Haden ordered a bowl of soup that, with crusty fresh bread, was as satisfying as a meal. If he asked enough people, he thought philosophically, something would happen. He gestured for the bill. When it arrived, he noticed that no sandwich or carafe of wine figured on it. Willi Hofer was a careful man.

Outside Vienna, traffic gradually thinned, and after Haden had turned onto the narrow road that climbed gently toward Bad Gastberg, he saw only one vehicle, a taxi heading in the opposite direction. He drove on through the silent, empty forest. The road behind him, clearly illuminated by the snow-reflected light from the merest sliver of moon, remained empty.

Back in his lavish room, Haden ordered coffee, which arrived promptly. He was beginning to dislike Dante and his epic work, and decided to fortify himself with a cheroot before reluctantly settling down to a spell of homework.

Both the book he had purchased in Charing Cross Road and the photocopy of the volume he had filched from Freddy's study lay open to the title page. Haden was leaning over them, sipping his coffee, his gaze sightless, when his eyes slowly focused on the page's ornamentation, intricate scrolls and whorls. He laid his cheroot in the ashtray and leaned closer, intently studying first one page and then the other. He moved his head away a little, but that did not help. He tried closing one eye. That didn't help, either. He tilted each page and peered sideways at it. Still he could not make out the difference.

Haden got up and crossed to the telephone. A desk porter answered.

"Do you have a magnifying glass?" Haden asked.

"I'm sure we have, sir," the porter answered, unflappable. "But the office is locked for the night. Would you like me to see if I can find one somewhere else, sir?"

"Please. And if you can find one, bring it up. If not, I'll ask at the office in the morning."

Haden took both books to a standard lamp and compared the two copies under a direct light source. It was no use. With the naked eye, he could not be certain if there was a true discrepancy or just his imagination at play. More likely, given the intricacy of the decoration on the title pages, he'd see an optical illusion.

He stood near the lamp, thinking. Harold Leyton had been certain that if there was something, it would be obvious. There was nothing wrong with Haden's eyesight, and if he was obliged to send for assistance to verify what he

120

thought he might have seen, it couldn't be anything obvious. Suppose, though, whomever he was supposed to have shown it to would have known exactly where to look? Suppose . . . ?

Haden was considering the various suppositions when there was a tap on his door. He blessed the efficiency of the establishment's staff. In a moment he would know. He laid the books on the couch as he passed it on his long walk across the room, and he opened the door.

"Hi," said Petra Baron. "Can I come in?" Haden stared at her. She had an impish, tantalizing smile on her lips. "My room's just across the way," she explained. "I thought I'd see if you were back yet." She paused. "Well, are you going to let me in?" she asked again.

"I suppose so," Haden said ungraciously.

He turned away. Petra closed the door and followed him as he picked up the books, clearing the couch. Her eyes remained on him as he pushed them into a drawer, and he could not tell whether she had seen what they were, or whether they meant anything to her if she had.

"Sorry if I'm interrupting your reading," she said.

"You're not. Sit down." Petra arranged herself on the couch. "What are you doing here?" he inquired.

"I thought I'd take the waters," she explained.

"They dig their ten-thousand-year-old mud from nearby," Haden said. "It's used to treat various diseases of the female reproductive organs, including infertility."

"I think my female organs are healthy," Petra said confidently.

"Whose idea was this? Janson's?"

"Mine," Petra said. "In case I could help. Show you where Alex and I went. I don't know—whatever. Anything you want." She leaned back and crossed her elegant legs. "Don't worry, I won't get in your way. Any time you need me is fine. If you don't, that's all right, too. Okay?"

"I'm thinking about it," Haden replied.

Her legs were long and slender. Her gaze was fixed. She had shown no interest in knowing whether he had made any progress. Whatever else was in that face, there was no strain or worry apparent.

"Ask me to have a nightcap," Petra suggested.

He thought there was the very slightest catch in her voice. Her expression was cool and composed, but her large eyes were bright and expectant. He needed no magnifying glass to read her message. Haden was standing several feet away from her, but the feeling was intimate, personal.

Haden did not see that he owed anyone anything. Certainly not Helen Lloyd. He had never met the probably long-dead Alexander Baronin, and whatever or whomever Petra Baron owed was her affair, not his.

"Have a nightcap," Haden said.

Chapter Seven

"Good morning, Mr. Haden," the receptionist said, with a pleasant smile. "You require a magnifying glass, I understand."

Haden thanked her, slipped it into his briefcase, and headed for the library. It was a facility little used during treatment periods, whereas his room had been taken over by someone from the housekeeping staff.

He settled himself at a writing table and was about to open his briefcase when he became aware that someone else had entered the library. Instead, he took a sheet of notepaper and began writing a short chatty note to Christa.

He was conscious of the man's presence on the periphery of his field of vision. In the dead silence he could hear the man's steady breathing, the light sounds as he fingered books and turned pages. Haden finished his note, read it through, and added a P.S. Still the man lingered. Irritated, Haden addressed an envelope, slipped the note inside, and sealed it.

The man spoke just as Haden put the envelope in his pocket and picked up his briefcase.

"If I would not be disturbing you, Mr. Haden," he said, "perhaps we might speak."

Haden looked at him only then. He had never seen the unobtrusively well-dressed man before.

"The receptionist said you might be in here," the man said. He was speaking with a vaguely American accent. His was the speech of a Russian who had learned American English, the language of the opposing superpower with whom important dealings would be effected.

"I always like to know who I'm talking to," Haden said.

"Oleg Tushin," the man said.

"Captain Tushin out of *War and Peace,* I presume," Haden said.

"Peace, let us hope," Tushin said. His face remained impassive. "I serve with the Soviet delegation in Vienna."

Tolstoy had described his Captain Tushin, Haden remembered, as having large, intelligent, and kindly eyes. His namesake did not. In a stony, expressionless face, his eyes were two deep-set pebbles, cautious and without emotion.

"Serve in what capacity?" Haden inquired.

"As a policy analyst," Tushin said. "But that has no significance."

"Something must, to bring you to Bad Gastberg first thing in the morning," Haden said.

"I am here to inspect facilities on behalf of some fellow delegates," Tushin said. "To speak with you at the same time is convenient. It is understood that you are interested in the whereabouts of a compatriot of mine."

"Alexander Baronin," Haden said. "I'm acting for his wife."

"No request for assistance has been made, or it would have been provided," Tushin said. "We are perfectly willing to help."

"Okay. Help. What happened to him?"

"What is known is this: Baronin was to contact a colleague of mine. Baronin did not turn up, and nothing was heard from him. That is all. I trust the information will assist you."

"Not a great deal," Haden remarked. "Baronin was under sentence of death. A known meeting with anyone from the Old Country sounds a bit risky. I wonder why he'd do that."

"Our laws require a trial before sentence for anything," Tushin answered. "No such trial took place. Perhaps you have been wrongly informed."

"That could very well be," Haden agreed. "So Baronin was in no danger?"

Tushin said, "He could have returned to his mother country at any time."

"Was that to have been the subject of the meeting?"

"No," Tushin responded. "Baronin was to make contact with what you would call a dissident."

"I see," Haden said. "Does this dissident have a name?"

"Naturally," Tushin said. He contemplated Haden thoughtfully. "Discussions could be resumed," he suggested. "I mention this, if it is of any interest."

"Not to me," Haden said. "Try Walter Gorman."

"It is not our place to take the initiative unasked," Tushin said.

"You're fishing in the wrong pond," Haden said. "I'm being paid by Mrs. Baronin. I've talked to Gorman just as I'm talking to you, but I'm not working for him. I don't support either team, yours or his."

"There are colleagues of mine in the German Democratic Republic who would not regard you as being quite so impartial, Mr. Haden," Tushin said.

"Like taxis, I'm for hire," Haden retorted. "It's not my fault if there's only one-way traffic."

"Well, your activities are their concern, not mine," Tushin said. "So far, anyway," he added.

Haden thought it possible that the slight twist of Tushin's

mouth as he said this might indicate that he intended his remark to be jocular.

"How do you feel about Alexander Baronin?" Haden inquired.

"For such a man, there can be no respect," Tushin said.

"Because he defected to the West?"

"Because he betrayed a trust," Tushin said.

"Love knows no frontiers, they tell me," Haden said.

"You refer to his foreign whore?" Tushin shrugged. "Perhaps she served his purpose. Perhaps he betrayed her, too. It is possible."

"I expect the Romans said much the same about Antony and Cleopatra," Haden remarked.

That time Tushin almost smiled. "And both met an unhappy end, as I recall," he said.

"Baronin has an eight-year-old son who misses his father," Haden added.

"This is sad," Tushin agreed. "But I am not responsible for the boy's deprivation."

"Suppose you could put it right?" Haden asked.

"Tell me how," Tushin said.

"I can't," Haden said. "Unless some more information comes your way. Would your feelings about Baronin stop you from passing it on?"

"Probably not," Tushin admitted. "It would not much trouble me to confirm his death."

"You know where to reach me," Haden said, picking up his briefcase. Tushin nodded stiffly. Haden left him scanning the shelves of books.

Having written the note to Christa, Haden thought he might as well send it. He handed it over to the receptionist and then loitered for a while, thinking about Oleg Tushin. Haden appeared absorbed in studying the notice board, which was full of suggestions for how residents could pass their leisure hours, including information about various

126

forthcoming entertainments in Vienna. Then, momentarily, he caught sight of Oleg Tushin again. The Russian was deep in conversation with Dr. Gottl. They moved out of sight toward the treatment area.

Still musing, Haden returned to his room. The wail of a vacuum cleaner was coming from next door. He locked his door, spread the contents of his briefcase on the desk, and sat down.

Haden considered it unlikely that Dr. Gottl would welcome weary Soviet negotiators to the secluded comfort of Bad Gastberg. When in doubt, however, he always adopted a worst-case scenario—this time, that Oleg Tushin represented the KGB. Still, Haden had to admit that the supposition told him nothing; if it was true, it would be no more than an indication that the Russian wariness of people whose activities were not sufficiently well explained more than matched his own. But why had Tushin sought him out, in effect putting him on his guard? A warning? Haden could think of no other explanation. Tushin had said practically nothing, except perhaps his veiled invitation to meet some "dissident." If that was intended to be a trap, would even a heavy-handed KGB man be so clumsy?

Haden set his speculations aside. Something more would either happen or it would not. The time to assess it would be later. He lifted the magnifying glass.

The powerful lens removed all doubt. His eyes had not betrayed him, it was no optical illusion. On the title page of the new volume, what looked like a decorative whorl was in fact nine tiny concentric circles. The artist had been indulging in some delicate symbolism.

But on the title page of the photocopy of the same edition that had belonged to Freddy, the corresponding whorl was made up of only eight concentric circles.

The ninth circle was missing.

How it had been done, there was no way of telling. Perhaps by the careful application of some bleaching agent. But there was no doubt about it. Freddy's copy had no ninth circle.

Haden's fragmentary boyhood recollection of Dante's work, a dim relic associated with the drone of his schoolmaster's voice, had been considerably sharpened by the more recent exercise of his line-by-line search for the discrepancy he had stumbled across, nearly by chance, and that was not in the text at all. Haden knew what the ninth circle signified.

He turned to "The Inferno," and read again Cantos XXXII, XXXIII, and XXXIV.

In Dante's concept, Hell was a descending cone divided into nine circles, in each of which the damned were confined according to the enormity of their sins. It plunged downward from those who sinned with carnal lust; to the gourmands; to heretics in red-hot tombs; to tyrants and murderers doused in boiling blood; to deceivers—seducers, thieves, and evil counselors; and, finally, to the lowest level, the Ninth Circle.

In the Ninth Circle, treachery, the most grievous of all crimes, was punished. It was a place of savage, unendurable cold. The damned lay clamped in ice for, as the commentary remarked, "treachery was a sin of cold blood," and the Ninth Circle was "the frozen cesspool of the world, into which drained all the streams of Hell."

There, tormented in the eternal ice, lay traitors to their kindred, traitors to their country, traitors to their friends, and traitors to their lords and benefactors.

Haden read once more Dante's account of Count Ugolino, who had conspired with the enemies of the city of Pisa in order to gain power for himself. Count Ugolino was later betrayed by his enemy, Archbishop Ruggieri, and with his children was confined in the Tower of Pisa, where they were left to starve to death. The Count died last, after having devoured the flesh of his dead children.

In his journey through the Ninth Circle, Dante saw both traitors forever locked in the ice, where Count Ugolino, racked with useless remorse and hatred, eternally gnawed on the head of the Archbishop.

A footnote from the translator observed that Count Ugolino's betrayal of his city would have been well known to Dante and his contemporaries. Dante would have placed Count Ugolino in the most fearful section of Hell not only for his crime of treachery but also because he had used his country's misfortunes for his own ambition and had plotted and schemed with whichever enemy faction promised to support his greed for power.

Haden read through to the end of the final canto, in which the giant black figure of Satan held the agonized figure of Judas Iscariot in one of his sets of jaws, chewing for all eternity on the archtraitor.

Haden turned back and read again a particular passage that had caught his attention: "Never did Danube in Austria or far off Don under its frigid sky made in winter so thick a veil on its course as was here."

Haden closed the book, lit a cheroot, and smoked it, watching the lazily rising coils of smoke.

The sheer power of the imagery, even in translation, with which Dante had evoked his abhorrence of the evil of treachery, depressed him. Reason told him that Dante, writing in the fourteenth century, was a man of his time, that the medieval concept of treason was far removed from that in the twentieth century. Today, there would be more than one view of the culpability of Brutus and Cassius, whom Dante had unhesitatingly placed alongside Judas Iscariot to share in equal measure his dreadful tortures. There would even, Haden reflected wryly, be more than one view of the true enormity of Judas himself. The age of certainty had gone, along with the belief in a frightful eternal Hell—or the rewards of Heaven, come to that—doled out by divine justice. Just the same, the extraordinary intensity of that long-dead poet's vision of the unimaginable was haunting.

Haden opened the book again and turned the pages slowly.

"Never did Danube in Austria or far off Don under its frigid sky . . ."

Written more than six hundred years before, the reference to the conjunction of the Danube, the banks of which he could see from his window, and the great Russian river unsettled him in a curious way. On any rational basis, it could only be chance. Yet, just a short time ago, he had been talking to a man who came from the land of the Don. The subject of their conversation had been Alexander Baronin, who had disappeared in a city that lay on the Danube. Haden stirred restlessly. The connection was too fanciful. Doubtless, if he scoured the world's literature, he could find innumerable coincidental references. The fact remained, however, that this one occurred in a work that happened to be in his possession. Haden found it hard to rid himself of the feeling that it all had some grim significance that lay beyond "so thick a veil" and that he could not pierce.

Very little, if anything, he realized, had become visible from behind that veil. He picked up the magnifying glass and played around with it, holding it at varying distances from the whorl from which the ninth circle was missing. It would not, perhaps, take as much magnification as he had imagined for the discrepancy to become immediately obvious.

Haden sat back and thought about that and about Harold Leyton. Anything was possible, and he might have beaten Leyton to it, but he considered the opposite safer and more likely. That devious little former spy knew his trade. By now he would have detected the missing ninth circle, but he hadn't called to share his interesting news.

Haden stubbed out his diminished cheroot and returned the books to his briefcase. Harold Leyton's silence most likely indicated that he had uncovered not only the key but the lock into which it fitted—or into which he thought it did—and that he could do without Stephen Haden.

Giving Leyton that copy of Freddy's Dante had resembled, at the time, a chess player's sacrifice of a pawn in order to defend a more important position on the board. As such, it had been necessary, and could not be regarded as a mistake. But a pawn could sometimes swing a game in unexpected ways.

Haden's depression lingered but was not entirely accounted for by Dante's apocalyptic description of his journey through Hell. Haden had a growing sense that he himself was a sacrificial pawn in someone else's game, in which he knew neither the players nor the objective, a piece capable only of limited moves until the time arrived to discard it.

He returned the magnifying glass to the reception desk, thanked them, and asked to lodge his briefcase in the safe. He felt the time had come when those books should not be left lying around. The receptionist nodded matter-of-factly at his routine request, asked him to wait a moment, and took his briefcase into the office.

During the few moments before she returned with his receipt, something about the notice board struck him as different.

"Thank you," he said, taking his receipt. He pointed to the notice board. "The list of what's on soon seems to be missing."

"Oh, dear. I'm sorry, sir," the receptionist said. "Perhaps one of the guests took it. They sometimes do. I'll see if we have another one . . ."

"No, don't bother," Haden said. "I'll take potluck at the opera sometime."

As lunchtime approached, he passed Petra Baron on the way to the sauna, each clad in a dressing gown.

"You've been playing hookey," she said playfully. "Where have you been?"

"Staring at blank walls," Haden said, continuing on his way.

He lay on the top shelf in the sauna and allowed his mind to float free while the perspiration gathered and then trickled down his body. Speculations came and went, were juggled, and failed to form any recognizable pattern.

The missing ninth circle recurred again and again, but did not seem to be an interlocking piece. He had made his discovery, but he did not know what it meant. The dead Freddy had alluded to some secret group. Did it call itself the Ninth Circle?

In Freddy's scenario of greed, or revenge, never now to be played out, that missing ninth circle must have been intended as some sort of shorthand threat, one that required no further explanation.

The nature of chance being what it was, Freddy could have been killed during a robbery that happened to take place the day before he intended to put that threat into execution. Why not? Doesn't chance dictate that a bridge player might be dealt a hand of cards, all of the same suit, from a freshly shuffled pack? It happens. Just not very often.

So, leaving aside that almost impossible chance, Haden knew about the threat that had brought Freddy's life to an end. He knew about the ninth circle. In that respect only, he had an advantage. If only he also knew what the hell the ninth circle meant, but he did not.

Without that knowledge the breakthrough would not give him command of the game. Sweat oozed and dripped from every pore. Haden knew he was worse off than before. Even though ignorant, he possessed the threat—and he was in no position to reveal it in any attempt to identify whomever it had been aimed at. Should he do so, he risked sharing Freddy's fate. Not only was he no farther ahead; he possessed a piece of knowledge that placed him in mortal danger should he make the slightest mistake.

Haden left the sauna, took an ice-cold plunge, and, shivering, returned to his top shelf.

There had to be something else. But what else? What? The shivering died away as his body responded to the dry heat.

The Ninth Circle. Dante. Dante . . . Freddy's obsession had started there, with Dante . . . but Haden did not know what Dante meant, either. Perhaps nothing.

No, Dante signified something, all right, or Frederick Webb, civil servant, would be alive and drinking. It couldn't be the name of a person; Freddy could have traced something that simple. A cover, then, a name by which something or someone was identified? Something secret, undercover, a code name, like Operation Valkyrie or Operation Dragon? Operation Dante? Could be. Or something else maybe, not quite a man or an operation . . . there was something nibbling at the back of his mind, some half-remembered fragment from a newspaper, read and then dismissed with other items of no particular personal interest at the time. It had been the French—that was it, something their secret service had been running that eventually came to light. Mitterrand had told Reagan about it, after which Franco-American relations had become much more cordial. What had they called it? *Adieu?* Something like that, anyway.

It might tie in with Alexander Baronin's periodic visits to

Vienna. That could make sense of much more about Baronin, too. "Dante" . . .

Did it really fit? Or was he becoming light-headed in the intense heat?

"Dante" . . .

Haden lay and sweated until he was nearly baked—and late for lunch.

"Dante" . . .

Eventually he roused himself from his dreamlike state with another cold plunge. When his mind was clear, the solution turned into no solution at all. It was only a miasma of a theory that, even if correct, resolved nothing. He set it aside to either gel or disappear. He needed to talk to Erwin Matz again.

They drove toward the lights of Vienna. Petra sat beside Haden, curled up defensively, her Bad Gastberg vivacity replaced by an almost sullen silence. The outing had been her suggestion, offered excitedly, as if she were a small girl planning an escapade, but now that the time was approaching, she seemed to find it an ordeal to be got through and viewed it with foreboding rather than anticipation.

"Do we have to wait around until it's the same time as then?" she asked, from the darkness beside him.

"Not necessary," Haden replied. That would clash with the arrangements he had made.

They stood on the steps of the Opera. Inside, a performance of *Aida* was going on.

"Whenever you're ready," Haden said.

"It's cold," Petra fretted, huddling into her upturned coat collar. "It was summer then. Warm."

"We'll make allowances for the temperature," Haden said patiently.

She gave him a look, her mouth downturned and showing no amusement, and hurried off briskly, Haden at her elbow.

"Try to walk at the same pace as you did then," Haden requested. "I'm timing it."

"Why?" she demanded aggressively. "What the hell will that tell you?"

"I've no idea," Haden answered. "Just do it." Despite her beauty, this was a woman who could be extremely trying.

"I'm freezing," Petra complained. But she slowed down to the casual strolling pace appropriate for a summer evening.

They arrived at Sacher's Hotel. Haden noted the route, and that they approached the hotel from the front. He also noted that the timing, which had little to do with how long the walk had taken, had been good.

"Well?" Petra inquired, hugging herself to keep warm. "What now?"

"Just a minute," Haden said.

Two men were standing some distance away. One glanced over his shoulder, turned his back, and moved into the shadows. The other remained clearly illuminated in the lamplight.

"There's a man standing over there on your right," Haden said quietly. "Tell me if you've ever seen him before."

Petra glanced sharply at the man and then looked away.

"No," she said, after a moment. "Never."

"Are you quite certain?"

"I've just said so. Who is he, anyway?"

"He claims he saw your husband being bundled into a car," Haden said. She looked at him, one hand unconsciously covering her throat with her collar. "Take another glance," Haden said.

Petra did so. The man caught her eye, stared back for a moment, and then turned away.

"I don't know him," Petra said. "Why should I? Do you think he's been following us or something?"

"As yet, I don't know," Haden answered. "I need to talk to him. It may take some time."

"Now? With me?" There was a rising note of apprehension in her voice.

"He's seen you, that's good enough," Haden said. He indicated the hotel's inviting entrance. "You wait inside. I'll pick you up later. That okay?"

"Fine," Petra said, relieved.

Haden watched her until she was inside the hotel. The two men were walking away. Haden followed them.

The walk through the biting cold night led past a café that Haden had expected his quarry to enter and then along a less well lit street that led to the courtyard of a shabby apartment house. Erwin Matz was waiting at the door. He led Haden into the dimly lit, empty hall and pointed to the stairs.

"His place is right at the top," he said. "He didn't want to be seen with you."

"What do you make of him?"

"He takes money," Matz said.

As he climbed the stairs, Haden heard the door to the street close behind Matz. The final flight narrowed and steepened before it terminated on the top landing. There was only one door. Haden tried it. It opened.

The foyer was small, little larger than a closet. Light streamed across it from a half-opened door. Haden heard a clink from inside and entered.

The man was pouring beer from a bottle into a glass.

136

"Close it," he said. His voice was deep and rasping. "I feel the cold."

Haden closed the door. The single large room was pleasantly warm, but the foyer was unheated. The furniture was basic and worn. In one corner of the room was a tiny kitchen area. The opposite corner was curtained off; behind it, Haden supposed, there was a bed. Everything was very tidy, meticulously so.

Hans Kinsky was in his seventies. His burly body and erect carriage belied his age. His face did not. The pale blue eyes had grown watery. The skin was lined and sagging, the thin lips bluish. The hair, close cropped to a stubble, was white.

"Well? What do you want of me?" Kinsky demanded belligerently.

"You've been told that," Haden replied.

"And you've talked to Hofer. I told him all I know."

"Okay," Haden said. "If you've nothing to add, give me the money back, and I'll go." Kinsky stared at him, his bleary eyes cold and hostile. Haden held out his hand. "The money," he repeated.

Kinsky gestured toward one of two wooden chairs at the small kitchen table. "Sit down, if you want," he said.

Haden sat down and unbuttoned his overcoat. "I was with a woman outside Sacher's," he said.

"Well? What of it?"

"Do you know her?"

"No. Never seen her before."

"I thought you might have."

"Why?"

"You say you saw Alexander Baronin being kidnapped," Haden answered. "She's his wife."

Kinsky topped up his glass and sat on the chair opposite Haden's, his back stiff and straight.

137

"She wasn't with him, if that's what you want to know," he said.

"Then the man you saw *was* Baronin."

"I thought it was. Later—well, Hofer will have told you about that."

"Yes," Haden said. "Can you describe the car or the other men?"

"I didn't take much notice at the time. I thought it was just some friends having an argument. It was only when I thought about it that I realized it could have been something else."

"So you went to the police," Haden said. "Was that when they showed up a number of photographs?"

"Didn't you ask Hofer that?" Kinsky inquired aggressively.

"I'm asking you."

Kinsky's frown added some additional wrinkles to his face.

"It was either the next day or the day after that," he said finally. "They sent for me."

"Perhaps they'd had to obtain Baronin's photograph from somewhere," Haden suggested.

"I wouldn't know," Kinsky said.

"How did Willi Hofer know you'd been drinking heavily that night?" Haden inquired.

Kinsky stared at him suspiciously. "He asked and I told him."

"When you picked out the wrong man?"

"Yes," Kinsky said. "Is that everything?"

"No. Why did you go to the police in the first place?"

"It was my duty as a citizen," Kinsky snapped.

"Not because you thought there might be something in it for you, like a reward?"

"If there'd been one, I'd have taken it," Kinsky said

curtly. "But since it seems I was mistaken, there wasn't any."

Haden reached into his breast pocket, took out a photograph, and held it up.

"Do you know this man?" he asked.

Kinsky leaned forward, his eyes narrowed into a squint.

"I do not," he finally said. "But I think it's one of those they showed me. Since you have it, I assume it's Baronin."

"*Could* this be the man you saw being hustled into a car?"

"No," Kinsky said definitely, shaking his head. "If it were, I'd have been able to pick him out."

Haden nodded, tucked the photograph away, and glanced idly round the functionally tidy room, somehow more reminiscent of a barracks than a home.

"You're an old soldier, I understand," he said.

"During the war I did my duty," Kinsky replied.

"In the SS," Haden added.

Kinsky smiled thinly. "You have been consulting old records," he said.

"You were tried for war crimes and served three years in prison."

The sagging old face split into a silent, mirthless smile. In its eyes were both pride and contempt.

"We lost," Kinsky said. "That was our crime."

"And after that?"

Kinsky shrugged. "After that, Austria was busy forgetting the Anschluss, pretending she had never really been involved. I refused to pretend—unlike some of my countrymen," he said, his derision and dislike apparent. "Why do you ask about such things?"

"Interest, no more," Haden said. "You live alone?"

"My wife is long dead. My son prefers to keep his distance. So be it. I don't need his help."

"But you need money," Haden said. "You accepted mine."

"I did not say my pension permitted luxuries," Kinsky said dryly.

"You could afford a few more," Haden said, "if you were able to remember anything you haven't told me."

"About my past?" Kinsky inquired. "What would you like to know?"

"Information about the man you thought was Baronin," Haden said evenly. "You'd be well paid. Very well paid."

"Nothing comes to mind," Kinsky said. "I will need some time to think."

Haden stood up and buttoned his overcoat.

"Think hard," he said. "Search your memory."

Haden made his way down the stairs and into the street. That aging relic, he was certain, was holding something back.

He wondered what it was that Hans Kinsky was concealing. And why? Fear? Haden considered Kinsky a pretty unpalatable specimen, but he did not think the old man kept company with fear very often.

Chapter Eight

Erwin Matz was sitting, an inconspicuous figure, in the lobby of Sacher's Hotel. Haden joined him.

"They're in the restaurant," Matz said.

"They've been there all this time?" Haden asked.

Matz shook his head. "They came downstairs together," he said. "Anything else?"

"Not for tonight. I'll call you."

"Stephen," Matz began, "I was talking to Berlin this afternoon, and it seems—"

"They'll get by," Haden cut in. "You're needed here."

"Okay," Matz said. "Good night."

Haden deposited his coat in the cloakroom and made his way to the restaurant, which was tucked away at the back. There, with its faintly *fin de siècle* atmosphere, service was taken seriously and waiters of sober mien glided decorously to and fro, intent upon their tasks.

Petra Baron saw him across the room and lifted her hand high in a wave of greeting. Her smile was brilliant. Haden walked toward the table. A waiter materialized, seemingly from nowhere, and held the vacant chair for him. Haden sat down.

"Meet Jerry Lander," Petra said. "He was in London—Ralph's friend, remember?"

Haden said, "His name was up outside the theater."

"I'm flattered," Lander said. "Not too many people notice the director's name."

"Haden notices everything," Petra said. She smiled sweetly at Haden. "We're ahead of you. Try the specialty, it's great."

"Just wine for me," Haden said.

"Jerry's here to direct an opera," Petra said.

"Yes, it was on the notice board at Bad Gastberg," Haden said.

Petra rocked with laughter. It came out rather high-pitched. "You see?" she said to Lander. "Everything. Every goddamn thing."

"Not quite," Haden said. "I wish I did."

She seemed not to hear him but frowned as if belatedly perceiving some contradiction. "The notice board?" she queried. "I didn't see it."

Haden gathered that either the bottle of wine was not the first or it had been preceded by a fair quantity of something stronger.

"Someone took it down," he said.

"Who? What for?" Petra wanted to know. Jerry Lander caught Haden's eye across the table and smiled slightly, with a small lift of his eyebrows. Petra didn't wait for an answer. "Anyway," she said, "when you dumped me in the cold outside, I decided to look up Jerry." Petra looked pointedly at Haden. "So we're invited to the first night," she said. "When is that again, Jerry?"

"Next month," Lander said.

"What? We may not be here," Petra said, as if she expected him to change the date.

"Rehearsing an opera takes a long time," Lander said patiently. "It's nice. Rehearsals are where the fun is."

Lander wore—or, rather, affected—a small beard and a thin mustache. His eyes were very brown and very bright. Haden thought his manner was almost certainly deceptive. No one who could handle notoriously temperamental artists, with an orchestra and a conductor thrown in, could be that mild and gentle.

"Have you directed many operas, Mr. Lander?" Haden asked, playing into the superficial drift of the conversation. He sensed that no real issues would be addressed that evening.

"A few," Lander said. "The first time, through Marianne, Ralph Janson's wife. She's an opera lover, a patron, an influential lady. The theater's where I make my living, but I enjoy the occasional opera. It's different. When I was offered this one, I accepted with pleasure. It's a Janáček. I like Janáček."

"Noise," Petra said. "Janáček is noise."

Again Lander gave Haden that small, tolerant smile with raised eyebrows and changed the subject, asking Haden about Bad Gastberg. Haden replied and added a question concerning Lander's line of work, although he did not inquire if Jerry Lander had, by chance, been directing at the Opera in Vienna the preceding summer, when Baronin had disappeared. That could easily be established by other means.

Petra finished the wine in her glass and sat in silence, looking from one man to the other as they talked, until there was a momentary lull in the conversation.

"I'm tired," she said then. "Let's go, okay?"

Petra fell asleep almost as soon as the Mercedes engine whirred into life and the heater began to hum. She stirred as they approached the village of Bad Gastberg but sat for a while without saying anything, staring through the windshield until the snowbound tennis courts appeared in the headlights.

"The man who saw Alex that night," she said, her voice subdued, "did you get anything from him?"

"The police didn't believe him," Haden said, "Nor do I."

She seemed to accept his reply and take it at face value. He heard her sigh.

"God, what an awful mess," she said, almost inaudibly. "It's not going to be any use, is it? There's nothing anyone can do."

Haden lay in bed for a while, considering Jerry Lander. The man was an American but seemed to work extensively in Europe. So did a number of directors. Theater was an international business. He seemed to know Petra Baron well but had not mentioned her husband. That could indicate nothing beyond consideration for her feelings.

Haden's original suspicion that Petra Baron had removed the item from the notice board so that he could not see it now seemed unlikely. Why do that and then sit with Lander in the middle of the restaurant at Sacher's?

But Haden was a man who viewed coincidences with immediate distrust. Jerry Lander had been in London, was now in Vienna, and—this still remained to be checked— just might have been in Vienna when Baronin vanished. Lander might be playing some part in this intricate game that Haden still did not understand.

Petra Baron was not exactly waiting around faithfully for a husband who might be dead. It struck Haden that her arrival in Vienna might have had more to do with Jerry Lander, who was an attractive man, than with his own attempt to find out what had happened to Baronin. In relation to that, Haden concluded in a moment of self-critical candor, he was merely floundering. He had achieved nothing more than isolating the missing Ninth Circle.

Haden yawned, closed his eyes, and turned over. As he was falling asleep, a hazy, half-formed hypothesis took shape in his mind. Suppose Petra Baron had removed the notice because she wanted to talk to Jerry Lander before introducing Haden to him? Like most dreams, it struck Haden as pretty fantastic. Why? He had no answer. If any more dreams invaded his mind that night, he did not remember them.

The telephone rang before Haden was fully awake. He peered at his watch in the early morning's dull light. It was 8:00 A.M. The voice at the other end spoke English, although with a marked accent.

"Mr. Haden, I think it may be desirable that we meet."

"Who is this?"

"I shall give you the name and address. You may wish to write it down. Are you ready?"

"Hold on." Haden got out of his bed to fetch pen and paper and returned quickly to the phone. "Go ahead." He listened to the name and address and queried the spelling. "What's this about?"

"Your presence in Vienna. Five o'clock this afternoon. You will be expected."

The caller hung up.

Chess was not obligatory in the café Haden walked into, but most of the patrons were hunched over boards, staring thoughtfully at the pieces. The atmosphere was quiet and ruminative, dedicated to the worship of the game. There was more thought and contemplation than conversation going on, and any talk was desultory, uttered in quiet undertones. No one took much notice of his neighbor.

Haden sat down opposite Erwin Matz and drew the white chessmen. They began to play.

"Coffee and a cognac for the time being," Haden said to the waiter, who nodded silently and withdrew.

"The opera Mrs. Baron went to see the night her husband disappeared had opened two days earlier," Matz said, bringing his knight into play. He spoke in the hushed murmur people instinctively use in church. "Your Mr. Lander was the associate artistic director."

"A work by Janáček, perhaps." Haden suggested, using the same undertone. Matz gave him a curious look. "He likes Janáček," Haden explained. Coffee, ice water, and a glass of cognac appeared at his elbow. Haden lit a cheroot and thought he saw an opening for his bishop. "How much can you tell from a man's name here in Vienna, Erwin?" he inquired.

Matz's eyes lit up.

"A great deal," he answered, and took one of Haden's pawns.

"Please explain how," Haden said. He studied the board. The loss of his pawn had left a nasty gap, and Haden considered how to close it.

Matz's normal brevity deserted him. He spoke with enthusiasm, a man expounding on a subject dear to his heart. While he talked and Haden listened, they continued to play.

"There is hardly such a thing as a truly Viennese name," Matz told him. "As the capital of the Austro-Hungarian Empire, Vienna attracted nationals of all subject peoples. From the north came Czechs, Slovaks, Poles." Matz counted them off on the fingers of his large, clean hand. "From the east, Hungarians, Rumanians, Bulgarians. From the south, Serbs, Croats, Italians, Slovenes. They came for

146

advancement, money, work, to indulge in social climbing—all that a great metropolis offers.''

"Okay, so you can tell where they came from. Anything else?'' Haden brought his queen out. It was a daring move but not, he felt, reckless.

"Yes,'' Matz said, oblivious, Haden noted with satisfaction, to the threat to his king. "Sometimes, you can deduce economic, social, and class backgrounds. For example, my own name, Matz, suggests proletarian, country origins—and, indeed, my ancestors were peasants in the Wachau. A Masaryk is likely to be middle-class, a Huber lower-class. It does not always work this way, of course. A Sternberg can be a count, with formerly enormous estates in Bohemia, or a Jewish dentist.''

"How about our friend Hans Kinsky?'' Haden asked. He advanced one of his knights, closing the trap.

"Kinsky is a Czech name and strongly indicates aristocratic origins,'' Matz said. "I did say the method was by no means infallible.''

"Perhaps his great-grandparents came down in the world,'' Haden suggested. In two moves he could strike with his queen.

"Checkmate,'' Matz said. Haden stared at the board in disbelief. "Bringing your bishop out like that was a mistake,'' Matz said blandly.

Haden sat back and sipped his cognac. His mistake lay in supposing that Matz could not talk and play at the same time.

"How about János Varga?'' he asked.

"Hungarian,'' Matz answered. "It is pronounced *Yanosh.*''

From his pocket Haden drew the slip of paper upon which he had written his early caller's name and address. He passed it over the chessboard to Erwin Matz.

"A Hungarian who now lives in Vienna," Haden proposed.

"I believe you may find he is a tailor," Matz added.

"That's very good," Haden said, impressed.

"Thank you," Matz replied modestly.

"A Varga is usually a tailor—is that how you could tell?"

"No. From the address. I think it is a tailor's shop."

At five o'clock, Haden opened the door of the shop and entered. The shop was small. Shelves laden with bolts of cloth lined the walls. A bald man in his fifties, wearing a waistcoat but no jacket, and with a tape measure hung around his neck, was speaking deferentially to a well-fed, shiny-faced Austrian with a bulging waistline. He excused himself and crossed to Haden.

"Good afternoon, sir. May I help you?" One eye was curiously fixed.

"My name is Stephen Haden. I'm here to see Herr Varga."

"Ah, yes. I am János Varga." He studied Haden's build with approval. "It will be a pleasure, sir. Did you have any particular style in mind?"

"Suppose I rely on you," Haden said.

"Of course. Will you come this way, sir?"

He led Haden through the shop, along a short corridor, and opened a door.

"The other gentleman has just arrived for a fitting, Mr. Haden. It will take a few minutes. In the meantime, I'm sure you can find a fabric to your taste."

Haden went into the brightly lit, windowless room. Before him were a full-length movable mirror, a table covered with books of fabric samples, and a chair.

"Perhaps I might suggest a mohair, Mr. Haden," János Varga said before he closed the door.

Almost at the same moment, abruptly, the light went out.

At once and instinctively, Haden dropped to one knee. Not a sound broke the silence. Still crouching, he edged to the door and tried it.

It was locked.

He thought he heard a sound behind him. He spun around. The darkness was absolute. He could see nothing. The sound was not repeated, but he was certain that there was someone else there.

Yet how could there be? Only a few seconds had elapsed before the light went out, and he was sure the room had been empty except for the mirror, the table, and the chair—no closets, no curtains, nowhere for anyone to hide.

But the feeling that he was not alone persisted. Haden eased the Smith & Wesson .38 from its shoulder holster. The weight of the butt in his hand was reassuring. With infinite care he inched away from the locked door. Trying it had been a mistake. In the pitch-darkness, sound equaled sight and would help his unseen companion to locate him. On the other hand, he could see nothing, and neither could whoever was there. If shooting started, Haden was ready for the first flash. He would gain a momentary advantage; he would know where to return fire.

Poised and ready though he was, the voice, when it came—low, scarcely more than a whisper—made him start.

"Mr. Haden, I must apologize for these precautions."

Haden said nothing. The voice, with its slight accent, was coming from the far wall, perhaps ten or twelve feet from where he was crouching. A blank wall, wasn't it? But it couldn't be.

"I must know if I can trust you—Mr. Haden?"

Haden aimed his revolver in the direction he thought the voice was coming from and rocked his memory urgently. He had only just started to look around the room when the light went out. Had there been a door in that blank wall?

There could have been . . . yes . . . painted the same color as the wall . . . that must be it.

"Answer me, please."

There was irritation in the voice. If that door was open now, there should be some trace of light, a glimmer, something. But there was none.

"You think you may be in some danger, is that the case, Mr. Haden?"

Haden thought the voice was coming from someone standing. Perhaps if he lay he could pick out a silhouette. He gently lowered himself and tried it. He could not.

"Quite the contrary."

The irritation had been replaced by a certain wry amusement. Haden was beginning to feel vaguely foolish.

"It is I who am risking my life, Mr. Haden."

"You've got that right," Haden said, changing his position even as he spoke. "You stand to get shot," he said, moving again. He found himself up against the full-length mirror. Both men were quiet. The other man spoke first.

"Yes. Well, then, you have the advantage, Mr. Haden. I am not armed."

"Let's have some light," Haden said. "Let me see for myself."

He wriggled behind the full-length mirror and stood. The sense of safety there was mostly psychological. Just the same, it was a sturdy, heavy object. It was something.

"You have not understood," the voice said. It still came from exactly the same position, Haden thought. "These precautions are because I dare not allow you to be able to identify me."

"All right, go ahead," Haden said. He leaned against the wall, behind the full-length mirror. His gun remained at the ready, although it was probably an unnecessary precaution. If there was going to be shooting, it would already have happened.

"You are seeking information concerning Alexander Baronin."

"Am I? Who told you that?"

"Mr. Haden, you have practically broadcast it."

Haden silently conceded the point. "Did you know Baronin?" he asked.

"I knew him," the voice said.

"How did you know him? Where?"

"That does not matter."

"Dante?" Haden said suddenly.

Again there was a pause.

"Dante? Now it is I who do not understand."

"I think you're Dante," Haden said. "Baronin's contact in Vienna."

"Who told you about Dante?"

"A dead man."

"How much did he tell you?"

Haden said nothing.

"Mr. Haden, this conversation is at an end unless you answer and I believe your answer."

"Just the name," Haden said. "Dante. Nothing else."

"And the rest? Where did the rest come from? Those who hired you?"

"No," Haden said. "My own conclusions. Guesswork, fitting pieces together. Baronin fitted with Dante."

"So now you seek Dante."

"If he knows what happened to Baronin, yes."

There was a long silence.

"It is possible that I could help you concerning Baronin, Mr. Haden, but I do not promise. It will depend on how you answer me."

"Is Baronin dead or alive?"

"From now on, the questions are mine, not yours, Mr. Haden. You claim to be working for Baronin's wife. Is that true?"

It was Haden's turn to pause for thought. Reason told him to maintain his cover story. Some stronger instinct told him that it was time to gamble with the truth.

"Petra Baron approached me," he said. "But there are others involved."

"Tell me about them, please."

"Baronin's former employers."

"You mean the CIA? Walter Gorman?"

"Not Gorman," Haden said. "A different section. I can't tell you who. People who think there's been more going on than they know about."

"I see," the voice said. "No one else?"

Haden said, "Someone who reports directly to the President of the United States."

The assertion made no noticeable impression. The low, accented half-whisper remained level.

"And what do you make of all that, Mr. Haden?"

"That maybe I'm part of a covert operation for which someone would like to maintain deniability. What the object is, I don't know. But I don't much like the prospect of being denied."

"Mr. Haden, you know more than you imagine. Too much for your own good. I would advise you to be very careful."

The voice fell silent, and after a moment Haden thought he heard that same slight sound that had preceded the man's arrival.

The lights went on suddenly. Momentarily dazzled, Haden blinked, and then, as his vision cleared, he found himself staring at a closed door, set in the opposite wall. At eye level in the door was a small sliding panel. Haden walked over and tested the door. It was locked. He opened the panel. There was a small storeroom on the other side. He saw no one. He closed the panel.

The other door opened, and János Varga bustled in briskly, his brow wrinkled in apology.

"I am sorry to have kept you so long, Mr. Haden," he said. "The size of the other gentleman's waistline appears to vary from day to day." He sighed. "Still, at least you have had time to make your selection." He smiled in eager anticipation.

"I'll come back later," Haden said.

"Soon I must close," Varga said. "Perhaps tomorrow?"

"Tomorrow isn't convenient," Haden answered.

Muffled up again, Haden stepped outside the shop. A light snow was falling. He looked up and down the street but didn't see Erwin Matz.

He turned right and found the narrow alley that ran along the back of Varga's shop. It was not well lit. He tried the back door of the tailor's shop. It was securely locked.

He walked through the alley until it joined a busy street and then retraced his footsteps and waited, as the gentle snow settled on his shoulders. Still Erwin Matz did not appear.

János Varga had his jacket on and was pulling down blinds when Haden walked back into the shop. Haden ignored the man's pained look.

"You can measure me now," Haden said.

"Of course, sir." Varga took off his jacket and led Haden to the same room. "If you would kindly slip your jacket off, Mr. Haden," Varga said.

Haden did so. Varga ran the tape measure over him, quietly murmuring measurements to himself and jotting them down.

He seemed oblivious to the shoulder holster and the gun, his eyes paying no more attention to them than to Haden's shirt. Only when he placed his fingers lightly on Haden's shoulders, and squared them, did he purse his lips thoughtfully and make his indirect inquiry.

"May I take it, Mr. Haden, that you like your suits to accommodate any accessories you may wish to carry from time to time?"

"That's right," Haden answered. "Can you do that?"

"Of course, sir. Leave it to me."

Varga slipped his tape measure around Haden's chest again, and Haden obligingly took the Smith & Wesson from its holster and held it casually.

Varga found the barrel pointing at his face. He seemed to have been about to make some remark, but reconsidered it and proceeded to take Haden's waist and inseam measurements.

The barrel of the revolver followed his face, inches from it. Still Varga said nothing, but his fingers shook as he wrote down more measurements.

"Tell me about yourself, Mr. Varga," Haden said conversationally.

"What about myself, exactly?"

"You just talk and I'll listen," Haden said. "Let's start that way."

Haden sat on the table and rested both hands comfortably on one thigh. Varga stood before him, his gaze on the barrel of the revolver, which was now pointing at his belly. Then he raised his eyes to meet Haden's.

"I was born in Budapest where I lived until I was a young man," he said. "I took part in the 1956 uprising, and when it was crushed by the Russians, I was one of the many who crossed into Austria. Is that what you wish to know?"

"It's a start," Haden said agreeably. "So you were there. You fought the Russians."

"We tried. But they had tanks. We had only rifles."

"And how did that make you feel about them?"

"The Russians?" Varga shrugged wearily. "As individuals, they were ordinary men, no more, like me. They were

154

doing as they were told. But for a little while, we had freedom. They took it away from us.''

'' 'He goes seeking liberty, which is so dear, as he knows who for it renounces life,' '' Haden said.

"I'm sorry? I do not understand," Varga said.

"Dante wrote that," Haden said. "Aren't you familiar with Dante, Mr. Varga?"

János Varga shook his head slightly. "My left eye is glass," he said. "You may have noticed. Many of my comrades, yes, they paid with their lives. For a while, the brief flowering, it seemed to be worth it.''

"How about you?" Haden inquired.

"Time has passed. Memories dim. Stalin died long ago. Hungary is not such a bad country today."

"Then why don't you go back?" Haden demanded.

Varga said quietly, "I cannot forget 1956. I prefer to live a free man."

"So you'd describe yourself as a dedicated anti-Communist," Haden suggested.

Varga said, "I fought once; but that was in the past, and I am no longer a young man."

"Half an hour ago, a man talked to me from behind that door," Haden said, pointing. "I thought he was Russian. Perhaps he was Hungarian. I'd like to know which. And who he was."

"There is nothing I can tell you," Varga said simply. "It is not my place to know of such things."

"You simply provide facilities," Haden suggested. Varga said nothing. "Suppose I wished to meet your friend again," Haden asked. "I assume you take messages, too."

"There is some fluff on your jacket," Varga said. He picked up the jacket and began to brush it carefully. "As though it had been on the floor."

"Quite right," Haden said dryly. "It was." He tucked his gun back in its holster.

"There, that's better," Varga said. He held the jacket up and helped Haden into it. "And now," he said brightly. "About the fabric you have selected?"

"I'll think about it and let you know," Haden said.

"At your convenience," Varga said. "Allow me to show you out, Mr. Haden."

Haden sat in the café, his cup of coffee growing cold. He had arranged the chess pieces on the board and was replaying his game against Erwin Matz. Without Matz sitting opposite, he won easily. In this respect chess was like life. Given sufficient hindsight, it is easy not to make mistakes.

Erwin Matz strolled in ten minutes later and sat down. "Ready for your revenge?" he asked.

"No," Haden said. "Start at the beginning."

"Okay," Matz said. "No one followed you to your tailor's." Matz himself had tailed Haden from the parked car, hanging well back. "Once you were inside, I kept watch for a while in case anyone else arrived. No one did, so I started walking back and forth. I was passing the rear alley when I saw a man walking away fast. It looked as though he could have come out of Varga's back door, but I couldn't be certain."

"Someone did. Can you describe him?"

Matz shook his head. "He was wearing an anorak with the hood up over his head," he said. "I managed to keep him in sight for a while, but he was being careful. In the end, I lost him. He could have hopped onto a bus— anything—I don't know. Sorry."

"Can't be helped," Haden said. "Where did you lose him?"

"Near the Hofburg."

The Imperial Hofburg Palace had recently been taken over for the East-West talks, to the indignation of Viennese

156

socialites, a number of whose most glittering balls had been displaced from their favorite venue that season, "in the national and international interest," as the Foreign Ministry had put it.

One kind of waltz making way for another, Haden thought. He eyed Erwin Matz.

"He just might come and go from the palace, Erwin," he said.

Matz looked dubious. "Not the way he was dressed," he said. "Didn't look the part at all."

"Perhaps that was the idea. He didn't want to be identified. Any chance you could pick him out again? Put a name to him?"

"From his walk, perhaps," Matz said. "It was slightly uneven. Distinctive."

"Don't make yourself conspicuous, that's all," Haden said.

Matz said, smiling, "I never do, Stephen."

"One man drew attention to himself and he's dead," Haden said. "So don't be too cocksure."

Matz nodded his assent, but Haden thought that the warning hadn't taken. If Matz, for all his caution, had a fault, it was the self-confidence of youth, the belief that things always happened to someone else. Haden knew better.

He looked at his watch. It was getting late, and he wanted a word with Petra Baron.

Dinner was over by the time he got back to Bad Gastberg. He found Petra in the bar, perched on a stool, nursing a vodka and tonic, which he judged was not her first.

"Don't you ever eat?" she inquired petulantly.

"Yes," Haden said. "I'll have a sandwich later."

157

"You'll get ulcers," she told him. "Where have you been all day?"

"Working for you," Haden said. "Remember?"

He ordered a cognac, took Petra's arm, led her to a corner table, and sat her down. She gave him an apologetic smile.

"I get bored on my own," she said.

"Am I being paid to keep you company?" Haden asked.

"Oh, Christ," she said, "suddenly you don't like me again. What have I done now?"

"Nothing," Haden said, wishing that he did not find her sulky ego appealing. "It's time for an hour of business."

"Well, let's get on with it, so we can be friends again," Petra said.

"After your husband disappeared, did the police ask you for a photograph of him?"

"Sure, but I didn't have one, not with me. I had Alex with me, why should I need a photograph as well?"

"A day or two later, they had one. Any idea where it came from?"

"No," Petra said. "It wasn't from me. Does it matter?"

"Probably not," Haden said.

"Okay. End of the hour of business."

She gave him one of her lingering, provocative smiles, one that would have elicited a response from any man not totally immune to women. Haden laughed.

"You owe me fifty-nine and a half minutes," he said.

Petra leaned back in her chair, finding a position that displayed her shapeliness to advantage. Her body, in Haden's judgment, was just about perfect, a fact she was well aware of.

"Put it on my tab," she said. "Will you be around tomorrow?"

"All day," Haden said. "But not here."

Petra made a comically plaintive face. It reminded him

of the expression Christa used sometimes when his plans did not match hers.

"I think I deserve a day off," she said. "Why don't I come with you?"

"You wouldn't like the man I have to see."

"I could do some shopping."

"True," Haden said. "Or call on Jerry Lander."

"What a good idea," Petra said. This time, her smile was sweet. "Come on. Don't tell me I have to explain my friends to you."

"Did your husband ask for explanations?"

The smile went. "I don't believe that's any of your god-damn business," she said.

"You're wrong," Haden said. "We're back on unexpired business time. If I want to know *anything* about how things were between you and your husband, you don't have to like it. You just tell me."

"I've already told you," Petra said. "Alex was different. I didn't expect to feel the way I did about him. That hasn't changed."

"Which implies something else did," Haden said.

"We stayed married," Petra said. "Most of my college friends are into their second or third husbands, and God knows how many lovers."

"Petra," Haden said, "that's a defense against a criticism no one's making. Your husband's state of mind might have had a bearing on what happened. Maybe not. But how can I judge if you don't tell me the truth?"

"I don't think you've ever called me Petra before," she said. "I don't suppose that's a breakthrough?" she inquired ironically. When he didn't answer, she said, "No, I thought not. Okay, you've guessed, anyway. I like men. You may have noticed. I have men friends, and I enjoy their company. Alex didn't understand. He was jealous. Not all the time—we'd go weeks, months, and everything would be fine. Then something would upset him and we'd fight. I don't mean he'd hit me or anything . . ."

"But there were quarrels," Haden said. "And if Peter was around, you spoke Russian."

She gazed at him curiously.

"It didn't happen that often," she said. "We both cared about Peter. We didn't want to hurt him."

"You weren't together all that often," Haden said. "Your husband was away a lot. And when he came back, you often flew to Washington."

She was silent for a few moments, during which she leaned forward and let her fingers play over the rim of her glass, although her speculative eyes never left his.

"I think you're a shit, Haden," she said finally. "You get little boys to gossip about their parents."

"Why Washington?" Haden asked, unmoved. "Were you on the payroll, too?"

"Not in that sense. I helped Alex with his work, that's all."

"He worked out of Munich, not Washington," Haden reminded her. "Perhaps you were in Washington because Ralph Janson was one of your men friends."

Petra sat silent for some moments, blinking. She looked like a child who had been slapped and was trying not to cry.

"Yes, he is my friend," she said quietly, at last. "Ralph Janson is a dear, sweet man, and I adore him. But even Alex at his most jealous never accused me of being unfaithful to him with Ralph. Quite apart from anything else," Petra said, "Ralph is a politician, a shrewd, cool operator. In that sense, he doesn't have girlfriends. Anyone who sees himself in line for the Oval Office needs to protect himself. People try to dig up dirt, and he means to make sure there isn't any."

Stephen Haden studied her. Helen Lloyd had referred to Janson as ambitious, but this seemed a bit extreme.

160

"Does he have a realistic chance?"

"Just one more political appointment," Petra said mysteriously. "If he gets that, just stay tuned to the next nominating convention. See who comes through as the retiring President's choice."

Haden finished his cognac and thought about the statesmanlike Ralph Janson, his handsome face, his discreetly graying hair. If nothing else, Ralph Janson looked the part.

"I'd like another drink," Petra said, gesturing to a waiter.

Haden pressed the doorbell repeatedly, but there was no answer. Flurries of snow were falling. He finally rang for the caretaker and was admitted.

Ensconced in the stuffy warmth of his cluttered apartment, the caretaker had been about to enjoy his mid-morning refreshment. He was a small, elderly man, who peered at Haden through his pince-nez. Haden inquired after Herr Kinsky.

"He's gone to stay with his son."

"Oh? How long will he be away?"

"Till the spring, I suppose. He paid three months' rent in advance."

"How? By check? In cash?"

"Is that your affair?" the caretaker asked. Haden took out his wallet. The man became more helpful. "In cash. But I gave him a proper receipt," he said hurriedly.

"I'm sure," Haden said. He took some bills from his wallet. "He may have left something for me. You must have a key. If you'll let me in, I can take a look around."

The caretaker hesitated, but if he had any objections, the money overcame them. He opened a drawer and began to inspect the labels on the keys inside.

They climbed the stairs to the top floor, where the caretaker unlocked Kinsky's door. Haden followed him in. The curtains had been left drawn, and the apartment was dark. The caretaker switched on the light. He stood riveted at the door, his fingers still on the switch, his body suddenly rigid.

"Holy Mother of God," he muttered.

A chair was on its side. Hans Kinsky lay crumped beside the chair.

The caretaker retreated, and Haden heard him stumble hurriedly down the stairs. He looked at the unpleasant scene.

As far as Haden could tell from the way the body was sprawling, Hans Kinsky had sat in the chair and then shot himself in the right temple. A Luger pistol was still in his hand.

The entry hole was quite neat, but the bullet had blown away the other side of his head. Blood saturated the carpet near his head; it had spattered all the way to the far wall.

Chapter Nine

Stephen Haden sat at Willi Hofer's regular table smoking a cheroot and contemplating what had turned out to be a long day. By the time he began sipping his coffee, he found it nearly as cold as the ice water. He gestured to the waiter, ordered another, and resumed thinking about the body of Hans Kinsky and the apartment in which it had lain.

He had skirted the corpse and, drawing on his gloves again, had parted the curtains that hid the bed. It had been made with fastidious neatness. Also behind the curtain were a wardrobe and a chest of drawers. Both were empty.

Two large suitcases had been standing in the living area, some distance from Kinsky's body. Haden had gently laid them flat, undone their straps, and opened them. Both were full of clothes, packed with a precision that had reminded Haden of his own training in the Swiss military.

Careful not to disturb the neatness of the contents, Haden probed delicately under the clothes but found nothing of any interest. He was interrupted by the approaching howl of police sirens. He had just managed to restore the suitcases to their former position when policemen strode into the apartment and he was asked to wait outside.

He had stood on the chilly landing accompanied by a

silent policeman who kept his eyes fixed on him. Soon afterward, men in plain clothes had climbed the stairs, representatives of the various trades associated with violent death. Among them had been Willi Hofer.

Hofer had glanced at him and gone into the apartment without saying anything. A few minutes later he had emerged and told the policemen to take Haden to police headquarters. There Haden had waited for a long time before being interviewed by Hofer in a neutral, efficient manner that included requiring Haden to account for his movements during the twelve hours before the body had been discovered. Haden had been glad that it was possible for him to tell the truth. Hofer might be on the take sometimes, in his careful way, but it had been more clear that that kind of cooperation did not extend to any favors during an official investigation.

"What was it you thought Kinsky might have left for you?" Hofer inquired.

"That was an excuse. Kinsky was short of money. I wondered where he'd got the cash to pay three months' rent in advance."

"Perhaps from you, Mr. Haden," Hofer suggested quietly.

"Not that much, by a long shot."

"So you did give him money. For what?"

Hofer knew the answer to that perfectly well, but not officially, and there was another detective in the room, silently recording the interview. But again, Haden was quite content to tell the truth.

Hofer returned to Haden's desire to see inside Kinsky's apartment, worrying away at it doggedly. Why? Hadn't he been told that Kinsky had left?

"The caretaker said he had gone to stay with his son. Kinsky had told me he could manage without his son. He seemed not to like him."

Hofer returned to that, and other questions, all from a variety of angles. In a way Haden admired the merciless thoroughness of the interrogation. The man knew his job.

"The caretaker says that he left you alone after you both discovered the body."

"I didn't touch anything, however," Haden said.

"You will not have any objection if we confirm that?"

Haden turned out his pockets. His belongings were examined, and he was asked to consent to a body search. That done, he was put into another room to wait while, he supposed, his statement was checked. It was late afternoon, and Haden was beginning to wonder if he might be held or charged, although for what he could not imagine, when Willi Hofer opened the door, another detective at his elbow.

"You are free to leave the station, Mr. Haden, but not Vienna for the time being, if you please. It may be necessary to speak to you again."

Haden went to the café and managed to contact Erwin Matz, who assumed initially that his boss had called to inquire about the identity of the Russian.

"You'll have to give me more time, Stephen—"

"I'm not calling about that," Haden said. "I'll explain later. Try to get hold of Willi Hofer. Say I'll be waiting for him, and you'll look after him next time you meet."

Matz promised to do so, but Haden had finished his coffee, read a newspaper, eaten a meal, and still Hofer had not arrived. Haden had almost decided that Hofer was not going to play this time, when the man walked in. He crossed to his regular table, sat down, and ordered a carafe of white wine and a bowl of soup. He looked tired.

"I had to be certain that I could meet you informally, Mr. Haden," he said. "I am now satisfied that you committed no illegal act." The trace of a smile flickered across Hofer's lips. "Apart, perhaps," he mused, "from initially harboring the intention to get rid of the caretaker and search Kinsky's apartment."

"If the courts could convict us for our thoughts," Haden said, "most of us would be in jail."

"There are countries where courts can do just that," Hofer said, "but not here." Whether he regretted that fact or not was not apparent. His carafe of wine arrived. He poured a glass for himself and emptied it with pleasure. He refilled it and gazed at Haden thoughtfully. "You expressed curiosity on two points," he said. "Money and Kinsky's son. What Kinsky's wallet contained would have been sufficient only for traveling expenses. Not a large sum. I have spoken to Kinsky's son. He lives in Düsseldorf and is a businessman of some affluence. He was shocked to hear the news of this father's death. Kinsky had telephoned him, asking if he might come and stay. His son was expecting him."

"Was he surprised his father had telephoned?"

Hofer considered the question as if it might contain some hidden trap. "He said that he had not heard from his father for a good many years," he finally answered cautiously. "But Kinsky was an old man. Old men tend to try to tidy up their lives before they go."

"Kinsky didn't strike me as a man who had any intention of departing this life before he had to," Haden said. "You must know his record."

"Probably better than you, Mr. Haden," Hofer said mildly. "He attended SS reunions. He was known to have contacts with an extreme neo-Nazi group. Were I allowed personal feelings, I would have disliked him intensely. But even men like him can come to have regrets."

"The only thing he regretted was that Nazi Germany hadn't won the war," Haden said.

"With all respect, Mr. Haden, you are not the keeper of his soul."

"He was an old soldier," Haden said. "The only certain way for a man to commit suicide with a pistol is to put the barrel in his mouth and pull the trigger. Kinsky would have known that."

Willi Hofer's soup arrived.

"Ah, good," he said and began to eat it. Haden sat in silence. Hofer finished his soup, polished the bowl with his bread, ate that, poured the remains of the carafe into his glass, and looked at his watch.

"I know," Haden said. "Your wife will be waiting. So am I."

"My vocation does not allow for a trusting nature," Hofer said. "Murder can be arranged to look like suicide. However, it is not easy and in this case there are no suspicious indications."

"There wouldn't be if it was done skillfully enough," Haden said.

"Forensic has found nothing," Hofer said. "Neither has the pathologist."

"A man arranges to go to see his son," Haden said. "He pays his rent in advance, he packs, he dresses. Then he decides to sit down and shoot himself. You think that makes sense?"

Hofer said, "Suicide is an act of despair. The moment can arrive at any time. If Kinsky thought he faced prison—at his age—he may have found the prospect intolerable."

Haden smiled at Willi Hofer, who was in a hurry to get home, yet had found time to be cryptic. "You know something I don't," he said.

"Concealed in one of Kinsky's suitcases were certain articles that appear to implicate him in Baronin's disappearance." Hofer paused to consider his words carefully. "The evidence also appears to corroborate the possibility that Baronin is dead."

"These 'articles' must be fairly incriminating," Haden remarked.

"A photograph of Baronin, similar to the one Kinsky failed to pick out at police headquarters," Hofer said. "Baronin's passport, bloodstained—believed to be Baronin's blood group. We hope to know for certain soon. A gold cigarette lighter, engraved 'For Alex.' Credit cards. In short, anything that might identify a body."

"You don't have a body," Haden pointed out.

"The Danube is often a convenient receptacle," Hofer said. "It is a great river. It flows from Austria through Hungary, becomes the border between Yugoslavia and Rumania, and then crosses Rumania into the Black Sea. A body carrying no identification could have been fished out downstream—in Rumania, for instance. We'd never know."

Haden toyed with a cheroot and lit it. There was nothing improbable in the idea of Hans Kinsky as a killer, presumably hired. Quite the reverse. Anyone who wanted Baronin dead would have done well to choose an instrument like Kinsky.

In that case, Kinsky's claim to have witnessed an abduction and then his "inability" to pick out Baronin's photograph would make perfect sense—a shrewd means of diverting any possible suspicion. It was good. It fitted. Almost.

"Why would Kinsky keep all this evidence?" Haden asked.

"Perhaps he thought it might prove valuable at some later date," Hofer suggested. "Blackmail, selling it to some other party, who knows the workings of a man's mind?"

"I was in the market," Haden said. "I'd have bought the passport."

Willi Hofer played with a toothpick. "Kinsky decided to leave Vienna soon after you called on him," he said. "He might have thought your willingness to buy was a trap. He knew you had spoken to me. Maybe he thought I was using you to get hold of evidence against him. Saw the net closing in on him and panicked. Thought of leaving, then imagined he was walking into a trap and saw no way out. The moment of despair had arrived.''

"It's neat,'' Haden said. "But there are an awful lot of 'mights' and 'maybes' in it.''

"None of which matters much. The fact remains, articles undoubtedly belonging to Baronin were in Kinsky's possession.''

Hofer paid his bill, leaving Haden's on the table in front of him.

"In your mind, then, it was undoubtedly suicide,'' Haden said.

"There is no concrete evidence to suggest that Kinsky did *not* commit suicide. I have informed the United States embassy of the circumstances.'' Willi Hofer shook hands politely. "Good night, Mr. Haden.''

It was late when Haden arrived back at Bad Gastberg. Petra Baron was sitting in the lobby. She stood up and came to meet him. Her makeup was flawless, but her face was tight.

"Can we go to your room, please?'' she asked.

Once there, she seemed disinclined to sit down. She refused a drink. Haden poured a cognac for himself and reflected that perhaps he was carrying his automatic defiance of Dr. Gottl's instructions to extremes.

"I've been told I can collect Alex's things from the police at any time,'' Petra said. "I called Ralph in Washington. He's coming as soon as he can. In a day or two. Something about having to meet with the President.'' She put her hand on the arm of a chair and then sat down, as though her knees had given way. Tears began to roll steadily down her cheeks. "Oh, shit," she said, trying to swallow. "No hand-bag."

Haden handed her the handkerchief from his breast pocket and sat sipping his cognac, watching her. There were no dainty, ladylike dabs at a few stray tears. She cried and cried, gasping and choking, the handkerchief held to her mouth. Finally she stopped and blew her nose with cere-mony. Blinking, she looked at Haden.

"Well, he's dead, then," she said dully.

"Is that what you were told?"

"Not in so many words. The guy at the embassy was being tactful. You know, the gently-preparing-me-for-the-worst routine. I suppose I always knew, really. But now, the passport and everything, the lighter I gave him . . . I hoped . . . Oh, God, I don't know what I hoped. Was he killed? Taken back to Russia, executed there? What differ-ence does it make? It comes to the same thing, doesn't it?" She gazed at him. Haden shrugged and shook his head. The corners of her lips curled down as if she were about to weep again. She said piteously, "Why are you staring at me like that? You think I'm putting this on, is that it? Whatever the hell you think of me, I never wanted him dead."

"What did you want?" Haden asked.

"I don't know. Everything to come out right, I guess." She sighed. "I don't think it was all my fault. It was the whole damn thing. I thought I could handle it, all of it. What a screwup."

"You're not telling me anything," Haden said.

She was gazing at the crumpled handkerchief she was clutching and seemed not to hear him. "Perhaps it's be-cause I was adopted," she said wearily. "I remember where we lived. It was big, so big, a long, low, ranch-style house, nice. He was a building contractor in Sacramento. Rotary, Chamber of Commerce, a pillar of the community. I had pretty clothes, dolls, toys—anything I wanted.

170

"You know what they did? They got divorced. Why do people do that? Take on a child, a baby, start to bring it up, and then quit? Oh, sure, I know I was the glue that held the cracks in their marriage, but it didn't work. People shouldn't do that. They really shouldn't. From the time I was old enough to be aware, I can remember the atmosphere in that house, the silences, the fights, hearing them shouting at each other when they thought I was asleep. When I was eleven years old, he ran off with his psychotherapist. What an American cliché, huh?" She raised her eyes to Haden's. She had screwed the handkerchief into a tight ball. "Some of this, I learned later, of course," she said. "At the time, I just knew he'd gone. My daddy had gone." Haden nodded.

"After that," Petra Baron continued, "the rest went, too. She wasn't unkind, but the glue hadn't worked and she was left with me as a symbol of her failure, I guess. She hated him then. She wanted revenge, which meant every penny she could get out of him. Only she didn't get it. The building business failed—I guess he'd neglected it—so then the house went. After that, it was crummy apartments, her working in some store, me a latch-key kid, lying in bed at night scared of the cockroaches, and then even more frightened by what I heard when she brought men home. In the end she married one of them. I didn't like him, and he didn't want me around. When I was twelve, I was sent away to school in the East. The money for that must have come from a trust fund they couldn't get at. Thank God for that, anyway. School was like being set free. I'd spend the vacations with other kids. I didn't want to see either of them. Since I graduated from college, I never have." She smiled ironically. "What a sob story, huh?"

Haden waited for her to continue, but Petra Baron remained silent.

"Did you ever find out who your real parents are?" Haden inquired.

"When I was thirteen, fourteen, I daydreamed about doing that. How I'd find a loving mother and father—you know, the whole fairy-tale bit. Later, when I got to be older, I thought I probably wouldn't like the ending much, after all. At school, and especially at college, my history and background didn't matter. I'd got myself together, I could take on life"—she gestured angrily—"or so it seemed then. This man and woman, whoever they were, who'd conceived me but didn't want to keep me, they could be anything, they could be the dregs. Suppose I looked at them and started worrying about my genes, or whatever? I could do without more bad news."

"Did Alexander Baronin know all this?"

"Some. A little. The past was done with. I'd disposed of it, like garbage. Only I guess you can't really do that. You can push it out of your mind, never think about it, but it's still there, inside somewhere. Eventually you have to deal with it. The thing with Alex, I wasn't ready for it. 'Love.' " She said the word with no little sarcasm. "I truly thought he was just another man, better in bed than most, enjoyable, washed away with the bathwater. Alex got a raw deal. By the time I realized I really felt differently about him, that it could all have been different, it was too late. Much too late. The past was there, a part of me I could do nothing about, beyond regretting it. I was chained to it."

Haden studied Petra Baron's bowed head.

"Somehow," he said, "that doesn't quite sound like a wife who's been married—for how long? ten years or so?"

"I wasn't much of a wife," Petra said, so quietly he could scarcely hear her. She gazed at the crumpled ball of linen in her hands as if wondering what it was. "I've made a terrible mess of your handkerchief," she said.

"They have fast laundry service here," Haden said. He

172

took it from her, extracted three more from a drawer and handed them to her. "Replacements," he said.

Petra looked up at him from swollen eyes that detracted little from the beauty of her face, but leant it a curiously childlike innocence.

"I'm sorry I yelled at you," she said. "It's true what they say. It does help to talk to someone. Maybe I should have tried it long ago. Anyway, thanks for listening."

Haden gave her one of his warmer smiles. "I'm a good listener," he said. "It's easy work. Though I'm not sure what to make of it all."

"If you ever find out, let me know," Petra said. "Because I don't, either." She stood up, glanced at him sideways, the sly, pert glance of a little girl, and said, "I really don't want to be alone tonight. I need to be with someone. Just for comfort, that's all."

"Come the morning, things'll look different," Haden said. "Your bag of regrets seems to be overflowing already."

"What the hell, one more makes no difference," Petra said. She produced a wavering, apologetic smile. "No, forget it. I'll take pills instead. Less fun, but you get more sleep. Good night, then, Haden. Thanks again."

Haden watched her walk toward the door. "Petra," he said. She turned and looked at him. "If you ever want to tell me the rest, I'm available for some more listening. At no extra charge," he said dryly.

"The rest? Dear God, I've told you more than I've ever told a living soul. There's nothing else. You've heard it all."

"All right, then," Haden said. "Sleep well."

After she left he sat eyeing the telephone. Petra Baron had been in a highly emotional state when she told her story. It had all come out in a jumble, which could easily account for any slight inconsistencies. So why was he still puzzling over it? As far as he could see, his job was over. But he couldn't rid himself of the sense that something was awry, all the more irritating in that he could not define what it was. A few mundane facts might help. Anna was good at that kind of thing—she knew all the shortcuts.

Haden lifted the receiver, called Zurich, and left a message on the answering device, adding one or two afterthoughts.

Then he checked his watch and dialed London.

"It's Stephen," he said. "Just to say hello and ask how you are."

"How about wishing me sweet dreams. I'd gone to bed," said Helen Lloyd. But her tone of voice was pleasantly warm. "I'm fine. How are things in the land of the waltz?"

"Since your embassy here knows that, I'm sure you do," Haden said.

"More or less, maybe. It seems you have your 'result.' "

"Ralph Janson's flying in," Haden said. "To check it out for himself, I suppose."

"Is that so? Well, well. That's interesting."

Haden wished he could see her face. Not that it would have helped him much, he supposed.

"All right," he said. "I'll take the bait. Tell me why."

"The rumor factory has it that Ralph Janson is in line for a job that would amount to a public sign of the President's confidence in him."

"Perhaps Marianne Janson's responsible for the rumors," Haden suggested.

"Could be," Helen agreed. "She uses her foundation to promote him, that's no secret. But he wouldn't leave Washington just now, even to see you," she said ironically, "unless it was cut and dried. That's why it's interesting."

"To me, hardly at all," Haden said. "Harold Leyton has gone very quiet. Have you heard from him?"

"He's been in touch," Helen said cautiously. "Why do you ask?"

"I'm making conversation, like you," Haden said. "What did he want?"

It had been on the tip of his tongue to phrase that question to include the word "Dante," but he had changed his mind.

"I don't know," Helen confessed. "He was pretty vague, even for Harold. Whatever it was, I guess he thought I was no use to him."

"Nothing to do with me, then," Haden said.

"Your name didn't come up. Should it have?"

Haden ignored that. "Well, I'll wish you a good night now," he said. "Next time I'll call at a more respectable hour."

"You may not find me in," Helen said. "I may need to visit one of the European offices just briefly. If so, there'll be a contact number on my answering machine."

"Since when did your job include the rest of Europe?"

"I've taken on some additional responsibilities," Helen answered modestly.

"Congratulations," Haden said. "Rising fast, like Ralph Janson."

The sound of her laugh again induced that nostalgic ache he could do without.

"My ambitions are a lot more modest than his," Helen said.

Stephen Haden was in the bar when he saw the headlights of the car as it wound its way along the drive. Ralph Janson had arrived in Vienna but not, as yet, at Bad Gastberg. Haden had seen Petra Baron at lunchtime. She had smiled and chatted, but her smile was waveringly distrait, and her conversation automatic. Now she was sitting in the lobby, waiting.

The headlights swept across the picture windows as the large American limousine stopped outside the main entrance. Haden watched Ralph Janson get out and walk toward the big double doors. He was accompanied by Walter Gorman. The driver remained outside, standing beside the car, mechanically surveying the empty wastes of snow. He appeared programmed, like a robot. Haden thought that the rumor factory might have got it right. Ralph Janson now rated a personal bodyguard. He moved closer to the lobby.

Petra Baron stood up with a smile of relief when she saw Janson, and went to meet him. He put his arms around her reassuringly. Haden could just hear the murmur of his deep, mellow voice.

"I know, I know," he was saying. "It's all right. It'll be okay now."

Haden put his glass down and walked into the foyer to join in the reunion. Walter Gorman flashed one of his empty, unnerving smiles. Janson's smile was welcoming, his handshake firm and vigorous.

"Good to see you, Mr. Haden," he said. "Petra, I need some time with Mr. Haden. We'll talk over dinner. Walter will look after you, won't you, Walter?"

"Of course, sir," Gorman said respectfully. "Shall we have a drink, Mrs. Baron?"

Upstairs, Ralph Janson made admiring noises about Haden's room, declined a drink, and sat down.

"On first impressions," he said, "you made a good choice in this place. I wish I were staying here myself."

"I'm sure that could be arranged," Haden said.

"I must have secure communications with Washington, which aren't available here but are in Vienna. Tell me, Mr.

Haden. You're known to be a careful man—have you been aware of any surveillance?"

"Nothing close," Haden said. "If there was any, it was too distant to be a problem."

He had found this freedom somewhat surprising, but Erwin Matz had been positive that it was so, and not once had Haden's own warning instincts alerted him.

"Walter was under instructions to leave you strictly alone, of course," Ralph Janson said. "I don't believe that made him happy, but he doesn't question orders."

"He left Baronin alone," Haden said. "If that was an instruction, too, it was an unfortunate one."

"We could discuss that, I guess," Janson said, "but it wouldn't change anything." Janson's silver hair glinted in the lamplight as he changed his position. "Anyone from the Soviets shown any interest in you?"

Haden thought about the voice in the pitch-black room in János Varga's tailor shop. "If so, they must be using the invisible man," he said.

Janson's smile was dry and professional. "I doubt their technology is that advanced," he said. "In any event, since they already knew what had happened to Baronin, they had no reason to try to stop you, or even to watch you. They'd had plenty of time to cover their tracks. Except for the man Kinsky. Would I be right in supposing that you offered him money for information?"

"Now I know how you've been spending your day," Haden said. He took out a cheroot and lit it. He studied the end. It was glowing nicely. "Kinsky wanted money for silence, and he got the silence," he said. "A fatal temptation, yes?"

Janson spread his hands wide, in a slightly theatrical gesture. "The police have their reservations, but they can't prove it wasn't suicide. If it was a fake, it was not the work of an amateur. Had to have been someone he knew. Maybe called to pay him off, and then . . ." He let it go at that.

Haden could picture the scene for himself. It was clear enough. Except for a certain fuzziness around the edges. "Hans Kinsky was an unrepentant Nazi," he said. "Hardly your average friendly hit man working for the Communists."

"Kinsky should have swung," Janson said, "for murdering civilian hostages. He was strongly suspected of violence in recent years. And he was short of money. He need not have known for whom he was working. They could have used front men, told him that Baronin was a Soviet spy. You met Kinsky. If he'd been hired to do that, would he have had any qualms, in your judgment?"

"None," Haden answered. He watched the coils of smoke rising lazily from his cheroot. It all seemed to fit. He was waiting for the final click, as all the facts slipped into place, but didn't get one. He didn't understand why.

"However, we have strayed into the realm of speculation, well founded or not," Janson said briskly. "I promised you that no unreasonable requirements would be imposed. And I always keep my word. In my view, you have achieved a result. It may not be the one I had hoped for. For Petra's sake, at the very least, I wish it had been otherwise. But a result it undoubtedly is." With his fingertips, he lifted the flat attaché case that lay on his knees, and passed it to Haden. "In one-hundred-dollar bills, as requested," Janson said. "Anything owing to you for expenses incurred, let me know."

"I'll work it out," Haden said.

The attaché case would go into the hotel safe, along with his copies of Dante. He would take care of that on their way down to dinner.

"Shall we go?" he asked.

Janson said, "We haven't finished."

Haden looked at the strong, handsome face, which was regarding him intently. "You're not satisfied that Baronin's dead?"

Janson said, "No one's going to present us with a grave and a headstone. Alex is either dead or as good as dead. That does not, however, end the matter."

"It sounds pretty final to me," Haden said.

Janson's smile of acknowledgment seemed strained, which, given his quietly commanding presence, was out of place—it was the smile of a man with heavy responsibilities who found himself obliged to intervene personally where he would have preferred to delegate.

"Few men impress me, Mr. Haden." he said. "You do. You deliver."

"You got what you paid for," Haden said.

"Too often, one does not," Janson said. "Somehow, you unveiled the Kinsky connection. No one else—not our people, not the Austrian police—traced it. That was good. Very good. Now," he went on, leaning forward as if impressing his views on a high-powered committee, "it seems at least possible that you also came across other information, which could be meaningful. You could be partway there."

"Partway where?" Haden inquired.

Janson sat back. "You are, of course, aware that Alex Baron had an appointment with someone the night he disappeared," he said. "It has become rather important that we know the identity of this person."

"Why is it 'rather important'?"

Janson shook his head somberly. "I don't know," he said. "I haven't been told. Perhaps cannot be told. Only that it is. From a source that carries complete conviction. So—is there any chance you could do it?"

Haden said, "Quite a lot would depend on who could be bought along the way."

"In that respect you have *carte blanche*. Any promises you make will be honored."

"Okay, suppose I could come up with an identity?"

"Then we would wish to resume contact. This person trusted Alex, but no one else. Once it is understood, through you, that an equally safe contact can be provided, your role would be over."

"You should be a salesman, Mr. Janson," Haden said. "You have a gift for making things sound easy and trouble-free."

"I hope they will be," Janson said genially. "I have the utmost confidence in you, Mr. Haden."

Haden stubbed out his cheroot. He felt a strange sense of calm, which he contemplated with some curiosity. It was as if some obstruction had been removed, as though everything so far had been a rehearsal for the real thing.

Now, as if fated to do so, he was facing this "real thing," except that Haden's innate skepticism included the concept of destiny. He wondered if Helen Lloyd had guessed, or hoped, or gambled that this moment would arrive. Or arranged that it would? No. Could she?

"Well, Mr. Haden," Janson was saying, "may I take it that we've reached an agreement?"

"I haven't heard your best offer for my services yet," Haden replied.

Chapter Ten

"You'll forgive me if I dine alone with Petra," Ralph Janson had said. "Naturally, she's upset, poor girl. I may be able to offer some guidance, help her to look to the future."

Haden's dinner companion was Walter Gorman, who ate busily and smiled frequently, indicating an eagerness for friendship.

"I hear you're staying on," he said. "Any facilities required are to be at your disposal. On the personal authority of Mr. Janson."

"What does that mean? Protective surveillance?"

"I just take orders," Gorman said. "What do you want?"

"To be left alone," Haden answered. "I prefer to work my own way."

"Then those are my orders," Gorman said. "It's your show. If you ever do need anything, you know where I am. For example, if anyone you don't like the look of shows up—you know what I mean."

The ease of picking out anyone he did not like the look of was one of the advantages of Bad Gastberg. The man who had called himself Oleg Tushin had hardly needed picking out. A Russian caller would surely have made Gorman uneasy.

"No stray Russian has shown up yet," Haden said, giving Gorman a self-confident smile. He suspected a strong streak of vanity in Walter Gorman, one that would be unable to resist a nod or a wink. Neither appeared. Gorman simply shrugged his broad shoulders.

"Why should they?"

"Perhaps they didn't know I had any interest in Baronin," Haden said, pushing his luck.

"What?" Walter Gorman snorted. "Short of appearing on television you couldn't have made it more public. Not that I'm mocking your methods, understand," he said hurriedly, a flash of a smile denying his disapproval. "It worked, and if it works, that's the only test that counts."

Haden devoted himself to his meal, reasonably confident that Gorman did not know about Tushin. Gottl had apparently thought it his civic duty to have the police informed that a man with the scars of gunshot wounds had arrived at Bad Gastberg, which was how Willi Hofer had known where he was staying. Haden supposed that the good doctor had found nothing suspicious about Oleg Tushin.

Walter Gorman, a man who believed that conversation should never flag, changed the subject mostly in the direction of tedious anecdotes about himself, one of which included a reference to "going home."

"What's that? Leave before you're posted to Finland?"

"Well, it seems that maybe I was being a little pessimistic," Gorman said coyly. "There might just be another assignment coming my way, something pretty special, but I'm not at liberty to say what it is."

Haden found that he could not look adequately disappointed by Gorman's reticence; he was not sufficiently interested to pry, so he excused himself as soon as he decently could, on the grounds that he had things to do.

"Right," Gorman said significantly.

Ralph Janson's driver was sitting in the lobby, in a spot from which he could watch the dining room. Haden said good night to the receptionist and went up the main stairs. He walked along the corridor and went down the secondary flight to the rear, which led to the treatment area.

There the quarters were dark, but the moon reflected on the snow outside cast enough light through the windows for Haden to be able to see.

Dr. Gottl's outer office, which housed his receptionist, had a Yale lock that yielded to the strip of plastic Haden carried for such an emergency.

The inner office was more secure, but Haden did not think that any further breaking and entering would be necessary. Gottl, a man who utilized his time to the second, was unlikely to have been available to spend any with a man who called unexpectedly.

The desk was scrupulously neat, everything in its place. Using a penlight, Haden soon found the doctor's appointment book, and in it the name "Tushin, O." There was also a Vienna telephone number.

Haden memorized the number, returned the appointment book to precisely its former position, and left the office. He slipped up the back stairs and went to his room, where he rewarded himself with a cognac and sat for a while looking at the telephone.

The reward, he supposed, was overly generous. His act of minor burglary only told him that the man had given the same name twice, not that it was his real one. Yet, there was the telephone number . . .

Haden found the warm esteem Ralph Janson had expressed less gratifying than the money that had changed hands, along with the tempting prospect of being able to more than double it. He had more or less blundered by chance into the "result" that had satisfied Janson. Nothing had really been explained, and inhabiting that large limbo was Oleg Tushin, who might or might not have a distinctive walk. Haden had really studied Tushin only when he was standing still in the library. Try as he might, he had not been able to recall how Tushin had carried himself during those brief moments as he had moved out of sight with Dr. Gottl. But the man had certainly spoken with a slight American accent. Haden very much wanted, as he sat with his eyes closed, as if in a pitch-black room, to hear Oleg Tushin's voice again. He reached for the telephone.

The woman who answered said something in Russian.

"I would like to speak with Oleg Tushin," Haden said in German.

"Who is calling, please?" Her German was slow and halting.

"I represent the *Neue Zürcher Zeitung*," Haden said.

"Excuse me? You speak too fast."

"Neue Zürcher Zeitung," Haden repeated slowly. "The newspaper. There is something I would like to check with Herr Tushin."

"This is not the number you want. You must speak to the press officer at the embassy."

"Thank you," Haden said and hung up. The press officer did not appeal. He was likely to be too well informed about accredited journalists.

He rang Erwin Matz instead.

"Erwin, among your many acquaintances, how about someone who takes an interest in these endless negotiations they shunt into Vienna? A local journalist, for instance."

"Not directly. Through a friend, perhaps."

"Fine. A simple piece of information . . ."

They talked for a while. "Call me back," Haden directed. "Tonight, if you can. Any time."

Haden put the phone down and rose. It rang almost at once. Haden sat down again and lifted the receiver.

"God, you're always busy. I've been trying for ages."

"Finally decided you need some help, have you, Harry?"

"Quite the reverse," said Harold Leyton loftily. "From what I hear, you're groping around in the dark. It seemed time to offer some friendly assistance."

"Friendly? Bullshit," Haden said. He was pleased. Several times he had been on the point of calling Harold Leyton. But it was better this way.

"I wish I hadn't bothered," Leyton said. "I'm too good-hearted, that's always been my trouble. But since you'll be paying for this call, I suppose we may as well compare notes. What have you got? If anything."

"The same as you," Haden said. He could hear the sound of Leyton's breathing. "But you don't know what it means, Harry, or you wouldn't be on the phone."

Leyton said, "Let me remind you that we have a binding deal. In return for my contribution, the poetical side is mine."

Haden sat back comfortably. Leyton was up-to-date. He knew that the emphasis had changed—from Baronin to "Dante."

"Okay, Harry," he said. "If you've got anything worth having, contribute."

"It's still a little vague," Leyton admitted. "But I'm on to something."

"Well done," Haden said. "In the meantime, while you're grubbing about, you can earn your keep. A Russian called Oleg Tushin. If he exists. What does your old firm know about him and his background?"

"My contacts in that direction are getting a little strained," Leyton said unhappily. "There's a certain feeling we should give it a rest."

"You've been using my money for your own ends," Haden pointed out. "Now I want something. Do it or I

185

start deleting some of your expenses and you'll have to pay for Ivan's keep yourself."

Leyton chuckled. "He's met a ballet dancer. Quite infatuated, poor love. So, as it happens, I do have my evenings free. I'll see what I can do."

Haden was in bed, reading, when the telephone rang again. "Oleg Tushin is an adviser to the Soviet delegation," Erwin Matz said. "Thought to be high-ranking, but very little is known about him. Sorry."

"That'll have to do, Erwin," Haden said. "Thanks."

He laid his book aside. The faint, almost indiscernible flicker, akin to anticipation—the mental equivalent of the darkness just before the first distant sliver of dawn—was there. The nearest comparison he could come up with was the way a dog paused and stood motionless moments before it actually picked up the scent, even though its muzzle was not pointing in the right direction.

That was a rationalization, of course. Haden had never been able to analyze or understand it. Nor was it always reliable. Sometimes the sense of approaching dawn when none was visible was false. There was an Oleg Tushin in Vienna, but someone else could have borrowed his name. Harold Leyton's call could be coincidental and have no connection with Haden's inquiry to Helen Lloyd.

Just the same, the faint flicker was there, the promise that he might soon be able to understand things. He decided to spend a relaxing day or two using the facilities of Bad Gastberg, until something happened.

Rather to his surprise, Haden came across Petra Baron working out vigorously in the gymnasium, endeavoring, she explained brightly, to tighten her tummy muscles. She was wearing a leotard and Haden was pretty confident that nothing about her needed any tightening. She took a breather and sat beside him, her face flushed. She looked, and quite evidently felt, very much better than the night before.

"I thought you might be in Vienna with Ralph Janson," Haden said.

"He's staying with the ambassador. It's a working trip for him. But I'm invited tonight—he's sending a car for me." She glanced at him sideways. "Are you coming? He didn't say."

Haden shook his head. "I'll be talking to Zurich, making sure things are okay. How's the future? All worked out?"

"More or less, I guess. Life is for living, the past is dead and gone, look forward, head held high, according to Ralph. Something like that, anyway. It's kind of catching." She stood up. "Well, back to work."

She resumed her floor exercises.

The telephone call came through at lunchtime. Haden took it in his room.

"Someone claiming to represent the *Neue Zürcher Zeitung* inquired for me, Mr. Haden," the voice said. "You come from Zurich. I presume it was you."

Haden shut his eyes: "What can I do for you?" he said.

"You said our friend had an appointment with someone. You suggested that assistance would be available if anyone wished to contact that person. At the time, I wasn't interested. Now I could be."

Haden kept his eyes closed as he listened to the reply, but when he hung up, he was still not certain. A man's voice sounded different when he was speaking in a low half-whisper. The accent was similar, though . . .

Time dragged that afternoon as Haden waited for another call, which failed to materialize. Having decided to force himself to relax at the pool, Haden swam his final laps with a growing sense of irritation. It would have been convenient if Harold Leyton had done his stuff before the meeting.

Leyton finally called as Haden was slipping on his jacket and picking up his car keys.

"Like his namesake in *War and Peace,* your man is Mr. Clean himself," Leyton said cheerfully.

"You don't have to prove you can read," Haden said, his disappointment showing. "Just back that up, and get on with it. I'm pressed for time."

Preferring to keep his arrangements for the evening to himself, Haden had not wanted to leave ahead of Petra Baron and provoke any curiosity. She had finally departed, after a seemingly interminable delay, keeping the driver waiting while she returned to her room for something. Now he would have to hurry.

"My, we are in a bad humor," Leyton remarked, amused. "Your man had long spells in the West, mostly at the U.N. in New York, some in London and Bonn. Not even a whiff of suspicion of any KGB connections. Enjoyed the West, took to smart suits long before Gorbachev set the fashion. Regarded as straight, friendly, and a good mixer."

"Are you sure you've got the right man?" Haden inquired. None of this matched Tushin's stony visage, his tense, stiff manner. Alternatives flitted through his mind. Harry had screwed it up. Harry was lying . . .

"Well, he's in Vienna now," Leyton said blandly. "When he's not being recalled to Moscow for briefings, anyway. He's come up fast. Believed here to be potential Politburo material."

"Well, thanks anyway, Harry," Haden said. His perspective was changing and with it his initial dissatisfaction. "Sorry to have troubled you, though. Someone's been having me on."

Harold Leyton's stock of credulity was close to zero. "Could be," he agreed. "Still, the weather here is horrible, pissing rain. I think I'll pop over and take a look at your snow."

"It's falling now," Haden said truthfully. He could see the thick white curtain descending inexorably outside his window. He swore inwardly. It must have just started. "You wouldn't like it, Harry."

"Love it," Leyton said. "Can't wait. It must be the schoolboy in me."

"There are people here who'd take note of your presence," Haden said. "You'd be too visible."

A pause indicated that Harold Leyton's wish to be on the spot had diminished. "Stephen," he said ominously, "I do hope your concern for my welfare is genuine. Should you be thinking of keeping to yourself certain information that belongs to me, I would remind you that a murder case is still open."

"I trust you, too, Harry," Haden said. "There's a dead body over here as well, which you may know about. So watch yourself. Someone isn't playing fair."

"How come you lead such a charmed life?" Leyton inquired. "Unless you're getting absolutely nowhere."

"Good night, Harry," Haden said.

Given the wretched conditions, Haden drove considerably faster than he should have; indeed, he found himself gaining on Petra Baron's limousine, which was being driven with more care, as he approached the outskirts of Vienna. Haden dropped back and followed at some distance until they reached the inner ring road, where he turned off, entered a multilevel parking garage, and drove up to the top level. His headlights illuminated only a scattering of empty cars as he circled the deserted area. It was a few minutes after the stipulated time, but he could see no one waiting. He reversed into an empty space, on the far side, close to the elevator, as he had been instructed to do, and switched off the engine.

If Tushin had been and gone, he could do nothing about that. But almost at once he heard the whine of the elevator ascending.

The doors opened. A small, slight man emerged, shoulders hunched; he hurried across to a Saab and got in. The engine fired and the headlights came on. The Saab swung out from its space, down the ramp, and was lost to sight.

Haden heard the diminishing sound as the Saab descended successive ramps. The elevator came to life, went down, stopped, and then went on down again. The oppressive silence returned and remained unbroken until Haden heard a very slight sound from somewhere behind him. He turned around in time to see Oleg Tushin, outside the car, reaching to open the passenger door.

The man must have been standing behind a nearby pillar. Tushin slid in beside Haden and closed the door. Haden still hadn't had a chance to observe the distinctive walk Erwin Matz had noticed.

"The heater, if you please," Tushin said. "It's cold out there."

Haden started the engine and let it idle. "I didn't allow for the snow," he remarked.

"I waited," Tushin said simply. He turned his head and smiled at Haden.

The smile abruptly changed Oleg Tushin's face to a remarkable extent. Unlike Walter Gorman's it was cordial and conveyed warmth. The pebble eyes had unfrozen and suddenly he resembled the likable diplomat Harold Leyton described. A man could have more than one face, Haden reflected. He should know that better than anyone.

Tushin took out a pack of cigarettes. He offered one to Haden, who shook his head.

"I smoke too much," Tushin said, his face lit briefly by the flare from the lighter.

"So did Baronin," Haden said. Tushin drew slowly on

190

his cigarette, as if considering some reply, but none came. "This contact of Baronin's?" Haden prompted.

"You may refer to him as Ivan, which of course is not his name."

" 'Dante,' " Haden said and left it at that.

Tushin's smile was beguiling. "Those who offer veiled remarks usually know very little," he said.

Haden said, "Perhaps you should rectify that. You want something, or you wouldn't be here."

"The same applies to you, Mr. Haden," Tushin said. "Money, in your case."

"I only get paid if I can show the right goods," Haden said.

Tushin drew on his cigarette, found the ashtray, and reflectively tapped the tip on the edge. "We have a dilemma," he said eventually. "I can say nothing that might endanger a man who is relying on me, and I myself could be at some risk."

"That's your problem," Haden said. "Mine is similar. For all I know, you could be bait."

Tushin did not dispute that or take offense. He nodded seriously. "The path of the go-between is strewn with suspicion," he said. The glowing tip of the cigarette described an arc as he gestured.

"If you're here to bargain for something," Haden said, "you'll need to come up with enough to provide convincing credentials."

"It depends on who needs convincing, Mr. Haden. Ivan would not find a local source acceptable."

"I don't report back to the local people," Haden said. "How much they know, I can't be sure. But decisions are definitely taken elsewhere."

Tushin gazed at him searchingly for what seemed a long time. "Very well," he said finally. "Some things, then, that I hope will validate my claim to represent Ivan—"

He heard a car approaching the final ramp, stopped speaking, and watched as it drove onto the upper deck. The car parked, and a couple got out and hurried across to the elevator. Tushin's cigarette smoldered until the couple disappeared.

"Do your people keep tabs on you?" Haden asked.

"They have no reason to. And things are pretty free and easy for us here in Vienna." Tushin smiled wryly. "Just the same, given the purpose of this meeting, one cannot help wondering."

"After he defected, was Baronin really sentenced to death?"

"There was gossip to that effect. But it was never officially reported inside the U.S.S.R. I imagine it was a smokescreen."

"To conceal what?"

Tushin said, "Baronin defected. He married. He found employment. Nothing happened for a long time. Seeds do not root overnight. There was no haste." Tushin stubbed out his cigarette and lit another. "Baronin's work for his radio station brought him to Vienna now and then. This is a cosmopolitan city and there are all sorts here, some of whom were useful to him."

"Did you meet him?"

"Once, in a café. He was looking for Ivan. After that, I don't believe I actually saw Baronin again. Ivan, you must understand, regarded himself as a man of conscience," Tushin said with a certain irony. "He was concerned about our treatment of dissidents, religious minorities, Jews. He was concerned about human rights in general and wished to bring about change. For whatever they are worth, these were his motives. He began to pass details to Baronin concerning internal oppression, as well as information on industrial, scientific, and technological developments. He pinpointed the sources of Soviet intelligence in the West."

"And you knew this was going on at the time," Haden said. It was a statement intended to provoke denial.

"You might turn off the heater," Tushin suggested. "It is too hot now."

Haden switched the engine off. The murmur died. In the silence, he could hear Tushin's small sigh.

"I was not completely out of sympathy," the Russian admitted. "This all began in the Brezhnev era." He broke off and sat, his head bowed, brooding. "But if you are pointing out," he said at last, "that I, too, could be implicated, I am all too well aware of it. Concern for my own safety more than equals my concern for Ivan's."

"Your name won't come into it," Haden promised. "And if we arrange it properly, only his new contact need ever know who Ivan is."

Oleg Tushin was studying him in a somewhat odd fashion. "Yes, I had supposed that the Americans might like to resume the arrangement," he said.

"You didn't have to meet me," Haden said, taken aback by the implication. "If you didn't want to resume contact, you could have done nothing. Had you not returned my call, I wouldn't have known where the hell else to look."

"I haven't quite finished," Tushin said. "During the years he was in contact with Baronin, Ivan also served his country faithfully—though that may seem a paradox to you. He ascended the ladder of rank. He found himself able to gain access to even more sensitive information, highly secret material concerning long-term policy intentions agreed upon at the highest level. This, too, he passed to Baronin, believing that it would aid the two superpowers to reach some relatively peaceful coexistence."

Haden said, "Your Ivan strikes me as an optimist."

"Probably," Tushin said. "Certainly, America has been consistently wrong-footed, not only in the propaganda war but in more serious ways. Of course, the policy documents to which Ivan had access were immensely complex and detailed, and he was not a specialist. Once he had copied them, he had to pass them on as quickly as possible. They represented a death sentence. He began to worry. Perhaps without reason, but he did.''

"What worried him?"

"Nothing he could check, much less prove," Tushin said, "but Ivan was suspicious. He had questions. When the leaders of the great powers meet, all the work has been done on both sides. They are there to sign documents, to smile at the cameras. A summit is a public-relations exercise. If one side believes that further major conditions may be imposed *at the summit,* conditions that will be completely unacceptable, then the side in question may have been relying on damagingly faulty intelligence about where the bottom line really is."

"Obstinate stupidity might be a more likely explanation," Haden suggested.

"I know," Tushin said. "It is one Ivan considered. He is not a man prone to accept wild surmises. But he is aware that there are powerful forces in my country, hard-liners within the military and the KGB, who do not want *any* agreement."

"The same is true of America," Haden pointed out.

"Yes, but just now I am dealing with Ivan's fears. He says there are other, recent instances where the Americans appear to have relied on bad intelligence. He believes this can be traced to the Baronin connection."

"And this revelation came to him when?"

"Just over a year ago. He passed a warning to Baronin. But nothing changed. The operation continued as before. Ivan himself dared not stop, for he had finally realized that the whole thing had been a setup from beginning to end. Baronin was, and always had been, a planted KGB agent. His defection was planned, his death sentence rumored to lend a little color. Ivan was posted to Vienna and the source was opened. Gradually, as he was given higher rank, Ivan was deliberately allowed access to highly sensitive information that looked genuine. It was not. The real business had begun. Then," Oleg Tushin said, "Baronin left the field of play. Or was carried off. Ivan's only contact had been with Baronin. He did not know which way to turn—until you arrived. I agreed to call on you at Bad Gastberg and fish a little. You did not bite. Or perhaps you were simply choosing to wait. Either way, here we are."

"The received opinion around Vienna is that Baronin was knocked off by the KGB," Haden said.

Tushin said, "They wanted Baronin in good health and functioning. Ivan, too, of course. He is safe while they wait for someone else to make contact with him."

"That's a possibility," Haden said.

"Ivan asked for nothing in return for his services," Tushin said, "except the assurance that he would be given the wherewithal to live decently in America if one day he was obliged to leave Russia. That is what Ivan now wants. He feels the Americans owe him that."

"And you'd go along with that?" Haden inquired. "Be involved? Make the arrangements?"

Tushin said, "Ivan did what he thought was right. He was used and betrayed by Baronin, a man he trusted. That is not so much of a crime."

"What do you want from me?" Haden asked.

Tushin said, "Ivan needs to get to the link beyond Baronin that has the authority to honor the promise he received. I believe you could achieve that, Mr. Haden."

"If that's the message," Haden said, "I'll pass it on."

Tushin opened the passenger door and got out. "Good night, Mr. Haden. You go first, if you please."

Haden drove down to the bottom deck, parked, used a

pay phone, and left a message with the duty officer at the American embassy.

He watched the ramp and the elevator doors while he was using the phone, but no car containing Oleg Tushin appeared, nor did he step out of the elevator.

Haden drove back to Bad Gastberg. On the way he considered how the proposition he was returning with might be dressed up as a "result."

Chapter Eleven

The snow had stopped during the night. Outside, the sun was shining. The Danube sparkled in the distance.

Ralph Janson sat in Haden's room, listening attentively. He had arrived at nine-thirty spruced up and fresh, accompanied by his driver and another man whom Haden did not know. The driver was standing guard at the limousine. The other man, Haden supposed, was alert to the potential dangers to Ralph Janson's person.

Haden gave Janson a compressed and edited version of his conversation with Oleg Tushin, whom he did not name. The trace of a frown crossed Janson's face now and then, but he did not speak or ask any questions until Haden had finished.

"I guess it checks broadly with the minimal information allowed to me," he said then, although with little enthusiasm. "At least we're indirectly in touch with this Ivan, or whatever his goddamn name is." It occurred to him that Haden might interpret his remarks as grudging, so he gave him a warm, appreciative smile. "My thanks to you for that, Mr. Haden. A fine piece of work." The smile disappeared. "Although, if any promise of asylum was made, I'm not aware of it. That will have to be checked." He

197

stared at Haden as if expecting enlightenment on the point. Haden said nothing. He had considered irrelevant the statement that Baronin had been a KGB man. Those involved in the game could sort that out later for themselves. It had nothing to do with him. "And why does he want to quit now, anyway?" Janson grumbled.

"Perhaps he's had enough," Haden suggested.

"When he's been doing it for years, for Christ's sake?" Janson demanded rhetorically.

Ralph Janson was really perturbed, Haden noted. Cracks in the man's urbane persona were showing. Dispatched on an errand by his master, perhaps he felt required to return with a prize, like a dog with a stick.

"It seems he thought some of the information he passed over could have been a bit dodgy," Haden said, watering the problem down somewhat. "I was told that he'd given a warning to Baronin and assumed that Baronin had passed it on," he said, a reasonably tactful dilution of the facts, he thought.

"Oh, Jesus," Ralph Janson said fretfully. "I don't know anything at all about that, but it has to be crap. Any warning and the whole thing would have been suspended; and anyway, all information would have been vetted and analyzed by experts in the first place." He stared at Haden, and his face set hard as another thought struck him. "Unless," he said grimly, "my briefing was sloppy. If so, God help the bastard concerned. Okay, I'll have that looked into, too, as a matter of urgency."

"In the meantime, there's a request to be dealt with," Haden reminded him.

"This is not what I'd hoped for, Mr. Haden," Ralph Janson said.

"You could parade him as an important defector," Haden suggested. "There'd be propaganda mileage in that. And a thorough debriefing should get a lot out of him."

It was the best he had been able to come up with as an offering. Ralph Janson's face told him that his lack of faith in its persuasive powers was well founded.

Janson sat back in his armchair, elbows planted firmly, his face grave and decisive, the attitude he adopted, perhaps, when summing up and concluding an important conference.

"Let us be quite clear, Mr. Haden," he said. "It is considered crucial in Washington that contact be reestablished with this Ivan. As to precisely why"—one hand flapped dismissively—"your guess is as good as mine. I am not privy to the reasons. What I do know is that this assessment comes from the top. Nothing else will be acceptable. The Ivan connection must be back in place, as it was before Baronin's disappearance. Okay?"

"He wants out," Haden said.

"That is not acceptable," Janson replied. "So you get him back in line. That's your job."

Haden gazed at him with some hostility. This, no doubt, was how Janson addressed a member of his staff who he felt had not responded to his charm and needed the spur.

Ralph Janson's antennae responded fast. He produced a warm smile and a change of tone. "Naturally, you may convey an assurance," he said, "that his request will be most sympathetically considered, *provided* he resumes contact on a temporary basis. That," he added significantly, "will qualify as a result. Would you be willing to proceed on that basis, Mr. Haden?"

It was a good performance, Haden thought. "No harm in trying," he said.

"I'm happy you agree," Janson said. "And I want you to know that you have my complete confidence, Mr. Haden. I can be reached directly at one of these numbers." He handed over a card and glanced at his watch. "If you'll forgive me now, I'm running a little late."

* * *

A large envelope from Zurich, as yet unopened, had arrived that morning. After Ralph Janson left, Haden placed another request to the *Neue Zürcher Zeitung* and received the same sort of reply from the same frosty lady.

He sat down, opened the envelope, read the brief, businesslike note from Anna, and studied its contents. Not much time had passed before the telephone interrupted him.

"This is a secure line," Oleg Tushin said. "We can talk."

Haden outlined the proposition, dressing it up, he thought, rather attractively.

"Hold on, please," Tushin said after a pause. There was another, longer pause, during which the mouthpiece at the other end was covered.

"In view of what you were told concerning the poor quality of the goods, the suggestion is not understood," Tushin said eventually.

"The quality will be reexamined, at the same time as the request. Meanwhile, contact should be resumed."

"A promise was made," Tushin said. "Good faith requires that it be kept."

"That's in hand. But my clients see it as a package."

"This is getting us nowhere," Tushin said. "I suggest you urgently restate the case to your clients."

"And I suggest you think it over," Haden replied. "Perhaps another meeting would help."

He hung up and resumed his study of the documents and other material from Zurich. Anna had done a good job.

Petra Baron did not appear at lunchtime. The waiter thought she had gone to Vienna on a shopping expedition.

Haden identified a new face across the dining room, a man reading intently as he ate.

The waiter approached and bent down with a murmured message as Haden was finishing his meal. Haden got up and walked out. He took the phone call in a booth in the lobby. As he was sliding the glass-paneled door closed, he saw the new arrival appear and speak to the receptionist. She smiled and handed him some brochures. Haden lifted the receiver.

"I have a new fabric which I believe you might like, Mr. Haden," János Varga said. "Would five-thirty this afternoon be convenient for you?"

"Perfectly," Haden said. Not much thinking time had been required after all. He left the booth and headed for the stairs. The new arrival was intent on his brochures.

"A nice place this," Haden said chattily as he passed. "You'll like it here."

The new arrival smiled vaguely, as if he did not understand.

Haden decided to leave Bad Gastberg earlier than was strictly necessary to be in time for his appointment. On his way down the stairs, a thought occurred to him that he was inclined to discard as too unlikely to bear serious consideration. The only thing in its favor was that it might explain in more plausible ways something that was bothering him. Still, he supposed it was worth making a phone call before he left, and he did so. Haden was a man who preferred to hedge his bets until he spotted a certain winner, and in the business he had become entangled in, certain winners were lamentably few.

While opening the door of his Mercedes and settling himself in, he took a good look around the parking lot. Volvos and Mercedes abounded, but he thought that the dark-blue

Volvo tucked away in one corner might not have been there before.

He drove through the village and then along the winding road. There was no vehicle in his rearview mirror. He resigned himself to having to kill time in Vienna.

He turned onto the main road and settled down to a steady cruising speed. After a while he noticed a dark-colored Volvo a long way behind him, too far to identify for certain.

Haden kept going at the same speed. The Volvo came no nearer.

Stephen Haden walked into János Varga's tailor shop at exactly five-thirty. Because it was easier to follow a car than a man, he left his Mercedes in a parking lot and took a tram, a taxi, and then the U-Bahn. It was likely that his innate suspicions were unjustified, but Haden could not help his nature. He preferred to be on the safe side. If anyone had been trying to follow him, he was confident that he was now alone.

János Varga greeted him with the same courteous respect he showed the first time they met. "Good afternoon, Mr. Haden. If you would come this way, please."

There was a bolt of fabric on the counter, a lightweight pure wool, in just the shade of soft gray Haden liked.

"Is this the new fabric?" he inquired, fingering it.

"It is," Varga said proudly. "Just arrived."

"Nice," Haden said. "I like it. You have my measurements."

"We must discuss the style," the tailor said. "A Varga suit is a creation." He eyed Haden with some professional interest. "If you wouldn't mind waiting for just a few minutes . . ."

He showed Haden into the same room and then retreated with further polite apologies for having to keep him waiting.

The door closed. The well-oiled lock was almost soundless. Moments later the light went out.

Haden groped for the chair, sat down comfortably, and waited. He heard the slight sound of the panel sliding open. Then he heard the same voice, the same low, deep half-whisper.

"Thank you for coming, Mr. Haden." Haden was listening intently, ears tuned, waiting for his senses to respond, still uncertain. The pause when he did not reply extended. "Mr. Haden, are you there?"

It came to Haden then, the faintest mental click.

"You're supposed to be dead," he remarked.

The man's momentary intake of breath was cut off as the panel was hurriedly slammed shut.

Haden sat where he was, took out a cheroot, and lit it. The lighter flame dimly illuminated the door and the closed panel. Total darkness returned after he snapped the lighter shut and put it in his pocket.

From somewhere at the rear of the shop, there was a collection of sounds—scuffling, half-audible muttered grunts, a door kicked closed—and then silence.

The light came back on. The door Haden was facing was unlocked, and a man stumbled in backward. He was clad in a thickly padded anorak, such as a street cleaner might wear. On his head was a woolen hat. At his throat, a small automatic instructed him to move with caution.

"All right, Erwin," Haden said.

Erwin Matz withdrew his automatic from the man's throat, closed the door, and casually waved the gun, inviting the man to turn around.

Slowly, he obeyed. His eyes, bright with animal fear, darted around the room and then settled on Haden.

"How do you do," Haden said affably. "No cause for alarm. There's no one else around except your tailor friend."

203

The man said nothing. He stared fixedly at Haden. The fear in his eyes changed by degrees to anger. The gray streaks in his full beard aged him. His long, unkempt black hair protruded from under the woolen hat that sat low on his forehead. His fingers bore nicotine stains, his fingernails were dirty, and his stout shoes were weather-worn. Haden thought the overall effect was pretty good—a far cry from the handsome, smartly dressed man whose photographs he had so carefully studied in case he met him.

"I was rather expecting to meet Oleg Tushin," Haden said thoughtfully. He expelled a stream of smoke. "Who seems to be something of a friend of yours."

"Tushin?" The deep growl was full of hatred. "Tushin tried to have me killed. Oleg Tushin is a KGB plant."

Chapter Twelve

Stephen Haden left his Mercedes at the airport in Vienna and boarded the plane. His moment of triumph, when he had been certain that he'd figure it out, had now passed, and he only felt listless and tired. If he could have seen a way out, he would have taken it. But there was nothing to do but keep going.

Ralph Janson had telephoned, his anxiety showing. "Where were you? I've been trying to reach you."

"Out on your business. Ivan has your message. He'll think about it."

"We need an immediate, positive conclusion to this business, Mr. Haden. I'm under a lot of pressure."

"Give him a few days to sweat. His alternatives are lousy."

Janson had conceded, but he had not liked it. Haden had not liked it, either. He had thought that his own alternatives were pretty lousy, too.

He had avoided Petra Baron but had left a message, together with his office phone number, with the receptionist, saying that he had been summoned to Zurich to deal with a crisis that had arisen and would be back in a day or two.

His overnight bag traveled in the airplane's cabin with

him. At Heathrow he took a taxi. It was evening. He had become accustomed to the rolling expanses of deep snow at Bad Gastberg. In London there was none. The sky was clear, and for England it was cold. The cabdriver chattily informed him that an overnight frost was forecast, but there was supposed to be a depression moving in from the Atlantic that would bring rain late the next day. Haden did not encourage any further details. A meteorological forecast came low on his list of priorities. The weather was not likely to kill him.

He put his bag down in the hall of the ground-floor flat.

"Can I make a phone call?" he asked. "I'll pay for it. It's long distance."

"Help yourself," said Helen Lloyd. She led him into the living room. "No need to pay. I don't. Is it private?"

"No," Haden said dialing. The voice answered almost on the first ring. "It's Stephen," he said. "Thanks for hanging on."

"One personal call for you, not long ago," Anna said. "I told him you'd just gone out, that you were with a disgruntled subcontractor who is threatening to sue, and I didn't know where to reach you."

"That has a certain ring of veracity," Haden said. "Am I supposed to call back?"

"He said it wasn't important," Anna said. "Just checking that you were here, I imagine. When can we have Erwin Matz back in Berlin?"

"I don't know," Haden said.

"There's a nice contract in prospect, but it's a difficult job. I wouldn't like to send anyone but Erwin. The client won't wait. We could lose the business."

"It's all right!" Haden said tartly. "I'll underwrite the loss."

"Whatever is wrong, Stephen," Anna said, "don't take it out on me. Those days are past."

Haden's lips twisted wryly. "Aren't we both lucky," he said. "I'll check with you again tomorrow."

He replaced the receiver and turned toward Helen Lloyd.

"A man in need of a drink, I believe," she said.

Haden took the glass of cognac and leaned his head back. Helen Lloyd was wearing a belted brown dress that would have looked sober on a hanger. On her it showed the slimness of her waist, the rise of her breasts, her slender arms.

"You must have one hell of a wardrobe," Haden said. "I haven't seen that before."

"You haven't seen me very often, period."

"That's true." Not many more than a dozen times, he supposed. "So how come you get to be so bloody perceptive about my needs?"

"You're a man who likes to fly solo through life, Haden. It makes you both interesting and impossible. Suddenly we have to meet, and it has to be right now, this evening. Also, you look like you have something on your mind, and it's not me."

Haden said, "I hope you didn't cancel anything interesting."

"It'll keep," Helen said dismissively. "So what's on your mind?"

"Suppose you're playing chess," Haden said. "You see a nice, tempting space, so you occupy it. From there you think you can dominate the play. Only you suddenly can't tell who's black and who's white. Where are you then?"

"Thoroughly confused, I should think," Helen said dryly. "You wouldn't know where it was safe to move, or which piece threatened you."

"That's how it is," Haden said.

He slid a cheroot from its packet and lit it.

Helen regarded him carefully. "You think it's time to quit," she said finally.

"I know it is," Haden said. "But I've been a bit too

207

clever. And a lot too stupid. I don't think I'll be allowed to resign from the game. And it's not even my game."

"You bought in," Helen reminded him. "Or, rather, you *were* bought in."

"That was your doing, I believe," Haden said.

"We could dispute the details of that statement," Helen answered. "Some other time, maybe. You want something of me. What is it?"

"Take an evening off," Haden asked. "Forget your oath of loyalty to whatever it is you think you represent."

"I don't think I can do that," Helen said.

"In that case, let's talk about the weather."

"I didn't realize how much you distrust me," Helen said.

Haden said, "Helen, what the stakes are, I don't know. But someone seriously intends to win. Two men are already dead. I'd rather not join them as a means to the ends of the United States, whatever they may be."

"I asked you to be careful," Helen said. "That meant something. Don't blame me because you got smart."

"I hear we're expecting rain," Haden said. "What do you hear?"

"A message I don't much care for," Helen said coldly.

"Too bad," Haden said. He studied his glass, drained the remnants, and set it down.

"You said you couldn't see how to quit," Helen reminded him.

Haden looked at his watch. "I have an extra few hours at my disposal to think about it."

Helen stood up, fetched the bottle of cognac, and banged it down on the low table beside him.

"Help yourself, you shit," she said. Haden gave her a smile and followed her suggestion. "That doesn't mean *carte blanche*," she said, sitting down opposite him again. "We take it point by point, one thing at a time. If I see my evening off coming to an end, I'll tell you. That's a promise. Will that do?"

"Baronin is alive and well and living in hiding," Haden said.

Helen's eyes grew fractionally wider, but she did not query his assertion. "Who else knows where he is?"

"Well, you don't, for one," Haden said agreeably. "Now it's time for your sample. What you know about 'Dante'?"

There was a considerable silence. Helen's lovely face gave nothing away, but he thought he sensed some inner tension. Helen Lloyd evaded, told half-truths, concealed, lied convincingly if she was obliged to, deceived with professional skill. But in one respect she was unbendingly, automatically straight, and that was that she kept the confidences of those who paid her salary, she did not risk betraying secrets. Haden was pressing her to bend. It was like asking a professional soldier to disobey orders. It hurt. He almost felt sorry for her.

Perhaps, in turn, her instincts told her what he was thinking, for a certain wry amusement entered her splendid eyes.

"A fine poet," she said. "I've only read him in translation."

Haden said, "I've mentioned 'Dante' to you before. You had no reaction. Yet let it slide past as though it meant nothing. That was an act. A good one, as ever. I believed you. Now I don't."

Helen said unwillingly, "It meant almost nothing."

"Define 'almost,'" Haden said.

"'Dante' is a word that has just appeared. It surfaced without anything attached to it," Helen said. "The meaning isn't known. Nothing's known for certain. That's what bothers people."

"One man knew," Haden said. "His name was Frederick Webb. He became Frederick Webb, deceased."

"He was British," Helen said. "The murder was outside our jurisdiction."

"He was British Intelligence," Haden said. "Aren't you speaking to them?"

"All the time. But in this case, on a matter that could be highly sensitive, no. Since you're so clever, you must know why."

Haden supposed she referred to the request for Webb's removal from Washington for—not to put too fine a point on it—doing some friendly spying on an ally. Also, possibly, that it would have meant revealing to the British just what was bothering "people."

"I'm not clever enough to know what this highly sensitive matter was," Haden said. —

"I said 'could be.' It's speculation, one guess among many, no more. The sort of thing you've wondered about, maybe. Or been told, maybe." She gazed at him expectantly.

"It's still your lead," Haden told her. "I check whatever you say, not the other way around."

"I could be your insurance policy, Stephen," Helen said quietly.

"I may need one," Haden agreed. "But they tend to carry exclusion clauses. Let's check the small print."

"This is positively the end of my turn," Helen said flatly. Haden nodded and drew on his cheroot. "Okay," she said. "My understanding is this. Over a period of years, detailed information was received concerning Soviet espionage sources. It varied in importance, but it was all good. However, it wasn't clear where the information was coming from. It just appeared, fed into the system somehow."

"That implies it didn't come from Baronin. He had no intelligence function."

"None," Helen said. "His Agency job was with the radio station, and that was it. He submitted no intelligence reports. Later a certain worry emerged about the way very important decisions were being made at the top. Sometimes they seemed to be based on assessments that were at variance with those submitted by the Agency.''

"Was this concern voiced?''

Helen said, "The President can take advice from wherever he likes. He also likes to delegate a lot. Combine that with secrecy and the machinery of government, and you have a maze on quicksand. Attempts to identify just where information originated got lost or swallowed. Nothing changed. There was something going on that the Agency didn't know about, but no one could find out what. On certain important matters the Agency was bypassed, and, however it was done, the operation was tightly knit. No loose ends. Of course, there were any number of guesses, "Dante' being one—except that it couldn't be established who or what it was, or if it had any connection with the apparent disjunction between intelligence and the top. It was just one unexplained item on a long list. But it was there.'' She smiled slightly. "That's why I didn't react when you dropped it. I had no real answers, and it seemed better to let you run with it.''

"I'm still running,'' Haden said. "But we're on the same track. Let me tell you Baronin's version. Years back, in Vienna, he met someone he'd known in Moscow. He was offered information. He asked for time to think it over. Later he agreed.''

"On whose authority?'' Helen asked, leaning forward intently.

"He says he was worried, wasn't sure if he should get involved. He talked it over with Petra. She suggested they fly to Washington and ask for Ralph Janson's advice. Her father figure, as Baronin calls him. Janson listened, asked a lot of questions, and said that he'd consult the director of the CIA, whom he knew well.''

"That would be the one who died awhile back," Helen said.

"Right. Later Janson urged him to go ahead. Said it was his duty, for which he'd also be well rewarded. That was the clincher. Baronin needed money."

"For Petra's expensive tastes," Helen supposed.

"For Peter's future was the way he put it," Haden said. "He was also under the firm impression that this offer was made on behalf of the CIA."

"There should have been something on record," Helen said, but her tone lacked conviction.

"The director at the time is now dead," Haden said. "Baronin received his 'bonus' separately from his salary, but the CIA channels its funds in peculiar ways." Helen looked at him as though she were about to say something but then shrugged and reconsidered. "The CIA is a vast apparatus," Haden went on. "Bits of it operate in secret and as if they were independent. At least that's what I've observed," he said guilelessly.

Helen had become restless.

"Okay," she said. "The point you're laboring is the subject of an ongoing investigation. Nothing's been uncovered. That doesn't mean it isn't there."

"Well and truly covered up, perhaps," Haden said mildly. "Baronin claims he had no further meetings with the Russian contact. Material was left at a shop belonging to a Hungarian. Baronin collected it from there."

"This Hungarian," Helen said. "A 1956 refugee?"

"So he says. Thousands of them crossed the border at that time. Quite a useful way to slip in a few sleepers, I'd have thought."

Helen did not dispute the possibility. "Who did Baronin pass the material to?" she asked hopefully.

"He says he doesn't know. It seems to have been worked out so that no one knew the next link. Baronin would take the material back to Munich, and the next day, Petra would fly with it to Washington and stay at a particular hotel. That night it was collected by a courier. He always wore a crash helmet, goggles, and a mask. He'd identify himself and she'd hand it over. In the beginning, the code phrase was 'Dante Delivery Service.' Later that was changed. When the word 'Dante' surfaced in Washington, I suppose."

"Have you talked to Petra about any of this?" Helen asked sharply.

"No," Haden said, noting Helen Lloyd's obvious relief. "Petra may not have known what she was carrying. Baronin says she didn't, that he'd been instructed to tell her he'd turned down the Vienna thing. True or not, who knows? It seems she was always glad to go, anyway, maybe for personal reasons. Things weren't good between them. There were other men."

"Petra is a warm-blooded lady," Helen observed. She eyed Haden thoughtfully. "But no one need tell you that," she said.

Haden let the remark pass. "According to Baronin he eventually began to worry about the material he was transmitting," he continued. "He became suspicious that the channel was being used by the Russians to plant information. But since he didn't know who to contact, he enclosed a note with the next batch, a warning. The response was a phone call from a man who didn't name himself, who told him everything was being vetted, but there'd be a double check. Not long afterward, Ralph Janson was passing through Munich, and he sent for Baronin. He said that someone very high up in the White House had privately asked him to reassure Baronin, tell him what an important job he was doing and that everything was okay. Baronin replied that he'd had enough. He wanted out. If he was right, the KGB knew what he was doing. If they suspected anything was going wrong, they'd get rid of him. Janson said he was sure there was nothing to get jumpy about and stressed that it was vital to keep the source open. He urged Baronin to do nothing to arouse anyone's suspicions. In the meantime, Janson would take it up again, to see if Baronin could be replaced. That made sense to Baronin, and in due course he went back to Vienna for the last time.''

"Someone got suspicious just the same," Helen said. "Who? Where was the leak? Has the KGB infiltrated somewhere along the line? And if so, how high up, for God's sake?''

"How about something to eat?" Haden asked.

"A three-course dinner is out," Helen answered. "You can have an omelette, like me.''

"Fine," Haden said. "I'll follow you around.''

He leaned comfortably against one of the worktops in the kitchen and watched her as she busied herself.

"Keep talking," she said. "I'm listening.''

"Petra had gone to the opera," Haden said. "Baronin suspected that the director was her lover. He left the hotel. He had a key to the back entrance of the Hungarian's shop. He'd let himself in that way. Just then, he says, he was brooding about Petra, wondering how something that had been so good could have gone so wrong." Haden stopped his story. "Sorry," he said. "Did you say something?''

"Nothing," Helen said. "It was just a derisive 'huh?' ''

"Well, Baronin supposes that's why he didn't notice the car until it was too late," Haden said. "Two men clamped a chloroformed pad over his face and hauled him into the back of the car. At first he struggled, which was the wrong thing to do because it meant the chloroform hadn't taken effect. He realized that in time and pretended to collapse. The car drove off. He lay on the floor of the car, nearly unconscious, trying not to pass out completely.''

"Make of the car?" Helen prompted as she whisked eggs vigorously. "Nationality of the men?"

"The car, he doesn't know. The two in the back spoke Russian. If the driver said anything, he didn't hear him. Baronin was pretty far gone at first, of course. He remembers them taking his passport and wallet, but nothing else. He still had his keys and some Austrian money he'd put in his back pocket for when he was ready to leave for the Hungarian's, the usual routine. The Hungarian maintained that he didn't want any payment for himself, it was always donated to a refugee welfare fund he supported."

"The passport turned up in the possession of Hans Kinsky," Helen said. "Could he have been the driver?"

"That's another unknown," Haden said. "The driver was wearing a hat, so Baronin only glimpsed the back of his head. He didn't see the faces of the other two at all."

"You can go and sit down now," Helen said. "Unless you want your omelette like rubber."

They ate off trays. The omelette was just right, the French bread fresh. Haden enjoyed it.

"Baronin lost all track of time," Haden continued, "and he didn't know where they were. He was only just conscious enough to realize that the car was coming to a stop. His first thought was that they'd arrived someplace where it would be safe to finish him off. Then he heard a train coming, fast, and guessed they'd stopped at a crossing. It seemed like the only chance he was going to get. He waited until the train came close, managed to find the door handle without anyone noticing, pushed the door open, and threw himself out and ran, blindly, from the car. He noticed the last lighted car of the train passing, and then, suddenly, he was falling. In that second he believed he'd gotten away from them only to fall to his death, but by chance the drop probably saved his life. He heard shots while he was treading air. He must have fallen into a small ravine. Some bushes partly lessened the impact, but he knew at once he'd hurt his right leg. He lay there in agony, listening. The train had gone, but he could hear another car arriving and saw the flash of headlights. Someone shouted in German, something like 'Get going. You're blocking the road.' The cars drove off, but he knew one of them would soon be back. He forced himself to walk as far as he could, away from the railway line, nearly crying with pain. When he had to rest, he looked for a niche in the rockface, pulled some undergrowth across it, and lay there. He passed out for a while, but came around when he heard the sounds of men searching. The noise went on for a long time, until they got close. He couldn't do anything about it except lie there, with his ankle throbbing, and try not to groan. But then they gave up, and he heard them moving away. He waited for a long time, until he thought it was safe, and then worked his way back toward the railway line. It was a dark night, without a moon, and it wasn't until he caught sight of a faint sheen on the horizon that he realized how close he was to the Danube. That, he imagines, is where he was supposed to have ended up. He found a stream, cleaned himself up as best he could, and soaked his ankle for a while. He made his way along the railway line until he came to a village. He caught the first morning train into Vienna, took a taxi, let himself into the Hungarian's shop, and passed out." Haden sat back and said, "That was an excellent omelette."

"Glad you liked it," Helen said. "That yarn was so enthralling, I didn't really notice what I was eating. I'll make some coffee if you're finished."

"Baronin has been in hiding ever since, courtesy of the Hungarian," Haden said. "They thought his ankle was badly sprained, but although it improved, there was still some pain. Finally he was seen by a doctor they trusted. Baronin had fractured a small bone. It had mended, but not properly, and required minor corrective surgery, but

Baronin decided not to risk that. He'll have it done somewhere else, when he thinks it's safe. So at the moment he walks with a slight limp. And he looks completely different. I doubt his own wife would know him.''

"Why has he remained in hiding so long after he could have been moved out?''

"He says the KGB must know he's still alive, and they won't give up.''

"KGB men are thin on the ground at the American embassy,'' Helen said impatiently. "Or so we fondly hope. All he had to do was make a phone call. Come to that, why deliver himself to this anonymous Hungarian? Why didn't he take a taxi to the hotel? Petra may screw around a little, but she's not heartless. She'd have called for help—and not from the goddamn KGB. It doesn't add up. Not unless he thought she'd betrayed him to the Russians in the first place. Is that it?''

"Baronin says that night was a traumatic experience. After that, everything looked different. He knew from then on he was a hunted man. He'd had enough of working for the Americans. And the one American in particular that he'd had enough of was Petra. She was never going to be the nice faithful wife he wanted. He just wants to go and live somewhere else, to disappear—away from the Americans, away from Petra.''

"Such things can be arranged, even without a passport,'' Helen said.

"But it's a bit more complicated. When he goes, he wants to take his son with him,'' Haden said.

"Does he, now? A happy family, minus mother, living in Paraguay? Is that the picture?''

"He's thinking of New Zealand, actually,'' Haden said. "Only, by the time he'd more or less recovered and worked out this scheme for future safety, peace, and bliss, two or three months had gone by. When the Hungarian called the

Munich apartment for him, a stranger answered, who knew only that Petra and Peter had gone. Baronin dared not risk giving himself away by making any more inquiries. So he hasn't been able to find out where Peter is.''

Helen's expression had remained thoughtful. "The possibility of your carrying out a little kidnap job hasn't come up, by any chance, I suppose?" she asked.

"It's been suggested," Haden answered. "And I think that much is genuine. Otherwise, there's a very different version of the whole thing, according to which Baronin was planted by the KGB and has been working for them ever since."

"Before you draw breath again," Helen said, "I think I'll make the coffee."

Haden watched her leave, impressed, as ever, by the natural unselfconscious grace of her movements. When she came back and they were sipping their coffee, he told her about Oleg, using his Christian name only, and about "Ivan." Helen listened, asking few questions.

". . . So, according to Oleg, Baronin was aimed at Petra right from the beginning, back in Moscow, and the defection was a fake, designed in due course to open up a channel for planted disinformation," Haden finished.

"Naturally Baronin denies that."

"He claims to be an innocent victim in a setup, later taken in by Oleg, the KGB officer who put the Dante source in place."

"There's quite a bit you're holding back, Stephen," Helen said. "Insurance policies require all relevant facts to be disclosed."

"The policy might not get underwritten at the head office," Haden said. "Someone in Washington was running the Dante source and wanted it protected, genuine or not. That someone still isn't identified and could be in your

Agency. Baronin's on ice, and Oleg's on hold. It's best if that's all you know right now."

"And both of them want something from you," Helen guessed. "And that's why they came out of the woodwork for you, while no one else could get anywhere."

"I attract such people," Haden said. "They think I can be used."

"So you can," Helen agreed. "Although your price is high."

Haden said, "I have two offers. Reunite father and son and arrange asylum in the States for 'Ivan.'"

"Other considerations apart, the first could mean allowing a Russian spy to disappear without paying for the damage he's done," Helen said. "And the second could mean granting asylum to an active KGB agent. It just depends on whom you believe."

"I don't know that I believe either of them," Haden admitted. "They could both be lying, setting me up between them." Helen's eyebrows rose inquiringly. "Perhaps the idea is for 'Ivan' to move to the West," Haden said, "while Baronin takes his son with him back to Russia, rather than New Zealand. It's just a thought," he remarked apologetically. "Or they could both be telling the truth, as they see it, of course."

"The way I see it," Helen Lloyd said, "you are both important and extremely unimportant. You've gotten close—but then no one's tried to stop you, either. Now, you're supposed to do something. If you don't oblige, or if you do the wrong thing, you could get killed."

"Accurately, if not tactfully, put," Haden said. "Only if I do the right thing, whatever that may be, I'm then no longer important. Which could prove equally fatal. It's a nice choice. By tomorrow I'd like to hear your opinion, which may or may not be sound. I'll decide when I've heard it."

"Stephen," Helen said kindly, "in the friendliest possible spirit, you are not in charge. It's too big, okay?"

"In the same cordial spirit," Haden responded, "you badly wanted me to look for Baronin. I obliged. I looked. It's done. No further instructions accepted. Right?"

"Wrong," Helen said. "You say he's alive. If so, you're now a party to concealing him, obstructing people who urgently need to question him."

"What people?" Haden inquired. "Check with your station chief in Vienna. You'll find that Baronin has been presumed dead."

"I know that, for God's sake," Helen snapped. "You don't expect me to join your private conspiracy, do you?"

"I expect Petra has the death certificate tucked in her handbag even now," Haden mused. "I wonder if Baronin left a will." He put his coffee cup down. Helen moved to refill it. "No more, thanks," he said. "Helen, it might be better if Baronin stayed dead for the time being. Think about it." Helen was pouring coffee for herself and did not look at him. "Well," Haden said, "when you've done your thinking, I expect you'll want to make some phone calls."

"Not until morning," she said. "I agreed to stay off duty tonight."

Haden smiled at her. "You may have to take orders, but you don't have to ask for them," he said.

She did not answer, and Haden looked around for his bag.

"You left it in the hall," Helen said. "Where are you staying?"

"I haven't booked a room anywhere," Haden said. "I'll find a place. It's out of season."

She was sipping her coffee, her hazel eyes regarding him speculatively over the rim of her cup. She put it down carefully.

"You may as well stay here," she said.

"Fine," Haden said. "Then we can talk some more."

Not a great deal of conversation took place. No thoughts of Vienna or the Ninth Circle remained in Haden's mind; they were erased as though they did not exist.

At first it was the greeting that follows a long separation, renewing the memory of warmth and touch; there were smiles of recognition and a gentle prolonging of the moment before reunion. But then they became impatient, and an urgent hunger set in; they came together, as if they would remain so forever, as if nothing else mattered, or ever would. There was that same remembered pleasure, the same shutting out of all but sensation, and yet, when the soaring climax had finally come, it was, in retrospect, subtly different. Something had changed, or shifted. Perhaps some trace of reserve, previously experienced, had gone.

They lay looking at each other. Haden reached out and touched Helen's shoulder gently, feeling its sculpted warmth, finer than any statue. He reflected with a kind of placid contentment on the nature of that strange, small difference. Perhaps it was his imagination. But perhaps their bodies had conveyed some message that remained unspoken. He wondered, dreamily, what exactly it was that had changed.

Helen took his hand and traced a pattern in his palm with her fingertips. Her eyes were large and dark in the subdued lamplight.

"I don't know what to do about you, Haden," she murmured.

"You're doing all right," Haden said.

She slipped inside his arm and pressed her body against his. The effect of that proximity was not subtle.

"Kind of like that, you mean?" she said. But he did not

answer. For a long while they said nothing, and then, with a sense of surprise at how profoundly relaxed he must have been, Haden realized that he must have fallen into a light sleep. When he opened his eyes and turned toward Helen Lloyd, her arms were around him at once, as if she had been waiting. Her fingers caressed the back of his head as they held each other.

"This doesn't count," she said, her breath warm against his cheek. "You know that, don't you?"

"I know," Haden said. "It's your night off."

"I guess there's still some of it left," she said.

There was, some. But when Haden woke again, although no light intruded from around the curtains, he was alone in the bed. Mixed up in the murmur of distant traffic, he thought he could hear Helen Lloyd's voice, although he heard no replies, no other voice. Haden did not bother to eavesdrop, or even to lift the bedside extension. He just lay there waiting.

He saw her shape dimly as she came back into the room, heard the rustle as she discarded her robe, and felt the bed dip as she slipped back in.

"I gather it's morning," he said.

"I played fair," Helen said. She groped for his hand and found it. "Just said there seemed to be a problem. It's been left to me."

"You must really rank since your promotion," Haden said.

"At my age, it's overdue," Helen said. "I deserve it. You ready to talk business?"

"No," Haden said, transferring her hand elsewhere.

This time, it was more of a goodbye. There was a certain regret, a touch of sadness in the way in which the moment was postponed.

Haden showered and dressed. The aroma of freshly

222

ground coffee beans reached him, overlaid with that of grilling bacon.

"Perfect timing," Helen said as he walked into the kitchen. "As usual."

That trace of sly mockery reestablished, intentionally or not, the old distance between them. She placed the plate of bacon and eggs in front of him and sat down across from him. They ate in a silence, which was less companionable than awkward. Finally Helen pushed her plate aside and refilled his coffee cup.

"Time to talk, Stephen," she said. "And suppose we do this my way for once, okay?"

Haden said, "I'm sailing under my flag, not yours."

"Meaning you'll be looking for a profit," Helen said. She gazed at him curiously across the table. "Don't you have any ideals at all?"

"I try to keep them in check," Haden said. "It's the people with ideals who cause the real trouble in this world."

"It is very important," Helen said flatly, "that we have Baronin, and right now."

"Baronin can wait," Haden said. "He's not going anywhere."

"You've already been paid for him," Helen said. "Now you're looking to get paid twice over. Suppose I told you you'll get nothing for this 'Ivan'?"

"I wouldn't believe you," Haden said. "Perhaps, being away from Vienna, I see things more clearly. Anyway, I've decided. Leave it at that."

She sat staring at him for a while. Finally she shook her head slowly, accepting defeat. "I have to be in on it," she said. "I'm the one who'll be held responsible. You could cost me my job."

"That would never do," Haden said.

* * *

Ian looked up and smiled as Haden passed the open door to the office. Haden returned the greeting and followed Harold Leyton into his study.

"He's back, then," Haden remarked as he sat down.

"During working hours only," Leyton replied. "If he's going to stray, that's it. A chap has to be bloody careful these days. I've no wish to depart this world prematurely and unpleasantly. God, when I look back . . . it doesn't bear thinking about. However . . . ?" He gazed at Haden significantly.

"It might now be convenient to gratify your desire to play in the snow," Haden said.

"Convenient for you is what you mean," Leyton said. "Which lessens the attractions no end. Persuade me. How much?"

"Halve the figure you first thought of," Haden said equably. "Then we'll bargain, bearing in mind that you really ought to pay me. This could be what you've been waiting for."

"Dante?" Leyton's eyes gleamed. "The Ninth Circle?"

"No promises, Harry," Haden said. "It won't be served up on a plate. But it's possible. It just might go that way."

Chapter Thirteen

It was like coming around after a major operation—the receding memory of unconsciousness, the gradual, creeping onset of pain.

Dully, but instinctively, he sought to return to that former, blissful state when he felt nothing, but the pain advanced to a generalized, bodywide ache, and local areas imposed themselves in separate torments.

Something hard pressed into his back, and his head was thudding abominably, as if it intended to explode. There was a lump on the back of it that was tender. He opened his eyes. Wherever he was, he might as well have been blind. It was as black as a tomb, and cold, too, a cold that bit into his bones as sensation began to return to him. He attempted to move and groaned out loud. His limbs were rigid, locked solid in the bitter cold. Tremors began to shake his body. His teeth clenched, forcing one hand under control, he groped for his lighter with numb fingers. He cupped it in both hands so he wouldn't drop it. It took several attempts before he succeeded in lighting it.

The small flame did not penetrate far into the darkness, but he could see that he was propped up against the bars on one side of a cage. He also saw, little more than an arm's length away, the crumpled form of a man, lying on his side. It was Harold Leyton, his face pallid and unshaven. At first sight, he looked to be dead, but then he moaned faintly.

Haden let him lie. He was better off as he was. It vaguely crossed his mind that he should hoard that small flame, and he eased the lighter closed. He rubbed his face and heard the rasp his hand made against the stubble. Harold Leyton? A cage? He tried to think, but no thought came. His mind was unable to record anything but his physical discomfort.

His mouth was dry as sand. He tried to lick his lips. They also were dry, cracked, possibly bleeding. He closed his eyes again, it made no difference whether they were open or shut. He tried to reconstruct what he had been able to see in the dim light from the flame.

It meant moving. His body issued immediate protests. Grimly he overcame them and managed to crawl the few feet across the cage. With one arm he groped between the bars and found the metal ladle and then the bowl alongside it, both only just within reach. When he tried to dip the ladle into the bowl, he found a thin layer of ice on top. With his arm outstretched and his head jammed against the bars of the cage, he succeeded in breaking the ice and spooned a few sips' worth of the ice-cold water into his mouth.

For a while he stayed slumped in his new position. Dimly he realized that what he was sitting on, although hard, felt like earth. Using the metal handle of the ladle, he prodded at it, and it gave a little. He prodded some more and then dug down with the ladle, his actions automatic, his mind blank. He soon gave up. A few inches beneath the packed earth were more iron bars, the floor of the cage.

He wiped the ladle on his overcoat and then groped for his breast pocket handkerchief to finish cleaning it. His fingers found his shoulder holster. It was empty.

London. He could remember London, a night of love-making with Helen Lloyd. Or was that a dream? It seemed

226

like one. But there was more to London than that. Days must have passed since then. Weeks, for all he knew. What the hell had happened to bring him to a cage in this cold, dark hole? There must have been some sequence of events. But his brain refused to work coherently. Think, for Christ's sake. Think. Do something. Anything.

Painfully, he checked his possessions, groping under his overcoat, identifying objects by their shapes, with half-frozen fingers. Nothing was missing but his gun and maybe his hat. Had he been wearing the fur hat he had sported on Vienna's colder days?

He opened his eyes in a sudden spurt of self-directed anger. What the hell did his bloody hat matter? Except that he needed it. Perhaps it was lying somewhere in the cage. If he groped around, he might be able to find it. Oh, for God's sake, were his senses gone? Forget the hat. Never mind the hat.

Haden was aware that he should force his limbs into some kind of movement, but he was disinclined to do so. Soon. He would do that soon. Until he knew something, anything, about how he had gotten here, there was no point. He should retain as much body warmth as possible in the meantime.

Gingerly he ensured that his heavy overcoat was draped over his legs. He buttoned it to the neck, turned up the collar, and thrust his numb hands deep into the pockets.

The overcoat surely meant that he had been outside, or in his car, when whatever happened that had brought him to this place.

Concentrate on that. Where had he been? Had he seen anyone? Concentrate. Belatedly he realized that his hands were touching something in his pockets. Thankfully he took out his gloves and pulled them on.

Then his mind responded. He was leaving a movie theater, putting on his gloves as he walked. The exit led into

227

a narrow, dimly lit passageway, and he had felt the deep chill of the night air after the warmth in the theater. He waited, watching the exit doors in case someone was following him. No one did, so he walked to the back of the cinema and around the corner. There, sheltered in a recess formed by another building, was Oleg Tushin, smoking a cigarette.

Was that when it had happened? No, it could not have been. Why not? He didn't know, only that it hadn't been then. All right, when was this? The day after he had returned from London? Two days later? Three? He didn't know that, either. But now he remembered what had been said.

"Mr. Haden, it is now urgent. There is very little time left." Tushin was very calm, just the same. "Ivan has heard that he is being considered for a Moscow posting. It is a hint. They are growing tired of waiting. Ivan *must* be moved out, and soon."

"There is no Ivan, for Christ's sake."

Wait. Had he said that? No. That was what he believed, but he had not said it. According to Baronin there was an Ivan, a trusted friend from his time in Moscow, who he believed was in Vienna, but he had not actually seen him there. Tushin had acted as intermediary in setting up the process, although not the delivery/collection point. János Varga, a man with many contacts useful to Baronin, had been Baronin's suggestion. So ran Baronin's story, anyway. Haden did not necessarily believe it. There could be an Ivan, hiding behind Tushin, afraid to come out into the open. Haden was not sure then—or now. So he could not have queried Ivan. He had gone along with it. So what had he said?

"It must be a day when Ivan will not be missed, from noon onward."

There had been a pause, as if for calculation. And then: "That might be possible. How?"

"By train. He can carry nothing with him, not so much as a briefcase. He will be escorted. At Innsbruck someone else will join the train. He will be taken to a safe place."

"I think he will need to know more than that."

"Then he goes to Moscow instead. I'll do my utmost to ensure nothing goes wrong, but there's always a risk. And not only to him. There are other people concerned. If he wants to go, what he gets to know is what I've told you and no more. It's up to him."

"Very well." Then there was a sigh from behind the cigarette. "I shall put it to him. With one stipulation, Mr. Haden. On the day in question, you play no part. You stay far away from Ivan, for everyone's sake."

"If you're saying he's already under surveillance, the whole thing's off."

"The risk is that you may be, Mr. Haden."

"I'm pretty certain I haven't been, so far."

" 'Pretty certain' is good enough for now. At worst, we have only talked. You have said you are in Vienna to look for Baronin. Baronin is now presumed dead. But you are still here. You are a well-known *Fluchthelfer*, a man whose business is organizing escapes. We are dealing with suspicious people. They may think it possible you are organizing a defection. The talk of a Moscow posting may be an oblique warning to Ivan, as well as a hint. Do you think it sensible to risk leading them to Ivan as he attempts to board a train?"

"I suppose not. Perhaps it would be best for me to try to get myself followed instead."

"By all means," he said jovially. "Be seen around Vienna. Behave as suspiciously as you like. But nowhere near the railway station, if you please."

Haden became aware that scrabbling sounds of movement, painful grunts and mutterings, were coming from the darkness. Harold Leyton was coming around.

Haden began to raise himself to his feet. He was only half standing when he cracked his head on iron bars. He swore and rubbed his head. He now knew that the cage was barely four feet high.

"Stephen? Is that you?" Harold Leyton mumbled hoarsely. "God, I feel ill."

"There's a bucket to your left," Haden said. "Meant for everything, I suppose."

"I didn't say I was going to be sick," Leyton said resentfully. Haden groped forward, found Leyton's recumbent body, and helped him into a sitting position. "Where are we?" Leyton groaned.

"In a cage," Haden answered. "Which I think is in a cave."

"Terrific," Leyton muttered. "Bloody marvelous."

"There's some water," Haden said. "Stay there. I'll fetch some."

Haden repeated his maneuver with the ladle and carefully drew it into the cage. He found Leyton's hand and closed his fingers around it. He heard Leyton slurping the ice-cold water, followed by the sharp hiss of an intaken breath.

"Now I know I need a dentist," Leyton muttered. "Big news."

"We also have a few chunks of bread as a main course," Haden said.

"Not yet. What time is it? What day, come to that?"

"My watch is gone," Haden said. It would have told them both.

"Mine, too," Leyton said after a pause. "It's the disorientation routine, then. With cold as a little extra. What do they want, Stephen?"

"I expect we'll find out," Haden said. "They've left bread and water. We're not supposed to die yet. Just get weaker."

"Except from the bloody cold," Leyton said, his teeth

chattering audibly. "Christ, I've never been so frozen in my life."

"Harry, we have to move as best we can. Crawl, do anything. But keep moving."

"I know," Leyton said. "But I don't think I can, not yet. Give me a few minutes. How did you get here?"

"I've been trying to remember," Haden said. "I can't. Only bits. They don't fit together. How about you?" He waited. There was only the sound of stertorous breathing. "Harry, don't go to sleep."

"I'm not," Leyton said from the darkness. "I'm thinking. They knew, Stephen. They knew the whole sodding thing."

"I guessed that much," Haden said.

"Me, yes, okay, I was there. But you weren't. You were doing your decoy act. But they got you, too."

"You say you were there. At the station?"

"That's right. Arrived on the dot. Bought my ticket. Went to the washroom. Started washing my hands. A chap began using the next basin. Identified himself. Walked off. Smooth as clockwork, I thought. A breeze."

"What did he say?"

"Exactly as arranged, word for word. He asked me for the time. I told him. He said, 'I think you still have British time.' Word for word."

"What did he look like?"

"Fitted the description you gave me, exactly. The chap you said you thought it would be. He was your man, all right."

"Well, that answers one question," Haden said. It had been Oleg Tushin and not any "Ivan." Whether, in view of their present confinement, Tushin had genuinely intended to defect, was another matter entirely. "What then?" he inquired.

"Watched him go, gave him one minute exactly, then

followed. Only he wasn't heading for the train. He was standing just outside, with two guys talking to him. So I walked around them, bought a paper, and parked myself where I could keep an eye on them.''

''Did you know either of the other men?''

''No. They'd have passed as young businessmen— smartly dressed, briefcase—you know. After a bit, they walked off with him, normal as you like.''

''Just that? They didn't use any force?''

''No. Hands in full view all the time. Didn't take his arm, never so much as touched him. Just talked to him. He didn't seem to be saying much. Just listened.''

''Did any of them look in your direction?''

''Not once. Just the same, I thought I'd better be careful. Your Oleg Tushin could have been fingering me. So I kept well back when I followed them. They were in no hurry. Walked quite normally. I knew your chap Erwin Matz was supposed to be backing us up somewhere, keeping an eye on things—''

''He was,'' Haden said, half remembering. ''He phoned me to say so, half an hour before the train was due to leave. I was at a café. We'd arranged it. I—'' He broke off—a lapse in his memory. He stared into the darkness. ''No, it's gone. Go on, Harry.''

''That's nearly it,'' Leyton said. ''I remember thinking they were probably going to take a taxi, or they had a car waiting, when someone bumped into me from behind. I stumbled, he said, 'Sorry,' in German and grabbed hold of me. Then I felt something in my neck, like a hornet's sting. And that's all I remember. Jesus. Whatever was in that bloody needle leaves one hell of a hangover. I feel terrible.''

''Sorry, Harry,'' Haden said.

''So you bloody well should be,'' Leyton said. ''You organized a complete balls-up that leaked in advance.''

"A woman used to answer his phone," Haden said. "Perhaps he said too much, and she didn't like it."

"Yes, it would be a woman," Leyton said with distaste. "Well, that'll teach Mr. Oleg Tushin. He'll be discussing the error of his ways with the comrades back in Russia by now, I expect." There was a pause, and Haden knew what he was thinking. "Which is where we could be, too, if they flew us out," Leyton said dolefully. "Or Hungary, or Rumania. Doesn't make much difference."

He lapsed into another gloomy silence. Haden forced himself to combat the inclination just to lie there and let the debilitating cold do its work. He groped through the bars, found the bread, and divided it in half.

"Come on, Harry," he said. "You know what they're up to. At least let's not go along with it."

"Oh, really?" Leyton said sarcastically. "We have all these other options, do we?"

He grumbled some more but complied by taking his share of the bread and eating it, complaining that it was utterly inedible, although when he had finished, he asked whether there was more. Haden felt the same. Even such disagreeable-tasting stuff reminded him how hungry he was. When every crumb, every hard crust was gone, his system cried out for more. He tried to assure himself that this was really quite a good sign, some semblance of a return to a degree of normality. His body remained unconvinced.

"I'm going to try to generate some body warmth," he told Leyton. "If you're not in the mood, don't get in my way."

"You must be delirious," Leyton said.

But in fact he joined in. In the pitch-darkness, like two animals, they circled painfully, unable to stand erect, grunting, resting, fighting the hunger pangs beginning again. The effects were scarcely invigorating, but at least Haden's muscles were easing a little, he thought, trying to persuade himself. He felt his crumpled fur hat lying in one corner and jammed it on his head with relief.

"We must look bloody ludicrous," Leyton said. He sounded slightly more cheerful. "I'm thawing out a bit, though."

"It won't affect you so much, Harry," Haden said. "You carry more fat than I do."

"I simply like to eat well," Leyton said. "Speaking of which, I'm starving."

Their crude movements had heightened their hunger pangs, but the enervating cold was the greater enemy, at least for the time being. It was then that very faint sounds intruded from the distance into the stillness. Another enemy.

A flicker of light reflecting off the rockface pierced the edge of the dense blackness, wavered, grew, and became two powerful flashlights that continued to grow in size and intensity as the sound of booted footsteps came closer. The sound finally stopped a few feet from them. The light from the beams illuminated the cage and its two crouching, disheveled inhabitants.

Haden screwed up his eyes and squinted, holding up a hand to shield his eyes from the blazing lights, but he could only dimly discern two silhouettes behind the beams.

One of them stepped forward and refilled the water bowl in silence. Then he put down a large thermos and removed the lid. Steam rose from the hot contents, along with the appetizing smell of goulash.

Saliva streamed into Haden's mouth. He could see the expression of yearning on Harold Leyton's face, as he swallowed, too. He also saw that the thermos was out of reach from inside the cage. The gift was conditional.

One of the shapes behind the glare of light spoke harshly in rapid Russian.

"He's addressing you," Leyton said.

"I don't speak Russian," Haden said. "You talk to him."

"He wants to know where Alexander Baronin is."

"He's dead," Haden said. "Where his corpse is, I don't know."

There was an exchange in Russian between Harold Leyton and the shape.

"He thinks you're lying," Leyton said. "He thinks that Baronin is alive, and that you know where he is."

"Tell them to check with their sources in Vienna," Haden said. "They'll find that Baronin is no longer listed as missing. He's presumed dead."

Leyton translated and received an immediate and lengthy reply. "I'm afraid he doesn't believe you," he said, his face pallid and drawn in the fierce lamplight. "The broad drift is that either you tell him or we stay here until we rot."

"I can't tell him something I don't know," Haden answered.

The interrogation went on for a long time—monotonous, insistent repetitions from behind the beams of light, Harold Leyton's increasingly urgent translations, Haden's repeated denials.

Finally there was a pause, followed by a short statement.

"He says you're being very foolish," Leyton said. "He may have a point."

Haden shook his head. Leyton sighed wearily. The shape nearest the thermos extended one foot and pushed it over. Goulash spilled onto the ground. He picked up the thermos, upended it, and shook it. The remainder of the goulash streamed out. The smell was unbearable. Then Haden glimpsed the gun in the other one's hand.

From sheer blind instinct he dived sideways, cannoning into Harold Leyton. There were three rapid shots. The explosions boomed deafeningly, echoing into the distance.

The bucket clanged, spun into the air, smashed against

the bars, and, ripped into jagged remnants, fell to the ground.

After a final angry outburst of Russian, the lights swiveled and retreated with the two silhouettes.

Haden watched them recede until the final vestige of light vanished and he and Leyton were returned to blackness. He leaned back against the bars.

"What was the final bit?" he asked.

"That the shots weren't for you," Leyton said. "Too quick, compared with starvation and cold. And that there is no time limit. This goes on until you tell them. Also," he added, "that from now on we can shit on the floor and live in our own filth." Haden said nothing. The cold was beginning to bite into his bones again. "I don't like that idea much, Stephen," Leyton said. "I'm a bit of an old woman about bodily functions."

"We're sitting on earth," Haden said tiredly. "It's hard, but it crumbles if you scrape at it hard enough. You can cover it up."

"Oh, well, that makes everything all right, then," Leyton's disembodied voice said. "I should never have listened to you, Stephen. Dante my arse. You're a worse con man than I am," he said, as if aggrieved by the discovery.

"I thought I nearly had it, Harry," Haden said. "It was there, just out of reach. I could almost touch it. Just one link to add, and it was complete."

That sounded familiar somehow. He wondered why. It took his deadened brain awhile to recall. Hadn't Freddy voiced somewhat similar sentiments before he met his end? And how about Hans Kinsky? But his brain had switched off, declining to function.

They sat sprawled where they were, in the timeless darkness.

"Stephen," Leyton said—how much later, Haden did not know. "Stephen?" Leyton repeated. "I don't think these people are bluffing. They mean it. Baronin doesn't strike me as a very good cause. You may think him worth dying for. I don't.''

''I don't either, Harry,'' Haden said.

''Then tell the bastards,'' Leyton said. ''And don't tell me you don't know. They don't believe that, and neither do I.''

Haden sympathized wholeheartedly with Harold Leyton. He well knew that the short, plump man would endure to the end for a cause he perceived as his own. But Baronin was not it.

''It's not mine, either,'' Haden said, answering his own thought rather than Leyton. ''Suppose I did know. Suppose I told them. What, then? Do you think they'd shake hands and escort us back to the West?''

''They might,'' Leyton said. ''They only want Baronin. Give him to them.''

Haden said, ''They'll keep us alive just as long as they think they can get Baronin. And no longer.''

''I don't know, dammit,'' Leyton complained. ''I can't see why they've put me in here with you, anyway.''

''Maybe to do what you're doing now, Harry,'' Haden said. ''To try to persuade me.''

''That way, at least we stand a chance,'' Leyton said. ''Your way, we don't.''

Haden did not attempt to provide an answer to that. He could think of no very good one, for Leyton was right. Given water, a man could survive for weeks without food, but not confined as they were, in this temperature. They would rapidly grow weaker. Within days, both ways would lead to the same end. His way, denying any knowledge of Baronin's whereabouts, could only prolong the ordeal. Another way must be found. He sat staring into the darkness and sought it. No answer came. He leaned his head back against the bars and closed his eyes, the better to think.

The sudden twitch of his body brought Haden's head up. His chin had been slumped on his chest. His heart was hammering. He must have fallen into a stupor induced by the dark and the cold. His subconscious must have malevolently taken command and produced its own scenario.

The invading paralysis of cold had returned, been a part of it. The growing, desperate hunger, too. In some dark, savage recess of his mind, he had still been in the cage, shaking with cold, driven mad by hunger. And with his fingernails, he had been tearing the flesh from Harold Leyton's dead body; he had been gnawing at the bloodstained bones.

Haden shuddered and fought to dismiss the monstrous, uncalled-for vision. Rationally it was simple enough. His errant, half-conscious brain had borrowed it and modified it only slightly. Just the same, the nightmare remained insanely real, a hint, or perhaps a warning, of the deterioration to come, the loss of reason, the onset of madness.

He had been lying in the same spot for too long. His limbs felt as though they were locked, and he didn't want to move them anymore. He forced himself to rise to the crouch that was the best the cage would allow. He staggered and then steadied himself against the bars. His bent legs threatened to give way, and he was obliged to prop himself up while he fumbled for his lighter.

Somehow the small, flickering illumination helped a little, just being able to see *something*. Unevenly he made his way around the cage, the lighter in front of him, peering at what little it showed. He came to the mangled bucket, bent down and examined it.

He was aware that Harold Leyton's eyes were open, that he was watching him.

"What are you doing?" Leyton inquired dully.

"Trying to keep moving," Haden said. "So should you."

"I'll wait until you've finished," Leyton said.

Haden completed his circuit of the cage. Then he put his lighter out. He was not sure how much fuel was left. Clumsily he took his gloves off and went around again, feeling his way, pausing now and then, and then he sank onto the ground.

"All yours now, Harry," he said.

He heard Leyton's grunts as he got to his feet and laboriously followed Haden's example. He circled the cage half-erect, apologizing when he collided with Haden. He sank to the ground, crawled to and fro, and finally collapsed with an audible moan.

"It's the stiffness," he gasped. "Takes some working off."

"I wonder when they'll come back," Haden said.

"Who knows? We've no way of measuring time, anyway."

"You know about the disorientation game. What would you do? Wait a few hours? Come back the same day?"

"I doubt it," Harold Leyton said. "Time's on their side, not ours. The weaker we get, the more likely you are to oblige. Food's going to be a lot harder to resist in a day or two."

"That's what I think," Haden said. "My guess is that when they called on us it was daylight outside. Why should they lose any sleep? Maybe I'm wrong, but it doesn't matter. How long do you reckon since they left?"

"Can't tell. I'm afraid I went a bit comatose. At least two hours. Perhaps four or five."

"But the chances are we've got about nineteen or twenty hours before they come back."

"Possibly." Leyton sounded more alert. "What's on your mind, Stephen?"

"This cage was transported here," Haden replied. "It's built to fold flat. There are hinges at the corners."

"Sadly," Leyton said, "I quite forgot to bring a screwdriver with me. Have you got one?"

"The hinges are the weakest point," Haden went on. "There's a sharp outcrop of rock three or four feet away."

Leyton considered that for a while. Haden heard him testing the bars.

"Can't shift it," Leyton said. "It's set in the earth."

"Only a few inches. Suppose we moved the earth?"

"Oh, I see. With the shovel you've got stuffed up your trouser leg."

"We have the ladle," Haden said, "and we have the ripped-up bucket. If we stamp on it a bit . . ."

He snapped on his lighter. Leyton blinked and crawled across to the bucket. With gloved hands he tested the long rip in one misshapen side. He sat down and used feet and hands, heaving. The weakened metal gave. He maneuvered the ripped portion between the bars of the cage and levered it carefully until a few inches of jagged metal protruded at an angle. Then he rammed it into the earth. It penetrated, not very much, but a little.

"I'd rather have a shovel," Leyton said. "This will take bloody hours and hours."

"Let's say we have twelve," Haden offered.

"Even if we could," Leyton said, "we'd have to make one hell of a noise. And if they've left someone on guard at the mouth of this bloody cave, we'd still be done for."

Haden put his lips close to Leyton's ear and whispered softly.

"There's what I think is a voice-activated tape recorder tucked behind that rock. My bet is that means they've left us to it." He drew back. Leyton's eyes sought the shadows behind the outcrop of rock. "That's the gamble," Haden said in his normal voice. "What do you say? Ready to have a go?"

"We could be somewhere deep in the bloody Urals," Leyton pointed out.

"You speak Russian," Haden said. "You can ask the way home. Look on the bright side."

"Well, it's something to keep us occupied, I suppose," Leyton said. "But if it doesn't work, you give them Baronin. Okay?"

"You always want to make a deal, Harry," Haden said.

"That's the deal," Leyton said.

He looked quite cheerful as Haden extinguished his lighter and they began work in the darkness.

Their cheerfulness soon evaporated. It was grindingly slow, painful work. Haden alternately knelt and sat to relieve his cramped muscles. With the pointed handle end of the ladle, he jabbed, jabbed, jabbed, laboriously loosening the earth. Then, with the ladle itself, a mere handful at a time, he took up the earth and deposited it outside the cage. He started in one corner, working down to expose the outside edge of the cage under its layer of earth. Leyton had started in the opposite corner. Haden could hear him chipping away doggedly, swearing under his breath now and then. They met somewhere in the middle and paused for a rest. Then they exchanged implements and worked their way back again, exposing an inch or two of the transverse iron bars beneath their feet.

Haden found that he could get on faster with the tortured bucket. When they met again, he handed it over with some reluctance and exchanged it for the ladle. The ladle seemed puny and ineffective by comparison. But every spoonful counted, and he kept on going, jabbing, jabbing, jabbing, ladling, ladling, ladling.

Neither of them spoke. Time meant nothing, it did not exist. There was only the loosening of compacted earth, its painstaking removal from the cage, handful after handful, as if they had been condemned to some eternal, meaningless torment.

Yet they had no eternity at their disposal. Outside the cage, time was passing, the sun was setting or perhaps rising, clocks were striking the hours, and time was another enemy. Its passage brought ever closer the return of their captors, and after that there would be no second chance.

Haden forced himself to use a steady, easy rhythm for his work. The painfully slow task was not the end, but only the beginning. Even if they managed it, it would be useless if they exhausted themselves utterly in doing so.

They met again, paused, rested, parted. This time, on his almost imperceptible progress to the edge of the cage, Haden counted steadily to himself, starting again at sixty, notching up the minutes. He noticed that he now had to extend his arm to tip the earth outside the cage.

He reached the edge of the cage, dug under the bottom bar, and rested on hands and knees. According to his mental count, it had been approximately thirty minutes since he'd met Harold Leyton in the middle of the cage. About an hour, then, in between each exchange of implements. How many times had they done that? Seven? Eight? He could not remember. Say at least eight hours since they had started. Perhaps more. He had the impression that their snaillike progress had quickened a little as they grew accustomed to the tedious work. It could be that nine hours had elapsed. Perhaps as many as ten. How long had they allowed themselves? Was it twelve hours? But that was only a guess. The Russians could come back sooner. Any minute, come to that. Part of him almost welcomed the idea. At least that would bring their laborious effort to an end. He must have been out of his mind. He could hear Leyton digging away methodically and suppressed his own inclination to give up. Haden gripped the ladle and stabbed at the earth, starting his long, slow return journey.

Eventually they met in the middle again, stopped, sat down side by side, and rested. After a while Haden took out his lighter and held it up. The flame was beginning to waver uncertainly. He tried to assess their progress. One more time? He was not sure that he could face it. And did they have another hour, anyway?''

Leyton was of a like mind. "I'm bored with this, Stephen," he said soberly. "One thing I do have is a good broad back."

"Worth a try," Haden agreed.

They stood a yard apart, with their feet carefully planted between the bars forming the floor of the cage that they had managed to reveal, braced their backs against the top of the cage, and heaved and strained. The cramped nature of the cage became an asset. Bent in half, thighs taut, and straining until it seemed their muscles would tear, they were able to exert maximum upward force. But the cage did not give; in fact, it did not move.

They stopped and sat, breathing hard, recovering. They lurched half-erect and tried again. "Come on," Haden urged silently. "Come on, you bastard." He had good reason to know that Harold Leyton's pudgy build concealed deceptive strength. The portly man was doing his full share. Had there been a slight movement that time? He was not sure.

They rested, gasping for breath, hearts throbbing and pounding, dizzy with exertion. When he could, Haden leaned forward, scrabbling and groping with his fingertips, seeking the transverse edge of the cage.

"I think she's shifting a bit," he said.

He heard Leyton groan as he, too, bent forward, the sound of his fingers scrabbling against earth and metal.

"Could be," Leyton finally agreed. "Or it could be wishful thinking."

"Either way," Haden said, "let's give it everything this time."

Leyton grunted a pained assent. They rose and braced themselves. They gripped the bars above them with their hands, adding strained biceps to the upward thrust of thighs and backs.

"She's coming," Leyton breathed.

"Hold it there. Just for a second."

Haden bent and felt. It was no illusion. The bars between which his feet were planted had angled upward perceptibly. He half straightened, settling his back against the top of the cage.

"There can't be much holding it now, Harry," he said. "Go for bust."

Spurred on by their desperation, they found reserves of strength. Slowly they felt the cage rise inch by inch, until the floor bars were scraping up against their calves, canting upward, although the edge behind them was still embedded in earth.

They lowered their small prison carefully, turned, and with ladle and bucket, frantically scraped and dug and chipped away at the earth. It was now or never.

They threw their implements aside, rose, braced, heaved. It was now. They had the cage on their backs, bending under its full weight.

Shuffling and panting, they edged the cage sideways, angled it, and set it down. Haden used his lighter briefly, the flame sputtering and spitting tiny sparks, to peer at the outcrop of rock.

"A few inches more, Harry," he said, "and bring your end around a bit."

They lifted and shuffled until the cage was in the required position, set it down, and took one more rest, until Haden touched Leyton's arm.

"Now we find out if it's all been a waste of time," Leyton

said. He positioned himself alongside Haden. They lifted. "Christ, this thing's heavy."

"More chance of it working," Haden said. "Okay, here we go."

The cage was mounted on their backs and shoulders. Carefully, a little at a time, they induced it to swing to and fro, to get the feel of it. Then they let it go through the full arc.

Unseen in the darkness, the edge of the cage struck the rock, the force of the collision jarring their bodies. There was a screeching clang that seemed to echo interminably along the cavern.

"Jesus," Leyton muttered, "they could hear that in bloody Moscow."

"Keep it going," Haden said loudly. "Again. Again. Again."

Successive horrendous clangs melted deafeningly, one into another, until, staggering, legs buckling, they were forced to stop.

Leyton sat and puffed. Haden crawled forward, gasping, felt with his hands, and risked another second or two with his dying lighter.

Then he sat, staring into the blackness, his breathing growing easier. He felt almost happy.

"The hinge has gone, Harry," he said eventually. "The frame's buckled. One bar's come adrift and splayed sideways."

Leyton crouched beside him and felt the damage for himself. "Right, let's get on with it," he said, renewed, "before those buggers decide to pay a return visit."

Working together, they lifted the edge of the cage and maneuvered it until the splayed bar was sitting on the rock.

"You're heavier than me," Haden said. "I'll steady it."

Cautiously Leyton placed his feet so that he was standing on the edge of the cage, his hands clinging to the bars.

Haden fought to prevent the cage from tipping sideways, to keep that splayed bar pinned where it was.

When both were satisfied that it was reasonably secure, Leyton began to bounce up and down like an oversized monkey.

The ease with which the bar gave was almost anticlimactic. Haden could hear the groan of metal; he could feel the bar bending outward with every enthusiastic bounce from Leyton.

They lifted the cage and dragged it clear of the rock. Haden was the first to crawl through the gap they had created. Getting the portly Harold Leyton out was more difficult. Leyton cursed and wriggled and twisted, while Haden pulled and heaved, but for a while it seemed that Leyton was irretrievably stuck where he was. Finally there was the sound of cloth tearing, and Leyton slithered out of the cage.

"You owe me a new overcoat, Haden," he said.

"Add it to your bill," Haden advised, "along with all the rest."

They groped their way blindly away from the cage, stumbling over the rocks. Feeling their way, they found that, after a while, the tunnel twisted and turned, grew narrower, and then steepened. They were climbing. Could that be right? Yes, it could, Haden told himself, but he was uneasy.

"There's another opening here," Leyton said suddenly. Haden stopped. He could hear Leyton groping around. "It feels like easier going," he began. Then there was a thump and he said, "Oh, shit."

Haden snapped on his lighter. In the brief flicker of flame, he saw Leyton rubbing his head in the low entrance to another tunnel. Then the lighter went out for good.

"They'd never have gotten the cage along that," Haden said.

"I hope you're right," Leyton grumbled.

They made their way onward by touch through the blackness, one cautious step forward after another. It seemed an eternity of groping forward, their progress inevitably slow without light. At least they had been able to stand upright all the way, Haden told himself. Surely that was a good sign, but without proof the argument was unconvincing. Doggedly, they kept going, one cautious step at a time.

"We should have seen daylight by now," Leyton finally said mutinously. "It must have been the other tunnel. I say we go back."

"You can go back, if you want," Haden said, "but there's daylight up ahead."

Leyton had stopped walking when he spoke, while Haden had moved on, around a twist in the tunnel. Leyton stumbled forward, grabbed at Haden to steady himself, and stood beside him. It was less daylight than a slight graying at the edge of the blackness ahead, but the promise was there.

Around a turn, and then another, and the feeble light increased by degrees until they could see where they were going. Suddenly they were outside, standing on a narrow ledge.

The dimness of the light they had approached was explained. Wherever they were was blanketed in heavy mist or low cloud. The ledge was packed with snow. It wound around a buttress, to their left, and out of sight. Before them, the tips of a couple of snow-covered trees close by and below peeped through the mist. Otherwise, there was no sky, nothing.

Haden picked up a piece of rock from inside the tunnel entrance and pitched it over the ledge. It seemed a long time before they heard it strike something.

"Well, we're not on the bloody Black Sea, that's for sure," Leyton said. He rotated his head to stare up, down, around. "We could be anyplace," he said finally. "But I keep thinking about that goulash we didn't get. If they just took us across the border into Hungary," he went on, hopefully, "there are people I know there. If we can get to a telephone, we'll be all right. If we *are* in Hungary, that is," he finished, less hopefully. "Otherwise, we could be anywhere, the Urals, the Carpathians, anywhere."

"If it's the Carpathians, there are people I know in Rumania," Haden said.

"Two to one sounds better odds," Leyton said. "Lead on, and let's find out. I'd hate to meet our chums on their way back."

Once around the buttress, the ledge turned into a reasonably negotiable footpath clinging to the side of the mountain. To their right, however, concealed in the mist, there could have been an abyss, for all they knew. The path was probably less dangerous than it seemed; it had to be, because somebody had carried a cage in sections up along it. Of course whoever it was probably was familiar with the route, whereas Haden was not. He tried to restrain his sense of urgency. Armed men might be on their way up.

The path straightened abruptly and leveled. They found themselves on a broad, flat patch of snow that had tire marks imprinted in it.

The tire marks led on to a rutted track. On either side the shapes of trees were half lost in the mist. Trees offered cover, Haden thought.

"We can't be far from a road," Leyton said.

They began to hurry, their ears straining for the sound of an approaching car above the noise of their breathing and footfalls and the eerie creaking of snow-laden branches.

Either the mist was closing in even tighter or, more likely, the day was ending. It was later in the afternoon than Haden had guessed. When the track they were following vanished inexplicably a few yards in front of them, Haden realized that they were very close to the road the track joined. Both men stopped instinctively, peering through the mist, trying to make out what lay ahead of them. The road was covered in snow, narrow, and probably winding, Haden thought.

The sound of an engine shifting down into a lower gear broke the silence before its headlights became visible. Depending on the mist for camouflage, Haden and Leyton crouched behind trees well clear of the track before the glow of the headlights turned and the vehicle began to crawl along the track away from them.

When he thought it was safe, Haden risked a look, but by then the vehicle was little more than an indefinable shape vanishing into the fog, the growl of its engine dying. Haden thought it might have been a small truck.

He stood up and found the track again. Leyton joined him. They were on the narrow, empty road before either spoke.

"They'll move faster than we did," Leyton said in a hushed voice. "An hour at most before they come looking." He glanced up and down the narrow road, and a bout of shivering overcame him. The temperature had fallen, and after only a minute or so of inaction, the cold was biting deep. His round, fleshy face was pallid under its dark stubble. He looked exhausted. Haden supposed he must look the same; he certainly felt it. "Half an hour if they've got a radio," Leyton estimated. "We have to find shelter, Stephen. We won't survive the night in the open."

"Just keep moving for the time being," Haden said, shivering himself. "We'll try going the way they came. There's a chance they'll think they'd have seen us if we were up this way, and they'll start looking the other way first."

He began to tramp along the road, Leyton beside him.

"There'll be patrols out both ways in a few minutes if they've got a radio," Leyton said.

Haden did not bother to answer. It was a likelihood they could do nothing about. The darkening mist was on their side. The cold, however, was not.

They hurried along as fast as they could, partly to put distance behind them, partly to fight the subzero enemy.

The road, just about wide enough to allow two cars to pass, wound and twisted erratically. Insofar as Haden could retain his sense of direction, the road even seemed to double back on itself, flanked by trees all the way. They heard the sound of running water somewhere out of sight and assumed the road must be following the course of a valley.

Because they were breathing hard, their hearts working overtime and the blood pounding in their ears, the approaching car almost took them unawares. Haden was not conscious of having heard an engine, only the faint swish of tires on the snow a second or so before the slow glow of the headlights rounded a bend in the road.

There was no time for concealment, only to throw themselves off the road, lie prone in the snow, and pray. They must have been visible, but the car drifted around the bend and passed them by without stopping, its windshield wipers clacking.

They had dived off the road on the inside of the bend, so that the driver, intent on negotiating the turn in the thick, freezing mist, had failed to see them.

The swish of tires and the low murmur of the engine receded and melded into the surrounding silence. Leyton sat up in the snow and stared at Haden. He had an idiotic grin on his stubble-strewn, dirt-streaked face.

"Well, I'll be damned," he said, and began to shake with laughter.

Haden grinned back at him, indifferent suddenly to the snow, the bitter cold, and approach of night.

What they had watched drive past them had been, unmistakably, an Austrian police car.

Chapter Fourteen

Stephen Haden and Harold Leyton sat in a huge room in which two double beds and two singles still left plenty of space. They were in a family room, whose ceiling sloped at the corners, at the very top of an inn. They were wearing someone else's dressing gowns, they were cleanshaven, they were relaxed after hot baths, they were warm, and they were eating the hot meal that had been prepared and brought to the room.

They had paused at the outskirts of the village and attempted to clean themselves up, but there was little they could do about their dishevelment—their dirty clothes, the jagged tear in Leyton's overcoat, or the sinister-looking stubble on their faces. The innkeeper's first reaction had been to eye the telephone and mutter something to his wife. He checked his suspicions, however, in the face of money, credit cards, and their proffered explanation. By prior agreement they professed no knowledge of German and spoke English. The innkeeper's grasp of English was slight, but what he understood must have struck him as plausible enough. The two Englishmen had left their car somewhere they could not identify, set out for a walk unprepared for the conditions, become lost, sheltered overnight in a hut, wandered again for another day, and finally stumbled onto the village.

Foreigners, it was well known, did not respect the snow and the cold; they did not know how easy it was to lose all sense of direction; they didn't understand the necessity for stout boots, equipment, special clothing. No, they had set off entirely unprepared, as though they were crossing some English meadow. It was just like foreigners to do such a stupid thing. The innkeeper had suppressed a smile and said as much to his wife in German, while the two grubby Englishmen had stood with blank, uncomprehending faces. But then he became brisk and kind. He showed them to the attic room, took their clothes, gave them razors and dressing gowns, and promised a good, hot meal.

Harold Leyton was shoveling his food down as fast as knife, fork, and spoon would allow. Haden ate more slowly and left some, cautioning Leyton to do the same.

"Your stomach won't like it," he said.

"My stomach says different," Leyton replied.

Haden shrugged and yawned. His eyelids were drooping. He struck a match and lit a cheroot. Just one, and then bed. Leyton finished and polished his plate with a hunk of bread.

"I wonder if there's any more," he murmured.

"Harry," Haden said, "you need to sleep, not spend the night in the bathroom vomiting. Wait till breakfast."

Leyton sighed, found some crumbs, disposed of them, sat back, and watched Haden smoke for a while.

"Sleep would be nice," he said finally. "Only, two tramps arriving in a village wouldn't be hard to find. Even though it's not their country, those chaps seemed pretty keen. Taking us out of this place in the middle of the night would be like rifling a child's piggybank for them. They could take us like that." He snapped his fingers. "Or you, anyway," he added. "I don't know where Baronin is."

"I made a phone call," Haden said. "Very soon, there'll be a watchdog outside, wearing thermal underwear and carrying a gun. You can sleep easy, Harry."

"Someone talked," Leyton said. "Not likely to have been your defector. Nor you. I certainly didn't volunteer to be stuffed in a cage. That leaves your man Erwin and Helen Lloyd."

"Yes," Haden said. He drew on his cheroot. The pleasure was wearing thin. The innkeeper didn't stock the brand he preferred.

"I just wonder how reliable your watchdog is," Leyton persisted.

Haden crushed his half-smoked cheroot into the ashtray.

"We'll wake up safe and sound," he said. "Remind me to buy a watch before we leave."

"So it was Helen Lloyd," Leyton said. "Why, for Christ's sake? Is she a double agent? A part of this whole Dante thing? What?"

Haden got up, threw the dressing gown aside, and crawled gratefully into one of the double beds.

"Turn out the light, Harry," he said, closing his eyes.

The next he knew, it was morning and they were being awakened by the innkeeper with breakfast.

There was a good deal of grunting and yawning over breakfast and very little conversation, but once the food and a shower had done their work, Haden realized that he did not feel too bad at all.

The innkeeper's wife returned their clothes, frowning and apologizing because she hadn't had enough time to deal to her satisfaction with the rents and tears. She had even less English than her husband, and resorted to gestures and appealing looks to express her regret. But in fact, the shirts were clean and ironed, the suits mended, pressed, and wearable. Haden took her hand, gave her a smile, and thanked her warmly. A look of modest pleasure crossed her face, and she smiled back gratefully.

"Doesn't your watchdog eat?" Leyton inquired, inspecting his shoes critically. The gleaming polish almost camouflaged the scuffs.

"Downstairs, I expect," Haden said. "I saw him walk inside half an hour ago." He began to dress. "It's come back, Harry, how they got me."

"The same as me?"

"Similar," Haden answered. "After Erwin Matz phoned me, I left the café. Strolled around a bit, went back to the garage. Took the elevator, no one in it but me. When the doors opened there was a man waiting to get in. He stepped back to let me pass. That's the last thing I remember. There must have been another one. They wouldn't have risked me coming around, but I can't find a needle mark. Chloroform, maybe."

"Followed you, and knew you'd go back to your car sooner or later," Leyton said. He eased on his shoes. "How did they get us, two dead weights, along that ledge and those tunnels?"

"Stretchers?" Haden suggested. "They had a truck." He paused before finishing knotting his tie. "There could have been a truck in the car park. I'm not sure."

"Quite a slick operation," Leyton said, a detached critic. "Not bad at all. Except that it didn't work," he said with satisfaction. "Not from their point of view, anyway." He studied his tie closely and picked with his fingernail at some mark on it. "Only I don't think they'll let it rest there. The Russians aren't good losers, you know. Persistent people—try, try, and try again, that's their style. I expect they'll do their best to make certain it works next time." He gave up scratching at his tie and looped it around his neck. "So, nothing personal, Stephen, but I'd rather we parted company at the earliest possible opportunity. They know I don't know anything, or so I sincerely hope."

"I'll be downstairs," Haden said. "Organize your own transport to the airport if you'd rather. I'll give you five minutes."

Haden expressed his appreciation for all the innkeeper had done in the traditional way, and the money was received in equal, and dignified, measure. Erwin Matz, waiting unobtrusively, followed him outside. They got into Matz's car, Haden behind the steering wheel.

The mist had gone and the sun was out, but it shed little warmth. The brief encounter with the cold reminded Haden of his ordeal. He started the engine and let the heater run.

"You want to bring me up-to-date?" Matz inquired, suppressing a yawn. His nightlong vigil had left his eyes heavy-lidded and watering slightly.

"Later," Haden said. "You kick off. Last night first."

"No prowling cars, nothing," Matz said. "Couldn't have been more peaceful."

It *was* a peaceful spot. Picturesque, too—the village in the valley, the trees marching into the distance, the encircling mountains, all snow clad.

"The station," Haden said. "You phoned me from there."

"I waited where I could see the washroom," Matz said. "Tushin came out. Two men intercepted him. I didn't recognize them. They stood talking."

"How about Leyton?"

"When he saw them he walked away. After that, I lost sight of him. There were a lot of people about. I kept my eyes on Tushin and the other two. They walked to the taxi stand. They talked again. Not for long. Then they got into a taxi. I took another and followed. I know that was something of a risk," he said apologetically, "but there was no time to get back to my car."

"You did the right thing," Haden said. A taxi following another cab was more conspicuous than an anonymous vehicle, but he would have taken the same chance. "Where did they go?"

"The Russian compound, where the delegates and their staff live," Matz said. "All three got out. The other two stood where they were. I thought they were looking at my taxi pretty hard, so I told the driver to keep going. When I looked back, Tushin was walking into the compound."

"Was any force being used?"

"No. If he'd wanted to make a run for it, he could have made it. The other two men were still standing there, eyeing everybody. The taxi was pulling away. I tried to contact you, left messages. I didn't know what to do."

"There was nothing you could have done," Haden said.

"You've been reported missing," Matz said. "Willi Hofer rang me to ask if I knew where you were."

"Who called him?" Haden was a little surprised. It seemed like forever since he had stepped out of that elevator, but in fact it had been less than forty-eight hours.

"I don't know. Mrs. Baron, perhaps. I don't think Hofer took it very seriously. He assumed you'd gone off somewhere without telling anyone."

"Tell him I had," Haden said. "I think Willi Hofer would rather not know what really happened." Harold Leyton emerged from the inn and was making for the car. "Get in the back and catch up on your sleep, Erwin," Haden said. "I'll take your gun."

Leyton eased into the passenger seat with an embarrassed smile.

"It occurred to me that it would be comforting to travel with a gun on board," he said. "And the local cabbie wasn't likely to have one."

"I thought you might feel that way," Haden said, and handed Leyton the gun.

Leyton checked the automatic expertly and rested it in his lap.

"Right, driver," he said. "Let's go."

Erwin Matz was curled up on the back seat, sleeping peacefully. Harold Leyton remained alert, his hand with the automatic in it relaxed but ready in his lap, his eyes darting everywhere as their car traversed the valley road and joined another that looped around the Semmering Pass and led toward Wiener Neustadt, where they joined the Graz–Vienna Autobahn.

Once on the Autobahn, with its constant flow of traffic, Leyton's vigilance increased, if anything, but the drive was uneventful.

A map at the inn had shown Haden that the village of Steinbach was deep in the Styrian Alps. A footnote recorded as a local item of interest a labyrinth of limestone caves. The network was thought to include some ten kilometers of passages, some possibly as yet undiscovered. Haden supposed that he and Harold Leyton had sampled one of them.

It took them little more than an hour to reach Vienna airport once they had crossed the Semmering Pass. Haden parked the car and switched off the engine.

Leyton sighed and handed Haden the gun. Erwin Matz stirred and then sat up.

"Take this," Haden said, passing him the automatic, "and go back to sleep."

Haden and Leyton stood studying the departures posted at the terminal.

"If I were you," Leyton said, "I'd get out of this place now. Catch the next plane before they pick up your trail again. Have your man collect your things from Bad Gastberg and send them on. I think you've used up your luck, Stephen."

"There is money lodged in the safe," Haden said. "They wouldn't give it to him."

"Well, it's your life," Leyton said philosophically, "but just in case you lose it in the near future, I'd like to settle up now—if it's all the same to you." Haden found a seat and took out his checkbook. "Cash, if you please," Leyton said firmly. "Checks either bounce or they're something for the grasping bastards to tax."

Haden showed him his wallet.

"The real cash is at Bad Gastberg," he said. "You'll have to come with me if you want it in full. You can take these few hundred schillings on account. Or you can have a check. I'm sure you can launder it somehow. It's up to you."

"I suppose I'll have to trust you," Leyton said grudgingly. Haden wrote the check and handed it over. Leyton regarded it, frowning. "You must still be concussed," he said. He tucked the check away. "However, it's not my place to query this unexpected generosity."

"For services rendered," Haden said. "I owe you."

"True," Leyton agreed. "You got me into it. All that crap about having cracked Dante, the Ninth Circle." He stared at Haden with sudden suspicion. "Have you got it worked out? Is that why you're getting rid of me?"

"I haven't and it isn't," Haden said wearily. "They're calling your flight. Go or stay. Make up your mind."

"You are concussed," Leyton said. "You should see a doctor."

He stood up and walked toward the departure lounge.

Haden went back to the parking garage, woke Erwin Matz, and drove into Vienna. The Mercedes station wagon was just where he'd left it, on the same deck in the same parking space. It did not appear to have been tampered with. Haden unlocked it and slid into the driver's seat. His fingers found the concealed compartment. The small Beretta was still there.

"What now?" Matz asked, smothering a yawn.

"I'm damned if I know, Erwin," Haden answered.

At Bad Gastberg, Haden stopped at the reception desk to ask if there had been any phone calls for him.

"Several, Mr. Haden," the receptionist said. "Mr. Ralph Janson, Mr. Walter Gorman, and Mr. Erwin Matz. They all asked to have you call back. And a policeman named Hofer asked if we knew where you were."

"Thank you," Haden said. "Nothing from a Miss Helen Lloyd?"

"I don't think so, Mr. Haden. Let me make quite certain." She double-checked. "No."

"Perhaps she didn't leave her name," Haden suggested.

"The call would still have been recorded," the woman said definitely. "No lady has telephoned."

Petra Baron was eating lunch. She waved and smiled when she caught his eye. Haden's overcoat was folded over his arm, and he thought his suit would pass inspection. He went into the dining room and sat beside her.

"You've turned up at last, then," she said, unconcerned, looking at him across her salad. "Ralph Janson has been asking for you."

"What did he want?"

"He didn't say. I think he left a message. I told him you were back from Zurich, but that you'd gone off again somewhere and I didn't know where."

"Right on all counts," Haden said. "How are things here?"

"Boring," Petra replied. "I don't know why I stayed on. You're never here. Jerry's working all hours rehearsing his damned opera. I think I'll check out when Ralph leaves. Fly to London and see Peter, maybe. I miss him a lot." There was a touch of defiance in her eyes. "I do miss him, all the time."

259

"Why shouldn't you?" Haden said. "He's your son."

"It's the way you look at me," Petra said. A waiter had arrived and was proffering a menu. Haden waved him away. "A glass of wine?" Petra asked. Haden shook his head. "Ralph thinks I should settle in the States." She stopped eating and pushed her plate aside. "I could go back on his staff. Or maybe work for the foundation, where I could use my Russian. But Peter is in school in England. I don't know . . . I always thought the British school would be a temporary thing. But he likes it there, feels safe. I can tell that, the way he talks about it, every time I call him. He has no father, and he's found a kind of security there he needs. I'm not sure I should take him away. Ralph says he'd be just as happy somewhere else. But I'm not so sure. And I wouldn't want to live in the States if he stayed on."

"You have to decide what you'd really like," Haden said.

"Oh, that's easy," Petra said. "I'd like everything to be different. I wish I hadn't screwed it up with Alex. I wish I could go back and start again. I wish I weren't me. Then everything would be okay." She smiled sorrowfully. "But then wishes come cheap, don't they?"

"Do you ever wish Peter had never been born?" Haden asked.

"God, no," Petra said. She stared at him, her smile fading into a look of reproach. "How can you ask that?"

"Because I wasn't quite sure," Haden said.

"On account of the way I am, you mean," Petra said, subdued. "I know how it must look sometimes, but he is my child, and I love him. Really. He's all I have now. As to the rest, I suppose I've always been looking for something, and when I had it, I didn't know it. So I lost it." She cupped her cheek in one palm and stared past Haden toward the window. "I wanted to be both married and free. I think Alex would have stopped the Vienna thing if I'd asked him to. But I didn't. When he was away, I could be free." Her eyes swiveled to Haden's. "So what happened to him was really my fault."

Not for the first time, Haden wondered if she had a need to dramatize all events in personal terms, if she found some enjoyment in it.

"I thought you were all sorted out," he said. "Look to the future and all that."

"That wore off," Petra said. "Now I don't know what to do."

"I expect you'll do whatever Ralph Janson thinks is best," Haden said.

"You think I'm some sort of Trilby to his Svengali, is that it?" Petra inquired, with rather more self-perception than Haden had given her credit for. "Well, maybe there's some truth in that. For a long time now he's been someone I could rely on. He's always helped me, known what's best for me. He could be right this time, too. I wish I knew. Tell me what you think, Stephen."

"You'll get no advice from me," Haden said. "You might take it and then blame me forever after."

"Sure. There's no reason why you should care about me," Petra said. Her lips trembled. "All I asked was a little help, for Christ's sake."

But her voice remained low-pitched. She was still very conscious of her surroundings, of the people at nearby tables. Haden smiled at her and stood up.

"I don't know if I can help you, Petra," he said. "I don't know if anyone can. If I can find out before you leave, I'll let you know."

Once in his room Haden discarded his clothes and took a long bath. He toweled himself dry, took out a shirt just back from the laundry and discarded its cardboard stiffener, and selected another suit. Reaction was setting in, fatigue gripped him, and his mind was fuzzy. He left the jacket on its hanger and lay down on the bed, thinking he would rest for just a moment. Almost at once he fell deeply asleep.

Daylight was just beginning to fade when he awoke. The sky outside was still bright, but only the tip of the declining sun showed above the distant hills. He reached for the guide to Austria that lay on the bedside cabinet and found the map of the area in which he had been confined.

He was feeling a good deal better, his mind clear. He laid the guide aside and studied the ceiling instead. As the physical effects of his ordeal began to wear off, his resentment increased. He felt he was entitled to a certain vindictiveness. Locating a target for it was another matter.

He lay where he was for some time, his eyes fixed on the ceiling, examining what he knew, what he had thought he knew, and how his previous hypotheses needed to be modified.

It was a mental game of chess, regarding the situation neutrally and attempting to eliminate any preconceived notions. He studied every piece remaining on the board. He replayed each move in the game so far, first from the point of view of black, and then of white. He wondered how the game would progress, what the next move would be, who would make it. The trouble was that one or more of the pieces bore the wrong color: black was impersonating white, white impersonating black. Which? Or suppose it was both?

Hanging somewhere over the whole thing was the Ninth Circle. Dante's definition of treachery as the ultimate sin. Again he considered Count Ugolino and his useless repentance for his crimes. That judgment, though, was Dante's, the received notion of the time. He wondered if *Ugolino* had considered himself a traitor. Probably not, human nature being what it is. More likely the Count was merely just an early exponent of the maxim that the means justify the ends.

In that interpretation, black and white were in the eye of

the beholder. Black need not be truly black, or camouflaged as white. Black could persuade itself that its moves were born of necessity, kept concealed at all costs only because they might be misinterpreted and lead to its loss of position—but underneath, black might consider itself pure white. The human animal was capable of persuading itself of almost anything. Haden was still musing along these lines when the telephone rang.

"Mr. Walter Gorman is here, Mr. Haden. He asks if he can see you."

"Send him up," Haden said.

Haden slid off the bed, feeling irritated by the interruption to his train of thought, and unlocked the door. He had just slipped on his jacket and was adjusting his tie when there was a knock.

"Come in," he called. He heard the door open and close and turned to face Walter Gorman.

Gorman was gazing at him with a look of concern, which melted into relief.

"I must be getting jumpy," he said. "Imagining things."

"You don't seem the type to me, Walter," Haden said.

"It's not like me," Gorman agreed. "Maybe I need a vacation." He flashed a self-deprecating smile of apology. "You see, I called you a couple of nights ago. You weren't here, no one had seen you. Early next morning, the same thing. And you hadn't been back. I kept trying, finally got really worried, called Hofer and told him you could be missing. Sorry."

"No need to apologize, Walter," Haden said. "You were right."

The earnest smile vanished and was replaced by a frown. "Something did happen?"

"The KGB took me," Haden said.

"Oh, Jesus. That's what I was afraid of. I did—No, forget it."

"You did warn me," Haden said. "and I ignored you. I know. I should have listened."

"Well, shit," Gorman said, embarrassed. "You're okay, that's the main thing. I mean, you look okay, anyway."

"Perhaps," Haden said. "The only thing I feel good about is that I got away."

Gorman nodded, planted himself in a chair, and became businesslike.

"What can you tell me? Any way we can identify the bastards and maybe take care of them?"

"Nothing," Haden said. "I didn't see their faces or the license plates of the vehicle they were using. Have you got any ideas?"

"As yet we haven't managed to penetrate the KGB," Gorman said. "More's the pity. Where did they take you? Across the border someplace?"

Haden showed him the location on the map in the guidebook. Gorman blew out his cheeks in outrage at what, it seemed, was a flagrant breach of some unspoken rule.

"Here in Austria?" he demanded, affronted. "Those bastards have a goddamn nerve." He met Haden's quizzical glance. "This is supposed to be a neutral zone," he explained. "Everyone keeps a low profile. Stunts like that are out."

"Perhaps you should lodge a complaint," Haden suggested.

Either Gorman chose to ignore Haden's sarcasm or he hadn't caught it. "I could take it up with the Austrian Foreign Ministry," he said. "I'd see a senior official. He'd make notes and inform the Russian embassy. The Russians would deny it." He spread his hands and shrugged. "End of story. What could I do? You're not even an American citizen."

"You mean I should deal with it myself?" Haden asked. "Go through the Swiss embassy?"

"You could try that, I guess," Gorman said, his expression doubtful. "God knows you have a legitimate complaint. It would help if you had some hard evidence."

"I don't," Haden admitted. "They spoke Russian. That's all I know."

"I'll have my people look around this cave," Gorman said, tapping the map. "See if we can come up with something."

"They'll have cleaned it out by now," Haden said.

"We'll check it out, anyway. You never know. What did those KGB bastards want? Just to scare you off? Or something specific?"

"Information concerning Baronin," Haden said.

"I don't get this," Gorman grumbled. "They know all about Baronin. Chiefly, that he's dead." He stared very hard at Haden. "Unless he isn't," he said.

"That's what they seemed to be wondering," Haden said. "Perhaps they haven't got a body, either."

"Who cares about Baronin, anyway?" Gorman inquired irritably. "It's beyond me."

"Me too, Walter," Haden said. "Anything else?"

"Yes." Gorman shook off his incipient depression. "Mr. Janson has to leave soon. He'd like to see you before he goes. That's why we were calling you in the first place."

"Fine," Haden agreed. "When?"

"He's pressed for time," Gorman said. "So the answer is now. Provided you feel up to it, of course."

"Suits me," Haden said. "Where is he?"

"I'll take you there, but I may have to stay over. Suppose you follow me in your car?"

"Give me a few minutes to get ready," Haden said. "I'll meet you outside."

"Okay," Gorman said. "I can phone Mr. Janson from downstairs."

He got up and nodded, smiling one of the bare-teeth smiles he seemed to believe were friendly, and went out.

Haden fetched his trench coat and found his fur hat stuffed in the pocket of his overcoat. A brushing improved its appearance, but it was still crumpled and shapeless. He thought it could use some stiffening. He cut some pieces of the shirt cardboard he had discarded, opening up the seam in the lining of his hat, inserted the cardboard, donned the hat, and gazed at the result in the mirror.

It looked pretty good now and stood up nicely. He took the hat off again and, while playing with it some more, dialed a number, laid the receiver down, and let it ring.

It took him a couple of minutes more before he was finally satisfied with the fur hat's appearance. The receiver was still monotonously emitting the ringing tone.

Haden hung up reluctantly, cutting off his lifeline. He had expected an answer. He had relied on an answer.

Soon after they passed through Bad Gastberg, the lights of Gorman's Audi went on in the gathering dusk. Haden, following, turned his on, too. Gorman turned away from the direction of Vienna and led him southwest. Gorman drove smoothly, unhurriedly.

Haden switched his radio on, turned the dial experimentally, found some Bach, and settled down to enjoy it as they drove through a sequence of valleys. It appeared that it was going to be a longer drive than he had anticipated.

It was dark night, but he could see the hills growing steep and closing in, the shapes of the mountains rising beyond. Bach had become Mozart by the time they turned off the valley road. They were climbing now. Haden thought they were somewhere in the Fischbacher Alps. Gorman turned off again. The grade increased, and the road became a series of tight S-bends. The timberline was thinning. They had climbed a long way. Gorman slowed and signaled his next turn well in advance, giving Haden plenty of warning.

Haden slowed, too. Gorman's car turned and was lost from sight. Haden made his turn. In his headlights he could see that Gorman had stopped at a barrier a few yards ahead. Beside the barrier was a one-story building. An armed guard wearing a greatcoat was inspecting Gorman's pass. Haden pulled up behind and lowered his window. He heard the guard say, "Thank you, Mr. Gorman, sir." The guard walked back to Haden's Mercedes and bent down to the open window.

"Would you kindly step out outside, Mr. Haden," he said politely, speaking, Haden thought, in the accents of one of the southern states of the U.S.A. "Leave your keys in the ignition, please."

Ahead, the barrier rose, and Gorman's car passed through and then stopped. The barrier came down again. Haden did as he had been asked. The air outside was thin and very cold. The building was overheated. Walter Gorman came in through another door.

"Sorry, Mr. Haden," he said. "We're entering a high-security area. Routine precautions."

He began chatting to the guard manning a bank of telephones. Haden went into the indicated cubicle. The greatcoated guard followed him and closed the door.

Haden took off his trench coat and handed it over.

"Your briefcase on that table, sir," the guard said. Haden complied. The guard checked the pockets of the trench coat, and then the rest of it, inch by inch. "Please raise your hands above your head, Mr. Haden, sir," the guard asked.

Haden lifted his hands high and leaned against the wall. The guard went over him thoroughly from the neck down and then turned to the briefcase.

"It's not locked," Haden said. The guard snapped it

open. Haden pulled on his trench coat. "Personal items," he said.

The guard made quite certain that was all they were and returned the briefcase to him.

"Thank you very much, sir," he said.

Haden followed Gorman outside again. His Mercedes was parked at the back of the guardhouse.

"No unauthorized vehicles are allowed beyond this point," Gorman explained.

Haden got into the Audi. Gorman drove on. The road crossed a bridge that spanned a ravine and then twisted into a long climb. Gorman took it in a leisurely fashion, staying in low gear. The headlights played alternately on rockface and empty space the other side of white barrier posts.

The road seemed to be climbing around the side of a giant buttress. Clouds obscured the upper reaches. There was no indication of their destination until the Audi went through a short tunnel, from which they emerged onto a huge, perfectly flat expanse—an enormous ledge, in effect.

Gorman stopped the car and turned off the ignition.

"We're there," he said, and got out.

Haden followed and looked around. The ledge also could easily serve as a helicopter pad. Lights emanated from the long, low windows of a large Alpine-style house, built into the rockface some fifty or sixty feet above them. A terrace ran in front of the windows the full width of the house. In daylight the view from that terrace down into the long, deep valley below them must have been spectacular.

"A nice little retreat," Haden said appreciatively. "Somewhere for the ambassador or important visitors to spend quiet weekends?"

Gorman looked around blankly, as though oblivious to the scenic attractions.

"Strictly a functional working establishment," he said.

The house perched above them appeared to be clinging to the side of the buttress. There was no obvious means of access. Gorman led the way toward the rockface. As they approached the seemingly impenetrable wall, a shadowed rectangle appeared. In a moment, it resolved into a steel door that Gorman opened.

Inside, a short corridor led to an elevator. Gorman summoned it, and they stepped in. The elevator moved smoothly upward. The shaft and the corridor had been driven through solid rock. Building this place must have cost a fortune.

The elevator stopped, the door opened, and they stepped out into a reception area. A handsome woman sat behind a desk, watching the screen of the word processor she was operating. She looked up. There were two telephones beside her.

"Please tell Mr. Janson that Mr. Haden has arrived, Carol," Gorman said.

"He's using the secure link to Washington, Mr. Gorman," the woman replied.

Gorman nodded and pointed. Haden sat down and waited. The woman resumed work, her fingers playing silently on the keys. When the light on one of the telephones beside her went out, she lifted the receiver, spoke into it, and then replaced it.

"Please come this way, Mr. Haden," she said.

"My stuff ready, Carol?" Gorman inquired.

"The file's on the desk, Mr. Gorman."

She led Haden along a narrow carpeted corridor, tapped on a door, opened it, announced him, and withdrew with a smile. Haden went in.

Ralph Hanson was sitting behind a large desk, the top of which was clean, save for the documents he had been studying. His glasses lay on the desktop. Behind him, floor-to-ceiling windows gave on to the terrace.

He stood and smiled as Haden entered, leaned forward, and shook hands warmly.

"I'm deeply obliged to you for coming, Mr. Haden," he said. "Please make yourself comfortable."

He indicated a deep leather couch angled at the side of the desk. Haden took off his trench coat and fur hat, laid them on the couch, and stood for a moment looking out of the windows.

"Somewhat reminiscent of the Eagle's Nest at Berchtesgaden," he said.

"It serves its purpose," Janson said indifferently. "Complete security and just a short hop by helicopter from Vienna. Do smoke if you wish." Haden sat down. Janson rotated his chair to face him. "We don't have much time," he said. "I'm expecting a return call from Washington, so if you'll forgive me, I'll leave it to Walter to offer you a meal or a drink, whatever you feel like." Haden nodded and lit his cheroot. Janson gazed at Haden with a troubled expression. "I'm deeply sorry to hear of your recent experience, Mr. Haden," he said. "I do hope it wasn't too bad."

"It wasn't too good," Haden said.

"Of course. And I blame myself. Allowing you to act without protective surveillance was a bad mistake, for which I am responsible. I should never have agreed."

"All the mistakes have been mine, Mr. Janson." Haden said.

"You've very gracious," Janson said. "The fact remains that Walter Gorman was very much against it, and because I disregarded his advice, your life was put in jeopardy. That must not happen again, Mr. Haden."

"A conclusion I've reached myself," Haden said.

"We agree then," Janson said, with a nod of his fine head and a slight smile. "You may also agree that it would be foolhardy, since you have been identified and targeted by the opposition, to continue your efforts to reinstate Baron's contact."

"I've already ruled myself out," Haden said. "I'll leave that to your people."

"Ah, but we don't know who the contact is," Janson pointed out.

"I do," Haden said.

"A 'result' in this case, as defined," Janson said, "was the resumption of the previous arrangement. A name is not a result."

"I'd say it was half of it," Haden replied. "I have done all the hard work."

Janson assented. "Very well. Half the fee to which we agreed for a result."

"The name is Oleg Tushin," Haden said. "He's a backroom boy with the Russian delegation."

"Fine," Janson said. "Fine." He leaned forward to write on a notepad, sat back again, and gazed at Haden thoughtfully. "Walter informs me that the KGB questioned you about Baron," he said. "What did you tell them?"

"That he was dead," Haden answered.

"Their interest could imply that he might not be," Janson said.

"I was relying on the evidence," Haden said. "Bloodstained passport, et cetera."

"The evidence is not entirely conclusive."

"No, but it's good enough for him to be presumed dead."

"In some minds, a doubt lingers," Janson insisted.

"I see," Haden said. "And how much would Baronin be worth?"

Janson's smile had become automatic, its initial warmth gone. "Does everything have a price tag in the world you inhabit, Mr. Haden?" he inquired.

"Nothing comes for free in my experience," Haden said. Janson took a deep breath and let it out slowly.

"Is Baron alive or dead?" he demanded directly. "And if alive, do you know where he is?"

"We still haven't established his worth," Haden said.

"He's an American citizen and Petra's husband," Janson said, a note of cool disdain in his voice. "That's his worth. Frankly, Mr. Haden, I find your habit of holding every little item back in case it has some market value quite tiresome. I do have to deal with you, but let's get one thing clear. No more dribs and drabs. *If* Alex Baron is alive, *and* you can tell me where he is, that information will be worth fifty thousand dollars."

"I might have something concerning Baronin," Haden admitted.

Janson said bleakly. "It's all or nothing. No bits or pieces."

"It comes in bits and pieces," Haden said. He took one of the books from the briefcase, leaned forward and put it on the desk. Janson looked at it, puzzled, and then at Haden. "Take a look," Haden said.

"Dante?" Janson frowned and began to flip through the pages.

"The title page," Haden said.

Janson went back, glanced at it, and then up at Haden, questioningly.

"What about it?"

"Try the artwork," Haden said. Janson did so, then lifted his glasses and held them several inches from his nose, peering through the left-hand lens. "There are eight circles," Haden said. "There should be nine. You know what the Ninth Circle represents?"

"You'll have to remind me," Janson said. "It's a long time since I read Dante."

"The region of Hell reserved for traitors," Haden said.

Janson returned his glasses to the desk with a gesture of

272

irritation. "Are you trying to tell me this has something to do with Alex Baron?" he inquired frigidly.

"It's one of the pieces," Haden said. "The people who killed Freddy Webb missed it."

Chapter Fifteen

Stephen Haden tapped ash from his cheroot into the ashtray. The silence was broken by the ringing of one of the telephones on Ralph Janson's desk. Janson lifted the receiver. "Yes?" He listened. "Say I'll call him back shortly." He replaced the receiver, sat back, and stared at Haden.

"Webb was killed while you were in London," Haden said. "You might have read about it." Janson shook his head—to all appearances, mystified. "Webb was a disaffected British agent," Haden went on. "He thought that missing ninth circle was worth a small fortune."

Janson laughed. "I can't imagine why," he said. "You're not being overly clear, Mr. Haden."

Freddy Webb had gotten one thing wrong. Either that or Stephen Haden had gotten everything wrong. It was too late to consider that now.

"Whether it began by chance or by design, I don't know," Haden said. "By design from the beginning would be my guess, but either way, Baronin, safely married to your protégée, was offered information in Vienna. He asked you what he should do."

"Perfectly correct," Janson said. "I took advice on the

matter and, on the basis of that, encouraged him to go ahead.''

Haden said, "For a long time, everything went smoothly. But then some unexpected factors emerged. One of them was Petra.''

"What about Petra?''

"She has problems,'' Haden said. "Like everybody. But hers run deep. She copes, she functions, but inside there's some kind of underlying neurosis, or suppressed guilt, or scars that won't heal—perhaps all three. Her college education didn't cancel out a lousy childhood.''

"Aside from your more dubious qualifications, you are also a trained analyst, I gather,'' Janson said sardonically.

"Tell me I'm wrong,'' Haden said.

"You're wrong,'' Janson said. "Petra had a poor start in life. So do many people. That's all in the past, and she got over it long ago. As you would expect from anyone with her qualities.''

"You wear blinkers, Mr. Janson,'' Haden said.

Janson looked at his watch, a barely controlled gesture of impatience. "If you have a point, kindly come to it,'' he said. "I have a call to make. You said you had information concerning Alex.'' He pushed the copy of Dante away with the tip of one finger. "Thus far, I've heard none.''

"The information is this,'' Haden said. "Baronin's work for the CIA was confined to the radio station in Munich. He had no authorized intelligence role.''

"Then I fail to understand,'' Janson said, "why you have just sold me the name of the man''—he glanced down at his note—"Oleg Tushin, whom you claim to have identified as Alex's contact.''

"He was,'' Haden said. "Through him Baronin acquired information. Petra acted as courier. She flew with it to Washington, where it was collected for onward transmis-

275

sion. That was the part she played, and she liked it. It gave her the chance to see old friends."

"I have no way of knowing whether that is true or not," Janson said, frowning slightly. "I certainly wasn't aware that Petra was involved." He caressed his cheek; the frown deepened. "But then I guess she wouldn't have told me," he said reluctantly. "Not if she was being used as courier on a highly secret link like that. I suppose it could be true," he admitted, "although I can't say I like it."

"With all the resources at the disposal of the CIA," Haden said, "you don't think it strange that sensitive documents hot from a Russian informer should be transmitted stuffed in a briefcase and carried by a woman traveling unaccompanied on scheduled flights?"

Janson shifted impatiently. "I can't answer for the methods of our intelligence services," he said.

"Ah, well, this wasn't a CIA operation," Haden said. "The CIA was bypassed. Once Petra handed the information on, every scrap vanished from sight until it turned up in the higher reaches of the White House."

Janson sat quite still, his gaze fixed on Haden, his face darkening as he took in the implications. "That's one hell of a serious allegation," he said slowly, at last. "You'd better substantiate it."

"You're better placed to do that than I am," Haden retorted.

"I can't start a hare like that, for God's sake, just on your say-so. You have no standing. They'd think I was crazy. If you're serious, you have to give me something more substantial. Some idea of who might be responsible."

"I rather thought it might be you," Haden said mildly.

"Me?" Janson queried, duly astonished. "Me?" he repeated, the mellow trumpet voice rising higher, his indignant outrage such that he half rose in his chair. Then he settled back slowly, his face rigid with anger, his nostrils

276

flaring as he controlled his breathing. He spoke very quietly. "What is this, Haden? You're a man who likes to line his pockets. Behind everything you do, that's the motive. Now it's crazy accusations. You must think there's something in it for you."

"There might be," Haden said.

Janson's head tilted slowly. The flicker of a humorless smile flitted across his face. "Your judgment is bad," he said softly. "I thought better of you."

"The evidence is circumstantial," Haden said, equally quietly. Had some subordinate opened the door and looked in, the two men would have appeared to be calmly engaged in discussing some usual, if weighty, business. "It hinges on the fact that for some years a complete shadow intelligence operation has been going on outside the knowledge of your official intelligence agency, entirely unsupervised. Run privately, mostly funded privately."

"Calling something a fact doesn't make it one," Janson said. "That's nothing but a wild assertion, with no foundation whatsoever."

"Yet you seem to object to initiating an investigation."

"Sure I do," Janson answered derisively. "I'd be laughed out of court."

"That's one possibility," Haden said. "The other is that you'd go to any lengths, and have done so already, to defend the power base it represents."

"When you start raving, you certainly go all the way," Janson observed judicially. "Now you've placed me at the center of some grand conspiracy."

"Well, someone is," Haden said. "At first, I thought it was a simple matter of betrayal. But that didn't fit. Then I wondered who might benefit most. That could fit nicely."

"You mean I don't get to be accused of being a traitor?" Janson asked, with a kind of tolerant jolliness. "Only benefit in some mysterious fashion. I guess that's something."

"The Baronin connection was code-named 'Dante' initially," Haden continued. "That got changed when, despite all the precautions, the word 'Dante' floated to the surface in Washington. That was when Freddy Webb first became interested in it. While the connection was operating, you rose ever higher in presidential esteem. You have a President who doesn't like detail or reading background documents. He likes it simple and easy from a handful of trusted advisers. His chief preoccupation was with Russian intentions. You gave him what he wanted, no mass of complicated detail, no ifs and buts, nice and simple, straight from the horse's mouth. He liked that. He came to rely on you absolutely. You're a man of unlimited ambition, Mr. Janson. With the President's trust and approval, you thought you'd be a good fit for his shoes, especially if he made it known that he backed the idea."

"We live in a democracy, thank God," Janson said tartly. "The President does not choose his successor. Your ignorance of our electoral system surprises me."

"The word is that you intend to run," Haden said. "You have access to the necessary money. You have influence. You believe you have the necessary qualities. If the President came out in your favor, your chances would be good. His backing would be essential, and you thought you had it. Then Baronin passed a warning. If he was right, the Russians knew all about the Dante source and were using it for their own ends. And if that was so, your whole campaign strategy was in ruins."

"If I may interrupt these lunatic accusations for a moment," Janson said. "I had that checked out immediately after you mentioned it. I was informed that every scrap of information received had been analyzed meticulously and verified."

"My guess would be," Haden said, "that it was assessed within the Burnham Foundation before you took it to the

President. I'm sure your wife employs highly paid and skillful experts, but they were dealing with Russian experts, and they weren't good enough to sift the disinformation from the information. So it slipped through and the President took it for gospel."

The only reaction Janson displayed was closer to veiled contempt than anything else.

"I love my country, Haden," he said. "I've served and defended America. If you really think I would do anything to prejudice her security, even by default, you're not just raving, you're insane."

"Freddy Webb got one small thing wrong," Haden said. "The missing Ninth Circle was intended to be a symbol of treachery. He'd spent his life working in intelligence, and that was how he saw it, how he was intended to see it. But there was another possible explanation he didn't think of."

"But your fertile mind has?" Ralph Janson asked. "What was it? Do tell me."

"That a man could want power so much, could believe so profoundly that he was the only man fitted to exercise that power, that he could persuade himself that any means, no matter what, were justified to achieve it. Of course, such a man would also be slightly mad. Maybe you did tell the people at the Burnham Foundation to double-check their analyses. But the information had to keep on flowing or you would lose your hold on the President's attention and favor. And Baronin had become a threat to that. When he disappeared last summer, the source dried up. There'd have been some information in the pipeline to keep the President happy for a while, but by the turn of the year, you were becoming desperate." Janson raised his eyebrows and smiled, as if the idea of his ever being desperate was ludicrous.

Haden went on doggedly. "That was why you employed me," he said. "Oh, not to find Baronin. That was just a blind. After a decent interval, *you* set up a 'result' for me to find. Then you offered me the real business. To identify Baronin's contact. You had to find out who he was, to get the source going again, phony information or not. The President was getting restless." Haden looked out the window. The clouds were breaking up. Beyond the terrace lay the spectacular landscape illuminated by the cold light of the moon.

"Someone did all that, Mr. Janson," Haden said. "It would take someone very ruthless and single-minded, someone in dire pursuit of something. All through history there have been men who would do anything for power. You wouldn't be the first. Nor will you be the last." Haden's expression was grim. Then he smiled. "But I'm an open-minded man," he said. "Convince me otherwise." He stared hard at Janson. "If you can," he challenged.

"It's not a bad smear, as smears go," Janson said reflectively. "Joe McCarthy would have been proud of you, Haden. Make all kinds of groundless accusations, and the more the victim defends himself, the more he digs his own grave. Meat for the press, I guess, even if it does stink." He toyed with his fountain pen, rolling it to and fro on the desk. "I begin to see the way your mind is working. You think you can squeeze me. Right?"

"You're the lawyer, but you haven't mentioned libel," Haden said. "I suppose you've already ruled that out."

"Libel? I'd call it criminal blackmail," Janson said, rolling his pen gently.

"Freddy Webb must have calculated that you wouldn't risk the courts," Haden said. "He got that much right. You could always step down, of course, resign from government service, try to cover your tracks. You could live in seclusion on your wife's money."

"In whatever capacity I am called upon to serve my country," Janson said, "I intend to do so."

"Freddy knew that, too," Haden said. "He intended to

280

use a front man, stay in the background himself. Freddy used to be a plant in Washington. I expect it works the other way, too. Someone realized what he was fishing for.''

Janson sighed and began to tap his pen monotonously on the desk.

"I'm tired of your fantasies, Haden," he said. "They verge on the demented. You house of cards has no foundation. The higher you try to build it—" He stood his pen upright on his desk. It fell over. "Don't waste your time," Janson said.

"I'll just add one more card," Haden said pleasantly. "This is even more speculative. Call it a guess."

"Such sudden modest forbearance," Janson said, amused. "Only a guess this time?"

"It concerns Petra," Haden said.

"What about Petra?"

"Her relationship with you seemed strange," Haden said. "A kind of Trilby to your Svengali. Her words, not mine. At first I thought she was sleeping with you. Then I realized she wasn't."

"You're missing a trick there, Haden," Janson said sardonically. "Accusations of adultery have killed other men's careers."

"You married your heiress wife the same month Petra was adopted," Haden said. "The adoption went wrong. Her adoptive parents were divorced. Instead of a prosperous, stable home, she was living in a shabby apartment, not much cared for, not much wanted. Suddenly there's money available for a high-class school in the East. Petra thinks it came from a trust fund set up by her adoptive father. Then she works in your private office. After she's married, you're always in touch. You're still close. I think she's your daughter, Mr. Janson."

Janson's face could have been carved from stone.

281

"I almost feel sorry for you, Haden," he said. "You burrow in the dirt like a man who loves it."

"I've only compared copies of certificates and thought about it," Haden admitted. "I expect a good investigative journalist could do better."

"You may see that as a threat," Janson said with deadly calm. "You don't know me very well."

"Whether you sent Petra to Moscow to get Baronin," Haden said, "used your own daughter as bait, I don't know. Anyway, she did it. You arranged his defection. They were married almost at once. You and Marianne have no children. Peter seems to have been a somewhat premature baby. I think Peter could be your son, Mr. Janson." Janson's set face was now the color of stone as well, although his eyes flamed with anger. "Tests could no doubt establish paternity," Haden added. "But the way it looks to me, you didn't mind Baronin's believing Peter was his. Petra, too, for all I know. After all, you left her alone. Become a friend, a father figure. You were satisfied. Even if he couldn't be acknowledged, you had a son. As he grew up, well, I'm sure you had that planned, too."

"Have you quite finished now?" Haden nodded. "And what precisely do you expect me to do?" Janson inquired icily.

"There's only one thing you can do," Haden said.

"Apart from telling you that you are a man who deals in foul and evil lies," Janson said, "which seems superfluous, I will repeat my previous offer for information concerning Alex Baron."

"We're not talking about Baronin," Haden said. "We're talking about you."

"This is where I offer you a small fortune for silence, is that it? Or possibly a large one?" Janson picked up the copy of Dante and threw it toward the couch. Haden caught it. Janson spoke into the phone. "Send Walter Gorman in, please." His voice was steady and controlled. He wrote on his notepad again, tore another slip off, and looked at Haden.

"I do not bow to blackmail," he said. "But once I have given my word, even to scum such as you, I keep it." Walter Gorman came in. Janson held out the two slips of paper. Gorman walked over to the desk and took them. "Mr. Haden cannot help us with Alex Baron," Janson said. "This is the final amount owing to him. Please see to it. As of now, Mr. Haden will no longer be working with us."

The news did not seem to distress Walter Gorman unduly. He retreated to the door and held it open. Haden gathered up his belongings.

"Goodbye, Mr. Haden," Janson said, as he lifted one of his telephones. As Haden went through the door, he heard Janson say, "You may place that return call now, Carol, if you please."

Haden followed Gorman back along the carpeted corridor and into the reception area.

"You're through now, sir," Carol was saying. Gorman checked his watch.

"You want something to eat?" he inquired. The grin spread across his face. "The food's really good here. The wine, too."

"Not for me," Haden said. "I'll eat at Bad Gastberg."

"Okay," Gorman said. He fingered the slip of paper. "I'll just take care of this and then see you back to your car. I'm staying over. Shan't be long."

He moved along another corridor and out of sight. Haden pulled on his trench coat, buckled it, and put on his fur hat. He flicked through a copy of *Time* magazine without taking any of it in. He had committed a serious error of judgment, a truly stupendous blunder. He should have known better. That'll teach you to think you can rely on bluffing and second-guessing, you arrogant bastard, he thought savagely. He wondered how to put it right, where to go next, and had no answer.

Walter Gorman came back, his overcoat over his arm, and handed Haden a package. Haden checked the dollar contents and put it in his briefcase. Gorman thumbed the call button, and the elevator door opened.

"Good night, Mr. Haden," said Carol, with a pleasant smile.

They rode down until the elevator reached its lowest level and stopped. The doors slid open. Haden was facing the wrong way. It was the side opposite the one he had entered when he arrived.

Gorman's face wore the relaxed expression of man who had a Magnum in his hand. The Magnum was pointed at Haden's stomach.

"After you, Mr. Haden," Gorman said, his teeth gleaming as his lips parted in a grin.

Chapter Sixteen

Haden knew at once where he was. His own house in Zurich possessed a modest nuclear fallout shelter. This one was on a grand scale, and air-conditioned. Strip lights illuminated the corridors, telephones hung on the walls at intervals. There were signs pointing in various directions: DORMITORIES, MESS ROOM, COMMUNICATIONS, DECONTAMINATION, ARMORY, STORES, SHOWERS, TOILETS, GENERATOR ROOM, FUEL STORE, SICK BAY.

Those American personnel of sufficient importance to command a priority place and within helicopter range would assemble here after the final warning to sit out a nuclear war and its aftermath. Deep within the solid rock of a mountainside, the chosen survivors would be comfortable enough, if cramped for space, during their long and probably fruitless wait.

Walter Gorman directed him to walk. Haden glimpsed bunk beds, already made up, and basic built-in furniture as he passed open doors. Somewhere there must be manually controlled emergency exits. The designer would never have relied on those double elevator doors, which might malfunction.

Past the sick bay was a steel door with a grille set into it at head height and a key in the lock on the outside. Walter Gorman told him to go inside.

It was a cell, perhaps for disciplinary use during the long confinement, perhaps in case any of the privileged survivors went insane. The small table and two chairs were bolted to the floor. There was a toilet in one corner. A fresh roll of paper hung ready. The adjoining washbasin had soap and a towel. Like the facilities throughout the shelter, it was equipped for use at a moment's notice.

"My quarters, I expect," Haden said.

"For a while," Walter Gorman said. "A little while," he added. "Sit."

Haden laid his briefcase on the table, started to unbuckle his trench coat, paused, and looked at Gorman inquiringly.

"Sure," Gorman said affably. "Make yourself at home." Haden took off his trench coat, hung it over the back of the chair, laid his fur hat on the table, and sat down facing Walter Gorman, who reached out and took the briefcase. "You won't need spending money in here," he said. "Everything's been provided." He sat back comfortably and grinned at Haden. He laid the Magnum flat on the table, although his fingers retained their grip on it. Haden could see the ugly round hole from which the bullet would emerge.

"It's your call, Walter," he said.

"I'm going to put one question," Gorman said. "I may as well tell you that I won't mind at all if you don't answer it. You're an asshole, Haden. I never did like you."

"I'll try to make amends," Haden said. "Ask me."

"Where is Baronin?" The words came out slowly and deliberately spaced.

"Presumed dead," Haden said. "You should know, Walter. You fixed the evidence."

"Okay," Gorman said happily. "That was your chance to have it the easy way. Fine with me. There'll be no psychological bullshit this time around."

"I seem to remember some lunatic suggesting kidnapped terrorists should be stuck in cages all over Europe," Haden said. "I suppose you and your Russian-speaking goons decided to make use of one of them."

"You like to be smart, don't you?" Gorman said. "You're not so smart, or you wouldn't be here."

"You never spoke a truer word, Walter." Haden said.

"Time to notify the specialists they have work to do," Gorman said.

"Let me make a suggestion," Haden said.

Gorman said, "Hurry up. I'm hungry."

Haden said, "We talk. Then you decide if you want to call in the specialists. Maybe we can work out a deal."

"There's only one deal," Gorman said. "Baronin."

"That's your angle," Haden said. "The way things look so far, I don't seem to have one."

His eyes strayed to the Magnum. Walter Gorman's fingers caressed it. "Go ahead," he invited. "Make a grab for it."

"You've gotten away with a lot, Walter," Haden said. "But so far, you haven't killed a Swiss citizen. That would be something else."

"Do you know something?" Gorman reflected. "I don't think the Swiss government would get too excited if you disappeared mysteriously."

Privately Haden acknowledged that Gorman's argument was only too accurate.

"Give me a few minutes," Haden said. "You might find there's something in it for you, as well as for me."

"People buy you, Haden," Gorman said. "You're for sale. Me, I'm not on the take. Forget it. My salary suits me fine."

"And your prospects," Haden said. "Don't forget your prospects. There's patronage, Walter, even in the democratic United States of America. You oblige, and the future looks bright."

Gorman switched on a vacant grin, but his eyes were sharp. "On merit," he said. "You wouldn't understand that."

Haden said, "Duty and the flag, and sleep like a baby, right?" Gorman shifted slightly in his seat. He was beginning to look bored. "Wake up, Walter," Haden said. "You could be looking at disgrace and prison. Put a price tag on that."

Gorman ceased looking bored and regarded Haden with flat astonishment, which turned slowly into a small smile even more unnerving than his customary empty grin. "I'm wide-awake," he said. "You must be either stupid or crazy."

"Keep listening," Haden said. "Last summer, the Dante source looked like it was coming apart. Baronin was restive, and questioned its integrity. He was judged no longer reliable. Needed replacing. Only now it mattered that only *he* knew who his contact was. You had him kidnapped at the back of Sacher's Hotel. Perhaps he was due to sit in a cage until he gave you the name." He waited for a moment, but Walter Gorman merely continued to gaze at him with superficial interest. "That went wrong," Haden continued. "He got away. I expect you kicked a few backsides." Gorman smiled faintly. "Especially when," Haden went on, "the Austrian police asked you for a photograph of Baronin, and you learned there was a witness, Hans Kinsky. You got to Kinsky. Unlike you, Walter, he did take money. He obliged by failing to pick out Baronin's photograph. I expect you went on looking for Baronin, but you didn't know where to start. He'd vanished. And it had been your mistake, Walter. The pressure was on. When you heard through channels there was talk of hiring me to find him, you saw that as an insult. You arranged for a couple of hoodlums in London to break my leg or something—to discourage me. Then you found out your chief was backing me—that he didn't want me discouraged. I don't suppose he knows you were at the back of that mugging. Walter. He'd have been quite cross about it.''

Gorman sighed and glanced at his watch.

''Is this supposed to be leading somewhere?'' he asked.

''Stay with it, Walter,'' Haden said pleasantly. ''By the time I arrived in Vienna, it was getting really hard to convince the top that there was no problem with the Dante source. There were withdrawal symptoms in the White House. You managed to kill two birds with one stone when I offered Hans Kinsky money for information. Whatever yarn you'd sold him in the first place, he realized what he knew was more valuable than he'd imagined. So he went to you for more. He got it. He also got a bullet in the head, a faked suicide, and phony evidence planted in his luggage.''

Gorman stifled a yawn. ''I always thought you did that,'' he said. ''To achieve a 'result.' ''

''Oh, come on, Walter,'' Haden said. ''Where would I get Baronin's passport and photograph?''

''From Baronin,'' Gorman said. ''Which is how we knew you'd found him and you were playing some double game.''

Haden smiled at him. ''Save that one,'' he said. ''You might need it.''

''You're full of shit, Haden,'' Gorman observed dispassionately.

''Sometimes I get lucky, too,'' Haden said. '' 'Dante' was ready to take a chance on me. He told me just enough. You knew he was the right man. I'd also passed on that he wanted out, which didn't fit your plans, but you thought you could iron that out, once you found out who he was.''

''We just have,'' Gorman said blandly. ''Mr. Janson handed me a note with his name on it. Oleg Tushin. You gave it to him upstairs.''

"You knew already, Walter," Haden said. "It came to your notice that I'd arranged for him to defect. That wasn't as per script. You had someone planted in the station washroom. He was identified. Then he was intercepted, and discussions took place: either he was handed back to the KGB as a defector or he went back of his own free will and carried on as 'Dante' with a new contact, supplied by you, in place of Baronin. Tushin didn't have much choice. That left you with one loose end. Baronin. If he was alive, he could still come out into the open, talk, and blow it. Baronin needed to be kept quiet."

"We're concerned for his safety," Gorman said. "Where is he?"

"The real question," Haden said, "is whether you're Tweedledum or Tweedledee."

"Where can Baronin be reached?" Walter Gorman persisted. "That's all."

"Perhaps you're what you seem," Haden said. "A man who just takes orders. But maybe that's a blind. This scheme was yours, you've run the Dante source from the beginning, and you've been using Ralph Janson. If so, all you can do is change your name and enlist as a mercenary somewhere hot. On the other hand, if Ralph Janson has been using *you*, you might still be able to get away with it."

"You know what you remind me of?" Gorman said thoughtfully. "A worm with a hook, in its guts, wriggling."

"You've been responsible for a good many crimes, Walter," Haden said. "Although I suppose you'd call them covert operations, regrettable but necessary."

"In my line of work, that's the way it is sometimes," Gorman said philosophically. "Where's Baronin?"

"I'll offer you this," Haden said. "You get me out of here. Now. In return, I'll back you up if you say that you took orders from Ralph Janson believing they came from the President. Put the blame at Janson's door. You won't get any medals, you'll never get the big job—director of this or that—but if you bargain hard enough for immunity, you should stay out of jail. In your position, that's a good deal, Walter.''

"I hear nothing about Baronin," Gorman said. He stood up. "I'll tell the guys you want to see them."

"You're not being very bright, Walter," Haden said. "If I know, so do others. It's all over. Don't you understand that?"

Walter Gorman picked up the briefcase with his free hand and stared down at Haden, his deep-set eyes hard, the Magnum steady. Haden remained very still.

"Understand?" Gorman repeated. "Understand what? All I hear is lies. Okay, if it was spread around, it might cause trouble, but who's going to spread it? Not you, Haden. That British asshole? That cave's been checked out. My people called in while you were with Mr. Janson. The KGB had left a tape recorder. We played it. Heard everything you said to each other, including how you got out. You didn't tell him any of this garbage. Maybe you think there's someone else." He grinned suddenly and ferociously. "You may think you have friends, Haden. Let me tell you something. You haven't."

"I didn't realize how completely you'd been programmed, Walter," Haden said. "The cover story becomes reality. You dare not risk disentangling one from the other. Your whole world would collapse. There's no point in talking to you. Go away."

Gorman stood where he was. It occurred to Haden that Gorman did not really want to enlist the help of his specialists in interrogation. He would prefer to obtain Baronin's whereabouts himself. Earlier Haden would have regarded that as a weakness, a chink to be exploited. Now he did not. The man was invulnerable. All Haden wanted was for him to turn and go. He fiddled aimlessly with his fur hat.

"If I go, you wouldn't like what happens next," Gorman said. "Give me Baronin," he said, almost pleading. "I'll make it easy for you. That's a promise."

"According to the official evidence, Baronin is dead," Haden said.

Gorman sighed reluctantly. "Okay," he said. "I tried."

"We both tried, Walter," Haden said.

Walter Gorman retreated toward the half-open door of the cell, still unwilling to admit personal defeat. He turned slightly and put out a hand to push the door of the cell open. Haden's fingers sought the lining of his fur hat.

Gorman started to turn around. "Haden," he began, "I'll—" Some instinct warned him. He broke off and, still turning, crouched and swung his gun hand around.

Haden's fingers had found the Beretta, tucked behind the cardboard stiffening. When the bullet hit Walter Gorman his finger involuntarily pulled the Magnum trigger. The two explosions were almost simultaneous. The bullet from the Magnum smashed into the table. Splinters flew.

Gorman had been slightly off-balance when the bullet struck him, and he had been sent sprawling back against the wall. His gun hand had fallen, too, but he was raising it again.

Haden, already on his feet, flung himself at Gorman, crushing him against the wall. Gorman screamed in agony. Haden jammed Gorman's right arm to the floor, but there was no longer any need for force. The arm was limp; the fingers had no grip.

Haden took the Magnum, stood up, and tucked it in his waistband. Walter Gorman stayed where he was. His face had turned the color of parchment; his eyes were watering with pain. He felt shakily inside his jacket with his left hand, and looked at his bloodstained fingers.

"You shot me," he mumbled in disbelief. "You shot me."

"You wouldn't see reason," Haden explained. "I couldn't think of anything else to do."

Groaning, Gorman raised himself slowly to his feet and propped himself up against the wall. Haden stepped back a bit and watched him. Gorman fixed him with a defiant stare.

"You think you can use me? Is that it? No way, you bastard."

"I know," Haden said. "You'd rather die first."

"So now what? Finish me off? Okay," Gorman said with dignified pride. "Do it. Get it over with."

"Oh, don't be so bloody silly, Walter," Haden said, vexed. He waved to Beretta. "If you can stand up, you can walk. Over there."

Chapter Seventeen

Walter Gorman moaned and grunted a good deal as he staggered unevenly across the cell. He collapsed heavily onto the bunk bed, where he sat, trying to catch his breath, his eyes screwed up with pain.

"Let's take a look," Haden said. "Only you'll have to help. Like you, I've only got one hand available."

His other hand was occupied with holding the Beretta, which was pointing at Gorman's face. Haden did not trust Walter Gorman not to try something heroic.

Between them they got Gorman's jacket off and loosened his tie. Haden ripped the bloodstained shirt open. Gorman caught his breath and emitted strangled squeaks as Haden dabbed at the wound with the folded handkerchief from the other man's breast pocket. Saliva dribbled from Gorman's mouth as he bared his clenched teeth, but there was no blood in it. Haden told him to lean forward while he pulled the torn shirt away from his back.

"The bullet's still in there," Haden said. "But you'll live." He handed Gorman the bloodstained folded hand-kerchief. "Hold that to the wound until I get back."

Haden left Gorman sitting on the bunk, locked the door of the cell, walked to the sick bay. He found a field dressing, selected a couple of ampuls of morphine, and went back to the cell. He glanced through the grille before unlocking the door, but Gorman was still hunched on the bunk bed.

"This is where your training comes in, Walter," Haden said. He handed him the field dressing. "Stick this on the wound." He laid the ampuls on the blanket beside Gorman's good hand. "Then give yourself a shot or two for the pain."

"I don't need it," Gorman said.

"Please yourself," Haden said. "Only that's all the help you'll get for the time being." He turned to go.

"They'll come looking soon," Gorman said. "You can't get away."

"I know all that, Walter," Haden said.

"Then what the hell do you think you can do?"

Haden said, "I'm thinking about just that."

"Shoot it out? You might get one of them. After that, they'd flood this place with gas. You don't stand a chance, Haden—"

Haden locked Walter Gorman in again and left him to his babbling. Inside the communications room, circuit lights glowed. The equipment was alive, ready for immediate use, as it had to be, given its intended purpose.

Most of the room was occupied by complex banks of radio and computer terminals, which were about as useful to him as he thought they would be for survivors come "the day."

Haden found what he was looking for, conventional telephones. The nuclear alert might not herald full-scale nuclear war after all. It might prove to be a false alarm. Or a war might be temporarily confined to conventional weapons, or chemical warfare, when ordinary communication methods could still be used. At least, for a while. So far, so good.

The remaining question was whether the system would bypass the switchboard upstairs. Haden told himself that it had to. They wouldn't leave someone upstairs, surely? There was only one certain way to find out. Gingerly he lifted one the of the phones.

No Carol answered. Instead he heard the humdrum sound of the dial tone. Relieved, he punched out the number. The ringing tone took over.

His relief began to seep away. The ringing went on and on, and monotonously on, while he thought about Walter Gorman's prophecy of gunplay and gas.

"For Christ's sake," he muttered in frustration and anger. But there was nothing he could do now except stand where he was, holding the receiver so tightly that his fingers began to ache, and hope against hope.

He was not certain, but he thought that somewhere in the direction of the cell he heard another telephone ring a few times and then stop. There was nothing he could do about that, either. He could only listen to the ringing tone in his ear. After the first minute or so, he began counting the rings as a kind of talisman. Before he reached one hundred, there would be an answer. Then he lost count. He could not remember whether he had gotten to two hundred or three hundred.

He started again. One . . . two . . . three . . . Perspiration was trickling down his face. He could think of no reason why there was still no reply. Perhaps there was a fault on the line, and no telephone was ringing on the other end. Seventy-eight, seventy-nine, eighty . . .

Suddenly there was a breathless voice on the line.

"Where the bloody hell have you been?" Haden snarled.

"Stephen? Is that you? The plane was delayed forever, and then I went out for a meal with some chums. I heard the phone ringing as I was opening the—"

"Shut up, Harry, and listen," Haden interrupted. "I've got what you want. There's no time to write it down. Tape it. Have you got that?"

"Okay," Harold Leyton said, his voice quiet and businesslike. "Go ahead." Haden spoke quickly, but in a level, controlled voice, leaving out all the trimmings, confining himself to the bones. When he had finished, Leyton said, with a note of awe, "Christ, Stephen, if this is true, I'm forever in your debt, old chap."

"You can repay it all now," Haden said. "Don't hang up. No matter how long you have to wait, stay on the phone. If you just do that, we're even."

"That's a bargain," Leyton said promptly. "The best I've ever made. Stephen, can you tell me—"

"Not now, Harry," Haden said, cutting him off. "Another time, given a lot of luck."

He laid the receiver down carefully. A film of sweat glistened on it under the fluorescent lights, and his hands were wet. He wiped them on his handkerchief as he walked back toward the cell. The wall telephone nearby began to ring as he approached it. He lifted the receiver.

"Mr. Gorman, Mr. Janson's been trying to reach you," Carol said.

"It's not Walter, its Stephen Haden."

"Mr. Haden?" Her voice lifted in surprise. "I thought you'd left."

"Put me through to Mr. Janson."

"He's busy right now—"

"He'll talk to me," Haden said. "Ask him."

The silence was brief.

"Yes, Haden? What is it?"

"You can have everything I know about Baronin," Haden said. "But only you. Not Walter. You, in person."

"Where is Walter?"

"Walter's here. You've won, Mr. Janson. But I need your protection. Shall I tell Walter it's okay to bring me up to you?"

"No. This is a highly confidential matter. I'm coming down."

Haden hung up. He took a look through the grille. Walter Gorman was still sitting on the bunk bed, but now he was leaning back against the wall. His face was relaxed, his eyes half-closed. Evidently he had decided to take a shot after all.

Haden took the Magnum from his waistband. Carrying the two guns he now possessed, he walked back along the corridor and chose his position.

He heard the faint swish of the elevator arriving. There was a moment before the doors opened. They stopped, halfway. Framed in the narrow aperture was the poised, half-crouching figure of a young man with a Magnum in his hand, which instantly sought and found Haden.

In a moment, Haden had his hands high above his head. The Beretta and the Magnum he had taken from Gorman lay on the floor at his feet, where he had placed them. The young man slowly stood up, his gun steadily aimed.

"Back up to the wall."

Haden retreated until he felt the wall against his shoulders. If the young man was one of the specialists, he did not look the part. Fresh-faced and handsome, with well-cut fair hair and broad shoulders, he looked as though, not too long ago, he had been the star of his college football team. He remained where he was in the half-opened doors of the elevator.

"Turn around. Hands against the wall. Feet back. More. More."

Haden did as he was told, until he was leaning against the wall at such an acute angle that any sudden movement would be difficult. The young man was satisfied.

"Stay there."

Haden stayed, staring at the concrete wall in front of his nose. He heard the young man speak on an intercom.

"It's okay, sir. He was armed, but he's surrendered. Yes, sir."

Haden heard the footsteps approach him, the elevator doors close, the faint swish as it ascended. Then the Magnum was jammed against his skull.

"Don't move."

Haden had no intention of doing so, and managed to refrain from flinching during the rough, thorough frisking. Then the Magnum was removed from his head.

"Stay as you are."

There was what seemed an interminable wait. Haden could hear the even sound of the young man's breathing; he felt the rough concrete against the palms of his hands; and the muscles in his legs began to ache as he maintained his contorted position.

There was the swish of the elevator doors opening again and the sound of footsteps. The footsteps stopped.

"Walter would never have allowed you to use the telephone, Haden," Ralph Janson's voice said.

"I know," Haden said. "But I had to see you."

"Stand up and turn around," Haden stood upright and faced Janson. "Now you see me," Janson said. "The required information first. Then Walter."

"There's an urgent phone call for you, Mr. Janson," Haden said.

"What?" Taken aback, Janson's eyes instinctively sought the nearby wall telephone.

"In the communications room," Haden said. "It's long-distance."

Ralph Janson's head turned. He stared at Haden, his eyes narrowing, the beginnings of a frown marking his distinguished features.

"What are you saying?" His lack of understanding found expression in the note of peevishness in his voice.

"It's urgent," Haden said. "It's about Baronin. With your permission," he said politely, "I'll lead the way."

The barrel of the Magnum swiveled in the young man's hand to follow Haden as he walked past, and remained trained on his back. The other two guns were no longer on the floor.

Haden could think of no very compelling reason why a nod from Janson would instruct the young man to shoot him as he started toward the communications room. They still needed him, but he braced his body for the impact, and the back of his neck seemed naked and exposed just the same. He felt slightly better when he heard footsteps following him.

He walked into the communications room and lifted the receiver.

"It's Stephen. Ralph Janson would like to hear the information you have."

He turned. Janson had stopped outside in the corridor. He seemed reluctant to move, as though he smelled danger.

"You—outside," Janson said to Haden.

Haden laid the receiver down and moved into the corridor. The young man circled as he did so, never for a moment allowing Janson's body to come between Haden and his Magnum. Janson's eyes followed Haden.

"Baronin is alive, Mr. Janson," Haden said. "I'll tell you that. The rest you get from the phone."

Janson's face cleared; dry amusement touched his lips.

"I see," he said. "A device. Concern for your own safety."

"That's about it," Haden agreed.

"Whatever you've arranged," Janson said, "don't rely on its working."

Haden shrugged. "If there's any more you want to know," he said, "I'll tell you afterward."

Janson nodded, strode into the communications room, and lifted the receiver.

"Yes . . . Ralph Janson speaking, who is—" He stopped speaking and stood, his back to the corridor, with the receiver to his ear.

Haden could just detect traces of the tinny recorded sound of his own voice. The young man continued to cover him, his all-American college-boy face untroubled by anything except his own role, to aim a Magnum, to be ready to fire if necessary. Yet another person who took orders without thinking.

Ralph Janson stood motionless while the seconds ticked by, the deathly silence broken only by that almost inaudible mechanical reproduction. Haden began to feel that he had used more words than were necessary, but they were holding Janson's attention, all right.

Finally Janson said in a muffled voice, as though speaking through some obstruction in his throat. "Who is this? . . . Hello . . . Hello—"

He replaced the receiver slowly, with infinite care, as if it were a task requiring great concentration. Then he turned toward the door. His face could have belonged to another man. Its pallor was the color of lead, and its firm lines had collapsed into sagging folds. His mouth hung half-open. He looked old and helpless. His head was bowed, and he stared sightlessly at the floor.

The silence dragged out until his appearance penetrated the young man's consciousness.

"Sir, are you okay? Sir?"

Ralph Janson raised his eyes and struggled to compose his features.

"Thank you, Jack, yes. Wait upstairs, if you will."

"Are you sure, sir?" The young man shot a worried glance at Haden. "Now?"

"I'll be all right, Jack," Janson said gently. "Thank you."

The young man stood uncertain for a moment; then he slid the Magnum into his shoulder holster.

"The Beretta's mine," Haden said. "I'll have it back, if you please. You can take the clip out."

Again the young man looked toward Ralph Janson with a mixture of bewilderment and appeal.

"Give it to him, Jack," Ralph Janson said. "I'm in no danger." Silently the young man took out the Beretta, unloaded it, and handed it to Haden. "I'll see you upstairs," Janson said.

The young man finally accepted his dismissal, shook his head slightly, and walked away. Janson waited until the footsteps had died away and they could hear the elevator doors closing before he moved. Then he stepped forward and leaned on the side of the doorway, not nonchalantly, but as though he were in need of support. His eyes were fixed on Haden.

"It doesn't mean anything," he said. "You could have left that tape with some accomplice, one of the ruffians you use." He gestured limply. "Waiting in Vienna, your Zurich office, anywhere."

"You were through to London," Haden said.

"You could be lying," Janson said dully. "There's no proof." But he was only speaking the words. His tone carried no belief in them.

"He's a former British agent," Haden said. "There'll be proof soon enough."

"Ask him to hold off," Janson appealed. "We could be there within hours, meet with him, both of us. Work out something. Whatever you want, whatever he wants. There's no price I can't pay. Anything. Your friend must need money. You work for money. There has to be a way."

302

"It was all a dream, Mr. Janson," Haden said. "Forget it."

Ralph Janson stood up, his shoulders squared, some semblance of his former pride and authority briefly returning. "I could have handled the job," he said. "I'd have been good. One of the best. I still could be. It's not too late. This thing can still be contained."

"It can't," Haden said. "You have nothing to offer. The tape is in the hands of a man who wants it more than anything else in the world. And he'll use it, you can be sure of that. How, I can't tell you, that's his business. But he'll use it. It's too late, Mr. Janson. No more Dante, no more great ambitions." He smiled sardonically. "Take your own advice, Mr. Janson. Look to the future. I don't suppose there'll be any Ninth Circle in it. That was medieval imagery. As to whether there's some modern equivalent, well, I expect you'll find out."

Haden turned away, walked back to the cell, unlocked the door, went in, picked up his trench coat, and put it on. Walter Gorman's half-open eyelids flickered as he became aware of Haden's presence. He emerged from his semistupor and focused blearily.

Haden retrieved the briefcase from where it had fallen from Walter Gorman's hand and set it on the damaged table while he buckled his belt.

"I'll take this now, Walter," he said.

Walter Gorman's eyes had shifted, and he was staring past Haden at Ralph Janson, who had entered the cell. He raised himself to a sitting position, about to rise to his feet.

"Stay there, Walter," Janson said. He crossed to the bunk bed, laid his hand on Gorman's good shoulder, and gazed down at him compassionately. "How bad is it?"

"It's nothing, sir," Gorman said bravely. "I'll be fine. I'm sorry about what happened, sir . . ."

Ralph Janson patted his shoulder absently and then took his hand away.

"It's all right, Walter," he said. "Don't worry about it."

"That goddamn guard on the gate," Gorman said breathily. It was an effort for him to speak. "Haden had a gun and he missed it. But I'm to blame. I should have made certain. I'm responsible."

"Not anymore, Walter," Janson said. "It doesn't matter. It's all over. Do you understand me?"

"No, sir," Gorman said, his eyes blank. "I don't. All over? What is?"

"Everything," Janson said, tired. "It's finished. Don't try to be loyal, Walter. Look out for yourself. Say that you followed orders in good faith. Whatever you have to say. In the meantime that wound needs medical attention. I'll arrange for it." He turned to Haden. "A brief word, if you will, Mr. Haden."

Haden followed Ralph Janson out of the cell and along to the elevator. Janson pressed the call button and turned to Haden.

"I'll have the gate informed that you are authorized to leave," he said. Haden nodded. "There's something else," Janson said hesitantly. Haden waited through a long pause. "You said some things concerning Petra," Ralph Janson said finally. "I don't believe they have any bearing . . . That is, I would very much hope that you wouldn't find it necessary—"

"I was only guessing," Haden said. "I've no intention of telling Petra, if that's what you're trying to say."

The elevators doors opened. A look of relief softened Ralph Janson's face.

"Thank you," he said. "None of it was true, of course. But it would have upset Petra. Hurt her. I wouldn't want that."

Janson stepped into the elevator, and the doors closed.

Haden made his way back to the cell, groped in Walter Gorman's pocket, and found his car keys.

"I'll leave your car at the gate, Walter," he said.

"Mr. Janson . . . he's letting you go?"

"You heard him," Haden said. "The whole thing's in pieces. It's every man for himself. Confession time for you, Walter."

Walter Gorman lifted his head and gazed up at Haden. His chin jutted proudly.

"I have nothing to confess," he said. "Everything I did was done in the best interest of the United States of America."

"If you want to try that on, good luck," Haden said.

It sounded like twenty-six-carat crap to him, but he supposed that Walter Gorman believed it.

The briefcase in his hand, Haden summoned the elevator, found the right button to open the opposite door, and made his way outside. In the thin, icy air, it was cold without his fur hat, and he was glad to get into Walter Gorman's car.

He had nearly reached the gate when he heard the clatter of a helicopter descending onto the pad of the aerie behind him. He supposed it had arrived to convey Walter Gorman to a hospital, or to take Ralph Janson wherever he was going.

Perhaps both. He dismissed them from his thoughts. His business was concluded, the final payment in the briefcase lying on the seat beside him.

What was left was more of a private matter.

Chapter Eighteen

Stephen Haden awoke late, but he still felt unrefreshed. He showered, dressed, and telephoned János Varga.

"How's my suit coming along?" he inquired.

"Ready for a fitting, sir."

"I'll be in. And I'll see our friend at the same time. Tell him it's about his son."

There was a pause.

"Can he believe that, Mr. Haden?"

"That's up to him," Haden said touchily. The shower had not done much to invigorate him. "I really don't care too much. I'll be there in a couple of hours."

He hung up and finished dressing. He was knotting his tie when there was a tap on the door.

"Come in," he called. Room service was prompt.

But it was Petra Baron who came in. She closed the door and stood where she was, looking at him. Her face was pale, her manner nervous.

"I've had a call from the embassy," she said. "Someone I don't know. He said I was to stay here, to remain available, until someone came to interview me. He wouldn't say why. Only that it was official and that I wasn't to speak to anyone."

Haden adjusted his collar and pulled on his jacket.

"Then you shouldn't be here," he said.

"I called back at once, and asked to talk to Ralph. They said he wasn't taking any calls."

"I expect he's got a lot on his mind," Haden said.

"But he's never refused to talk to me before," Petra said. "Never. Something's wrong. What is it, Stephen?"

"Whatever they want to know, just tell them the truth," Haden said.

"About what?" she asked, puzzled. "I've done nothing wrong."

"So there's no reason for you to be anxious," Haden said. "You'll come out smiling."

"No," Petra said. "There was something about those voices on the phone . . . I don't know . . . distant . . . as though something bad had happened. I couldn't bear it if anything happened to Ralph. I just couldn't."

"Petra," Haden said kindly. "I think it's time you stopped relying on Ralph Janson."

"But then I'll have no one," Petra said. "Without him, without Alex, I have no one."

"You have your son," Haden reminded her.

"I know," Petra said sadly. "But he's a child, not a man. I'm not built that way. I can't be all alone, I just can't. Aren't you going to tell me what it's all about?"

"Official business is American business, not mine," Haden said. "Go back to your room and wait, Petra. If you really don't know anything, it's best that I don't tell you anything. Convincing ignorance is any beautiful woman's finest weapon."

In the small fitting room to which János Varga had led him, Haden tried on his new suit. He gazed with approval at his reflection in the full-length mirror.

"You're a fine tailor, Mr. Varga," he said.

"Thank you, sir," János Varga said. He looked quite pleased with his handiwork himself. "You're not wearing your accessories today, of course, but just the same—"

"It'll be fine," Haden said. "How soon can you finish it?"

"There's very little left to be done," Varga answered. "If you're in a hurry—this afternoon?"

"Provided you can have it delivered to Bad Gastberg."

"Of course, sir," Varga said. "And now, if you'd care to change, Mr. Haden, you know the way."

Smiling, Varga closed the door behind him. Haden put his own suit back on, walked along the corridor, unlocked the door to the back room, and entered.

Baronin was smoking a cigarette restlessly.

"My son," he said without preamble.

Haden propped himself against the door.

"First, let's talk about you," he said. Baronin tensed and stared at him suspiciously. Haden opened his jacket wide. "I'm not armed this time," he said. "All decisions today are yours, except one."

"What does that mean?" It was hard to detect any expression behind the full beard, but the eyes were wary.

"Mr. Baronin," Haden said, "you were trained and groomed for the role you played. The American girl, defection, marriage, minor employment with the CIA, and the eventual opening of the Dante source—it was all set up from the start. And you knew all along that only part of the information transmitted would be genuine. The good information was the bait. Once the hook was in, misleading intelligence would follow."

"No, no," Baronin said, agitated. "That's not true."

He crushed out his cigarette and lit another at once.

"I think it is," Haden said, not unpleasantly. "I believe you when you say that you tried to pass a warning. Why doesn't concern me. Whether you'd become disillusioned or you believed that if you could stop playing double agent you might be able to patch things up with Petra doesn't matter. Of course, Petra was the one thing you hadn't bargained on—that is, that she'd come to matter, that you'd be jealous.''

"And Peter," Baronin said. "I didn't expect to father a son."

"And Peter," Haden agreed. "The point is that your KGB bosses know nothing about any of this. You could go back to the Soviet Union, your job done."

Baronin was shaking his head vigorously. "You're forgetting that they tried to kill me."

"That wasn't the KGB operation," Haden said. The wary eyes widened a fraction. Haden took out a cheroot and lit it, leaving Baronin to work out the rest for himself. "So you could go home," Haden said, "and be given a medal, or however they reward their agents."

"Only if I could take my son with me," Baronin said.

"Of course, there is an alternative," Haden said. "Things have changed. The Americans are hunting bigger game than you now. You could come out of hiding and remain a United States citizen." Baronin inhaled cigarette smoke and looked at Haden. "My guess is they'll need a star witness," Haden said. "That's not such a bad hand to play. You could probably do well out of it."

"I decide nothing until I have my son," Baronin said obstinately. "You said you knew where he was and could arrange it."

"He's at a boarding school in England," Haden said. "It wouldn't be too hard to have him flown out to Vienna. My stepdaughter is at the same school. She could bring him. There's only one obstacle."

"More money," Baronin said at once, his teeth showing. "I must keep enough to take us to New Zealand. But very well, I agree. János will find the difference. He will trust me to repay him.''

''New Zealand's a pipe dream,'' Haden said. ''But if you're set on it, I'm not in the business of kidnapping children. There are people who will, though. You'd better hire one of them.''

Baronin looked as if his frustration were likely to be expressed in physical aggression.

''Mr. Haden,'' he said, his voice little more than a menacing whisper. ''I came here for my son, Peter. You can give him to me. I don't need anyone else.''

''You have a wife,'' Haden said. ''Peter's mother. You need her consent. At least you do if you want me to help you. If not, find someone who doesn't care.''

Baronin moved his head in a small nod of understanding. He unclenched his fists and shoved his hands into the pockets of his anorak.

''Even if I knew where she was,'' he said flatly, ''even if I thought she might agree, I wouldn't ask her. No. Never.''

''Well, it's up to you, Baronin,'' Haden said. ''It's all up to you.''

Stephen Haden had paid János Varga and shaken his hand. He drove back to Bad Gastberg for what, he thought with some relief, was to be the last time. The route had become tiresomely familiar.

There was an official-looking car in the parking lot. The driver was reading an American newspaper. Haden went straight into the dining room. His stomach was beginning to remind him that he had skipped breakfast. It was the tail end of the lunch period, but the service was as courteous as ever, and the waiter assured him that there was no hurry, that he should take his time. He was the last to leave and, feeling better, walked into the foyer.

310

"Oh, Mr. Haden," the receptionist said with a smile, "I didn't know you were back."

"If there are any messages, I'll be in my room," Haden said, taking his key.

He laid out his suitcases and began to pack. The tap on his door was not long delayed. He opened the door wide, turned away, and went back to his packing.

"I rather thought it might be you," he said.

Helen Lloyd came in, closed the door, and stood looking at him.

"Abandoning the scene of the crime, I see," she said.

"Since no Austrian policeman seems to wish to interview me concerning a shooting incident somewhere," Haden said, "yes, I am."

He collected his hairbrush and odds and ends from the dressing table. Through the window he saw a van, tastefully emblazoned JÁNOS VARGA, TAILOR, pull up.

"I thought maybe you'd rather talk to me," Helen said.

"You have no jurisdiction," Haden said. "Whatever your role is today. Miss Squeaky-Clean, on the outside, at least, come to sweep up, I suppose, or cover up."

"Something like that," Helen said.

"Sit down and keep out of my way," Haden said, carrying a pile of shirts across the room. "So, tell me all about yourself," he said. "How are you?"

Helen Lloyd sat on the couch and crossed her legs. Haden wished she were wearing trousers.

"Ralph Janson has flown back to the States," Helen said. "He's in a sanatorium with some unspecified illness. Walter Gorman is being uncooperative." She watched Haden as he closed the first suitcase and placed it near the door. "Stephen," she said. "I need Baronin."

The telephone rang.

"Excuse me," Haden said. He lifted the receiver and

listened. "Fine," he said. "Ask him to bring it up." He replaced the receiver. "Sorry. What was that?"

"Your hearing is perfect," Helen said acidly.

"You'd better ask Petra," Haden said.

"I have. I've been with her for two hours or more. She says she thought he was dead. I believe she does think so. Come on, Stephen. Where is he?"

Haden turned away from the wardrobe, holding two of his suits, and faced her.

"The last time I saw him was in Vienna," he said. "I haven't seen him since."

Their eyes held for several moments before he resumed what he was doing. He laid out his suits on the bed, ready for packing.

"You were paid," Helen said. "There was an agreement, which I've inherited. I'm holding you to it."

"I was paid to find him," Haden said. "I found him. I wasn't paid to deliver him."

"Ah, so now we're into the small print," Helen said coldly. "How much is it going to cost?"

"I didn't much like your insurance policy, either," Haden said.

Helen was about to say something in reply. From the expression on her face, it was going to be in anger. The rap on the door interrupted her. She let out a deep breath and closed her well-formed mouth tightly.

Haden opened the door. A man wearing an anorak stood holding a suit on a hanger; it was cloaked with a dust cover bearing János Varga's insignia. Haden took it from him.

"Ah, thanks," he said. "What was that? Hang on, I'll direct you."

He looked at Helen Lloyd's set profile. "He has another delivery," he said. "I shan't be a minute."

Helen glanced at Baronin standing in the doorway and turned away in irritation.

312

Haden led the way along the corridor and tried the door. It opened.

Petra Baron was lying on the bed, her face averted.

"Oh, sure," she said harshly. "Feel free. Walk in."

Her head moved. She saw who it was, and sat up slowly, staring.

"My lovely companion is CIA," Haden said softly, to Baronin. "Lock the door and don't answer the phone."

Baronin nodded, stepped inside, and stood gazing at his wife. Neither said anything. Haden closed the door and left them.

Back in his room, Haden held up his acquisition.

"I thought I might as well buy a suit while I was here," he said. "Would you like to see it?"

"No, I wouldn't," Helen Lloyd said. "Show off in front of someone else."

"Pity," Haden said. "You'd like it." He laid the new suit on the bed with the others, sat in the armchair facing her, and lit a cheroot. "There seem to be hard feelings on both sides," he said.

"You came to me," Helen Lloyd said, more quietly.

"Yes, that's true," Haden said. "I did."

"You needed me," Helen said. "You didn't know which way to turn."

"At that time," Haden reflected, "you seemed marginally less lethal than anyone here."

"Well, now I need you, Stephen," she said, apparently disregarding his comment. Haden reached out and tapped his cheroot over the ashtray. "If you want to be paid again," she said tiredly, "I'll try to arrange it. If that's what it is."

"I forgot something, Helen," Haden said. "I forgot that in our mad world Oleg Tushin had to stay in place. Keeping the Dante source in operation had to be your top priority. Never let the enemy know what you know," he said dryly, "being the first imperative. Or something like that."

There was a definite tenseness in Helen Lloyd's composure. She sat quite still, her eyes unwavering.

"The Dante source is corrupt," she said. "But now that we know it, we can learn a lot from the proper analysis of information the Soviets want us to have."

"Yes, that's what I had overlooked," Haden said. He drew on his cheroot. "The irony is," he said, "that Oleg Tushin was the only one in the whole damn setup who was playing it straight. But you're going to leave the poor bastard where he is. To hell with what happens to him, right?"

"We'll get him out eventually," Helen Lloyd said. "Nothing lasts forever. When it's decided that the Dante source will serve no further purpose, then Tushin will be given asylum in America. It's the only logical thing, Stephen."

Haden said. "Your logic nearly killed me."

"How was I to know that taking action to keep Tushin in place would endanger you?" Helen said.

"Would it have made any difference if you had known?"

A faint flush heightened the color of the skin over Helen's high cheekbones. "I seem to remember," she said tightly, "that it was I who wanted Baronin moved out of Vienna first. He could have been flown straight back to the States, where he'd have been safe. But you were too goddamned pigheaded to listen. If we'd done it my way, everything would have been okay."

"That's crap," Haden said, his own irritation showing. "With Walter Gorman on the scene, Baronin would never even have gotten to the airport. He'd have turned up dead somewhere, and you know it."

"No one appreciated the extent of Walter Gorman's involvement at that time," Helen said. "And if you knew, you didn't say so."

"I didn't know," Haden said. "I suspected. But then I suspected every bastard. Except you. Not until I sat in that bloody cage and realized that only one person knew enough about the arrangements to have put me there."

Helen Lloyd sighed and her slender fingers gestured dismissively.

"Circular arguments are pointless," she said. "In my opinion it was your damned arrogance that landed you in that cage. Naturally, you think differently. But what's important now is Baronin. Without his evidence everyone concerned can plead that they didn't know, or that they thought the President had authorized it, just the way it's happened before. It's my job to take Baronin back with me. For God's sake, Stephen, what do I have to do, beg?"

"No, you don't," Haden said. "I can't help you. The decision belongs to Baronin, not me, not you. I'm sorry if that impedes the upward mobility of your career, but there it is."

Helen Lloyd stood up and walked out of the room. The door closed sharply behind her. Haden sat where he was and finished his cheroot. Then he got up and slowly finished his packing. He was tempted by the idea of a drink, but he had a long drive in front of him.

He thought that he might have heard Helen Lloyd rapping on a door along the corridor after she'd left, but he was neither certain nor interested enough to look. What happened now was no longer his affair.

He called the desk for a porter to come to collect his luggage. He pulled on his trench coat and gloves and went downstairs.

As he crossed the foyer, he saw Helen Lloyd and Petra Baron. They were sitting in a glass-fronted alcove that offered a pleasant view across the terrace outside. A coffeepot and cups stood on the low table beside them. They were intent on their apparently serious conversation and did not notice him.

Haden went outside. János Varga's van was still parked

in the same place. He walked to the parking lot. The driver behind the wheel of the official-looking car was no longer reading. He was asleep.

It was not as cold as it had been, and the snow glistened in the thin sunshine. A thaw was setting in. Haden drove his Mercedes around to the main entrance, retrieved his remaining belongings from the safe, and paid his bill.

As he turned, he found that Helen Lloyd was standing close to him, her eyes on the briefcase in his hand.

"I guess you've come out well ahead on this deal," she said.

"I'm in profit, thank you," Haden said.

"Suddenly Petra just might have some idea where Baronin is. Provided she receives all kinds of guarantees. Isn't that amazing, Haden?"

"A stroke of luck for you," Haden said amicably. "Your career rescued, and you don't need me."

He went across to the alcove. "I'll say goodbye, Petra," he said. She took his hand. Hers felt cold. She tried to smile as she looked at him.

"Everything all right?" Haden asked.

Petra Baron said, "There's this feeling . . . that I could be about to make the biggest mistake of my life."

"Well now, that would have to be a monumental one," Haden said. "One for the record books."

She smiled again, shakily. "It's such a big commitment," she said. "Just now, I feel like backing off. If I could only talk to Ralph . . ."

"There is no Ralph in your life anymore," Haden said. "From here on, you decide what you want, on your own."

"I'll probably screw everything up again," Petra said glumly.

Haden said, "Then again, without Ralph, you might not."

As he walked toward the door, he glanced at the slim,

elegant figure of Helen Lloyd, still standing near the reception desk, and gave her a polite smile.

She nodded slightly in "Goodbye," but there was no answering smile.

Three weeks later, a letter postmarked London arrived at Haden's Zurich office. He slit it open. It informed him, from an address in Wembley, that due to the pressure of work on a government contract, Harold Leyton had sold his franchise operation to Ian, who wanted to know if Haden intended to pick up his option on the Swiss marketing rights.

Haden smiled and filed the letter in the wastepaper basket.

The card that had arrived a few days earlier was more interesting. It read: "Things are more or less okay here. I've cooled off. How about you? Helen."

The wording had struck Haden as ambiguous. Tempers? Feelings? If the one, yes; if the other, no.

Stephen Haden supposed he would test the ambiguity sometime, when the opportunity arose. In the meantime the card would remain in his pending tray.

ESPIONAGE FICTION BY LEWIS PERDUE

THE LINZ TESTAMENT (17-117, $4.50)
Throughout World War Two the Nazis used awesome power to silence the Catholic Church to the atrocities of Hitler's regime. Now, four decades later, its existence has brought about the most devastating covert war in history — as a secret battle rages for possession of an ancient relic that could shatter the foundations of Western religion: The Shroud of Veronica, irrefutable evidence of a second Messiah. For Derek Steele it is a time of incomprehensible horror, as the ex-cop's relentless search for his missing wife ensnares him in a deadly international web of KGB assassins, Libyan terrorists, and bloodthirsty religious zealots.

THE DA VINCI LEGACY (17-118, $4.50)
A fanatical sect of heretical monks fired by an ancient religious hatred. A page from an ancient manuscript which could tip the balance of world power towards whoever possesses it. And one man, caught in a swirling vortex of death and betrayal, who alone can prevent the enslavement of the world by the unholy alliance of the Select Brothers and the Bremen Legation. The chase is on — and the world faces the horror of The Da Vinci Legacy.

QUEENS GATE RECKONING (17-164, $3.95)
Qaddafi's hit-man is the deadly emissary of a massive and cynical conspiracy with origins far beyond the Libyan desert, in the labyrinthine bowels of the Politburo . . . and the marble chambers of a seditious U.S. Government official. And rushing headlong against this vast consortium of treason is an improbable couple — a wounded CIA operative and defecting Soviet ballerina. Together they hurtle toward the hour of ultimate international reckoning.

Available wherever paperbacks are sold, or order direct from the Publisher. Send cover price plus 50¢ per copy for mailing and handling to Pinnacle Books, Dept.17-305, 475 Park Avenue South, New York, N.Y. 10016. Residents of New York, New Jersey and Pennsylvania must include sales tax. DO NOT SEND CASH.